# STARBORN VENDETTA

# STARBORN VENDETTA

## THE CLUSTER CYCLE

## VOLUME ONE

# THOMAS WRIGHTSON

DRAGONBRAE

DRAGONBRAE

An Imprint of Roan & Weatherford Publishing Associates, LLC
Bentonville, Arkansas
www.roanweatherford.com

Copyright © 2023 by Thomas Wrightson

**Library of Congress Cataloging-in-Publication Data**
Names: Wrightson, Thomas, author.
Title: Mercedes: Starborn Vendetta | Cluster Cycle #1
Description: First Edition. | Bentonville: Dragonbrae, 2023.
Identifiers: LCCN:  ISBN: 978-1-63373-861-4 (hardcover) |
ISBN: 978-1-63373-862-1 (trade paperback) | ISBN: 978-1-63373-863-8 (eBook)
Subjects: | BISAC: FICTION/Science Fiction/Space Opera |
FICTION/Science Fiction/Action & Adventure

Dragonbrae hardcover edition October, 2023

Cover & Interior Design by Casey W. Cowan
Editing by Laura Lauda & Amy Cowan

*To my late father.*

# PREFACE

THIS BOOK HAD such an obscure beginning. Watching the anime *Gankutsuou,* an adaptation of Alexandre Dumas's seminal work of revenge fantasy, it struck me. Why not attempt my own retelling. It all began with a test, a single page. A ruined palace with a woman standing within it, ready to take back what was her's, and another at her side in for her own gains.

But the story wouldn't be what it is without its central character, Mercedes. She may have changed from that first fleeting image in the ruined palace, but her core remained consistent. An intelligent, determined, almost cold-blooded woman who would do practically anything in pursuit of her goals. She isn't a heroine, she's a protagonist. Sounds odd, but that was what this story became. A book without heroes or heroines, only protagonists and antagonists.

Much changed from that first concept to the finish project. The characters took on lives of their own, the narrative became a more nuanced look at the distorting power of petty schemes and revenge, and most of all it began an entire series. A universe filled with classical parallels and a look into a society far beyond our own, yet also very much tied to our own.

# ACKNOWLEDGMENTS

TO MY FAMILY, who supported their wayward child to the fulfillment of his dream. To Frances Hardinge, who reviewed my early scribbling. To Sarah Ash, a wonderful person who encouraged and enjoyed my work. To the team at Roan & Weatherford who brought forth unexpected but welcome changes. And to whatever muse has been working themselves to the bone providing me with this stream of ideas and prose.

# STARBORN VENDETTA

# FILE 1

## BIRTH OF PRISONER 74

*All the worlds mourn when a woman's virtue is taken. All the worlds rejoice when a man suffers a similar fate. This inequality of the sexes is an overlooked aspect of our modern times. While not to be encouraged to the degree of returning to the bad old days of women being second in all things, true gender equality should merit an equal quota of both sympathy and condemnation when discussing male and female characters. None should be exempt.*

—Extract from Fingal Dee's "Views on Devolved Morality"

THE PRISON TRANSPORT Shuttle *Hypnos* cast its shadow across the sunward windows of the d'If. In Docking Port 5, Squad Captain Gaspard Atarex opened a comm channel to the ship's captain.

"You're late again."

Gaspard's flat accents were not polite. Working in a prison would dent even the toughest of hearts, removing care and softening. Long forgotten were the days of courtesy, of natural politeness that sorted the green from the grizzled. The Ship Captain of Prison Transport Shuttle *Hypnos* was not in the mood for Gaspard's manner.

*"Late again. Late again,"* came the echoing, angered reply through the comm. *"I don't need you to tell us that. Why the hell did the warp engine have to fail like that…? At least we got here. But who's gonna get it in their bonus?"*

"Not you, that's for sure. Get ready for your approach to Docking Port 5."

*"Docking Port 5, copy."*

Gaspard looked through the dock windows at the *Hypnos,* its rough exterior matching the decrepit look of Prison Station d'If. This place, with its visiting barges of infamy, had been his home for five years. Built inside an asteroid and named after an infamous Ancient Earth prison, the d'If orbited the Ares twin star system. Human run, human powered, staffed mostly by Feles who could be trusted to keep quiet. Prisoners from all the Cluster peoples were kept here, prisoners too dangerous or embarrassing to be kept anywhere else. It was here they were sent to be forgotten, along with the guards and staff assigned to them.

This was his home, his own little prison, though he walked free among the entrapped. If possible, he would have left years ago. But in the Outer Worlds, who would accept him? A Feles without a tribe, without any affiliation beyond himself. None trusted such as he. Scum worse than the lowest, no spine or scruples. He didn't deceive himself of that but accepted it as who he was.

The same routine as in previous years played out like a piece of stock footage in a long-running series. The *Hypnos's* warp rings powered down, docking signals were exchanged, and thrusters gently guided it toward Docking Port 5. The twin stars' unfiltered sunlight threw the scene into cruel relief, giving shadows edges sharper than tempered steel. The *Hypnos* was not pretty, an outdated Blue-class passenger freighter with rocky warp systems. Beyond the Capital Worlds, older models were more common and kept maintained within tight schedules and tighter budgets.

*"Breakdowns, breakdowns, breakdowns."* The voice came through on the comm again. *"At least this place needs it, too. Doesn't get the funding it used to."*

Time blurred momentarily. Gaspard lost himself in musings and little mental rituals, wiling away the minutes of monotonous boredom that had long since crushed his soul into the mold of "Squad Captain." Clearance codes being transmitted, the light of Ares blocked out by the ship's bulk, the docking ports connecting, thrusters disengaging. Like the culmination to a well-rehearsed act, the pantomime of his life.

The docking procedure was completed, and a few crewpeople from the Hypnos appeared ahead of the prisoners being shuffled along like the cargo they were. One of the crew was an engineer Gaspard recognized from earlier trips, a Feles like himself. She noticed him, and he waved in a pathetic imitation of normality. He didn't bother deceiving himself. This place wasn't normal. It was abnormal. Anyone trying to be normal here was only imitating, and poorly at that.

"Hi there." The female Feles approached with a springing gate, fiddling with the matted locks of her mane and scruffiness of her fur. "We're all done out here in the Outer Worlds. How many times do I have to get assigned to this bloody run before I qualify for an upgrade? Seriously need a shower. When I get to the next space habitat, I'm not going to leave my bath for an hour."

Gaspard wrinkled his nose at the crewperson's odor, sweat mingled with engine fluids and the natural neglect born from near-constant overtime. "You may have to change the water a few times. What're the cargo like?"

"Mostly the usual. Sullen, meek, and foul-mouthed."

"So more of the usual shit, that's just great. Like we haven't got enough here already."

Mediocrity persisting for yet another day, draining his self ever more. The engineer was still talking, letting fly traces of outside normality as the latest batch of prisoners were shunted inside. Only nine this time, surrounded by a tired-looking corps with rifles looking older than the Skirmishes. They were a sorry lot, wearing tattered prison scruffs given after being stripped by security during the transfer between Capital and Outer territories. All walked with heads bowed, their spirits broken.

No, that was wrong. Not all. Eight were as lowly and subservient as others before them, but the ninth was different. Gaspard's ear twitched, his curiosity piqued by that ninth figure.

"Who's that there? That tall human female in the middle. She's... different."

The engineer looked. "I did say they were 'mostly' usual. She's the exception. Got a look at her old clothes before they were taken for recycling. Very fine, good quality stuff. Natural fibers, not synthetic stuff off the street. Looked tailor-made."

"Know her name?"

"No names after processing, you know that. And we're not allowed to talk to them."

"Pity. If Witton has his way, she'll only be a number soon. Or less."

Just thinking about the warden brought a little sick into the back of Gaspard's throat. The human chief of the d'If, a detestable little wart and figurative king among scum. If Gaspard were anyone or anything else, he would be away and working for someone else. But he wasn't, so he stayed. Brushing away Witton's ugly presence and his own burdens from his mind, Gaspard refocused on the woman.

A special one. Yes, she had something, had been someone who didn't bow and nod politely, but commanded and expected obedience. Not like the others. Those sorry, cowering, colorless wrecks. Even the other guards. Even him.

As the prisoners were scanned, he took in every discernible detail. Dark-skinned, a lush head of chestnut hair, slim without being weak, a figure alluring but modest. She held herself upright and looked about her with a stiff grace all the others lacked. This alone turned her colorless convict clothes into almost a badge of honor and dignity. What stood out most were the markings across the right side of her face. Flat and thin keloid scars, like scratch marks or narrow burns, accentuating rather than marring her charisma.

All the time Gaspard stared, the woman's eyes were scanning the room, taking in every detail. Suddenly, without warning, her eyes focused on him. It took all of Gaspard's willpower to restrain an involuntary salute. Clenching his hand into a fist behind his back, he spoke with more emotion than he'd used in years.

"I wish she hadn't been sent here. She's dangerous. That kind of authority could rally the other prisoners. I'll advise she be put into solitary confinement for the duration of her imprisonment."

"That's probably wise. But I'm not sure she's a threat."

"Really? Why?"

"You didn't see her on the journey here. She looks in control now, quite poised in fact. But while we were en route, when I was on an errand near them, she looked deflated. As if she'd been winded and hadn't recovered."

Meek Gaspard may have been, but when his eyes saw, they saw truly. Beneath the woman's regal facade, there festered a layer of fresh despair and anger smothering who she might have been. Her eyes were harsh from some deep hurt, her hands clenched and unclenched in subtle motions, and at times she struggled to retain that poise. She was marshaling her entire will into restraining some strong emotion. Was she fighting like those bouts in the arena on the ClusterNet? Maybe even fighting for her life?

With the prisoner exchange finalized, the Hypnos crew were allowed to depart, relieved their last delivery of the working year was over. It didn't take long for everything to be done. It never did. Speed was the essence of keeping prisoners in line, away from the temptations of ship hijacking. The prisoners remained in the holding area until the *Hypnos* was beyond the buffer zone and jumped into warp. Within the day, the *Hypnos* was lightyears away, leaving Gaspard on the d'If, alone in the Ares system, superheated giants his only unchanging companions.

———————————

THE PRISONERS WERE lined up in the processing chamber. Gaspard stood beside prison governor Witton Mondego, who looked over the newcomers like a merchant eyeing produce. The nine looked exhausted, with only the woman holding herself straight, eyes focused on the near-invisible figures behind the lights. Witton was focusing on her above the others. Again, her presence, her strength of will, even under this glaring light and open depersonalization, overawed him. She had become an imposing and untouchable figure, a towering vertebrate amongst cowering worms.

Witton pointed at her. "Who's the human girl?"

Gaspard yanked his attention away with an effort. He repeated his ignorance, a guarded version of his opinion. Witton smiled unpleasantly. Gaspard understood the expression and suppressed a groan. The Warden's unchained libido was as deplorable as his manners.

Gaspard put all the conviction possible into his words. "I presumed being in the solitary wing might be best. That is, until we've got a better idea of who she is now, not who she was when sentence was passed."

"I think that's a wise suggestion. Talking of newcomers, has the Ambassador arrived?"

Gaspard knew full well to whom Witton was referring, and again felt a little sick. F'thodish Azd Laffw, a senior administrator and ambassador for the Kavki people, assigned to a sector of the Capital Worlds. Witton may have used her formal title, but he showed little reverence or respect, only contempt. Regardless of Laffw's reputation, even Gaspard knew to show the proper respect to his betters.

"No, she hasn't. She canceled her visit."

Witton scowled. "A good client she may be, but I sometimes wish we'd have someone more reliable with their visits and purchases. She's so busy with administration these days, who knows when she'll–" He pulled himself together. "Move those prime picks back to their cells, and make sure they're not damaged. Also… hmm…." He smiled a little, looking at the scarred woman. "I'd like to see her in my offices immediately."

"Yes, sir."

Gaspard knew what was coming. Female inmates were often sized up by Witton just in case. He struggled to compose his face as he left but didn't stop himself punching a convenient chair back when no-one could see. It wasn't much, but it stopped him releasing his fists onto the prisoners or guards. Or Witton.

Within the hour, he was escorting the woman into Witton's private office. On the point of leaving, Witton recalled him.

"Just a moment. I think you'd better stay."

Even as he closed the door, Gaspard heartily wished himself a million miles away. Witton tripped the lockdown function, sealing the office off from the outside world. Gaspard settled into a corner. He hated what was coming but dared not intercede. He could only watch, a powerless spectator.

The prisoner's eyes met Witton's with an implacable steeliness. The warden got up from his desk and circled the woman, giving her body looks which made Gaspard's stomach churn.

Witton was obviously impressed. All the others he had summed up in this degrading manner would cower, cringe, or flinch as he moved close to them. A few even gave in and pleaded in some manner before he had risen from his chair. This one remained erect and impassive. As he placed a hand on her shoulder, Gaspard could have sworn there was the slightest twinge, a muscle spasm quickly suppressed. Witton spoke softly, using the voice of a father or a lover rather than a warden.

"You're quite a woman."

The woman remained silent, although the corner of her mouth briefly lifted in what Gaspard could only interpret as a contemptuous smirk. Or she was struggling to contain a flattered smile? Best to consider both possibilities until he knew more.

Witton, ignorant of the expression, continued to speak. "Your control is admirable. How you're holding up is a mystery to me. I've met many women in my time, but you're the only one to remain so calm."

He circled her again, still trying to figure her out. It must have been like looking at a bulkhead without markings and trying to judge its age or manufacturer. Gaspard and Witton saw the clue at the same moment, the small line of tattooed markings across the edge of her hairline. Her height could place her among half a dozen tribes, her coloring among twice that, but those marks made it certain.

"So, you're from Argo." Witton was not bothering to hide his contempt. "A moon filled of softies, I'd thought. But then, I'm an Outlander, so what would I know? You know, you're more composed than all the other prisoners in this place put together. Where're you from? What did you do?" He bent close, his mouth creasing into a winning smile. "What's your name?"

The woman remained silent but looked directly at the warden. There was a clear contempt in her eyes. Gaspard could've cheered as Witton's gorge rose at this defiance. He clenched his hand until the palm almost bled as Witton placed his hand on her shoulder, allowing it to drift up toward her pulsing jugular. He felt what Gaspard had seen with narrowed eyes, the slight trace of nanotech implants lying beneath the skin.

If he knew anything about the d'If and its population, he knew the size and fragility of Witton's ego. He refused to be denied by anyone, especially someone he wanted. He had never been denied before and would not take it well now. And Gaspard was powerless. But why did he even want to do anything? Why now, after all these years?

Witton's voice punctured Gaspard's thoughts. "Such a fine form you have, well toned and firm. You're the kind men would fight for in older times. A shame if such form went to waste or withered away in a cramped little cell. But if you do come across, I can give you so many things. And I must tell you, no-one resists me for long, my d—"

"You're right."

Witton was visibly shocked by her voice, and Gaspard's heart skipped as an overexcited child. The voice held a medium tone, but its regal accent and timbre of authority made him start. Witton pulled his hand away and sat behind his desk once more.

"Right about what?"

"My place of origin. And on Argo we have a saying. 'He who seeks the unaffordable knows only disappointment.'"

The sting in her words was powerful. Gaspard felt the command of generations behind it, stirring his moribund senses. She was not just a woman. She was power and majesty. In a world of insects, she towered over all as a majestic predatory bird. Struggling to keep his composure, Witton picked up a datapad and flicked through its contents.

"You've got two options ahead of you. One has a cell in the solitary wing with only two meals per day and no human contact whatsoever—aside from myself for your yearly review and one chosen non-human guard. Any insubordination or violent acts will see you confined automatically to the punishment cells. The second option is a cell in low security, good conditions, light work, comfortable furnishings. And my personal attention."

Witton clearly expected her to cave. Most of the others had. Those same promises whispered to them, and they had given themselves willingly. Well, the human ones. Witton preferred humans, not the few alien females kept in this place. Those could rot with the others in the d'If's overcrowded Factory Level for all Witton cared.

Gaspard struggled to retain his composure, and Witton's face blackened abruptly. Where in others there had been a submission or a forced sensuality, here there was only defiance. The woman remained aloof, proud, undaunted. Witton drew himself up to his full height, demonstrating more forcibly that she was several inches taller than nearly every other human in the d'If.

"It's unwise to antagonize me, my dear. You realize that, don't you?" Witton's voice had become normal, a hard tone without empathy. "You're not your own person here. If I want, you'll be known and talked of only as a number. Two digits, if you're lucky. Here, I'm the supreme ruler. If you want to use archaic terms, I'm the king of the d'If. And you're all, guards and prisoners alike, my subjects."

The words seemed to sting her, as they did Gaspard. Witton must have thought himself a king before, but using it so openly was rare. This woman, who stood like a rock against the tide, seemed to shift a little under this analogy. For a moment Witton smiled, thinking he had succeeded in breaking through her shell. Instead, she focused her gaze upon him, and her voice became venomous.

"Your use of the word 'king' disrespects it in every possible way. You're no king, Warden. Merely the petty tyrant of a backwater prison. And I will never kneel before a tyrant. For as anyone knows, in history, a tyrant will inevitably be overthrown. The day I accept your attentions or even call you by your name, Warden, is the day you will lie dead at my feet."

Oh, shit. *Now* she had done it.

Witton turned purple with fury, rounding the desk and slapping the woman hard across the face. Her scarred cheek came up in an ugly red welt, and Gaspard's own cheek sang in sympathetic agony. Witton spoke again, his tone darker than he ever heard it before. It made Gaspard feel small, a little ant in a vast colony under the absolute rule of its 'king.'

"I'll make you regret the day you were born, girl. You'll be getting worse than normal solitary. Count on it. You're not a woman anymore. You're an object. A number. You're Prisoner 74. Unless you reconsider."

The woman smiled. "I don't. And as Prisoner 74 I shall survive, Warden. Until the tyrant's fall."

There came another hard slap across the other cheek, another sting of pain in Gaspard's mind. Then the lockdown was lifted, and Witton ordered her to be taken to the most remote cell in the solitary wing. Gaspard was recalled with a sharp command.

"Squad Captain Atarex, take Prisoner 74 for processing. You're to stay with her at all times. Report back to me when it's done. I want to know how she takes it."

Like an automaton, Gaspard ushered Prisoner 74 along two corridors into a padded cell with a reclining chair. Strapped into it, she was stoically helpless as a female doctor entered and first injected a general antivirus and antiseptic, then got a chip gun and punched the tiny tracking capsule into her right shoulder. Was that a slight wince registering at the corner of her eye?

As much as he wanted to look away, Gaspard kept his eyes on the helpless form. The doctor then got a thin shock collar and looped it round the woman's neck, fastening it snugly before activating its contact welding strips to fuse plastic to plastic, locking the collar in place. Then further injections, including another layer of tracking using nanomachines. The woman more clearly suppressed the winces of pain as each procedure took place. Gaspard could barely stand the unfolding scene. Pained empathy clashed with his duty and the bewilderment at these stagnant feelings reborn by a human woman.

Words flowed in his head, taking the place of tears from his eyes. Please,

please, please Gods Beyond let it end. Let anyone else suffer this, but not her. Not this one.

The procedures complete, Gaspard escorted Prisoner 74 to a large transport pod. The transport tube's walls were transparent, giving her a view on several portions of the d'If as they cruised along. In one section human males were kept, a wrestling match was being staged, where it looked like the loser was being slowly choked to death. Another part of the prison housed the male non-human occupants. The female part of the prison passed unseen behind them.

Gaspard clenched his hands, focusing his eyes on the near distance. The reflection glared back at him in sullen mockery. To many looking on, he presumed himself not too poor a sight to behold. At least for any of the Feles in the d'If. A muscular form supported by wrapped digitigrade legs, soft gray fur showing around his prison uniform, the dye-cleaned mane of the casteless cropped short aside from a single long strand falling above his emerald eyes. Even his face had its qualities, though many humans saw only an echo of the tiger of Ancient Earth. Every day he glimpsed his reflection somewhere and sought in it an iota of worth.

In the solitary wing, cells large and small held the d'If's most dangerous inmates, or those who had roused Witton's anger. Prisoner 74's cell was the last in the wing, slotted against the station's exterior wall. Its roof was sloped, so the only place to stand up straight was pressed hard against the interior wall. The bed was in one corner, the bathroom facilities in a tiny adjoining cubicle. It was a pitiful little place, a mockery of home.

Gaspard all but pushed Prisoner 74 inside. As the forcefield door hummed into life, his growling voice spoke above the noise. It sounded forced to his ears, as if he were acting out a mocking version of himself in a play.

"We should be clear about who and what you'll be here, Prisoner 74. You're not a person now, just a number. Ever seen that human A-show? Quite fitting. Someone who defied the state, stripped of all identity. A toilet with shower and sink, a bed, and this door to look through. That's your world. You'll be given two meals a day. Won't taste good, but they'll keep you alive. And don't try crossing this field. Do it, and you'll get some very nasty burns. Only we can deactivate it. And don't think of charming us either." He grinned without malice, surprising himself. "I, for one, don't swing your way."

The woman looked hard at him, frowning a little. "What's your name?"

"Excuse me?"

"I think you heard what I said."

"Trying to get to me?"

"No. It's just that when I get out and meet you again, and you aren't in my good books, I'll want to know who I'll be punishing."

The response and its serious delivery made Gaspard's spirit at once jump and quell. He glanced at the field, which showed strong. He began shuffling away slightly, but the woman's eyes followed him. Eventually he shrugged and replied, his voice shaking a little.

"What the hell. You're not getting out anyway. The name's Gaspard. Gaspard Atarex."

With this final remark, Gaspard moved out of sight. Back in his office, on an impulse he activated the small hidden camera in Prisoner 74's cell. He had to see her without that look, without her being able to see him. He must know what she was really like.

What appeared shocked him more than her in the flesh. As the view flickered into life, Prisoner 74 was slumped on the bed, her poise fallen, tears of some strong emotion creeping down from her eyes. She snapped erect as the observation drone passed, turned, and moved away again. Alone, she crumpled once more, head sagging between her knees, the picture of despair. Another impulse made Gaspard switch on the audio feed for a few seconds.

He heard no sobs, no telltale signs of grief or despair. His ears were stung by words suffused with tones of purest rage. That level voice, which had awoken his heart, now shook with a raw emotion, something he never heard before. He distinguished a name amid the woman's emotive growls.

"Duncan Vorn-Solari." She was repeating it over and over again like a prayer. "Duncan Vorn-Solari. Duncan Vorn-Solari. Duncan Vorn-Solari. Duncan Vorn-Solari. Duncan Vorn-Solari."

He shut off both visual and audio. Sweat was flowing from him, tickling the skin under his fur. Seated at that console, he breathed hard like someone who had been running for his life. Or running toward something. He stared at the controls, at where the woman's face and voice had been projected. His voice was a hoarse entreaty to nothing.

"Who the hell *are* you?"

---

OVER THE NEXT few days, Gaspard was living two lives. The outer life was one of dreary routine and dour suppression. The other half, the secret scandalous half, was looking forward with fervor to his daily visits to Prisoner 74. Witton appointed him as her minder for the first month or two. He would supervise her meal deliveries and make sure the medical and tracking procedures were producing no side effects. Over those first days, whenever he saw Prisoner 74, she seemed lost and alone despite her aloof manner.

There was only one way he could have described it to anyone else. It was like she stared into darkness without any real hope. She was completely controlled in company, but alone she became a different person entirely. Perhaps she needed a psychiatric evaluation.

On the third day, as the food was passed through a gap in the forcefield, he again took notice of the scarring on her face. Those strange markings that on him would look ugly. On her, they took on a measure of beauty.

"Erm, excuse me, but could you tell me where you got those scars?"

The woman looked up with a dull expression but perfect rectitude. "I was born with them. They're an inheritance from my mother. My only gift from her. She's been dead these past ten years."

"Why didn't you get them fixed?"

"Because I don't believe in hiding one's unique features. It's dishonest, shameful. If you have something like this, bear it as a part of yourself. Don't let it be shunned and demonized as a mark of low quality or corruption or hide it out of fear. Let it be your badge of honor, and let all those who fail to push you under flail in their impotence."

The words struck like stab wounds to his soul. She turned away and sat on the bed, showing a wish for him to leave. If it were any other prisoner, he would have stayed there and tormented them with his presence, a means for him to feel any kind of power. But instead, he meekly departed, his mind teaming with ideas. Ideas of loneliness, of sorrow, of isolation that had not been there before.

That night in his private quarters, Gaspard tossed and turned on his bed, unable to sleep. Closing his eyes and thinking inconspicuous thoughts was useless, as was trying to use his usual quota of erotic fantasies. His mind was focused entirely on the woman in the cell. Prisoner 74 with her scarred face and proud posture. That woman's face was behind his eyes, dominating his imagination both waking and eventually sleeping when his eyes finally closed. Words from Witton, from his first days there as a raw and casteless recruit, rose from the back of his mind.

No fraternization with any prisoner of the opposite gender, under any circumstances, is allowed.

Of course he would say that, the bastard. Do as he liked, and all others must follow the rules. After all, what were they, the staff of the d'If? The untouchable dregs, those no other facility would touch. The Cluster's worst guarded by the worst, unable to talk or touch or feel. Except for Echo....

The thought of Echo made him sleep out of sheer brute force. He slept like death and woke to a nightmare of a grinning Feles astride him and pounding his chest with pleasure. Wash out the filth with more filth. That was the thing to do. But during breakfast, looking into his chosen portion of soup with fresh greens, Prisoner 74's face floated in the oil slick. He grimaced and destroyed the apparition with his spoon.

Why? Why did he feel like this? Sexually he was repelled by her. Human women, women of any kind, left him cold. But there was something about her poise that commanded respect and obedience. A prisoner she may be, less than a slave in the courts of Tezta or some indentured worker in the Cruqia Mines. But while all others allowed the d'If to slump their shoulders and bend their necks, she remained erect. It was wonderful and terrible, like staring into a black hole from the outer limits of its gravitational pull.

That day, long before he was due, Gaspard visited Prisoner 74. Standing outside the forcefield, he stared at her for several minutes. The woman's face remained turned away until the door opened, and he passed inside. She glanced round and up, her face remaining a mask of defiance.

"What is it? You're not due for an hour at least."

Her voice demanded a response. Gaspard struggled to find the words, any words that would not be a concession or an apology.

"I'm—Well, I *was*... intrigued. I didn't want to presume... I mean, no, that's wrong. I don't—ah. Gksuk."

An unexpected smile lit up the woman's face. "You needn't be so reticent. It's understandable, seeing me in this cesspool."

"I… yes." His cheeks flushed scarlet beneath the fur.

"Don't be embarrassed. I was brought up with an answer to any situation. If it comforts you, you needn't bother showing sympathy. Prisoners don't deserve sympathy, especially those like me. It's not as if your Warden's going to give me any special privileges." She glanced at him, a glance like a blow to the chin. "Unless you are drawn by more than curiosity. Is that it? Are you, perhaps, interested?"

"I told you—"

"You know I didn't mean my sex appeal. I can read people, you know. But in this modern age, audiobooks are perhaps more informative than the written word. Why not provide some narration for me?"

The words came painfully, like biting on the tongue. "I don't want you hurt."

"Then don't endanger either of us with a passing curiosity. That's all it is, and all it should be in a place like this."

"And if it isn't passing?"

"Don't get yourself into trouble on my account. Now I wish to be alone."

Gaspard was lost for a response. He could only turn and walk away, leaving the prisoner to her solitude.

Over the next month, Gaspard found excuses for visiting more frequently than his duty needed him to. Slowly but surely, Prisoner 74 opened up a little, allowed her poise to fall just a fraction. They talked cautiously about this and that, but neither revealed anything about the other. It was two strangers' careful talk over a garden fence more than the close confidences of friendship. After all, the power dynamic was wrong. She was his inferior in everything but spirit, and he didn't have the guts to break the code. It almost killed him every time.

Finally, at the end of another cautious talk, as Gaspard was about to leave, Prisoner 74 spoke up. "Pardon me, but could you stay a moment?"

Gaspard stopped—something he would never do for any other prisoner. "Yes?"

"I would ask you something. Why are you here in a place like this? I couldn't imagine you sticking around willingly."

"Well…."

This was his moment, his chance for a clean break. He envisioned turning on his heel and leaving, showing this woman he was the one in charge. But the resolve broke like thin ice under a booted foot.

"If you're willing, let's swap. I'll tell you why I'm here, and you tell me why you're here."

The woman considered. "Steep terms. All right. I'm here because I was betrayed by a vile serpent, a base worm unworthy of name or title who stole the heart of my own flesh and blood. I was sent here because death was too risky and exile too costly. I'm to rot here without name or position while he struts about like a king of Ancient Earth. Your turn."

Gaspard considered. "I don't know anymore. I didn't want to do it. It's like that job you take when there's no other option. Sorry if that's a bit weak."

"I understand. A casteless Feles has few opportunities in the Cluster regardless of territory. There is little to tell in such tales."

"If you knew already, why ask?"

"I guessed. You confirmed it. I take it kindly that you held up your end of the bargain."

She turned away, and Gaspard left. This time she did not recall him.

---

IT WAS TWO months later when Gaspard stood in the Warden's office, his mind and spirit still conflicted and dissenting. Automatically Gaspard stood to attention, seeing Witton's preoccupied face, and stood waiting until the Warden spoke.

This was not the day to be anything but obedient.

"Officer Atarex. I want your opinion on something."

"Yes, Sir?"

"You've been spending some time with the newcomer, Prisoner 74. I'm interested to learn what you think of her."

"I think she's harmless."

"Harmless. Is that what you think? I see. I will speak with her again. See if she's changed since our last interview."

"As you wish, Sir."

For all his bowed head and submissive attitude, Gaspard knew how to manipulate. His tone was enough for Witton's eyes to flash. No implicit suggestion, nothing reprehensible, only that slight tonal shift which spoke to the Warden's own insecurities.

"I'm not sure this'll go well either, so you can drop the mannered tone. If she's still like she was, I'll know exactly how to… mellow her."

Picking up his datapad, Witton led the way from his office to Prisoner 74's cell. When they reached it, she was erect on her bed. She deliberately met his gaze as they approached, keeping her eyes fixed on Witton. Gaspard could barely contain his admiration at such unflinching rectitude.

"I've given you plenty of time to think about my offer. What's your answer?"

"The same one I gave you before, Warden."

"You're being quite stubborn."

"Take it how you please."

"Fine. Solitary isn't doing anything, so we'll try something different. Officer Atarex, get Prisoner 74 prepped for transfer to work details in the Factory Level. You'll be her handler. I trust you can manage it?"

"Yes, sir."

After a few desultory matters were settled back in the office, Gaspard was allowed to depart. Once alone in his office, he paced up and down, equally and alternately cursing his cowardice and Witton's cruelty. He should have spoken, done something and faced the consequences. Instead, he watched and nodded. How was she supposed to survive down there? Few other females had.

The Factory Level. Worse than any infernal realm of folklore or religion. Two days down there, and she would snap like a rusted girder. If not from the harsh working conditions, then from the nastier inmates confined there. Any female sent down there was sure to turn up dead within the week if they were lucky. If they were unlucky, then within a fortnight they would be brought for reevaluation by Witton to see if they 'improved.' It was the seedy, slimy underside of the d'If, the part Gaspard knew was there. The part he ignored with all his force of will.

A prison off the map, somewhere the worst can be sent. Yeah, they got that right. Witton's the worst, ten times worse than anyone else in this shithole. He raised his hand, ready to smash it down into the console. It hung suspended in mid-swipe. Gaspard let out a horrible sound, something halfway between a cry and a sob. His hand dropped limply to his side, as impotent as his courage.

What would breaking anything change? Nothing. It was time to stop looking away. Time to do something for her. Past time. But how could he do anything? The last time he tried, he almost screwed it all up. If it hadn't been for Echo....

He sickened at the thought of their last encounter, that ugly welt in his mind that until now closed his heart. But what else could he do? Nothing, though he might rack his brains for hundred years.

An hour later, in one of the interview rooms on the Factory Level, Gaspard paced up and down with nervous expectancy. He stopped and turned as Echo was pushed inside. The prisoner, a brown-haired Feles with platted locks emerging from his mane, stared at Gaspard for several minutes as the shackles were taken from his wrists and the other guards left. Once the door shut, Echo gave a smile that to all but the knowing would come off as friendly. Gaspard felt sick upon seeing it.

"Nice to see you again, Gaspard Atarex. It's been so very long since that little issue I helped resolve. I've barely seen you since then. I'd almost think you were avoiding me."

"I'm not here to talk about that. You said back then that if I never needed a favor related to one of the prisoners, I should come ask you about it. You stick by that?"

"Depends. Say what it is."

"There's a human female being sent down here. She's new, and she's gotten on Witton's bad side. Make sure no-one down here lays a finger on her and get her onto the easier work schedules wherever possible."

Echo frowned, fingering one of his locks. "Tricky. I'll see what I can do—though I'll need to get several of the guards in on it. And she might not cooperate."

"Are you kidding?"

"Just messing with you."

"Bastard. Keep her safe, you hear?"

"Goodness, such energy. I can but do my poor best." The smirk turned into an expectant smile. "But something that complicated would entail, I think, a bigger payment than last time. And no vague promises. I'm not in the mood."

"Look at the camera."

Echo glanced up at the small camera patches on the walls. They were dull, disconnected for the duration. Echo grinned as Gaspard went to the desk and sat on its edge. He spread his legs a little and reached with a hand to unfasten the interlinked folds of cloth that made up the uniform trousers. Echo's grin broadened like an animal shown a treat.

"So, this is it?"

"Yeah."

"Sweet, hopefully. Want a blindfold?"

"No. I'll manage. Just do what you want."

Echo pushed forward and thrust Gaspard down onto the table. The impact jarred his neck, and his back arched. Echo's hands began to probe and prepare. Random thoughts passed through Gaspard's head reflecting on the present and future. He could have struggled against that grip, forced this "payment" to be on his own terms. But no, he lacked the raw nerve for that. He lay still, dulled to the brief spikes of pain within his loins, and thought of the woman in the cell. For her, for that fire which brought some fragment of life back into his dulled existence, he would endure anything.

# FILE 2

## TEN YEARS LATER

*In matters such as the running of a planet or territory,
her skills were little to brag about. But when it came
to manipulation and making alliances, she was unmatched
in her class. She could reputedly charm the state robes
off an Ekri shaman, and win over the most skeptical
human without once raising her voice. She is missed.*

—Excerpt from Fingal Dee's "Politiká"

IN THE ADJOINING bathroom of the largest suite aboard the long-distance luxury cruiser *Hated Brilliance*, a Kavki was taking a bath. The bath lasted three hours, and its occupant picked up the gilded hand mirror to assess the visage she must present to the lowlife staff of Prison Station d'If, the most remote and embarrassing of such locations.

F'thodish Azd Laffw—known to her few friends as "Mephi"—smiled at the reflection, admiring the narrow mouth as it curved up and across. Eyes of a misty gray gazed out above a flattened nose, and a high forehead reached back to the slick scalp and its five atrophied fins. Such relics of the Kavki's aquatic past were useless physically, but it was better to keep her people's most defining trait. She ran a finger along the soft line of her jaw, azure-tinted skin glistening from the bath water.

*"Attention, attention. Approaching Prison Station d'If. All personnel—"*

"Ah, at last." Two loud claps, which sent droplets spraying across the room, summoned her two Kavki serfs. "Ali, I am ready for drying. Bapti, prepare my robes."

"Yes, Mistress."

The drying cubicle was almost icy compared to the bath's sultry warmth, and Ali's gentle assistance with a hand towel did little to ease it. The one distraction was a floor-to-ceiling mirror in the cubicle, giving a view of her total impact. It was good, and not a trace of surgical scarring to betray the additions. Nails shaped to resemble claws, her chest curving with human-like breasts of modest size, the digitigrade legs that looked as if she were standing on tiptoe with elongated feet. A far cry from the normal flat, flipper-like feet her people were born with.

"I see what humans mean about such legs. Like someone wearing high heels. So they do and look so alluring. Be that which others desire, so you might charm them. Do you not agree, Ali?"

Ali's nod was more eloquent than a dozen words. All the confirmation needed. To look her best for all, from the highest ruler to the lowest of vermin, was her role and calling. Whatever the mission, it was time and money well spent. Stepping from the cubicle, she slipped into the flowing garment brought by Bapti from the room-filling ambassadorial wardrobe. Made from the lightest silk produced by one of the Kavki vassal worlds, it flew rather than rippled as she passed from bathroom to dressing room.

Before another mirror, Bapti and Ali presented separate boxes with different accessories and adornments. Her long hands played over them, feeling and considering as she judged their aesthetics. Finally, she selected four items. Clip-on earrings for the narrow pit-like ears, a bracelet of platinum for the right wrist, and a smooth band of gold set with opals for the left third finger. The effect was admirable, though such a waste.

"Why must we don such things for the dross of this universe?"

"We all must do as instructed in this universe, Mistress."

"True, Bapti. Very true." She raised one of the long, flowing sleeves and let it fall and dance in the air. "I have little doubt this will get soiled somehow. Did you treat it beforehand?"

"Yes, Mistress."

"Good. I hope to reuse this, and these fabrics stain so easily."

Under normal circumstances, to don some of her best clothes for someone as lowly as Prison Warden Witton was unthinkable. But today was a special day. It was government business, and she might find a new serf along the way. Ali and Bapti were still her favorites and the best she could wish for, but there was still one thing she wanted. A human to serve her, to be her own for the rest of their natural life. It would be the talk of Kavki social circles, and many Capital Worlds. Not many could boast of having a human serf. And it could prove an interesting memento before she consigned the d'If to history.

"And to think the Feles tried to outlaw serfdom across all the Cluster. Heinous. We can but thank the Seventeen-Fold Cycle the Synod saw fit to remember that the Cluster Culture Protection Act exists for a reason."

Ali and Bapti remained silent, as was their place. Their role was to respond and serve, not critique her random bursts of speech. As they proceeded to the main docking area, Laffw turned to Bapti.

"Is everything ready for our departure? Once the business is done, we must be swift."

Bapti nodded as she spoke. "All is ready when you are. Nothing has been left to chance."

"Correction. One thing has been left to chance. Whether I will find anything worth salvaging in this rat hole. If I make a purchase, ensure it is swiftly retrieved before we leave. I do not want to waste anything here."

The *Hated Brilliance* approached the d'If's buffer zone and deactivated its warp bubble, slowing on its approach to the station's docking area. Laffw walked to the boarding zone at her own pace. No need to hurry herself. Witton would wait for her even if she took all day. He knew the prices she paid for new serfs and would never insult her with impatience. Besides, the honor guard needed to get into place, and the outfit would not stand going at a run or even a trot. This slow and stately speed was both choice and necessity.

"Are the soldiers in position?"

"Yes, Mistress."

"They know their orders?"

"Not to move until your signal."

"If any disobey, they die."

"Yes, Mistress."

The honor guard formed a corridor along the docking tunnel. Laffw waited until they were all in place and the doors wide open, then began her progress. Ali and Bapti followed a half-pace behind. Her eyes, enhanced with nanotech zoom functions, spied out Witton Mondego and four squad captains framing him. One of them was a gray-furred Feles. A newcomer since her last visit eleven years before. Oh well, more people to impress and bluff in their remaining time.

She walked with the utmost grace and drama, the folds of her mantle billowing without crumpling. Ali and Bapti walked with a stately calm, which provided a perfect foil for their mistress. The Kavki guards appeared like Ali and Bapti, outwardly unaltered in form and function. For them, it was true, they were as nature made them, untouched by secret technology. None stirred an inch as she passed each pair, never even glancing at their cold, focused eyes.

Her long-established protocol came into play. Be the greatest, the biggest, the utmost. The translation chips in ears helped with that, removing all the frowns and slowed speeches that had hampered early interactions between the peoples.

It was gratifying to see the d'If squad captains give an appropriate salute as she emerged into the hanger of Docking Port 2. Witton merely gave a gentlemanly bow, otherwise remaining still until she was within reach.

"Ambassador, I'm pleased to see you so resplendent." He took her hand and gave it a very light peck. "May the Three Suns of the Kavki homeworld shine ten thousand years beyond their appointed lives."

"And may the human worlds endure even as their own fades into history." Laffw returned the appropriately archaic greeting. "So many things have changed in these many years, yet you have remained constant against storm and tempest, my dear warden."

"You flatter me too much, Ambassador. And you do me wrong, having stayed away so long."

"Sadly, matters of state demanded my attention. The Human-Ekri Conflict is not so far past that a small skirmish on the new borders could not reignite it. Such negotiations do take years, in this case upwards of a decade. But it appears the time was not wasted here. I am pleased to see the d'If so much... improved." She pondered briefly what incentives or threats had made the prison cleaning details do the hanger floor properly this time. "And I look forward to seeing your stock. I heard it was a most promising selection. Nothing too damaged, I hope?"

"Not at all. Any damage there may or may not have been has long since been healed. They are the best of the best, and fine choices for your retinue."

"Do not all salesmen say their stock is the best? We shall see. By the way, I notice you have a newcomer among your ranks. You must introduce us."

Laffw gestured toward the gray Feles, and Witton introduced her. "Ambassador Laffw, Squad Captain Atarex."

She was all courtesy, as befitted their relative positions. She, one of the Cluster's most powerful figures. He, a homeless and casteless thing given the chance to do something useful. Though not for much longer. At a sign from Witton, Gaspard accompanied them. The journey from Docking Port 2 to the viewing area was short, and she took the opportunity to continue commenting on her surroundings, throwing out small compliments and only the occasional disguised slight. As expected, Witton noticed only the compliments. He made up for his dull wit with animal instinct and institutional fear.

He showed Laffw into the viewing room, a modified observation room for one of the interrogation chambers left over from the d'If's early days as a military detention center. A two-way mirror bisected the room, and those prisoners selected for her consideration were seated on the other side in shadow. Only the spotlight into which they would be called lit up the otherwise darkened chamber, and they could not see Witton and Laffw descend into luxurious tailored seats to view the display.

Settling herself, her legs decorously crossed and her robe flowing out like water across the chair, Laffw prepared herself for the usual dross. It was consoling to remember the wheat she had picked out from similar selections of chaff, a few even from this place. That fine young Feles who died bravely in the arena, a young Ekri with more than suitable qualifications to become her spy. Though none like Bapti, loyal to her since tender adolescence, and certainly none like Ali. Faithful and patient Ali, now waiting outside the room with Bapti and the Feles Atarex.

"How many today?"

"Just eight." Witton sighed, his tone clearly calculated to show disappointment and commiseration. "Most people sent here these days are the ugliest looking bastards you never want to see. Just eugh. I know how much you like beauty, so I chose only the best. Refreshments?"

"Please. How many humans among them? I will take someone from the other peoples if I find one I like, but I did come hoping for a human."

"There are several. I ordered in some special tea, Kavki blend. Just for you."

"You always spoil me."

Ten minutes after Witton pressed a button, the Feles Atarex entered and set the tray down on a hovering table between the two. Once each had their drink—tea for Laffw and some strong-smelling alcoholic distillate for Witton—the first prisoner was called into the light. It was a scrawny-looking human female with a fine figure but terrible coloring and glassy eyes.

"This one, Prisoner 32, real name Hyra Ven, is from Y'jayn. She was sent here three years ago for killing her family. She's got spirit but can easily be trained."

"No." Laffw was immediate and harsh. "She is too dull. Her eyes so weak. Next."

This set the tone for the following several minutes, names and designations followed by a potted history and flavor text. Sipping the vile ill-balanced brew, she considered prisoner after prisoner. They all had some fault. Overblown muscles, unpredictable behavior, wasted figure. But above all else, their eyes were dead. No spark of life remained in them. They were as cold and uninspiring as the eyes of the guards, of the squad captains. And all the time Witton talked on like a vulgar commentator or salesman. So irritating. With the viewing finished, she sat in silence for some minutes.

"Bring out Montmartre and Maiv Kanh again."

Witton nodded and pressed the comm button. "Prisoners 23 and 43, step forward."

A shabby-looking human and a brutish Feles returned to the spotlight. Laffw looked long and hard, then nodded slowly.

"I think Prisoner 23, the human. Montmartre."

"Very well. Would you like to wait in my private quarters until the transfer is ready? We can discuss payment. And perhaps further refreshments?"

"Of course, my dear warden."

Laffw allowed herself to be guided. If not for her clandestine reasons for coming, she would dub the whole affair as a waste of time and money. That disappointed weakling would barely last a week without disciplinary action. But one must keep up some pretense, even if Witton would not live long enough to collect his fee.

As she was passing a row of holding cells, she glanced through the windows at their sullen occupants. Then one figure arrested her attention. She paused, looked again, sure she had been mistaken. Such poise, such pride. Even with the alarm collar given to prisoners brought to the upper levels for medical check-ups, her stance was free and defiant. Witton noted her fascination, but his charming smile faded once he saw its focus.

"I'm sorry, Ambassador. She's not for sale."

"What do you say?" Laffw almost touched the glass, her lips parting. "But such a creature, with that incredible, luminescent spirit. It is like seeing an undiscovered world."

"She's dangerous. *Too* dangerous."

"All the better. I must speak with her at once."

"No."

Laffw looked directly into Witton's eyes. "Mondego, you just said 'no.' Did I not tell you on an earlier occasion that nobody sane says no to me?"

They glared for some moments. Laffw had withstood such obstinacy before and could play the waiting game with the best of them. Ultimately it was Witton who caved, and the lowly warden unlocked the door for the ambassador. His face was a mask of barely suppressed rage and apprehension.

Laffw approached the human woman, who turned to look at her visitor. Even before she saw the scarring on her face, Laffw recognized that poise and strength. No name or circumstances came to mind at once, but she knew she had found a treasure among humans. She approached slowly, causing the human to stiffen. Not with fear, but a solid wish to keep herself from showing any emotion. Laffw would have applauded the effort under different circumstances. She bent close, whispering so Witton would not hear.

"Who are you?"

The woman replied at a matching volume. "Prisoner 74."

"No. Who are you, truly?"

A pause, a flash from those shining eyes. For the first time in years, Laffw's hand tensed as if preparing for a duel. This was a woman worthy of her steel. That glance could not be misread. The human was summing her up, assessing her.

"Maybe if you get me out, I could tell you."

That voice held such an unusual quality. There was a clipped, measured tone almost equal to her own. She had long grown used to Human and Feles speech, so rough and ready and often truncated. All those don'ts and can'ts, so many unpolished phrases. The Kavki and Ekri had no need to rush in their speech. They had more time for refinement and pacing. Perhaps it was the differing lifespans. Humans and Feles were lucky if they reached 120 years and change, though Ekri could still outstrip a Kavki's 160 average by some decades.

Laffw stifled a snigger. "None before you have had the gall to say anything like that to me before. Most refreshing. You ask a high price."

"I've heard a lot about you." The woman assumed a familiar expression, the person with something valuable to sell. "Someone spoke to me about you. A gray-furred guard. I think you'll be interested in what I can offer. More than favors and passing amusement, I promise you."

Laffw gave her lips the briefest of licks, intrigued by this mysterious promise. Then she feigned disinterest and pulled away. Rejoining Witton in the corridor and watching Prisoner 74 through the window as the door was sealed, she smiled. Yes, this one would do nicely. Better than that flaccid Montmartre she had agreed to buy. He would have been a poor consolation prize.

Sitting in Witton's private quarters with more foul-tasting refreshments, Laffw steered the talk away from anything concerning Prisoner 74. The look in the warden's eyes was enough to guess his agitation. Whoever the prisoner was, she was important as well as dangerous. This chance meeting between Prisoner 74 and Laffw had been unplanned, and it worried him. So be it. Let him worry. Let him grow ever more agitated, reveal more of his stake in the strange woman's situation.

The breaking point came as Laffw steered the conversation back toward the mating habits of the Whixy Gadfly for the third time in a row. Witton's manners collapsed like a house of cards, and he banged his fist on the table with enough force to knock its hovering adjustments out of sync.

"Cut the chatter, Ambassador. What's your game?"

"Game?"

"You're interested in that girl. Prisoner 74. Well, I'm telling you, no matter how much you try and persuade me, she's not gonna get out of here alive. I'm making sure of that."

Laffw could read Witton like a book. "Oh, dear. You finally found a woman immune to your charms? That must sting."

"That's got nothing to do with it. She's a political prisoner, dangerous and cunning. She'll get to you. Perhaps she already has. I saw you talking with her."

"Not eavesdropping, I hope."

"Ambassador, whatever you do, I'm not letting her go."

"Have I mentioned her in all the time we talked up to now?"

"No. That's the problem."

There was a knock at the door. Witton's head snapped round, and he spoke in something between a bark and a growl. "What is it?"

Atarex entered and gave a short bow. Ali and Bapti were just visible beyond the half-closed door.

"Apologies for interrupting, but there's an emergency in docking transfer. Prisoner 23 is being difficult."

"Urg. Fine. Ambassador, please excuse me."

"Of course."

Witton left with a loud snort, clearly frustrated at both Prisoner 23 and his interaction with Laffw. Left on her own, Laffw considered her possible courses of actions. After a minute's thought, she tapped one of the two small gems on the collar of her cape, a customized comm. On the point of speaking, her eyes flicked back to where Atarex was still standing, left in limbo by Witton's rapid departure. His face was pinched, his movements stiff. He was anxious about something. Two and two clicked together in her mind. She looked him up and down, then spoke with the sharp tone of command.

"Squad Captain Atarex?

"Yes, Ambassador Laffw?"

A smile crossed her lips, the first true smile since meeting the human. "It is good to hear someone use my full and proper title."

"I believe in showing respect to my peers."

"Yes. Tell me, do you want to save someone?"

The Feles remained silent. That silence was answer enough for Laffw. She placed her fingertips together.

"It is that girl, Prisoner 74, is it not? She said something about a gray-furred guard. I at first thought she meant 'gray-haired.' Was she referring to you?"

Clearly this Feles had trained himself well in hiding his emotions from the local rabble. But Laffw was not of their stock, seeing through the facade with no effort.

"You need not say anything. Silence speaks volumes. But since the human spoke of you so, I assume you mean something to her. So I may as well tell you that the d'If will be floating debris within minutes of my departure."

"What?" Atarex's jaw dropped.

"Try to keep your voice down. In the current political climate, it does not suit the interests of the Synod for such a place to exist. Off the grid, where anyone may be held for the right price, holding more secrets than their secret files, and twice as damaging. Its existence may be rediscovered, and before anyone can investigate more fully, it must vanish. A tragic accident."

"And you were picked because?"

"Because I was coming, anyway. So, do you want to save her?"

"Yes."

"You must be quite smitten. It matters not to me. Ali, Bapti." The two serfs entered and awaited their orders. "I would have you aid this Feles in his mission. The woman called Prisoner 74 is to leave with us, and with this one if she so chooses. I presume you wish to come, Officer Atarex?"

"Y-yes."

Her eyes quivered up and down, taking in his frame. "I have little under-standing of what drives the Feles mentality."

There was no reply to this jibe. Ali and Bapti were standing by the door-way, and the three went as a body. Laffw tipped the rest of her drink onto the floor, listening as the trio vanished down the corridor to where Prisoner 74 was being held. It was a simple matter to close the door and seat herself. Best to wait it out here until Bapti could return. As the chaos slowly unfolded beyond, she sat and smiled.

---

OPENING THE CELL door proved easy for Ali's practiced hand. Such huge, primitive circuitry was at least a century behind the times. No liq-uid-based ducts, no plasma, no nothing. All solid-state, eminently breakable. If asked, she would have memorized the code Witton put in to open the door. But Laffw had not asked or even indicated, only engaged in the duel of wills which quelled the human warden and watched as he acquiesced. Just as all ultimately acquiesced to her mistress.

The door popped open, and Ali had to flatten herself against the frame as the Feles Atarex rushed in. Through the door, she took in the human woman identified as Prisoner 74, her scarred face turned and looking warily at the opened door. Even as Bapti was distracted by a call from their mistress, the Feles extended his hand.

"Come. Quickly."

The human narrowed her eyes. "What game is this?"

"No game. We're going before the place gets blown to atoms. Ambassador Laffw's giving us a free ride."

"Hardly free, I'd guess. But are you serious?"

"Completely. Well?"

Prisoner 74 seemed deep in tortured thought, but it lasted only a moment. Ali almost grimaced at this false display, all for the Feles's benefit. He must be completely under her thumb. So like a human, using their wiles to get under everyone's skin in one way or another. Like in the Human-Ekri Conflict's aftermath, persuading the Synod that they were in the right as the victors.

As Atarex all but dragged Prisoner 74 from the room, the collar round her neck began screeching. The Feles quickly used his control wristband to disable the alarm. It was just two seconds of noise, but that was still two seconds too long. Footsteps sounded behind them. Two guards responding to the call, human by sound of their stride. Before they were round the bend in the corridor, she slipped through and behind them, delivering two swift blows with the small dagger hidden in her tight-wound sleeve. The men fell with a choking cry, their spinal cords severed at the neck.

The Feles was clearly shocked by the swift dispatch. The human merely nodded and spoke directly to Ali.

"Impressive. Your name?"

Ali looked at the woman without even opening her mouth. What was the point? There was no voice to answer. Though she could not blame the human for not knowing. The ring adornments round her neck hid nearly all the scarring from those injuries of long ago. The wounds from a human's rifle weapon which had torn her voice away. Bapti stepped in and introduced the two of them with a bow.

"Forgive my companion." She spoke in the same honey-like voice that always grated upon her nerves. "She is mute."

Ali and Prisoner 74 stared at each other for several seconds. Then Prisoner 74 shrugged and looked at Bapti.

"What's going to happen?"

"This prison will be destroyed within half an hour. It appears our mistress wishes to save you."

"So, she's accepted my offer."

"That is none of my business."

"And Witton will die?"

"Yes." Atarex answered this time.

Prisoner 74's face took on an odd, unsettling expression. "So, it doesn't matter if he's dead a little early?"

Atarex struggled to reply. "What do you mean?"

Prisoner 74 raised an eyebrow at the Feles. It was a look Ali recognized from other humans touched by the lust for blood, for retribution by fair means or foul. That look which said, *Do you have to ask?* Atarex hesitated a moment, then drew a long shock baton from his belt and gave it to her. The human tested its weight and activated it, causing a spark to flash across the two tiny prongs at its tip.

"Perfect. Where would our dear warden be now?"

"In Docking Port 3 Transit with Prisoner 23. They'll be loading him aboard the *Hated Brilliance* within the next few minutes."

"Would you accompany me?"

The Feles again hesitated, and this time shook his head. "No. I can't. I *won't.*"

"Why not?"

Ali gave no time for Atarex to answer. The discomfort in his body language was painful to watch. She stepped forward and motioned with her hand. She was willing to accompany the human. Bapti gave a dismissive snort.

"Well then, I leave you two to your quest. I must ensure this Feles remains safe. And in case you missed it, Ali, I received a message from Mistress. Prisoner 23 is no longer desired. Their fate is open."

Ali nodded. Open fates were a good thing to have, until they closed about one's neck like the arms of a vice to choke you.

While Bapti took Atarex back to where Ambassador Laffw was waiting, Ali followed Prisoner 74 down a sequence of corridors. Once or twice, the human would stop and glance at a few directional signs stamped into the metalwork,

then resume her fast walk. A miracle she could walk at all, she looked so malnourished. Whether stubbornness, some hidden energy, or plain insanity was
driving her, Ali neither knew nor cared to know. She had offered to accompany
this human her mistress seemed to value and would do so.

The pair entered the hanger of Docking Port 3 on a metal gangway running along the upper story. Looking down into the poorly lit space below,
they spied Witton and a group of guards brutally restraining Prisoner 23.
Harsh words and blows from batons were gradually quelling the inarticulate
human, forcing him into submission. A wonder he resisted so. Perhaps he was
afraid to leave?

Ali averted her eyes as a brutal blow all but broke the man's chin, but Prisoner 74 watched on impassively. Typical human, numb to brutality except
when placed beneath it.

"Come now," Witton's voice echoed from below, "be a good boy and get
into that cage. Or you'll be getting some more lessons in obedience."

What lessons might have followed none would know. From Docking Port
2's hanger came muffled sounds of stun fire, some kind of shouting, all deadened by the metal walls separating the two spaces. The guards were clearly
objecting to her mistress's plan. Witton's voice snapped like a whiplash.

"What's that? Squad Captains, respond."

There was no reply. Not even the comm was functioning. The *Hated
Brilliance* was blocking local channels, as per instructions. Witton ordered a
guard to investigate. Prisoner 74 eyed him with the look of a wounded lion,
anger and caution commingling. She glanced at Ali.

"Whatever you do to the others, I want Mondego. Got it?"

Ali understood, better than this human did. Everyone on the d'If would
be dead or dying very soon. To kill those down below now would be a kindness. Better she did it than the Feles, or this strange prisoner with her eyes
of hatred. A quick leap took her over the railing, and Ali was on the ground
within the small circle of soldiery. The grunting hiss within her legs was a re-
assuring sign, the old implants still working their magic. A quick contraction
of the wrist muscles, and a single-edged daggers shot into each hand.

It would be the work of seconds to kill such ill-trained rabble, and less
than easy to grant them mercifully quick deaths. Heart or spine, quick with
little pain, never prolonging their demise. It was her way, and it worked.

Nearly all attempted to fight, their slow reactions no match for enhanced speed and the skill born of war. The one nearest the door rushed to help her comrades and was dispatched with a single thrust to the heart.

As could be predicted, Montmartre was taking advantage of the situation. He grabbed a guard and choked them, backing away to a door he must assume was unlocked. A typical human response, run and hide to snipe from safety. With barely a second thought, she darted behind and sliced at both their necks, severing their spinal cords. They dropped like limp marionettes. The whole process had taken less than twenty seconds.

Prisoner 74 lowered a nearby ladder and clambered down from above. Witton tried to flee himself, but Ali's long arm reached out and threw him against the side of the prisoner cage. He stared up at her, then began shuffling and scrabbling as if he might climb up the cage wall. Prisoner 74 approached at a slow walk, the sparking baton in hand. The fear was clear in his eyes, though not fear of the human female. It was Ali's imposing presence that kept him in place.

As she drew level with him, Prisoner 74 reached round to her shoulder with a deliberate lack of speed. The mark of the tracking chip was clear, similar to Ali's own buried in the skin above her chest. The human barely winced as she pressed the baton against the scar, sending down a charge that would destroy the implant. It was difficult not to admire such pure nerve. Barely a wince of pain, hardly a twitch. Then Prisoner 74 lunged forward, thrusting the baton down at Witton like a blade. It struck his groin, and he screamed as the electric shock rippled through his body.

Ali watched as the woman thrashed, struck, and prodded Witton's most sensitive parts, the shocks prompting spasms of agony. What started as cries of pain and anger degenerated into inarticulate wails of mercy, like a beaten child begging their tormentor for succor. It recalled memories of an unsanctioned interrogation complex Ali raided over thirty years before. Those same cries, that same degradation of self in the name of information. But here, pain was the only goal.

After five minutes, the panting Prisoner 74 took a step back. Witton uncurled himself and stared up with tear-filled eyes. Her face suddenly became pleasant, an expression more terrible than rage or scorn.

"About your proposal, Witton. Do you remember what I told you when we first met? He who seeks the unaffordable knows only disappointment. I must respectfully decline on the grounds that you won't be alive to receive it."

With a motion like a striking snake, Prisoner 74 drove the baton down against Witton's forehead, at the same time pushing the voltage up to max. The warden writhed in his death agony, his brain shocked beyond endurance. The woman's face shone with savage joy, an abused beast allowed to take revenge on its captor. After ten seconds of screaming convulsion, Witton's cries ceased, his body going limp aside from the spasmodic aftershocks from the weapon. His killer backed away from the grisly sight, tossing the baton away. She spoke to the twitching corpse.

"It's over. It's finished. I did promise, Witton Mondego."

Typical human. All culture and truth when it suited them, then just as barbarous as any other people in the Cluster. Prisoner 74 turned and looked Ali straight in the face.

"I trust you can take me to your mistress? I haven't got all day."

Ali nodded. What else could she do? Hers was to obey and protect her mistress's property. And, for the moment at least, Prisoner 74 was her willing property. Without another word, Prisoner 74 followed Ali from the room into Docking Port 2, leaving behind the scene of death they had together created.

---

LAFFW, THE BOREDOM building in her, waited by Docking Port 2. "I trust she will not be too long."

A small legion of soldiers and staff moved the bomb-containing box on its floating platform into position near one of the power lines. A simple bomb based on energy feedback. One signal, and the bomb would trigger catastrophic overload in every mechanism in the d'If. And before that, the last flourish of an override signal opening every cell door, allowing the inmates to run riot.

She was on the point of returning to the ship to wait when a door opened and the small party appeared. Ali and Bapti, escorting the haggard-looking Feles and a triumphant Prisoner 74. The latter approached with an upright poise which made Laffw smile. There was new confidence in her stride and a burn mark on her shoulder. Even with graying hair and the malnourished look all prisoners shared, she was to be noticed.

Laffw directed her question at the prisoner. "I take it you are ready to leave this place?"

"I've done what I must, so yes."

"I see. But before we leave, there is something I want to know."

"And what's that?"

"You said you would tell me your name if I helped you escape. I think this qualifies."

Prisoner 74 glanced at the hovering crate behind them, then back at Laffw with an odd smiling expression. Laffw bent, and Prisoner 74 whispered her name into Laffw's ear. Memories emerged from obscurity and attached themselves to the face. The smile on the human's lips mutated from grin to laugh.

"Surprised?"

"Somewhat." Laffw looked at this woman with the scarred face and modest clothing. "This is priceless. Of all the places in the Cluster, in the galaxy, in the universe where one could find you, I find you in a cell of the d'If. And they say irony is dead."

"Irony brought me here, perhaps." The woman's cool voice broke her smile. "But my goals are plain. For a decade I've languished here, and you've given me the opportunity to find myself again."

"Now, now. I do not talk business when I am already on the job, as you humans say. Save that for after the d'If is disposed of. Atarex has told you?"

"Yes. I'm surprised it didn't happen sooner."

Laffw guffawed. The cold detachment was like nothing she had heard, and coming from such a one was downright hilarious. Bapti and Ali had stayed at a distance with the Feles until now, and with a gesture they were all called over. Atarex hesitated, unsure. Laffw pointed him out to Prisoner 74.

"What of him?"

The woman looked at the Feles and spoke with a level detachment. "I would have him safe. Let him come."

"As you wish." Laffw gave a mocking bow. "Let us then return to the ship. We all deserve some *proper* refreshment. Warden Mondego always chose the most dreadful teas."

The woman's voice was cool. "Well, he won't anymore."

"I see." Another guffaw. "This will be amusing. For that, I shall slightly delay my planned spectacle until we can both view it in comfort."

Within a few minutes, the group was aboard the *Hated Brilliance*, and Laffw ordered that the woman be brought fresh clothes.

The woman nodded her thanks. "Let's meet when I can make myself presentable."

"Indeed we shall… Mercedes Angael Quistor Solari."

# FILE 3

## THE END OF PRISONER 74

*To freedom we fly, its close caress,*
*and despair ignore, it needs no less.*
*To a life fulfilled we sprint at speed,*
*to depression's yoke we pay no heed.*
*Let this stricture be our guiding light,*
*we scale the pyramid to its height.*

—Stanza from Fingal Dee's "Ode to Life's Folly"

HAVING HER NAME spoken by another person again, let alone the fish-like face of a Kavki, washed Mercedes clean of a decade of inadequacy within a second. Bapti departed with the Kavki ambassador. Ali lingered and waited for Mercedes and Gaspard. The Feles looked fidgety and unwell. She bent close and spoke softly.

"For you, no need to remember titles as yet. For now, I'm Mercedes."

Before Gaspard could respond, another Kavki entered saying she was assigned to escort him to his quarters. Mercedes looked into the face of the Feles who had spent a decade protecting her, then turned to Ali.

"I'm ready now. Where are my quarters?"

Mercedes was led to what she assumed was an annex of the ambassador's suite aboard the ship. Ali conducted her into a bathroom twice the size of her cell in the d'If and left her to herself. A heaven lay about her in shades of blue, cobalt, and pure white. The closest she had been to a bath was a quick soak in lukewarm scum-flecked water during work duty in the d'If's Factory Level, arranged by that strange Feles character Echo. As the bath water roared into the basin, she tore off the old prison clothes down to the last tardy scrap of underclothing. Turning, she caught herself in the room's full-length mirror. The ravages of ten years in prison struck like a blow, scouring eyes that hadn't seen a proper mirror in all that time.

She barely recognized the woman looking back at her. A shell of her former self, her rich dark hair was thinned and graying in places, her skin tone sallow and unhealthy, and she could in places see the outline of ribs and joints in her malnourished form. It looked like someone in the middle of being skeletonized for posterity. Slipping into that bath was a shock, like stepping into a house unseen for many years and finding it completely unchanged from sweet memory. There was a datapad on the table next to the bath, and she picked it up.

Everything was roughly the same. Thank goodness for Technology Unification Laws. No huge changes, even a good signal. Laffw must have a ClusterNet signal booster in the ship's core. Now she needed to find up-to-date information.

The news was all as expected. New trade routes opened between the Lutheyan region and Ekri border outposts as "a sign of unity following war." The multi-species Axiom was flourishing once more, its population reintegrated after decades of separation. An economic depression in White Oil produce was causing stock market issues, prompting the Synod to meet and discuss potential market salvage. She flicked through these wider issues, then searched for news of her home, New Dubai. The headline words burned her eyes before she even pressed the link.

### QALAA'S PROSPECT TRIAL POSTPONED

In recent developments, representatives of the Ekri immigrant population Qalaa's Prospect have asked for further time to consider their defense regarding disputed claims to the Alasaya region of New Dubai's southern continent. This arid region is contested by the Ekri immigrants as having been ceded to them in ancient treaties with the people of New Dubai as part of agreements during humanity's early days in the Cluster.

Grand Prosecutor de Granger, who is handling the case for the Duchy, contests that the aggressions demonstrated in the

Human-Ekri Conflict render such agreements null and void, and that Qalaa's Prospect is an unsanctioned settlement that must be dismantled and its population moved by force if necessary.

This marks the third consecutive delay to the trial which will decide this legal battle. Said Granger's spokesperson during pre-trial press conference, "We feel confident that—"

Her teeth clenched in anger. Were she still Duchess, the Ekri wouldn't be fighting for their homes. They had a right to that land. Georges de Granger, that human-centric mountebank. He'd stoop to anything to win a case, to preserve the status quo and impede the rightful word of his leaders. She should've turfed him out ten years ago.

She wondered....

It took little effort to find archived news from the beginning of her imprisonment. The next article made even more painful reading.

We regret to report the sad death of Mercedes Solari, who until six months ago was the 50th duchess of the planet New Dubai and Demesne of Argo. Originally forced to retire following three years in the role due to health issues, her post was filled by the newly ennobled Duncan Vorn, husband to Duchess Solari's younger sister, Gretchen. Named Duke Vorn-Solari, he took the former duchess's place and managed power until the reported death of Mercedes Solari following a prolonged illness.

Among the duke's notable achievements is the recent White Oil boom. A key ingredient to the creation and maintenance of modern White Engine technology, White Oil was previously restricted to several planets within Kavki space after the original human-controlled mines on New Terra were destroyed during the Human-Ekri Conflict twenty years prior. New Dubai confirmed White Oil deposits two years ago, and Duke Vorn-Solari has successfully negotiated export rights at the human-staffed mining centers.

Reports from New Dubai indicate that supporters of the

late Duchess Solari attempted to prevent Vorn-Solari from inheriting the position through marriage, but the movement was quickly crushed based on an earlier marriage-based inheritance cited by his legal representative Georges de Granger. Aided by the tactical actions of General Henri Laurent-Leblanc, Vorn-Solari's chosen legal and political representative presented proof that Mercedes Solari had entrusted the dukedom to her brother-in-law's care.

Following national mourning for the duchess, Duke Vorn-Solari and his wife have announced that Her Grace is pregnant with their first child."

With an unrestrained roar, Mercedes threw the datapad across the room, hearing its frame and screen crack as it struck the wall. Her world, her people, made to watch and nod under that usurper's hand, read words put into her absent mouth. His cronies, all high and mighty on their stolen thrones. And Gretchen, poor Gretchen, who never did see that tick for what he was. Those three, those men with their smiling masks, had forced her from power, then stolen ten years of her life along with her throne. She would show them.

"Yes. Yes, I will."

Her laugh bubbled like the foam enveloping and cleansing her body. She would show them. In that cell in the d'If, it was all pipe dreams. But one chance look through a window and she got the perfect tool in the palm of her hand. But how to use it? And what would Laffw accept as a price?

For ten minutes, brushing and scrubbing and grinding away the dirt and scum of a decade's prison time, her mind turned. At the end of that time there came a knock at the door, and Ali entered to help dry and cloth her. The process was very impersonal, and Ali's eyes never lingered for long on Mercedes's time-bruised form.

Then it was on with a bathrobe and into the outer room where a dress waited for her. It was a style she recognized as Neo-Tudor, harkening back to Ancient Earth. Great sleeves fell over a long-hooped skirt, the kirtle was as light as gossamer, and a high starched collar spread out like a leaf. Its main modern concession was a slimmer skirt for ease of movement. There were also embracing boots with the slightest heel. The whole ensemble was made of sumptuous fabrics in difficult shades and adorned with exotic embroidery. Laffw had good taste.

Mercedes donned the dress, then followed Ali to where Ambassador Laffw was waiting. She felt the barely perceptible jolt as the *Hated Brilliance* detached from its moorings and began moving away from the d'If. Ali led her to the ship's stern-side observation room, now illuminated by the tempered light of the Ares twin stars. In one of two chairs, Laffw reclined in a different and, if possible, more resplendent gown. Seeing Mercedes, she gently clapped her hands.

"A true vision, Mercedes Solari."

Mercedes smiled. "I'm surprised you know about human high fashion."

"It is my business to know other peoples. That is what an ambassador must do. The Cluster would be nothing if the right people did not know about their neighbors and partners. Also, those prison clothes did not suit you."

Mercedes looked at the copious sleeves. "Hydreen fur, embroidery from New Dubai's Royal District, footwear by deSartre. Perfect taste."

"If you are who you say you are, you deserve those clothes. But if not, then you are…. Oh, what is the human expression? Mutton dressed as lamb?"

"It's lamb dressed as mutton, and that's not the right expression. You could say I'm a wolf in sheep's clothing. Or dressing above my station."

"Thank you for the correction. Now let us refresh ourselves. I assumed you might want to see your former home's end."

Mercedes smiled, her depraved glee tempered by years of training. "Thank you, Ambassador. I'd love to. May I know your full name?"

"F'thodish Azd Laffw. Mephi to my friends, merely 'the Ambassador' to some contacts and most of my enemies."

"Ambassador Laffw will do. If you wish, I can simply use 'Ambassador.'"

"Both are more than acceptable."

"Good. And yes, some refreshments would be most welcome."

"Of course. Ali, help Bapti bring the refreshments."

Ali bowed and departed. She was gone less than ten seconds, then she and Bapti brought in the refreshments. As they were laid out, Mercedes noted Laffw taking in her poise and grace. It took less than a second for Mercedes to sum her up. A dangerous person, acting the fop but as sharp as a razor, and cunning as they made them. Laffw checked the small timepiece which hung from a part of her necklace, then looked again at Mercedes. Mercedes gently sipped from her glass and looked at the sea of stars around the d'If.

"I believed you were dead. So New Dubai's news said."

"I was." Mercedes spoke bluntly. "I died ten years ago when the uprising failed, and I was sealed in the d'If by a foul usurper. I've spent ten years without a name or anything to call my own. I was Prisoner 74. But that moniker tarnishes me no more. I'm myself once again, and I have you to thank."

"Do not thank me." Laffw's smile was toxic. "I never do anything out of charity. I have taken a chance, gambled, and won. Now I have in my hand one of the best bargaining chips anyone could possess. A dead ruler returned to life."

"Perhaps we should discuss the matters when we are safely away from the d'If. And after the d'If is no more."

"Of course. Anything for an asset."

"Is it so simple for you? Use me and throw me away?"

"Not throw away. Remember, I was there to buy someone as a serf."

"That's different. Your laws aren't ours. They never were and never will be."

"True. What you see as slavery we see as a natural part of life. But I think we should leave those discussions until we known each other better. Oh, I forget, do you enjoy a little stimulation? Bapti."

From some obscure corner, Bapti brought what looked like an opaque beaker perched on three legs with a long pipe feeding from its neck to a head shaped like the mouth of an archaic wind instrument. It was a Smoker, a high-end device based on Ancient Earth hookahs, filled with various stimulants both subtle and malign. Mercedes's face puckered in undiluted disgust.

"No. I don't. I prefer not to dull my senses."

"Ah yes, of course." Laffw took a long draw from the device before continuing, "I forgot human biology is so fragile. We can take ten times the amount you do before it begins impacting our senses. For me, two blows every few weeks is more than enough to keep me satisfied. Not like those poor slobs from your home planet who needed such stimulation in flammable paper tubes hundreds of times in a day."

"I have no interest in discussing the fallacies of my ancestors."

"As you wish. Perhaps discuss something more appropriate. Like why you care for that Feles. He is such a pitiful thing."

Mercedes stared directly ahead as she answered. "He can be useful. Also, he kept me safe. He defended me from the others in there. It's poor sport to abandon one's helpers to death when their worth is proven. Speaking of which, will they all die trapped in their cells?"

"Not at all. After we boarded, we arranged for not only the planting of a bomb, but the opening of every cell door and security gate in the place. I would guess that for the past few minutes, the place has been running riot as prisoners do whatever escaped prisoners do."

"Escape?"

"Or taking out their anger on the first guard they see. I pity those who run into a prisoner who thinks death is too easy. Some may escape, and that would add to the story if it were told at all. A riot leading to the overload and collapse of the d'If's power system. A tragic incident, plus total destruction of all information storage."

"Clever. And expensive."

"When the central government of the Cluster gives you a mission, no expense is spared. Enjoying your drink?"

"Excellent." Mercedes sniffed the dark blue liquid. "Synxiyn wine."

"Our people's name for it is 'T'hrakki.' But I think human terminology is applicable in this case. It is a fine wine."

"Not as good as some of my planet's vintages."

"A bold claim. Maybe you could show me one day."

"It would be a pleasure. Assuming that day comes. And you let it come."

Laffw smiled again, then checked her timepiece. "I think we can watch the spectacle now. You can see some smaller shuttles trying to undock. Good luck to them, we sent a feedback loop into the clamping system. The only way they will leave is by tearing themselves to pieces."

"But if any do get away?"

"I will certainly not let them aboard my ship." Laffw activated her comm. "Captain, stop engines until further orders and trigger the bomb. If any shuttles try docking, take all action necessary."

"Understood."

Laffw looked at Mercedes with a smile. "This should be interesting."

Mercedes and Laffw watched. Ten seconds passed. Twenty. Forty. Then it happened. With little warning, the vast structure fractured along a natural fault, blowing several of the walls. The whole power system had undergone catastrophic failure, rupturing its innards. Any flames there may have been died instantly in the vacuum of space, and heat-scarred debris shot in all directions. From within, through breaches in the d'If's walls, objects were propelled out as the atmosphere evacuated. The shuttles were torn away and sent adrift. Living people met the void, twisting for a bare ten seconds before succumbing to their fate. Guard uniforms and prisoner overalls were indiscernible at this distance. The last pockets of atmosphere were being consumed by the chain reaction.

It was horrible and arresting, like watching an execution. Mercedes was unable to look away no matter how hard she might try or how terrible the sight. Not that she wanted to. She felt no pity for those dying in and around the d'If. All she felt was a sense of terrible triumph. She had saved the one person worth saving. All the rest did not matter. She would enjoy the spectacle and take satisfaction in this indirect retribution.

Mercedes turned to Laffw. "Are you always this ruthless?"

"On official business, my feelings do not matter. I will take life when I must. Or rather, I will order life to be taken. And now that we have satisfied your wishes and my business, maybe we can talk. Or would you rather wait?"

"Where are we heading?"

"Cape Life. I have a home there."

"I would discuss matters further at Cape Life. Also, I would like to speak with Gaspard."

"The Feles? Very well. Ali, take her to Atarex's quarters."

Ali, who had been waiting out of sight, came forward and gestured gently toward one of the doors. Mercedes followed Ali along the curving corridor to a transport pod, which carried them to another part of the ship. She was led down a long corridor lined with simple doorways. They came to one marked Z-B3, and Ali opened the door with a light touch on the pad beside its frame. Inside, Gaspard was sitting in a simple chair, a half-empty glass in his hand. He glanced up, seeing Mercedes enter.

"Ali, leave us." Mercedes's voice was firm.

Ali nodded, the door hissing shut behind her. Gaspard turned away from Mercedes as she approached. She could tell by his lolling head, vacant expression, and forced speech that he was drunk. Or at least he appeared drunk.

"Gaspard Atarex?"

Gaspard looked up with blurry eyes. "Yeah? What is it, oh, grand Mercedes Solari? Want a drink?"

"No. I wanted to see you."

"You've seen me. That's all sorted. Hey." He seemed struck by a thought. "I didn't ever get to see the penal mine shafts. They always told me there was gold down there. Never got to find out. Heh. Laughable."

He struggled to make a sound like laughter, then burbled and hid his face. Mercedes struggled to hide her disgust at his condition.

"You seem more than distressed. I would think you were glad to leave that place."

Gaspard answered dryly, his voice slurring, his blurry eyes staring directly at Mercedes. "Oh sure I'm distressed. That place was one of the only jobs I could get along with scraping out engine coils. I've thrown it up, let my co-workers die, helped some Kavki bitches kill my superior. Then there's you, a prisoner for whom I gave up more than she'll want to know to survive that hell. And here I am, drinking shit and getting hollow sympathy."

"You might not be as drunk as you seem. I know that defense. Cruel words may be taken lightly when spoken through a fog of alcohol."

"You think I'm not drunk? Here." Gaspard snatched up the empty bottle from the floor by his feet, got up with an effort, and waved it under Mercedes's nose. "All that. In under half an hour. Tell me I'm not drunk after that."

"So, you're drunk. What of it?"

"So, I've betrayed everyone I know, left them to die. For some bitch called Mercedes Solari. It was better when you were Prisoner 74."

Patience exhausted, Mercedes snatched both bottle and glass from Gaspard's grip, then pushed him back into the chair. Pinned by her booted foot, Gaspard gaped at her, an expression of terror warping his face. Mercedes's voice became hard, venomous.

"I have no patience for those who hide in drink. Measure yourself anew, Feles, or risk losing my respect. The d'If is in ruins, its prisoners and staff dead or dying. You have nothing to regret, nothing to tie you to that fetid life. I offer you the choice to come with me and aid my quest. Or you can be dropped off at the nearest habitat with a bar to wallow in your sentimental self-loathing."

Gaspard looked at Mercedes for a moment, then burst into hiccupping sobs and hugged her leg. He was like a child before her, and the sight softened Mercedes's heart for the first time in years. Gently extricating her leg from his grasp, she helped him over to the large bed, trying not to wince at his drink-sodden breath. Laying him on the bed, she watched as he cried himself to sleep. Only when he was snoring did she leave and ask for Ali to lead her to her own room.

"And," added Mercedes, "when he's able, please have him come to my room."

Ali nodded, as silent as she always had been. As they rode back, Mercedes took the opportunity to study her companion. She noted the multilayered choker about her throat, the pinprick edges of scars it just failed to conceal on her long neck. She also noted the hairline scarring partially masked by make-up across Ali's fern-colored skin.

Back in her own room, Mercedes sat in her chair, her eyes closed, waiting for Gaspard to come. It was a full hour, and a slight snooze later, when the door opened and Ali showed Gaspard in. His eyes were sunken, and he looked like someone had hit him over the head. He came over and stood before Mercedes.

"When I woke up, Ali was outside the door. Brought me here."

"I asked her to. I think I owe you an explanation about myself." Mercedes quickly gave her name, titles and former position. "Now do you understand why I wished to escape?"

Gaspard's eyes had grown wide, then doubtful. Maybe he thought she had gone insane during the years of confinement. Tempering her voice, she spoke with the soft tones of a mother to a confused child.

"I can guess what you did to help me. In return, I can help you. I don't offer safety or an easy life, but I can offer a place to belong. That's what you've wanted all along, isn't it?"

Slowly, Gaspard dropped to one knee and bowed his head. "Mercedes. Mistress. Your Grace. I accept this and will give my all to repay you."

Mercedes looked at Gaspard, then rose and held out her right hand, asking curtly for his left. Gaspard extended it and started as she took it in an iron grip. Mercedes fiddled with one of the nails on her left hand. It slid away, showing the tiny laser inside. Witton had wanted to remove it, but it could do nothing to the systems of the d'If, so it remained as a useless accessory until now.

Before Gaspard could react, Mercedes activated the laser and played its beam across his palm. He winced, and Mercedes knew from other reports that it stung like salt across a scab. It took less than a minute to finish, and when complete, it was all but invisible.

"You now bear the sigil of New Dubai, a symbol given only to those retainers closest to the Dukedom. You belong for as long as I need you and you need this. In return, you will serve me in any and every capacity until whatever instigates release from this charge. Desertion or betrayal are not options. Is that understood?"

Gaspard slowly nodded his head. Mercedes gently dismissed him, her eyes following the Feles back out through the door. There was a new lift in his shoulders, a sense of self that had not been there before. Good. She needed a confidant, and he had become one.

Left alone, Mercedes drifted into the bathroom. Her old prison clothes still lay on the floor, untouched by any. Picking them up, she noted the number printed in black across their right breast. 74. It took a second to locate the waste chute, an inconspicuous little doorway in a dark corner. Teeth gritted, she flung the prison clothes down the chute to meet their fate. As the chute door slammed, she turned away, smiling in triumph.

At long last, Prisoner 74 was dead.

---

"HMMMFFF. HMMMMFFF."

"I'm sorry." Echo was completely insincere. "You know there's not enough air recycling capacity for two in here."

Echo adjusted the guard's uniform across his chest. It fit him well. He pulled the manual release of the shuttle's inner door, trapping the bound and stripped guard inside.

"You know, the one thing I didn't think I'd be able to do is space a guard. You were on my ass ever since I came to the d'If. And to think I found you clinging on to that door handle like a frightened baby. Not so tough now, eh?"

Then, with an effort, he flipped the manual release on the outer door. The guard floated out into the ether, body tensed and prepared to last as long as possible. Useless for more than a few seconds, but all creatures clung to life given the right circumstances. Echo pressed his face against the door's porthole.

"I'm gonna enjoy every second of this."

And he did. Every second of the guard's agony, the futile struggle against space. But all good things had to end. Turning away from the now motionless and slowly twisting form, he jetted himself over to the main circuit control panel. It was a small miracle the gravity field systems still worked, though he had needed to reroute and overload the main lighting system to shock the docking clamps open. Such were the benefits of an engineering background.

Repairs done, the shuttle hummed into life. With an effort, Echo pushed the panel back into place and began plotting a course. Those Kavki saboteurs had been careless. Sending out unencrypted signals when he was working on the d'If's comm system. A simple matter to do a little work, find out what was happening, and when the chaos began, make his break. Also simple to catch their passenger names and their destination. Now he plotted his destination, however long it took to get there.

"Cape Life."

# FILE 4

## ORIGINS OF COLLABORATION

*Layton: I have no desire to be associated with you, Lady Colliq.*
*Colliq: Why ever not, Sir Clyde?*
*Layton: Because one profits so little from theft.*
*One either condemns or is condemned.*
*And condemnation is so often a check on one's social advancement.*
*Colliq: And if I say you could profit enormously from it*
*and enhance your reputation without risk to your position?*
*Layton: Then I have every desire to be associated with you, Lady Colliq.*

—Excerpt from Fingal Dee's "Lord Ingshell's Eye"

MERCEDES COULD ALMOST taste the approaching space habitat. The *Hated Brilliance* had taken a week to reach its destination at top speed, only dropping down to normal speed near the buffer zone. Laffw impressively gestured at the scene for Mercedes and Gaspard, who waited near the docking port of the *Hated Brilliance*.

"Well? What do you think? Quite a sight, hmm?"

Mercedes took it in with an appreciative gaze. Located in the human-dominated New Sol system, against the backdrop of the Class-VI gas giant Inferno and its second moon, Cape Life was one of the first space habitats of its kind. Huge, imposing, ugly in its improvised modifications, it held two centuries of history as a trading hub, a place where independence was sought, where the four peoples held sovereignty over it, each in turn. Now it was a place without any one owner, a population of over 40 million, embassies on every level, and the perfect place to hide from the Synod. Or anyone else for that matter.

"A beautiful place to be one's self." Laffw sounded almost normal. "I shall go with Ali and Bapti on the usual route, but you shall go separately. Best you not be seen with me yet."

Mercedes understood. She was unproven, still a gamble. If anything went wrong, best to be separate. And even if all went well, best to be inconspicuous. The *Hated Brilliance* docked at Main Level 3, near the top of the station close to the communication and transmission areas. The environmental controls and much of the recycling system were near the bottom of Cape Life. There had once been wars between factions calling each part home, but now all recognized such conflicts as worthless before trade profits. The small group entered a docking port and reception area three times the size of any Mercedes had seen on the d'If or around New Dubai.

Once through the processing lounge under the grace of diplomatic clearance, Laffw led Mercedes and Gaspard to an exclusive-looking transport pod, its spherical shape perched on cushioned rails, its interior softly furnished. "You will be going outside Cape Life's gravity field. Best strap yourselves in."

Laffw departed with her serfs. Mercedes entered first and secured herself, followed by Gaspard. The door closed with a hiss, and for a few moments Mercedes basked in the seating, positively decadent in its comfort compared to the d'If. The pod started moving sideways, then abruptly slowed. Mercedes felt a falling sensation in her stomach, and both her hair and Gaspard's fur drifted up slightly as they passed beyond Cape Hope's gravity field. Her armrest had an exterior viewing panel, and she switched it on.

The panel flashed into life, and the New Sol star was revealed in all its glory. The pod began ascending, pushing all hair down and around. A smile spread across Mercedes's face. She had not felt this free and relaxed in a decade. Her mind traveled back to when she first went into a zero-G environment as a four-year-old accompanying her father on a trip to Argo, her family's ancestral home. Mother, heavily pregnant with Gretchen, had stayed on New Dubai. After so long divorced from that floating feeling, the flashback was almost frightening.

"Ever felt zero-G before?"

Mercedes started, surprised at Gaspard's question. "Several times when I was younger. If you mean recently, I never got job assignments on the d'If exterior, remember?"

Gaspard nodded slowly, though his face showed the pain that the memories of the d'If still prompted. The pod finally ended its ascent and slid back into Cape Life's gravity field, allowing clothing and hair to fall back into place once again. A quick flick with the hand and her hair was in order once more.

She decided to introduce a different subject. "I hope this place of Laffw's is as grand as she promised. Her bathrooms are positively garish."

"Grand? That wasn't the word for it. It was spectacular. Y'fthu."

"Eh?"

"A word only the Kavki can claim. I learned it from one of my squad."

The pod stopped, the door opened, and Ali stood waiting for them. She escorted them down a tastefully ornamented pedestrian corridor. At the end was another ornamental door, which Ali opened by touching a pad. There was a moment of blinding light as the door opened, then everything coalesced into reality as they entered the space beyond. Mercedes gasped and glanced to see Gaspard gawking like an idiot.

They were looking down the path of an artificial garden at a miniature mansion, the area bathed in a combination of artificial sunlight and filtered light coming through vast reinforced windows in the roof. The greenery was unprecedented, and the insects buzzing and flapping and humming from flower to flower made Mercedes momentarily forget they were inside a space habitat. Ali led the pair to a large pond set in one quadrant of the garden layout, where Laffw sat at a table and chairs, with Bapti bringing a delicate but nutritious meal for them.

As she was invited to sit down, Mercedes struggled against the impression of dream-like fantasy. It was like an Arabian fable of Ancient Earth. Sipping her drink and eating a flavorful paste sandwich, she watched a black amphibian springing across the pond's lilies with one of its fellows. Large-winged violet insects settled on garlands of magenta flowers hanging from weeping bushes, and in the water iridescent fish swam in a shoal. It was like a dream memory played back for her, and she struggled to remain composed.

Gaspard was sensually overawed, but his attention remained focused on Mercedes as he mechanically ate and drank, offering suitable praise for tastes and textures he barely noticed. Laffw was utterly arrested by the arrival of one of her local pets rushing out to greet its mistress. She stroked and fondled its large cheek flaps and watched as it played with its two companions. Mercedes likewise observed this and noted the way Ali looked at them, an odd mix of loyalty for her mistress and contempt for the newcomer. Laffw's attention had focused entirely on her pets, and she spoke only to Bapti. It was as if Ali were an invisible shade.

This quiet scene lasted for half an hour, then Laffw asked if the pair could talk in private. Gaspard was offered entertainment in the house's kitchen quarters with Ali and Bapti. After a look from Mercedes, he accepted. She was now alone with Laffw, with only the bubbling water, rustling leaves, and humming insects to disturb them.

"So," began Laffw, "I understand you want something from me. I presume you want your planet back?"

"The current duke is a usurper, a betrayer of his people and planet. The White Oil was ours. Ours to own and ours to mine." Mercedes slammed her fist into the chair arm. "I would have raised our planet to glory from our own power, made us a world to be proud of, to accept and integrate the peoples of the Cluster on our terms. But no, he betrayed our sovereignty, asked for help, allowed his cronies to make concessions and keep humans on top. He took the easy route, typical of him."

"The reports said illness."

"And you know what that means, I'm sure. My father was many things, but not a good judge of character, and Gretchen was easy prey for someone with the duke's manners. When the White Oil was discovered, the duke made short work of getting me voted out. Voted out! As if those sycophants ever sought democracy in their lives. I tried to keep the upper hand, but I was an unmarried woman."

"And that meant anything?"

"On New Dubai, yes. He was the charming and personable Duncan Vorn-Solari, married to the sweet and beautiful Gretchen. The good sister our father called her. Then when those who were truly loyal attempted to restore my place, I was banished to the d'If. I read that news report, very touching. It makes me sick."

"I heard something about a smashed datapad. Easy to see why you are so angry. I will admit to understanding your frustration."

"Oh, you don't. You really don't." Mercedes all but glared at her host. "You've no idea what it's like to have the man your sister wed allow his cronies to hoodwink my allies, win my own flesh and blood over with his charms, take my family's name and use it to enrich himself." She regained her composure with an effort. "I lost everything to that bastard, including my sister."

"And now you would work against her, if only by proxy."

"I'd think the Inheritance War would've armored a Kavki such as you to squabbling between in-laws."

"That was many centuries past. Even by our standards, a long time."

"You can't know how well humans hold grudges."

"On the contrary, I think I know better than you. Some humans never give up their resentments, but allow it to fester like a gangrenous growth, poisoning their minds."

"Consider mine poisoned." She paused. "I assume Duncan's cronies have moved up in the world since then? I read that Granger managed to con himself into being a Grand Prosecutor. What about Laurent-Leblanc?"

"Yes. Granger's prowess in law raised him to the rank of Grand Prosecutor about three years ago. He is charged with handling New Dubai's most high-profile cases. Even his most common opponent in the courts, Grand Attorney Glas, pales in comparison. As to Henri Laurent-Leblanc, he is now Viscount-General. A noble title in recognition of his services both military and political." Laffw's face became inscrutable. "And now, to terms. What do you offer in exchange for my help with your problem?"

"What would you propose?"

"It is difficult to decide. You are in a good position, about to become head of a prominent stellopolitical power, the head of one of the most influential trading planets in the Cluster. Exclusive trade? Co-ownership of the mines? Either of those and others might do."

"What about trade preferment?"

"Too nebulous. You can do better than that. And no symbolic positions. They change status as often as political establishments."

This was the awkward part. The prize had to be grand, splendid. Only one thing would tempt this person. Mercedes smiled.

"I do have something to offer along those lines. Something a little more substantial, though it rolls those others into it."

"I am intrigued."

"How about this. Your government shall have suzerainty over New Dubai for my lifetime. That means a cut of all mining and trade proceeds, and supporting you with either political, financial, or military aid in your dealings with the Synod and any internal troubles. In addition, I can grant your people fifty percent access to all White Oil produce from the new mines during their lifetime. And considering how much White Oil was down there, that's several centuries worth of business."

"At the cost of other trading partners?"

"We would still be selling on our terms. It's just the majority cut would be to our ultimate rulers, and afterwards to, I hope, very profitable partners. So, do we have a deal?"

The light in Laffw's eyes was painfully clear. Greed, ambition, shining like diamonds behind her pupils. Her body remained relaxed, and Mercedes didn't invite any motions of agreement or refusal. This fish was hooked. No-one could refuse the right price, and for politicians the price was always power.

Eventually Laffw spoke, her voice a flow of honey. "Revenge for riches. Far more pragmatic than a noble quest for justice. You may consider me deeply interested. But do you have a plan?"

"I have yet to consider all options."

"Then do you have a general strategy? I would prefer to know if we are to be partners in this business."

There was a long pause, during which the two looked at each other. Mercedes remained poised and defiant, Laffw assured and amused. Each exuded the kind of confidence only true politicians could have. The assurance that their plan would work, no matter the obstacle.

Finally, Mercedes spoke. "Perhaps I should use an analogy. Do you know a human game called Chess?"

"I have played it a few times."

"I didn't enjoy it. Gretchen was terrible at it, and always winning gets boring."

Laffw smiled, clearly pitying such a statement. "But you must understand that a game cannot be won with one piece. Even if it is a case of one versus one, the most which can be achieved is a stalemate. You need multiple pieces to win, even against superior forces."

"Life isn't an eight-by-eight square grid."

"True, but the principle stands. You are one woman. And you are up against at least three adversaries, not counting their subordinates and the popular will of people who may not want you back."

Mercedes gestured illustratively. "In the average Chess game, if you take out the most mobile pieces while preserving your own, it gives you an advantage."

"But one must also not discount the pawns as viable players. They can take your pieces and rise up to replace ones that were lost."

"So, make the pawns change sides. Without pawns the opponent is, according to your logic, at an even greater disadvantage."

"How do you make the pawns change sides?"

"By undermining the image of their king."

Laffw whistled. "Interesting. Daring. And very risky. Do you think you could pull it off?"

"Confidence in one's abilities is more than half a victory. An old Argo proverb."

"There is another matter I might mention."

"My appearance? I hadn't forgotten." She placed a hand on the scarring. "The afternoon knows what the morning never suspected. I wouldn't worry about that too much. People who knew me well would recognize my face with these scars. Certainly my brother-in-law would. But ten years in prison changes you. I saw myself in a mirror in that bathroom and almost didn't recognize myself. Cover up the scars with makeup or a mask of some kind, dye my hair, change my dress style. No one will recognize me. And it's amazing how few people actually look at faces."

"And your sister? Your brother-in-law? You may meet them."

"I'm sure I will. And if I do, and they recognize me, I'll handle it. But now I need some time to construct my new identity. If you've a library, that would help. And if you wish a contract of some kind."

Laffw seemed to think for a moment, then smiled. "Maybe once you have your identity ready. Until then, you are my guest." She gave a slight tap to her comm. "Bapti, come at once." Bapti appeared with surprising speed. "Take Miss Solari to the library. If you need refreshments, my dear, Bapti will be waiting just outside."

Mercedes looked directly at the Kavki. "You're most accommodating. I will ask Bapti to call you when I'm ready."

Mercedes followed Bapti, leaving the Ambassador seated by the pool. Laffw's face could be read as easily as a large-print datapad. Mercedes had given her the chance of enriching the Kavki beyond anyone's wildest imaginings. But their wits were of a kind, and she deserved careful treatment. Mercedes was fully aware of her position in Laffw's eyes. As Ancient Earth had it, "Timeo Danaos et dona ferentes." Beware Greeks bearing gifts. Not an exact parallel in this case, but close enough. Though another phrase came to mind. "There is no free lunch." Well, she would keep that motto in mind.

An hour later, Mercedes put away the book she had been reading, having finally constructed her identity. Her search history included Le Fantôme de l'Opéra and Les Trois Mousquetaires. Both old and rather hokey, but adequate. Calling Bapti, she asked to see Ambassador Laffw once more. Surprisingly Bapti was reluctant.

"The Mistress is busy."

"It doesn't matter. I must see her. Where is she?"

"She is in the dueling room."

Mercedes couldn't help but smile. Dueling was something of a dying art in these days of peace and guns. The blades of modern dueling were beautiful constructions. A frame of metal and strengthened materials fashioned into a saber concealed a plasma core which heated the blade's edge up to white hot temperature. Most fencing was competitive, leaving the plasma core inactive. When it was serious, the heat could take off a human limb with a single stroke and leave permanent scars in skin and tissue.

Laffw was clearly surprised as Mercedes pushed her way into the room, but quickly recovered composure and assumed a charming smile. Mercedes nodded and took stock. She had surprised her, therefore she could be surprised.

Laffw went straight to the point. "Have you invented a suitable identity?"

Mercedes walked over to the sword rack, running her fingers along the hilts. "Maybe we could talk over a sparring session."

"I did not know you could duel."

"My family's been dueling for many generations. No need for visors."

Laffw looked on in surprise as Mercedes picked out a blade. "These are not practice blades. They can take fingers off with the wrong handling. And you cannot have had much practice in a prison."

"I know. I grew up with these. My mother was the top duelist in the Capital Worlds for two seasons. And you'd be surprised what a few mimed actions in a cell during detention can do for muscle memory. So," she concluded with a smile, "shall we?"

Still wary, Laffw took up her stance, waiting for Mercedes to follow. After a quick bow, the two began their duel. Mercedes regretted exaggerating the benefits of mimed actions in a tiny cell. The old moves quickly came back to her, and she knew how to keep her skirt from tripping her up. But age had worked against her, and Mercedes in her forties was not the spry woman of twenty-something that had fought Duncan Vorn to a standstill during a practice match while he was courting Gretchen. Laffw won two bouts, and Mercedes conceded each with grace. As they dueled a third time, she talked.

"My name is the Baroness Charlotte Clarisse. I'm of New Dubaian extraction but have spent much of my life around the border between the Capital and Outer Worlds. I'm, of course, extremely rich through my family's third-party trading connections. Father and mother both dead in a tragic accident. The accident also left part of my face scarred beyond repair, so I wear a mask."

"Somewhat old-fashioned."

"New Dubaians are notorious for their pride, and I retain that. A reconstructed face would be worse than no face at all. To continue, I'm good friends with Ambassador Laffw, who had also dabbled in third-party trading with the Outer Worlds?"

"Correct."

"My servants are Gaspard, who acts as my steward and confidant, and one of your two serfs, who would be my valet de chambre and secret weapon. Plus your eyes, of course, but that's confidential. I've spent my life up to now far away from my ancestral home, but now." A duck and parry saved her from another loss. "I'm returning to reclaim my roots and have decided to take splendid apartments on the Upper Residential District in New Dubai's capital Amasian City. Which, as it happens, is also where the seat of the Dukedom is located, and where the current duke is in residence for the coming festive season."

With a half-remembered thrust and twist, Mercedes succeeded in pushing Laffw over the edge of the dueling zone, scoring her first win. Breathing hard, Mercedes saluted and returned her sword to its place. Laffw followed her with her eyes.

"Fine duelist you may be, with an active imagination. But I must put a lot of faith in you. This opening gambit not only involves a false identity which might not stand up to scrutiny, but some very expensive scene dressing."

"Think of it as an investment. What I'm offering for your help easily eclipses any expenses on your part. Besides, you won't need to contribute much."

"What do you mean?"

"You didn't think I was the stereotypical penniless deposed noble, did you? The Solari family haven't survived since the first human colonists arrived in the Cluster without having secret savings."

"What kind of savings?"

"I checked on the *Hated Brilliance*. My alias, one distinguished Lady Wilmore, has roughly seventeen million in actual money, shares, and secondary trade interests unrelated to the New Dubai Dukedom. You see, Ambassador Laffw, your investment will purely be one of research, personnel, and social support. Help find the chinks in the current duke's armor and that of his cronies. And then, slowly and systematically, we exploit them in full. If that's satisfactory, shall we sign off on this?"

A non-networked datapad was produced within a second. The terms were in place, almost as Mercedes had stated them. The data signature was given, the deal signed, and Laffw secreted the datapad deep inside her clothing. The Kavki grinned.

"You are truly devious. And trust me when I say that, whether on my person or secreted among my belongings, this shall never leave me." Assurance and threat in one sentence, as one might expect of the perfect politician. "Your analysis of our targets?"

Mercedes stood, drumming her fingers on the sword rack. "The first, Laurent-Leblanc. I knew him when I was young. He was just a common soldier back then, a hateful man if somewhat dashing. Later I found him less repulsive than I once did, so he became a key ally. At the time. He keeps an Ekri female from his days at the wars. A former royal-turned-POW apparently. At least he did when I knew him. I don't know now."

"And the other?"

"The second, Georges de Granger. His family's been on New Dubai almost as long as mine, and he comes from a powerful political dynasty. Despite his current high position, his grandparents were traders from the Outer Worlds following a shortfall in his family's status. When I was born, he was already a respected pillar at his law school and considered a possible match for me if not for the taboo."

"Taboo?"

"Other social classes and the nobles of other worlds may indulge in pre-arranged marriages, but the Solari family don't."

"Then your successor has a further crime to answer for. I heard about it some time past, but only now see its significance. Duke Vorn-Solari and his wife have one child, a son named Malcolm. He is at present engaged to the youngest daughter of House Berggarten."

"Berggarten?" Mercedes's nose wrinkled, "That insular pile of dross? When did they become anything worth bragging about? Last I heard they were just a two-bit trading family on the outskirts of Amasian City. Barely had enough to keep up their licenses, and too much up their asses to just be normal and trade outside the human population."

"They made quite a killing in the White Oil boom." Laffw spoke in a level tone as if reading a report. "They are among the planet's new rich. And their daughter is apparently quite the beauty, though she is only thirteen."

Mercedes's face became a mask of rage. She knew Duncan had little respect for change, but regression was another matter. With an effort, she controlled herself again, then turned a determined face to Laffw.

"I want to know everything. Laurent-Leblanc, de Granger, my brother-in-law, even these Berggarten people. I want everything about them. Once I'm up to speed on the last ten years, we leave for New Dubai. The eccentric and staggeringly rich Baroness Clarisse shall make her entry onto the social scene. I just need one more thing."

"What would that be?"

"Mercedes Solari always acted and appeared alone or with her sister. I need someone to be window dressing. But it can't just be a servant. It needs to be someone related to the baroness."

Laffw smiled. "Someone we can rely on to help, but also someone we can dispose of if they become a threat. Someone who won't be missed. Someone like an assassin?"

"Yes, if you think that would do. Do they still have a registry, or must I use the DarkNet?"

"Just use my terminal. You can access the Synod databanks and take your pick. Varying levels of reliability, but nearly all eminently disposable."

Less than ten minutes later, alone in the room and seated in a sumptuous chair designed for a Kavki physique, Mercedes began scanning through the lists. Laffw had spoken true about its comprehensive nature. Sorting alphabetically would be a good start. She slowly flicked through the lists of names, selecting a few and often discarding two out of three. Dozens of A's, then she moved on to the B's.

"Bellaroso. Be'ly. Bemfi. Benalti. Bernedetti." She stopped, eyes growing wide. "No. But that's…. It can't be."

What was she seeing? Was the picture wrong? Had she fallen asleep? She expanded the snapshot image, rubbed her eyes, checked the name again. Impossible. Completely impossible that this face should be there. She brought up the life history, the work history, the place of birth. The DNA record flashed up, marked with a classified stamp. Her wide eyes slowly narrowed, and her lips broke into a grin.

This was beyond her wildest dreams. Her low laugh echoed through the chamber. And they say birthdays come but once a year. The only real problem now was if they recognized her. If they did, Granger would make sure she was dead this time. Then there was Laffw. And that contract.

# FILE 5

## GENESIS OF LEGEND

---

*A person kills a relative, inheriting a large amount of money.*
*But no one finds them out. This person now has the means of*
*establishing themselves. They become a member of society,*
*eclipsing their other relatives in power. If they are found out,*
*they are decried as a callous murderer and condemned.*
*If not, they are hailed as an upstanding member of society.*
*And many whose crimes remain unknown are called "Rulers."*

—Extract from Fingal Dee's "Views on Devolved Morality"

"WILL PASSENGERS ABOARD *the 23523 flight from Axiom to Cape Hope please prepare for docking procedures. Gravity field shall be reinstated in ten minutes. All passengers must return to their seats and fasten their safety belts. I repeat—*"

Bernedetti snapped awake at the smooth yet harsh announcement. Automatically he checked his belt, then made sure no personal effects would be floating away. Around him, some people were scrambling to get back into their seats, an amusing sight. An Ekri flight attendant, off-sandy scales shimmering in the shuttle light and digitigrade legs propelling her along, stopped by his seat. A smile broke across her short-snouted face with its rows of spiked teeth.

"Excuse me, sir. Do you need anything before the docking procedure?"

Bernedetti smiled, a sight to charm any from across the Cluster. "No, thank you. I'm used to it."

The attendant passed along, leaving him to his contemplation. He was not embarrassed by this special little attention. He stood out from the crowd, and he knew it. About an inch shorter than the average human, skin paled by a lifetime of exposure to artificial light, he had a kind of lofty manner associated with diplomats and politicians that violently clashed with his common attire.

He once heard someone trying to place him and failing. Most space-faring types were laborers, made both bulky and sickly from a lifetime of heavy work in low-G environments. He, by contrast, was slender to the point of lankiness. He had shoulder-length blonde hair pulled back violently from an angular face, deep gray eyes that looked almost white in low light, and a classy voice fluctuating easily between soft tones and harsh lashes.

As the ship dropped out of warp and the gravity system shut off, Bernedetti considered the message that had summoned him from Axiom. An offer he supposedly wouldn't refuse, a simple job with a bonus for completion. An interview at the Kavki Ambassador's mention in Sector Q, Main Level 1, reachable from Pod 19 in Docking Port 12. If he failed, the passage would be refunded. Hopefully it would be an interesting job. That message had taken him away from a most entertaining feud between four Feles brothers. He was here now and wondered if anyone else had been summoned.

With the shuttle docked, Bernedetti followed the instructions to reach Pod 19, sitting for the ride to Sector Q. It took nearly fifteen minutes, with stoppages and a slow pace while the route was confirmed by the outdated transit algorithms. The mansion was indeed breathtaking, and a Kavki with scarring hidden by neck jewelry led him down the impressive pathway to it. He was led into a large anteroom on the ground floor.

The anteroom's design, blending Ancient Earth Baroque with the geometric Kavki F'testu school, wasn't anything to ignore. But Bernedetti focused on the other occupants, for all shared his profession. Assassination, sabotage, confidence scams, general skullduggery of the dirtier kind. An eclectic selection to be sure. Seating himself in a corner chair, his trained eyes took in the more recognizable figures. The Feles lounging in one of the larger chairs was of the u'Botu clan, hunters by tradition and mercenaries by trade. He immediately recognized the one Kavki, leaning with a relaxed air against a bulky statue, as a notorious bouncer with his own fan following. The crimson-scaled female Ekri fiddling with the matching leaves of a potted plant, scanning the room with her one good eye, he pegged as a veteran of the Human-Ekri Conflict. Tough competition to be sure.

No-one approached him, and everyone waited in near-silence for close to half an hour, during which time all but the Kavki and the Ekri helped themselves to a variety of drinks from a large sideboard. All moved with varying degrees of professionalism. After the half hour, the doors opened to admit a different Kavki with a smug-looking expression and old broken nose. With her was a human woman in her forties, maybe fifteen or sixteen years his senior, with graying hair and undeniable charisma. All eyes focused on them, though the Ekri merely glanced with her good eye. Bernedetti looked, and for a second his heart froze over.

Unpleasant memories and desires were associated with that face. She was speaking to them in a level, cultured voice about each requiring an interview for the post, guaranteeing remuneration regardless. The nondescript memory crystallized into hatred and wounded pride. All the time, his face was placid and measured. The woman had finished speaking, and her Kavki assistant distributed datapads. The reward for completion looked tempting indeed, the sum of twenty average jobs combined.

The Kavki bouncer spoke in a curt tone. "Just have us in when you are ready."

The woman gave a slight bow. "I'm glad about that. I assume that goes for all of you?"

All nodded, and the human woman smiled in an odd way. Bernedetti saw it. The Ekri clearly saw it. None of the others seemed to notice. It was the smile of an executioner when the condemned prisoner appears before them. A mocking acknowledgment of acquaintance and farewell. He swirled his drink in his hand, at last noticing the tiny spiderweb of cracks that had appeared when he clenched his hand upon seeing his prospective employer. This was no longer a mere assignment. It was essential he get it, by hook or by crook.

After a half hour of watching the others passing out and in, Bernedetti was summoned by the Kavki with the broken nose. He was led up one of the two stairways into the "east" wing of the mansion before being shown into a small room with a vast window looking out across a pond large enough to be home to a giant squid. Sitting in one of two chairs in the otherwise barren room was a gray-furred Feles. He wore a tight jumpsuit covered by an embroidered chintz waistcoat and a flowing cape now draping over the chair arm. Bernedetti sat with a courteous smile.

The Feles spoke with the slight drawling accent of the Outer Worlds. "Your name?"

"I've got several. At present, I go by the moniker Bernedetti Bel–"

"And what's your *real* name?"

"I prefer to keep that to myself. Professional etiquette and all that."

"That complicates matters."

The pair eyed each other, like soldiers across a trench. The Feles turned back to the datapad in his hand, which displayed Bernedetti's profile and photo. There was a small round of routine questions, the kind of boring fact-finding any interviewee could answer in their sleep. Finally, the Feles smiled, a surprisingly winning expression.

"You seem suited to the role."

"So it seems." It might be best to take a chance here, find out whether his recognition was accurate. "The duchess planning her comeback?"

The throwaway remark was perfectly timed. The Feles almost dropped his datapad, then shot up and glared into the man's eyes.

"I don't know what you mean by that."

"I wouldn't play coy if I were you. I recognized her the moment she entered the room. Most may forget a face after ten years of wear and tear, but I don't. Does that make a difference?"

The Feles typed in a few notes. "Remains to be seen."

Bernedetti put on his most winning expression. "I'm going to be honest with you. I have my own reasons for getting to New Dubai in an unofficial capacity. I've been there before, have some contacts there she wouldn't want to know, and know more about the recent intimate social life there than she would. Not to blow my own horn, but if I were her, I'd snatch me up at once."

The Feles frowned and sat back down. Bernedetti could read what the Feles must be thinking. This strange man was a risk, but also potentially an asset. Bernedetti had guessed his prospective employer's secret and was effectively trying to coerce them into taking him on. They could just kill him, but he had the verifiable advantage of having been on New Dubai before. From the faces he had seen, Bernedetti doubted anyone else had been there recently. Risky, but he enjoyed a high stakes gamble.

The Feles appeared to dismiss the subject with a shrug. "You've said enough. Please wait with the others downstairs."

"Of course."

Bernedetti rose, bowed politely, and left. Back in the waiting room, he waited with the others for a further fifteen minutes before the door opened once more. It was the two Kavki servants, each bearing a tray of drinks. A general treat before the grand reveal of who would be accepted.

The scarred Kavki approached Bernedetti first and handed him a glass. All others took their glasses, including the Ekri assassin. As Bernedetti raised the florid drink to his lips, he watched the Ekri. She paused, her snout-like face twitching, eyes flickering round the room, then discreetly tipped the drink into the pot plant's overflow dish. The two Kavki servants remained in a corner, watching. Best to wait a time before he drank.

Within thirty seconds, the first signs appeared. A few yawns, rubbed eyes, some unsteadiness. One of the number sat down, passing a hand over her forehead. Another dropped a drained glass onto a table with a loud clatter. Everyone began knocking into each other, and there were slurred attempts at speech. One of them tried to reach the still-conscious Bernedetti, but his legs gave under him, and he collapsed.

In two minutes, everyone but him was slumped down somewhere in a stupor, all breathing heavily and some snoring. Even the Ekri slumped in mock unconsciousness. He was the last remaining conscious candidate in the room. He'd won. Grinning, he drained his glass. After a minute or two, the door opened again, and the woman entered with a tall physically-altered Kavki, obviously the owner of the property. The woman glanced round the room, taking in the unconscious candidates.

Bernedetti stood from his chair. "What happens now?"

"Now," summed up the newcomer Kavki, "they will be taken by my staff to suitable locations and wake up without any memory of the last few days. Ali, Bapti, please tidy them away somewhere. They are causing such a mess."

The pair nodded, and the one with the broken nose began moving the Kavki. The other approached the slumped Ekri. Then she paused, her eyes narrowed, and sprang back just before the Ekri whirled round and stabbed out with a concealed blade.

Bernedetti watched fascinated as Ali tried to retreat, twisted round a slumbering form, then fell backward over an unseen chair pushed awry by one of the drugged guests. The Ekri shot forward toward her, dagger arm outstretched. Then the sound of a pulse shot echoed round the chamber, and the Ekri sagged, a cauterized hole in her forehead. Bernedetti turned with everyone else to see the woman, Duchess Solari, holding a small pistol in her hand.

The lead Kavki's voice was cold. "Where exactly did you get that?"

"One of your drawers. I thought it wise, just in case. Was I wrong?"

"And what about that?" She gestured at the fresh corpse. "I dislike bodies on principle, especially when killed with one of my weapons."

"Yes. Gaspard, I know there were unaccounted deaths in the d'If. How were the bodies disposed of?"

"In the energy flow conduits. The body will be disintegrated."

Solari turned to the lead Kavki. "Would you mourn the loss of one gun?"

"After this, no. I hate the things anyway."

"Then Gaspard can dispose of that, too, would you?"

Solari's back was to the Kavki, and the tone was completely natural. Only Bernedetti could possibly see the slight knowing smile on Mercedes's face. The smile was gone in an instant, and she turned to him and beckoned. He followed her out of the room, out of the house, and over to an area of the surrounding grounds next to a large pond. They stood and spoke in soft voices, as if it was just a chat between friends.

"You knew who I was from the start?"

"You should seriously consider wearing a mask over those scars."

"I planned to wear something along those lines on New Dubai, but I didn't think anyone out here would recognize me after ten years. Can you also guess what my goal is?"

"Who wouldn't want to reclaim their throne?"

"My aims are slightly more complex than that. There are others who were key in my betrayal. I'll have my revenge on all of them. But I need someone to help me, someone who will be an accomplice. Not the real thing, just…."

"Close enough to pass muster? What made you choose me?"

"Firstly, you look the part. Secondly, you recognized me and guessed my intent, something none of the others did. And thirdly, you made a very good impression on Gaspard."

"Gaspard? Ah, the Feles."

"Yes. By the way, can you speak using a New Naples country accent?"

Bernedetti smirked. The dialect of his home country of New Dubai was distinct. Still best not to say he was born there.

"Yes."

"Good. Use it. Also, you said you had many names."

"The truth is I don't know if I ever had a true name when I was born."

"Is there a name you use more often than others?"

"Yes. It's one I've never used for my less savory work. Andréa."

"Well then, you've got the job, Andréa. And from this point on, you'll obey my instructions. It will take a month to firmly establish our identities and perform the required research. Plus any social training needed to be pitch perfect for the sycophants we'll be meeting. I trust that's acceptable?"

Bernedetti, now Andréa, gave a half mocking and half sincere nod. "Your Grace, for the pay you're offering, I think I'd put up with anything."

———————————

A MONTH IS a comparatively short span of time. But for Andréa, it had been like a whole year of training in etiquette, poise, and a dozen other subjects which he half-knew or thought were not worth knowing. Waiting in the departure lounge near where the *Hated Brilliance* was docked, Andréa went over that month in spite of himself.

It had been a drag drilling the planned storyline into his head. He was the Honorable Andréa Manfredi, ward and punitive heir to the rich and reclusive Baroness Clarisse. The biography read like cheap fiction, a combination of saccharine and snobbery for a young man in his early thirties. Born to a good family on the human-dominated New Naples space habitat, parents killed in the Human-Ekri Conflict, given into Clarisse's care shortly thereafter, heir to both his own estates and Clarisse's own as she lacked children. Now he was thirty and marriageable. He had queried why he was not already lord of these claimed estates.

Mercedes had answered, "You forget, on New Naples, men don't reach age of discretion until they're forty."

Andréa had understood the reference. "True. All years until then are considered ones of indiscretion."

That had been during one of their planning sessions. Mercedes loved to sprinkle in little classic references and tags worked into cutting remarks and hard-edged jokes. All to try and catch him out, test his cover. Simple tests meant to catch out people far less intelligent than him.

Finally, Mercedes appeared at the door. She still wore a Neo-Tudor style, but otherwise might have been a different person. She walked slightly differently. Her hair was a perfectly dyed blonde, and the scars were hidden beneath a beautiful gilt-edged fabric mask. She also looked healthier than when they first met, with fresh tanned skin and a month of good meals giving her a healthy figure. The age lines were still there, but her poise and grandeur disguised them well. Had he not been there throughout that month, he would have never recognized her.

They made eye contact, and Andréa went to meet her. "All sorted?"

"Yes, we have officially opened our accounts at the Interplanetary Bank. And when we arrive, purchase shall be agreed upon regarding our residences on-world."

"How much did you deposit? You wouldn't tell me before."

"You'd have been too excited. For me, an opening current account of four million, and a savings account of six million. For you, a sub-account containing a further three million. Thirteen million in all. The poor clerk fumbled the typing when she heard the sums."

"Thirteen out of seventeen. Keeping some in reserve?"

"Naturally."

"Speaking of money, why are we using the *Hated Brilliance* to reach New Dubai? Wouldn't you be able to afford your own ship?"

"We are good friends of Ambassador Laffw, and consequently travel as guests aboard her ship. Didn't you read any of your brief?"

"Of course I read it."

"Then don't ask idiotic questions. Even on purpose."

"Guilty as charged." He smiled, giving a slightly exaggerated bow. "So, do we depart now?"

"Yes. Laffw is waiting for us in the *Hated Brilliance*. Within the next week, we shall enter the society of New Dubai."

Andréa followed his employer aboard the *Hated Brilliance*, its engines already humming and ready for takeoff. Just as they passed inside, Mercedes paused and looked out one of the windows. He understood the sentiment, taking a last look at somewhere which had been home for any length of time. Gaspard had been waiting for them inside and now approached his mistress.

"I've spoken to Laffw. Your suggestion is acceptable."

"Good."

Gaspard moved away. Andréa raised an eyebrow.

"What suggestion?"

"I asked that Ali become my second servant."

"Why her?"

"I saved her life. And she works well with me." Her voice became low and powerful. "Soon, very soon, it will all begin anew. Ten years of suffering, a month of negotiating and waiting and training. But we have everything now. New Dubai, here we come. And to be clear, I shan't pry into your business so long as it doesn't impinge on mine."

"Oh, don't worry." Andréa suppressed a smirk. "You won't ever know what I'm doing."

# FILE 6

## ANTICIPATION

*When you look at a cake, many would say "How nice" without thought.
We typically see and take most notice of its sweet or gaudy covering,
never thinking much of the many foundations of meal that forms the
larger whole. With some cakes, there is sweetness further in, such as
a layer of chocolate or jam or other confection. But this may be seen
in two lights. You may enjoy what you experience. Or you may find
it grates upon the tongue and leaves one grimacing from an unwanted
taste. How many of us think of the varied ingredients—fresh, fine,
and foul—that went into this great and glorious cake that is 'society.'*

—Extract from Fingal Dee's "Views on Devolved Morality"

DUNCAN VORN-SOLARI was startled from a snooze as Gretchen called
across the gardens of Qas'tan House toward where her son Malcolm was playing a chase game with imaginary enemies as represented by a small flying
drone round one of the bushes. The gardens were full of plants both local and
exotic, all safe but still worth calling out a warning.

"Malcolm, be careful now. We've got that walk planned, and I wouldn't
want you to trip and sprain anything."

Malcolm's voice, still in the process of breaking, called back. "Okay Mammy, I'll be careful."

Duncan smiled, turning his glass of deep blue local vintage. "This is the
life. Here with my wife and kid in the sunshine."

"I think that toy was a good find. Set it off, let Malcolm toss a ball, then
chase it around."

"Simple pleasures. He'll grow out of it soon enough and learn about using treadmills and things when he can't get out for walks."

"Speaking of which, I'm noticing you've let out your belt a notch."

"Yeah, it was that reception thing. An investiture for one of Granger's protegees. They served all those sweet dishes."

Gretchen's laugh was a thing of beauty. "Well, that's settled. Cutting down on portions, upping the protein and greens, and a bit more exercise for you, my lad."

"Yessir, ma'am."

"Goofy."

They laughed at almost the same moment. When not guiding New Dubai to greater upon greater prosperity as its duke, nothing gave Duncan more pleasure than sitting with his wife and watching his son enjoying himself. Bathed in the glorious sun of a New Dubaian summer in its northern hemisphere, everything seemed worth it. The horrors of the succession problems and aftershock of the insurrection, dealing with his ministers and Synod Representatives, negotiating new trade deals while retaining human control at Granger's insistence, putting new administration levels into place. All of it had been worth it if it allowed him to sit in peace in his garden watching his son playing.

It was also worth it for Gretchen. He drifted back in spirit to twelve years prior, when he had been courting the young noble. He, an upstart from beyond Argo, came and met and fell for the beautiful daughter of New Dubai's ruler. She walked with a cool grace like Mercedes had but lacked the sharp corners and hereditary scars. She also lacked the coldness of her late father, something Mercedes had also inherited. Gretchen was bright and unmarked, like looking at a sunlit reflection of a younger Mercedes.

Remembering Mercedes brought him back to the message he had received a month ago through unofficial channels. The d'If had exploded, gone completely. He had breathed a sigh of relief that day. Granger and Laurent-Leblanc had said it was necessary Mercedes be sent away to a place where no one would look, be declared dead with all suitable proofs provided she had given the throne to him. Of course, Granger had wanted her dead, but Laurent-Leblanc had sided with Duncan in exiling her. All she'd done was annoy the nobles, nothing worthy of cold-blooded murder.

Now the d'If was in ruins, and he was safe forever more. It was amusing to recall briefly falling for Mercedes's stern beauty, but it was Gretchen's sweet nature and lively conversation that won him. That had given him this life and their greatest treasure.

"Yes," he mused, "Out here in the sunshine. Enjoying my own little sun."

Gretchen chuckled at the pun and was quiet for a time. While Duncan would have been more than willing to sit in silence, Gretchen liked to talk as she rested from the burdens of office. Her voice became casual but incisive in its will.

"Duncan, have you heard about the new arrival?"

"New arrival?"

"Yes. Surely you've heard."

"My dear, you know I don't have time for gossip these days. The spring diplomatic reception and charity ball is somewhat pressing, plus that investiture, and then there's the whole business of the trial. Who is this new arrival?"

"I don't know if you could call her *new*. Her family's from here apparently, made a fortune in trade among the Outer Worlds. Now she's returned to have New Dubai benefit from her extensive wealth."

"Where did you hear this?"

"My secretary's brother works at the local branch of the Interplanetary Bank, and unlike my dearly departed sister I prefer to treat my secretaries like people, so they tell me the most interesting things. I'd heard about some new arrival causing a stir and asked her if she knew anything. And she told me."

"Gretchen, you can be infuriating. Told you what?"

"It seems that this mysterious woman opened a set of accounts at the bank worth…."

Duncan sighed. Gretchen's dramatic pauses during her talks were one of the few things that put his back up. It was all in good fun for her, but he wanted things done and dusted quickly. Like the old matter of Mercedes.

She finally concluded, "Accounts worth around thirteen million yuren."

His eyebrow rose significantly. "Thirteen. That's the import-export revenue from some of our larger trading houses over a few days."

"You don't have to tell me. I worked it out."

"Surprised the Outer Worlds could provide that kind of cash. Who is this woman?"

"She's called the Baroness Charlotte Clarisse. Everyone's talking about her."

"Not so I can hear it. And she's here alone? Dangerous. Some of the young men around here are worse than gnats for attaching themselves to a succulent feast."

"No, she's not alone. She came here with a young man who is her ward and heir. His name's the Honorable Andréa Manfredi. Family from New Naples killed in the Human-Ekri Conflict. He's got an inheritance of his own, but it's in trust until he turns forty."

"That's space habitats for you. So, you're saying two hugely rich people have just dropped out of the blue. You couldn't just say it without all the faff?"

Gretchen's smile was winning. "You know that's not how I like to talk. And they haven't just dropped. The baroness has taken one of the best apartments in the Upper Residential District. And she's got herself a country house to go with it."

"Sounds more like splashing money about to make an impression than distributing money to help people. We'll see if she can do anything but spend it on her own comforts."

"Duncan, you can be so cynical."

"And you're far too good-natured."

"We'll never know unless she's invited to the ball. Why not send her an invite if you're curious?"

"My dear, a personal invite to the ball is a serious matter, especially at this late stage. It shows at least interest and at most favor toward someone. You know how most of the others are about favors, all very nice until you give them to someone else."

"But aren't you interested?"

"Hmm. We'll see. Ah, I think our boy's finished. Malcolm, you've finished?"

Malcolm ran over to join them, panting, his clothing soaked with sweat. "Yes, Pappy. Mammy, did you see? I beat the machine once."

"That's wonderful, darling. But you'd best get inside at once and get cleaned up. You're not fit to be seen, and you've lessons in half an hour."

"All right. I'm going. We're still going to the Big Splash Ball tomorrow night, right?"

"That's your father's decision. And please remember *not* to call it the Big Splash Ball."

"Then you'll take me to the Ball, Pappy. Won't you?"

"Malcolm, you mustn't pester. Rest assured you'll go. Maybe not this year, but certainly sometime. You must be patient."

"Yes, Pappy."

"Now," she took charge, "go inside and wash up. I'll be inside shortly."

"All right, Mammy."

Duncan frowned as the young boy ran inside the house, his large shirt sleeves billowing like a young bird's wings. "I'm a little worried about him still using 'Mammy' and 'Pappy.' He'll be ten next year."

"Duncan, you told me your parents tried to make you grow up too fast. It's not as if he's half-witted. One shouldn't visit a parent's sins on their children. Now let's head in."

It wasn't any use arguing with Gretchen on that point. Duncan and Gretchen rose to follow when a small servant drone flew toward them from the main door. It stopped beside the two and spoke in its mechanical sing-song voice.

"Henri Laurent-Leblanc and Georges de Granger to see you."

"Oh, damn." Duncan turned a pained face to Gretchen. "Sorry, my dear. It's always business, business, business. Sometimes I wonder why I bother with being the duke."

"I could take the post if you like."

"Gretchen, I've seen how you handle your affairs." He grinned ruefully. "If you became duchess, the office would be a mountain of unanswered messages and pending matters in a week flat."

Gretchen scowled for a moment, then gave a final smile as her husband went toward the meeting. It was sad leaving behind the family time, the company of his wife, the playful joy of his son, the beauty of the gardens. But the duke of New Dubai was a servant to the state and must serve its needs and the needs of its controlling figures. He covered the distance to the patio window of his office at a brisk pace, passing inside to see the visitors, five seated secretaries and two standing men. These men were Granger and Laurent-Leblanc.

As he made the usual greetings, the tinny little voice in Duncan's mind wondered why he tolerated them so much, for in appearance they were not pleasant for him to look at. Granger, going against the conventional stoic image of a Grand Prosecutor, wore a suit in twin bold colors of scarlet and green festooned with gold thread. Laurent-Leblanc contrasted this showy opulence with a simple mauve suit belying its military origins.

"I trust we don't disturb you," said Laurent-Leblanc with something approaching courtesy.

"No, of course not." The lie felt tacky on Duncan's tongue. "Let's discuss this in private, shall we?"

Both men nodded, and they followed Duncan through into his starkly-functional inner office. The secretaries' gazes after them were palpable. As the door closed with a soft hiss, Duncan tapped a small pad on the corner of his desk to activate the sound-blocking software built into the office walls. Duncan turned, and the two visitors bowed.

"Your Grace." Both men spoke as one.

Duncan smiled with difficulty. "Surely we've gone beyond *that.*"

"Of course, Duncan." Granger's smile seemed genuine. "But it never hurts to remind ourselves of the order of things. How's Malcolm?"

"Doing splendidly. He'll grow up to be a fine man. And a fine duke."

"And Gretchen?"

"Likewise. She's the best wife I could wish for. But I take it you're not here to talk about my family affairs. Is this about the ball?"

"No." Laurent-Leblanc's voice was characteristically cold. "We've all three been summoned to a meeting with the Synod on an urgent matter."

"Eh?" Duncan was as startled as he sounded. Even across its centuries of existence, direct scheduled meetings between the Synod and any of the Cluster's semi-independent planetary nations were a rarity. Even rarer was being called out of the blue.

"When are they calling?"

"At once, in your comm room. We came as soon as we were messaged."

"All right. Let's go."

Beyond his office, there was yet another even starker chamber, a small, black-paneled room contrasting against the baroque exterior of Qas'tan House like chalk and cheese. An illuminated white circle with retractable seats and comm-desks stood in the midst of a black-walled squared area. This was the long-distance volumetric comm room where planet-to-planet calls were done through private ClusterNet connections. Even to the Synod, if needed or wanted.

All three seated themselves, the call sign flashed, and Duncan acknowledged it with a gesture. The ceiling lighting vanished, replaced by a virtual space where other desks floated on the paneled floor like boats in a sea of data. Behind one desk was a Kavki and her entourage. She typed a few symbols into her console, and other figures from all the peoples of the Cluster appeared. The Kavki spoke, her voice a piecing beam of authority.

*"The Ministers of the Synod acknowledge the transmission of Duke Duncan Vorn-Solari, current ruler of the human territory of New Dubai. This meeting of the Core Synod is now in session. We wish to speak with you on a most urgent matter."*

"I hear and comprehend, Minister H'dryn. Please say whatever you must."

*"Thank you, Duke Vorn-Solari. The Synod calls the Ekri Ambassador D'payn Paya to recap her report to this body."*

The said Ekri Ambassador, a scaly snouted form clad in shimmering robes, appeared from beyond the display zone like an Ancient Earth stage effect, bowing her head to Minister H'dryn. *"Ministers of the Synod. Duke Vorn-Solari. An incident occurred on the New Sol space habitat Cape Life, which has caused great concern among certain elements of our current government. One month ago, an assassin known to many of us as the Dagger disappeared from the radar. Her remains have recently been discovered on Cape Life. She was murdered."*

"With all due respect," Laurent-Leblanc cut in, "what does this have to do with us?"

Minister H'dryn's voice became a little harsher. *"It was discovered that the Dagger had been summoned to a meeting on Cape Life with several others of her kind, though all were found to be alive. When questioned by our Enforcers, several professed complete ignorance of any such journey."*

Duncan spoke with a due tone of deference. "With all due respect to the feelings of the Ambassador and the Synod, one might say this was a good thing. Whether useful or no, assassins are dangerous people."

D'payn Paya nodded reluctantly. *"Given her recent actions against representatives of the current government, it was. But the Dagger was also a decorated war hero from the Human-Ekri Conflict. Her exploits following the war are not on official record, nor do the public greatly care what their heroes do if they can be granted the abeyant status of martyr, a victim of discrimination from humanity's imagined post-war reprisals."*

"Have you any leads that lead you to contact us?" asked Granger.

*"We have nothing direct, but there is some circumstantial evidence. The few witness reports and security recordings we have indicate that some of those summoned were taking transport pods for an upper area of Cape Life, where the more exclusive residences are located. A recent arrival there was the Kavki Ambassador to the sector, F'thodish Azd Laffw, who came with some unknown guests. A month later, a human woman called the Baroness Charlotte Clarisse opened an account with the Interplanetary Bank worth many millions. Both she and Ambassador Laffw have now come to New Dubai with others that we currently cannot identify."*

Granger's eyes narrowed. "You think this baroness is involved in the murder of the Dagger? Is that not something of a stretch?"

*"Our Enforcers are confident there is some kind of connection, though there is no direct evidence tying them together."*

Duncan nodded. The Synod Enforcers were notorious for both their apparent leaps of logic and the correctness of those leaps. They were the best of the best of law enforcement and investigation, and for them to only have this much was unsettling. Any other investigating body would have found next to nothing. Granger chose to be direct in his counter.

"If you have this information, why not arrest her? The Synod Enforcers have unlimited jurisdiction, as you have often reminded us."

Duncan winced and gave Granger a look. With difficulty, he restrained a relieved sigh as Ambassador D'payn Paya ignored the slight jibe, as did the rest of the Synod ministers present.

The Ambassador continued. *"There is a further layer to this. If we were to proceed in the usual way, it could cause complications. Tension between the Ekri and human communities remains high, and the Ekri imposing on a human world might be taken in the wrong spirit. Cooperation is necessary for both our sakes."*

Minister H'dryn took up the narrative. *"We think the baroness may have information to share on the matter, but we cannot approach her directly. She is on your world legally, and our investigations show no indications that her funds were obtained through criminal or even questionable activities. She also appears to be a close friend of Ambassador Laffw. It seems to indicate a possibility that the Ambassador was also somehow involved in the incident."*

Ambassador D'payn Paya broke in. *"In all fairness, the latter point has yet to be proven conclusively, though it must still be considered. Nevertheless, if we were to approach Baroness Clarisse or Ambassador Laffw through the expected channels, things could become difficult. We do not wish to trigger an embarrassing diplomatic incident, especially with one as influential as Laffw."*

Duncan nodded. "I quite understand."

*"In addition, I have been informed that your position, while currently favorable, is still open to difficulties. You are a comparatively new ruler by Cluster standards, especially given the circumstances surrounding your accession. We do not wish to cause you undue trouble. We wish to offer the chance for you to make your own investigations before we become more firmly involved."*

"You have my gratitude. To serve the Synod's wishes, I can investigate the matter covertly. I was considering offering this baroness an invitation to a social event being held coming this evening. That could prove a good opportunity to speak with her without arousing undue suspicion."

A Feles minister with a mane in a tight bun spoke now. *"I for one call that an excellent approach. If you can safely draw her out on the subject, it may give us something to go upon. It would be better than approaching Ambassador Laffw directly. Minister H'dryn, I would not detain the duke any longer now the matter has been brought to his attention."*

Minister H'dryn nodded. *"I concur. Duke Vorn-Solari, I would ask that you keep us informed of the situation. Our own agents will investigate on Cape Life. If Granger could use some of his contacts to investigate the baroness's antecedents, we would be grateful."*

Granger nodded. "I can also position some agents in discreet areas. And if you give your permission, I can also arrange observation for Ambassador Laffw. They will never be out of our sight, should you wish it."

*"I think we can leave such measures for the moment. If it must be done, let it be done with our knowledge and with circumspection. If the Ambassador suspects she or her associates are being watched, it could cause an even greater diplomatic incident."*

"If surveillance is used, we shall use the utmost discretion, Minister."

*"Then we shall leave you to your duties. The Core Synod thanks you for your time, and bids you farewell."*

The transmission shut off abruptly, and the lights sprang back to life. Duncan leaned back, his muscles relaxing, scratching the wispy beginnings of a beard on his chin. As the three rose, Duncan turned to face the others, leaning on the desk with serious eyes and nonchalant pose.

"Your thoughts?"

Laurent-Leblanc spoke first. "I don't like it. This smells wrong. I don't think you should invite this woman to anything."

Granger threw an odd glance at his colleague. "Snubbing her is just as dangerous as inviting her. She's the friend of a powerful political figure. It would be expected for her to be invited. If she isn't, regardless of all this, what kind of message will that send?"

Duncan nodded slowly. "We can't let anyone suspect anything about this. Any other tongue can be made to wag. Until the Synod says otherwise, this stays between the three of us. Understand?"

Granger nodded. "Of course."

"Lips sealed." Laurent-Leblanc's reply was flat.

"Then let's return to normality. This conversation never happened."

After a time, back in the garden, Duncan walked through the small maze in the brightest corner of the garden, face pinched and brow furrowed. To Granger and Laurent-Leblanc, precautions might seem preposterous. Duncan knew only too well about the tensions born from the Human-Ekri Conflict. His father fought in it and lost a leg. A neighboring family had sympathized and fought with the Ekri at the cost of an entire branch dying during the Siege of Cataaka. It had taken the united force the Synod and large factions from both the Ekri and humanity to stop conflicts of reprisal spreading across the Cluster following the decisive bombing of Cataaka, the Ekri home world.

And now this. A decorated war hero of the Ekri found murdered on a space habitat created by humans. However tangential the connection, it was an explosive combination. Just the history of Ancient Earth had more than enough examples of insurrections born of revenge killings to make him wary of such idiocy. His own lifetime also bore those scars when those obstinate idiots led by his equally obstinate sister-in-law tried to overthrow him. True, he had blackmailed her into giving up, but there were reasons for that. Excellent reasons.

A quick tap to the cheeks brought him back to reality. No time for dwelling on the past, only thinking of the present. At present, there was the ball and who he'd have to mingle with. That famous writer and wit Fingal Dee and her partner. The Berggartens of course, with their daughter who would one day be Malcolm's wife. Then to send off a last-minute invitation to the

Baroness Charlotte Clarisse and her mysterious ward. He left the maze with a forlorn sigh. This was going to be a long day.

———————————

"BUT HERMA–"

"No!"

Hermathruda Berggarten—or Herma to close friends and family—threw her mother's arm off her shoulder with the frenzied strength of anger and distress. Her father's voice came from behind her, taking up the argument.

"It's tradition."

"I'm not going."

"Herma, you're being selfish."

"Go if you must, but I'm not gonna be seen with that prig."

Her father's voice became harsh. "Herma, don't use words like that. It's not ladylike. Have you been playing that stupid game again? I told you–"

Mother again, defensive this time. "Hans, please don't make this worse."

"Eileen, this is important. We can't have our girl learning those words until she knows when and how to use them. Then she must be taught never to use them at all."

Herma's little voice bellowed in an uneven screech. "Just leave me alone."

Herma rushed from the room into the apartment corridor, then up into her own room. She slammed the door, typed in her special locking code, then fell on the bed and struggled not to cry. Shouting at her parents always took it out of her, but sometimes it seemed the only way to get through to them. If they thought she would be going to that boring party thing and meeting that horrible little tyke Malcolm Vorn-Solari, they were mistaken. That was all.

An hour later, Herma still laid on her bed. The tears had dried up, but she was still deeply miserable. It was as she lay in this torpor that her mother knocked at the door.

"Herma? Dear, are you all right? Can I come in?"

Herma glanced up, then tapped the control to open the door. Her mother could easily have forced her way in with her passkey, but it was not her style. Father was the one who always did that. As the door opened with its usual sigh, Herma's mother came over and sat on the bed beside her, her eyes soft and comforting.

"It's all right, Herma. Cheer up. Your father will calm down soon."

"It's not that." Her voice was quite level. "I just don't want to see that boy."

"You can't avoid him forever."

"I can if I try."

"My dear, you're being selfish. I know you two aren't getting on right now. But that'll change in time."

"Will it? He's frosty now, but I prefer that over him talking down to me like I should be grateful he acknowledges my existence."

"That was two years ago. He's matured a lot since then. And just between the two of us, I think he regrets it."

"Regrets it? I doubt he even remembers it." Herma looked directly at her mother. "I don't know what's happened to us."

"Happened?"

"I may not remember when we were poor, but I remember when things were just settling down. We were a family. We were enjoying ourselves in our new house, I was looking forward to some nice friends. Now what are we? A commodity?"

"Herma, you're being too hard on yourself. These kinds of things happen all the time to people. It's just how things are."

Herma shook her head. "No, it isn't. Other kids I know just live their lives, make friends they want to make, have parents who care."

Her mother was audibly shocked. "Herma, how can you say such a thing? We love you and care for you. Of course we do. You're our only child."

"Then why not think of my happiness? Why not break off this stupid match and let me go on with my life as if I'd never met that little oaf?"

Herma glanced at her mother. She was unable to answer. How could she? A child's simple logic could almost always defeat the smooth manners of adulthood. They both knew why the match was non-negotiable, at least for them. Marriage of the Berggarten line into the most powerful social and political force on the planet was key to their future. The Berggartens had not always been rich, and her father shrank from the idea of being poor again.

She was key to preserving the family's fortunes, to having an impact on New Dubai equal to or greater than the glory days of their pioneering ancestors before the rise of the Solari line as the planet's ruling dynasty. Through all this, Herma realized her mother's own suffering, the knowledge of the toll it took on both of them. It all hinged on Herma coming to accept the arrangement. If she did not, then the duke might end the match and find someone more compatible for his precious son.

Her mother spoke gently. "So, you don't want to go to the ball?"

"Not if that boy's there, no."

"There's no guarantee he'll be there."

Herma turned to look her mother in the eye. "Can you promise me he won't be there just because we're invited?"

Her mother again was silent, and Herma turned away. She finally let her head slump once more into her arms and asked quietly to be left alone. From the corner of her eye, Herma watched her mother's retreating back. She clearly wanted to stay, perhaps persuade her into accepting the situation with good grace but knew better than to go against her daughter when she was in this state.

Alone once more, Herma shuffled into a kneeing position and looked through the selection of physical books she had, gifts from parents who once doted on her. She picked out a slim volume of surviving fairy tales from Ancient Earth. She flicked through its pages and saw the heading of one in particular. Sleeping Beauty as interpreted by Charles Perrault. She slowly turned the pages until the end, reading up to when the prince passed unharmed through the barrier of thorns and found the princess, waking her from enchanted slumber with a kiss.

Herma snorted and slammed the book shut. No real prince for her, merely a prince in all but name. A Marquess without manners or sense. Her eyes flashed toward the window. New Dubai was a relic. She had seen the Cluster-Net. She had seen what life could be like if you want it beyond this system. She didn't want this. She didn't want any of it. She just wanted to be happy. Was that too much to ask?

She almost winced at her last thoughts, slumping on the bed once more and letting the book fall from her hand to the floor.

---

"PASSPORT PLEASE."

"Certainly."

"I see. Hmm. Very well, all in order. Pass through. Your luggage is being checked now. If it's all in order, you'll find it in the collection area."

"Thanks."

A brief smile, the picture of the pleasant visitor. Echo was utterly charming, as he had been since reaching Cape Life in that battered little shuttle. With the spry walk of the free and free-thinking, he walked through the terminal gate into the larger reception area of Amasian City Shuttle Port on New Dubai. He glanced through the windows, looking down the great tower's length toward the beating suburban heart of Amasian City far below. There, presumably, lived the office workers, White Oil refiners, and other professionals that made this planet what it was. In the near distance, the shining grandeur of the city center's Neo-Bourbon architecture formed a stark contrast to its utilitarian suburbs and the futuristic tower.

Picking up his luggage, Echo boarded the main messenger lift and took in his fellow travelers. Mostly Feles and Kavki females here for a good time, but some among them were strapping Feles males with muscular loins and noticeable bulges in the right places. Must be some big event on. Maybe he could try his luck? He rapidly suppressed the thought. He was on a mission. Exiting the shuttle port's saucer-like base, Echo hailed a taxi and was driven to the apartment building in the Lower Residential District. His room there had already been arranged by some local contacts.

Leaning back in the seat and sighing, he contemplated his journey. And what a journey it had been. Following the intercepted comm data, Echo had pushed the little shuttle in pursuit of the Hated Brilliance. The warp core was shot, so a long-distance distress beacon was his only chance. The d'If's supply ship had picked him up, and he had passed himself off as a guard using his stolen clothes. It was a simple matter to reach Cape Life, and an even simpler one to rediscover some old contacts and find out where Gaspard had gone. Then it had been a waiting game.

His new home was in one of the area's higher buildings fully furnished with good signal, a view of the Upper Residential District, and a direct link to the Commercial District. Just what he needed for a little hunting. When he arrived, he quickly finalized the rent payments with some of those contacts' old repaid debts, settled the deal with a handshake, and moved in immediately. There was little luggage, just a case full of clothes bought at Cape Life and his few tools. A quick glance showed him the state of the room. The color scheme was less than ideal, but choosiness was not on his agenda for the coming weeks.

He unpacked rapidly, then threw off his stifling clothes and strode over to the kitchenette, getting a glass of chilled water. Even official guides on the New Dubaian summer had not prepared him for this. His fur stuck behind his ears, which twitched almost incessantly as if warding off midges.

That evening, as he showered in the coldest water setting possible, Echo ran over the information on hand. Gaspard was in league with an ambassador and whoever that woman was from the d'If. They had departed with someone else on the Hated Brilliance and arrived here, setting up in the Upper Residential District as the Baroness Clarisse and household. There was also some large country estate that had been abandoned for years, bought remotely and renovated to order.

She had the chops, he'd give her that. He was beginning to see why Gaspard was so infatuated with her. Infatuated, no that was the wrong word. Arrested. Yes. He was under arrest.

A weak joke, but Echo guffawed with laughter. It had been easy to trace the schedule of the *Hated Brilliance,* and easier still to find some old contacts and debtors, gaining networked help from one and fresh funds or favors from the other. The money in his pocket would last a few weeks, even on this world where the inflation was ridiculous. Plus, there was nothing stopping him picking up odd jobs.

If he knew anything about that woman from ten years of keeping her out of trouble, it's that she loved trying to get herself in trouble. Riling up Witton all those times, but never using overtly reprehensible language. Oh yes, a sly one. He wondered if anyone here could find out who she was? She must've been someone once. Why else would she come here of all places and be so flush with cash?

More questions, not enough answers. And no answers at all as to when he should approach Gaspard again when he found him.

The old ache pulsed inside him. On impulse, he turned the water temperature up to a steaming warmth and leaned against the cubicle wall, slowly passing his hand over himself. Gaspard, he had so missed him. That fine, able, compliant yet defiant form. Those had been the best half-hours during his stay in the d'If. True, there had been others willing to bestow favors, but none had willingly taken them. That young innocent had wised up quickly under Echo's expert handling.

"Gaspard… Gaspard…."

The water hissed down, Echo's teeth bared, and his free hand clawed at the wall as he climaxed at the mere thought of him. For the moment, he could be satisfied with fantasy. Eventually he had to find him again, hold him down, make him his own. Whatever laws governed the universe, be they fate or random chance, had granted him this opportunity. Beyond the walls of the d'If, he could freely pursue his fantasies and turn them into reality.

# FILE 7

## THE BARONESS

---

*I never saw anyone like her, nor believed any like her existed.*
*She seemed a fae creature from a time before humankind.*
*All turned and were attached to her, all men looked and loved her,*
*all women looked and envied her. She was that which humans have*
*called "beautiful." But in her face was a dark shadow marring that*
*beauty. It was not physical. It was more like a wavering darkness*
*that might denote some sourness of mind or temper. She seemed,*
*from the moment I saw her, the embodiment of "wolf in sheep's clothing."*

—Excerpt from Fingal Dee's "On The Tragedy of New Dubai"

MERCEDES ADJUSTED HER cloth mask, looking in the mirror display on the back of the driver's seat. In the front, Gaspard kept an eye on the autodrive display while Ali appeared to be reading something. Next to her, Andréa was preening himself, getting his hair into exactly the right angle. He had done that three times on the drive already, but there was little point stopping him. In effect, he was playing his part.

Mercedes threw a quick question in Gaspard's direction. "How long until we reach the building?"

"Ten minutes."

"Right." She finished adjusting her mask. "I'll switch on the network and see what kind of crowd there's going to be."

A quick switch of settings and the mirror became a video display showing 24/7 Cluster's live coverage of the spring season diplomatic reception and charity ball, or the Big Splash Ball as most informally called it. The view showed all those attending, so many Mercedes despised. The old rich, the new rich who modeled themselves on the old, every suit of the highest quality representing every single mainstream and haute couture fashion without a thought for cost or fabric. From across the Capital Worlds there were diplomats, oligarchs, royals, elected heads, and financial figureheads from all the peoples, the types that should have been calling New Dubai home. Not the money-bloated humans now infesting its streets.

"Disgusting."

Andréa glanced over, finally satisfied with his fringe. "Excuse me?"

"The people here. It revolts me. My father or Gretchen would've stood for it. Not me."

"What?"

"If you can't see it, it's not worth talking about."

"I'm beginning to see why they kicked you out."

Andréa's tone was enough. Mercedes shot him a look which had him shuffling uneasily in the car seat. The voice of 24/7 Cluster's Kavki reporter, commonly known by her human name Margaret Maye, stopped any further conversation. Mercedes started paying attention in the middle of a sentence. The reporter's skin looked more fish-like than usual under the glaring colored lights of the event.

"…transports for Henri Laurent-Leblanc and Georges de Granger arrived a few minutes ago, but I'm afraid we missed them during our last interview. As you know, the Grand Prosecutor is…." An elongated and dramatic summary followed of Granger's case against the Ekri of Qalaa's Prospect and the planned resolution of the case at the Grand Assizes. "And coming toward us now is Herruk Falak, the famous Feles dramatic actor. He has just finished filming Sorrowed Catechism. This is the latest entry in the highly successful 'Furious Six' series, a hexalogy set during the Early Colonial era. Falak has famously refused to use a stunt double for even the most difficult sequences." There was a quick interview with the Feles, who easily brushed off any spoiler-related inquiries and continued inside. "I also see over there the famous poet, wit, and author Fingal Dee with her partner, apparently here to perform a recital later in the evening. And…." The reporter tapped her earpiece as if to clarify a point. "Yes, we have confirmation that the Kavki ambassador F'thodish Azd Laffu will arrive shortly. She is said to be a close friend of the mysterious newcomer, but no-one has been *able to interview her since her arrival a few weeks ago. Yes, here she is. I will try and grab her as she comes this way."*

"Right." Mercedes switched off the screen. "We need to get ourselves ready. Gaspard, you wait with the car until I call you. Ali, you come in with me." Both Gaspard and Ali nodded. "And as for you, my ward, act your part well."

"Don't worry, Auntie Charlotte."

"Aunt, not *Auntie*. Auntie isn't a word used here. And cut down on the contractions. I want you to make a good impression on the non-human guests. And remember the accent."

Bernedetti shifted his accent and tone ever so slightly. "Of course. How foolish of me, Aunt Charlotte. I think I must have been unduly influenced by our present surroundings."

"That's better. Right, here we are. And out we go."

The car stopped. Ali got out and opened the door. The floating trains of Laffw's gown sailed into the building. It was probably making fashion news just taking those opening steps. Andréa came up next to her, and the three advanced like a military jet formation from ancient human history. Approaching the cavalcade of media representatives, Mercedes suppressed a sigh as Maye approached them, clearly determined to get some kind of comment. Oh, well, best not avoid it.

"Excuse me." The reporter was almost yelling above the whirring and shouting and buzzing surrounding the entrance way. "Excuse me, please. Excuse me, Baroness. May I have a few words for our viewers?"

Several other reporters waited ahead, hoping to snag her if Maye failed. Might as well submit to the first available ordeal. The reporter asked a series of questions about the baroness's history, her recent purchases of notable properties on New Dubai, and her antecedents. The answers flowed with a calculated tone of boredom. Finally, after answering a question about Andréa, she looked about for him. He had been distracted by someone waving to him. It wasn't hard to play the concerned and slightly annoyed aunt.

"Andréa. Come along now, don't dawdle. We can't linger here all night."

Andréa returned to Mercedes's side. "Sorry, Aunt Charlotte."

She rapidly excused herself, leaving the reporter with an ecstatic look on her face. She probably managed to get the scoop of the evening. Andréa was smiling smugly, and Ali's face remained composed and neutral. The pair entered the building, passing through the reception area into the main hall. This was it, the moment of truth. The riskiest moment in her plan. If she was recognized here, it would be all for nothing. Death would be her certain reward. Clenching her fists, she willed herself over the threshold.

The interior was both dark and light with illuminated pathways across smooth surfaces and automated drink and refreshment trays at every turn. Music played around a stage where volumetric dancers were accompanying the admittedly sweet tones of three singers performing some of the surviving orchestral and vocal songs of the Ancient Earth song master Okabe. Andréa scowled.

"What a chaotic mess."

"I know, but whoever arranged this has good taste in music." She glanced at Ali. "Make our donation. Ensure it ranks among the top five donations, but not at the top. We don't want to be ostentatious."

Ali nodded and vanished into the crowd around the donation console. Andréa separated from her and moved toward a small group of women. Mercedes, left on her own, found a quieter corner on an upper balcony after picking up a serviceable drink. It was a good place to watch those below, the sycophants and power players who thought they owned this world and its people. She found herself close to a pair she vaguely remembered her father speaking of. Her dear, silly, archaic father. It was Fingal Dee and her partner Chatterly. She might have moved, but Dee spotted her first and affected introductions.

Mercedes smiled. "I'm glad to meet you, Miss Dee. Or is it Miss*us?* I take it you're life partners?"

"We are, but Miss will do. Don't worry, no-one knows quite how to address us. Don't see why, we're both clearly women."

"This planet can be a bit backward."

"Don't we know it." Chatterly laughed. "Can you believe some of the people here tonight? Such a glittering array of cold masses. I feel like I'm inside a crystal cavern."

Dee was smiling, eyeing Mercedes's outfit. "I hope you won't take this personally. That has got to be one of the most audacious dresses I've ever seen. And yet the most tasteful."

"Thank you. I don't know much about fashion. My ward said it was a little over the top."

"My dear, on New Dubai at present, to be conservative is to be daring, and thus to be tasteful. Look at me. Ten years ago my writing was scandalous, but now I'm the talk of the sector. You seem to know who I am."

Mercedes smiled and half-lied, struggling to remember the snatched sentences of wit from illicit copies of Dee's *Views on Devolved Morality and other Essays*. "I've read your work, though it was some years ago."

"Must've been when my books were banned under the old duke, but it's not like they still aren't banned elsewhere. Archturia still destroys copies when they find them. One almost feels you have to be boring to get attention."

"So, things have changed here."

"If you look at the surface, it's difficult to see. The rich grow richer, and the poor remain as poor as they ever were. But the old duke's daughter was a liberal sort, and her successor positively encourages the daring arts. Though not much non-human stuff."

"Is he racist?"

"Not that I've heard. I think it's those cronies of his, but they help him run the planet, so what's the alternative? Do you know them at all?"

Mercedes made an effort to remain light in tone. "Not personally, no. But I've a friend of a friend, plus some gossip. I do remember the old duke didn't take kindly to your work. Rather unfair, I thought."

"Yes. I remember him saying that 'the day I let one of your plays be broadcast or one of your poems be read is the day I die.'"

Chatterly spoke again. "I seem to remember you saying 'As you have commanded, so it shall be. I'll write a suitable eulogy for your funeral.'"

Dee smiled wryly. "The foolish wit of youth. I had people accusing me of making a death threat for months after that."

"I seem to remember you did read it."

"Yes, thanks to his daughter. The whole congregation was sniggering. Oh look, there's darling...." Some series of names Mercedes didn't know or care to remember passed around her ears. "Please excuse us."

The pair moved away, and Mercedes was again alone, staring down into the crowd. Like watching a pathetic reenactment of Ancient Earth decadence. Or like one of her father's god-awful state functions. Gretchen hadn't ever minded, but Mercedes had always bowed out as soon as possible and gone to do studies in her rooms.

Maybe she hadn't given them enough parties. She glanced to left and right of her. Wouldn't that be an interesting reason for insurrection. Sheer boredom. Her eyes suddenly focused, seeing her prey, Duncan Vorn-Solari, socializing with a small group on the opposite end of the balcony. So, he was here. Well, he had invited her. Though he was on his own. Where were his precious cronies? Better to approach them first, not someone who might still remember her from her sister's face. She scanned the crowd until she spied one.

The balcony she was on extended round the floor below like a severed garland, and on the other side almost directly opposite was Henri Laurent-Leblanc and an Ekri wearing a fine gauze robe. His wartime trophy, or "house guest" as he still insisted on calling her. If it weren't for the prejudices on New Dubai, Mercedes might have said unwilling mistress. Surely it was madness to approach him directly.

She laughed at her thoughts. How many times had she mentally rehearsed her escape plans in the event of being recognized? No, it wasn't madness, especially if he didn't recognize her. And who would recognize her now? Ten years of hard life, some different clothes, dyed hair, this stylish mask, and an identity ready for his inspection. And what if he did recognize her? She'd never know if she just stood here. She smoothed her skirt and sleeves. No sense in dawdling. Time to do what she had never done before, engage in casual small talk.

With a pounding heart, she walked briskly round the balcony, dodging around a couple of party goers who were talking loudly. Approaching her target, she gave a light cough, then bowed her head as Laurent-Leblanc turned.

"Please forgive me, but I wished to speak with you. I recognized your appearance from a mutual acquaintance, but your name escapes me."

Laurent-Leblanc seemed willing to tolerate this. "Of course, your servant. I'm Viscount-General Henri Laurent-Leblanc. And you are?"

"Baroness Charlotte Clarisse, likewise and more so at your service." Mercedes gave a suitable bow. "I ought to have known. Who doesn't know the great wartime exploits of Viscount-General Laurent-Leblanc? Your name is, on New Dubai, second only to the duke himself in grandeur."

"You flatter me." Was that an undertone of unease she detected? "I think myself fairly low in general affection. I would say my two friends stand above me in that, though we are equal in our mutual liking. But forgive my manners, I must introduce my companion, Hydee Satkireae."

The Ekri bowed her head and spoke in the hissing, formal tones of her people, translated by the tiny chip implants all had within their ears in this cosmopolitan age. "I am pleased to make your acquaintance."

Mercedes eyed Hydee and smiled, showing nothing but calm friendliness. "Charmed. I'm pleased to have met you both. I didn't know who would be at this function. Viscount-General, could you tell me of your two friends in case I bump into them?"

"It would be quite hard to miss them. Georges de Granger and Duncan Vorn-Solari."

"Few can claim friendship with both a duke and a Grand Prosecutor. I can barely claim a passing acquaintance with an ambassador. Where are these illustrious persons?"

"One of them's down there. Ah, and so's the other. Look."

Laurent-Leblanc pointed down at the floor below. Mercedes looked and noticed Granger's familiar and repulsive form next to Duncan. She tightened her hand very slightly on the balustrade but otherwise remained calm.

"That human in the suit over there." Hydee was speaking now, her tone dull. "He is being very loud. I can hear him even over here above the music."

"Human?" Mercedes looked, resuming her role. "Oh, yes, that's my ward, Andréa."

Hydee bowed her head, apologetic to a fault. "He's your—I beg your pardon, Lady Clarisse, I had no idea."

"It's all right. You can criticize him as much as you want. He needs it."

"Is he a little… wild?"

"You could say that. I love him as a ward, but I don't overlook his faults. He's got no sense of style and can be utterly nauseating when he chooses."

Laurent-Leblanc spoke now. "You, on the other hand, have excellent taste in clothing."

"Thank you. It's not really me. My servant Ali is my fashion savior. Mind you, I'm sure my ward would call me something not quite as nice."

Laurent-Leblanc looked at her with appreciative eyes, almost disquieting. Hydee also looked, but her face showed something more. The Ekri leaned in and whispered something into her companion's ear. Strain as she might, Mercedes couldn't catch the words. Laurent-Leblanc gave the subtlest of nods and returned his attention to Mercedes. Had they recognized her somehow?

"Pardon me if I appear forward, but I'd like to introduce you to the duke and Granger, if you wish."

Mercedes concealed her unease behind a smile. "I'd be honored."

As Laurent-Leblanc and Hydee moved down the nearby stairway to get his two friends, Mercedes hid her triumph behind a stony veil. She had done it, spoken to him who had been her closest adviser. And he hadn't recognized her. Hydee's expression had been strange, but there was no sign of recognition there. It was worth keeping an eye on her though and restricting their meetings from this point forward.

Laurent-Leblanc returned with his two allies and friends. Time hadn't altered them a bit. One was a devilishly-handsome man with true blonde hair now graying, and the other a smug-looking type with a slicked hairstyle and angles within his generous proportions. Laurent-Leblanc introduced them, and Mercedes again gave the bow due to their station. Had she gone this low a month before, poor living and hard wearing from the d'If would have left her stricken, but a month of healthy food and daily sparring had built her physique up again into a figure of strength and poise.

She gazed at her two enemies as they bowed in turn, the duke giving a shallow but sincere nod. No signs of recognition—at least not yet.

"Prosecutor de Granger. Your Grace. I'm honored to meet you both. This I never expected."

"My wife Gretchen heard of your arrival." Duncan's smile was arresting. "She's the one who persuaded me to invite you."

Mercedes's smile was perfect. "I'm flattered the duchess should take such an interest. I've heard she is a vision of grace and so devoted to her family. You have a son, I believe."

"Yes. A dear boy. There he is now, over there. Talking with…. Oh, dear. Please excuse me."

The duke broke away quickly and went downstairs, leaving Mercedes alone with Granger and Laurent-Leblanc. Duncan's face had been plain to read, and from her information she could guess what had caused his sudden departure. Best to be sure, though. She continued a casual conversation for some minutes, deliberately avoiding the topic of the duke's sudden absence before subtly turning to it as they began a conversation about families. She spoke in the most informal, off-hand tone she could muster.

"It seems to me that people blessed with children aren't aware of their luck. So many in this modern age still suffer from severe reproductive problems, and not all of them through genetics or compatibility. Just take that terrible scandal a few years ago with the lack of radiation shielding on Seventh Air transport shuttles."

Laurent-Leblanc winced. "Yes, it was terrible. The duke nearly had a fit when he heard his wife and son were on one of those shuttles."

"Is his son's health fragile then?"

"Not at all." Granger spoke as if rebuffing a scandalous news story. "His health couldn't be more robust. No, it's the matter of…. But of course, you wouldn't have heard. His son and the daughter of the Berggarten family are engaged. They will marry when both are of age, but the girl is not entirely willing."

"Forgive me, but I'm not of this world. Is it right that they should be attached at such a young age? I thought His Grace's son was…. Is it eight or nine?"

"He will be ten next year. But this match is one of two families who have long shared good relations. The Berggartens have also become very wealthy from the White Oil boom. As have so many you see here tonight. Though they're probably being careful with their funds due to mining being temporarily suspended."

Mercedes showed surprise. "Suspended? Why? I thought the Synod shipyards needed all the White Oil they could get with those new Black-class cruisers being developed."

Laurent-Leblanc's face fell, and with a quick excuse he abruptly drew away with Hydee. Granger shook his head slightly and spoke in a conspiratorial tone.

"He worries too much about that Ekri's feelings. The mine owners are worried about sabotage. It's this dratted land dispute. You may have heard about it. Qalaa's Prospect versus… well, me. It's causing a quiet panic with the White Oil trade and exploitation executives. They think closing down the most vulnerable mines will discourage any rash action on the part of any malcontents among the Ekri refugees."

"Isn't there still such a danger?"

"The equipment is quite safe when inert, but when functioning it allows more than enough access to crude White Oil. The last time some crude was set off the mine burned for a century. Completely ruined any untouched deposits. If the Ekri refugees were to…. But forgive me, Lady Clarisse, talking shop at such a time is unforgivable."

"Not at all. I do it all the time. Drives my ward to distraction. You were saying about those Ekri refugees."

Might as well get the story from the other side, the side who believed they were in the right and weren't. He spoke of the land as his by rights, that the Ekri were illegally claiming it as part of damages following the Human-Ekri Conflict. The same old yarn used to justify keeping land for oneself. It made her sick, but she smiled and nodded and gave appropriate exclamations. Granger concluded with one of the smuggest backhanded comments on "winning a fair victory" she ever heard in her life.

"I see." She nodded slowly. "How interesting."

There was a silence, and when Granger spoke again there was an edge to his voice. "I'm curious to know, do you know Ambassador Laffw well?"

Mercedes shrugged. "A passing acquaintance. We met at Cape Life, spent some little time there, and my ward and I had arrangements to make regarding my finances and travel to New Dubai."

"I didn't think Cape Life was the Ambassador's kind of place."

"Perhaps, but she is a person of original tastes. But…. Oh dear, that's my comm. Would you excuse me for a moment?"

"Of course."

Her excuses made, she withdrew from earshot. Best to do so now before Granger could probe any further. Best he not know too much before she was ready. Mercedes had kept her hand on the balustrade, then gently raised her ring finger when Granger's inquiries started. This was the signal arranged with Ali, who responded at once with an instant ring through to Mercedes's comm bracelet. The farce enacted, she returned apologetically to Granger.

"I'm sorry, but that was an urgent call. I have to leave early. Please give my apologies to the duke and Laurent-Leblanc."

"Of course."

Walking back down to the lower floor, she struggled not to skip with delight. He hadn't recognized here. None of them had. She also struggled not to tear the mask away from her itching cheek. As she approached Ali, Mercedes stole a glance to the side where Duncan was standing. He appeared agitated standing beside Gretchen and in front of a young boy who appeared upset. A boy who had the hair and posture of Duncan, but the soft face and eyes of his mother. Mercedes hesitated for a moment, then moved on before they spotted her. She drew level with Ali.

"You will remain here and keep an eye on Andréa. Signal to Gaspard I wish to leave. I've had enough of this place."

Ali nodded, and Mercedes quickly made her way to the side entrance where cars could park and pick up guests who wished for an early departure. She wasn't kept waiting as the car drew up within seconds of her arrival at the curb. She got in and quickly gave the order for her home in the Upper Residential District. For some minutes, they were driven in silence, Mercedes slowly calming herself down.

She had feared this when she first took office, when the first requests for favors and special dispensation had come in from her father's old cronies. The riches of White Oil had made New Dubai decadent and self-centered. She wore their dresses, but her heart felt nothing but contempt. At first thankful for the sumptuous fabrics that clothed her, she now wished herself stripped of them. She pulled her mask away, rubbing the itches that had sprung up under it like a dozen insects crawling on her cheek. Best find some alternate material for other masks.

The traffic was thick, so nearly half an hour passed before they drew up in front of the Yakam Apartment Building. Mercedes had chosen it at Laffw's suggestion as one of the most luxurious and expensive homes in Amasian City. Her part was a ten-room complex some would have killed to possess. It had a living area, comm room, two bathrooms, servants' quarters, and catering provided by some of the best in the city. Pure luxury, and not of a kind entirely distasteful to her.

Once inside, Mercedes gave her order without hesitation. "A drink. Now."

She kicked off her shoes and waited by the floor-to-ceiling window as Gaspard got it for her. A month's training had done impressive things for him. He moved properly, could prepare and mix a variety of drinks and beverages, and even spoke with a little more culture and restraint. How different he was from the confused, blubbering mess she had awed into loyalty. He gave her the drink, then stood waiting in her peripheral as she drank it down at a drought. The sharp fluid bit into her throat, awakening her from the approaching gloom of memories and sour encounters. She gazed out across the blazing cityscape, a view of nighttime conjured from a fever dream.

"All those years ago, I never imagined Amasian City would be like this. I thought I'd be glad. But I hate what it's become. How can anyone live here? How can anyone stand such a place? It's so decadent. And I'm forced to don its stupid wears to blend in."

"Here, maybe. Not in this apartment. Mistress, you should rest. You haven't been sleeping properly since we left Cape Life."

Mercedes gestured at the illuminated scene out the window. "How can I sleep properly with all that outside? So noisy, so bright. Even when blocked from my room, I can sense it. All those people down there, like ants tunneling through my beloved home. It's Vorn. He's allowed this to happen. My family would never allow such—"

"Wasn't Amasian City always like this?"

Mercedes turned. She couldn't deny it. Under her father, her grandfather, so many before her, it had been like this to some degree. Consumed by itself, peopled by sheep and ants with no eye for worlds beyond their own. She had tried to curtail it, but Duncan Vorn-Solari had let it flourish. If only those idiots hadn't forced her out, she would have brought them to heel.

Her gaze returned to the window, and her tone became relaxed.

"You see those buildings there? All this was where the working population lived once. The developments here are nearly all new. There's the city center that was always there. But the rest of it. All those green parks. Where are they? Where are the birds which sang, the natural clouds passing overhead to throw natural rain across the fields? Gone. Now it's localized weather control towers and volumetric trees. I didn't even grow up in the center. I grew up in the country or on Argo. I loved living there. Loved the outdoor spaces, loved the people. The d'If was a hell in more ways than one."

Gaspard pulled into her vision and looked out at the scene with her. "I grew up in a place like this, a big city. My family came from the slums, hence my casteless state. It isn't that strange to me. In fact, it's comforting. The d'If was a prison for both of us. Here I can go where I want and do what I want."

"When you're not serving me, yes."

Gaspard nodded. "You know I'm yours to command."

"Yes, I know. And I know one day you'll leave. When I've done what I came here to do. I won't stop you."

"What about Ali?"

"Ali?" Mercedes grinned, amused at the thought of Ali having any will of her own beyond Laffw's instruction. "Yes, she's a good servant for me. And with some semblance of loyalty after I saved her at Cape Life."

She breathed a deep sigh, finding relief in an overview of her status. She had introduced herself, made friends with those who maintained the status quo, and with Gaspard's help left an appropriate trail at Cape Hope. Granger's interrogative techniques were good enough for dullards and rich idiots, but to her they were see-through. She could lead them on at her own pace. Gaspard was fidgeting, and Mercedes flashed him a look.

"Is something troubling you?"

"I'm worried. About Laffw."

"Rethinking your part in this?"

"No, of course not. But what if she finds out before you're ready?"

Mercedes's eyes narrowed. "I understand your concern, but on that front I won't show even one part of my hand until I'm ready. She may play the fop, but she's cunning and ruthless. With her, I must seem as ignorant as my own quarries are."

"And Andréa?"

"He'll remain as long as he's useful."

"How's that little brat useful as anything but window dressing?"

"You'd be surprised. You never got to look at his DNA profile, did you?"

"No."

Without further explanation, Mercedes picked up a datapad, opened a saved file, and thrust it into Gaspard's hand. She watched him read it and saw the change in his face, eyebrows rising and breath drawn in with a startled hiss. His eyes flashed back to her face.

"Is this true?"

"DNA doesn't lie."

"But why hasn't anyone else—"

"I doubt anyone bothered to look. I only recognized it by chance. It's best you know so you don't make foolish mistakes with him, but tell no one else. If you do, on your head be it."

Gaspard seemed to gain a measure of confidence. "May I speak frankly?"

"Please do."

"After working with you for a month, I've got this idea of you. It won't stop me serving you, but it helps me understand. If you were under threat from any of us, I think you'd willingly kill me, Ali, Bapti, Andréa, and even Laffw without batting an eye."

"Rulers are called upon to be ruthless if needed. I was raised and trained from birth to be a ruler, a politician, a player of the odds. I'm also bloody good at chess and know when pieces need to be sacrificed to aid the greater game plan."

"My God, you're different from how I first saw you."

Gaspard sounded slightly shocked. Mercedes eyed him coldly.

"The d'If taught me many things. You should know what a good teacher prison can be."

Gaspard struggled not to wince and failed. He clearly didn't have as clear a view into her as he imagined. All the better. Servants who saw too much were the most dangerous. He was loyal, and even if his insights were clear, they were also shallow. Mercedes turned away, ending the topic. Gaspard gave a slight cough.

"Will there be anything else, Mistress?"

"Nothing. I'll stay up for a while, then go to bed. This day's been long. You can do as you like."

"Thank you. Good night."

A slight smile broke almost unwillingly across her lips. "Good night."

Gaspard left for his quarters, somewhere beyond Mercedes's view or need to know. Left alone, she sank into the nearest chair and closed her eyes, her mind returning to her long-planned schemes. She ran a hand through her hair, which felt odd and out of sync with her head. But the feeling was short-lived. Just thinking about the horrors she would inflict in the coming weeks brought a smile to her face.

"Soon." The words came as she half-slept in the neon lights. "Very soon."

# FILE 8

## CHÂTEAU AUTEUIL

---

*Never wake the dying man.*
*Never stop that once began.*
*Never trust the meat to hang.*
*Never shed the dagger's tang.*
*Never does the snake lack fang.*
*Never vengeance give for pang.*

—Stanza from Fingal Dee's "The Bell, It Rang"

LAFFW GAZED WITH the eye of the naturalist connoisseur at the scenery below the small transport shuttle. New Dubai was a planet of many ecological communities, from the arid dustscapes of the southern continent, the transient cold and ice of the polar regions, and the snake-like oceans separating landmass from landmass. She recalled her first look at the planet so many years before. It had looked like a bed of serpents curling in and around each other with tongues of cloud flowing across them. Beautiful indeed.

Out of all the areas she had seen or visited, the lush wilderness covering the tens of miles around Amasian City were her favorite. Small, paved footpaths threaded out from visitor centers between marshland and islands filled with trees or covered by lush grassland. The flora and fauna were the envy of other human-dominated worlds. From bright purple Anzil blossom to the mastodon bellows of Aupheleen, it was a wild yet safe paradise. With air travel becoming the norm, the old roadways had all but vanished, leaving the surface beyond towns and cities all but pristine.

"How long until we reach Château Auteuil?"

Bapti checked the shuttle's report. "About ten minutes."

Laffw looked critically at her nails. They were a new kind for her, artificial sheaths covering her natural nails to exemplify their claw-like quality. No need to wear them for Mercedes. Casually unclipping them one by one, she spoke to Bapti.

"You know what I like about human worlds?" asked Laffw.

"I believe you said they love greenery."

"You know why, do you not?"

"Now that you mention it, no."

"According to their records, their Ancient Earth was once very green. Greener than many Cluster planets. But a great catastrophe struck, and humanity was forced to leave it behind. They separated, driven by petty divisions. The most diverse chose the route of least hope. And found the Cluster."

"And helped found what we have today."

"But in doing so, they left their world far behind. Even if they wanted to return, what would remain? Their home is remembered as a lost wasteland. All that remains of it are the archives. They are a pitiable people."

"We, too, once sought in desperation for others like us."

"But we did not need to travel as far as humans did." Laffw glanced out the shuttle window as it began an arcing turn. "I believe we are here a little ahead of schedule. The winds have been favorable."

The shuttle was beginning its approach toward a large building inside a transparent dome set on a large artificial island amid swampland and shallow rivers, bought long before the *Hated Brilliance* arrived from Cape Hope. Through the dome could be seen a luxurious garden of local flora trained to perfection, and at its heart the building itself. Though named for a piece of Ancient Earth architecture, it bore little resemblance to the throwback buildings of Amasian City.

It was a matter of seconds for the shuttle to pass inside through the dome's one entrance and set down on the large landing pad, throwing out a buffeting wind which made the larger plants nod and bend. Through the window as the shuttle touched down, Laffw got her first good look at Château Auteuil. A three-story building, its elongated tree-like shape was supported by four large pillars reaching out like roots. She had seen pictures on the sales sight of course, but never had she been in person until now.

Stepping down from the shuttle and walking leisurely along the winding path toward the building, Laffw smiled at their achievements so far. It had been a week since they arrived, less than that since the charity ball where both had made their social debut. Mercedes had been hesitant to invite Laffw too soon, but now she summoned her with positive eagerness. And in Laffw's possession, secured in a pouch at her belt, was the final results of her extensive research. Every little dirty detail she could find on Laurent-Leblanc, Granger, and the duke himself.

"Mercedes shall see I hold up my end of bargains." She spoke into a large sickly-sweet flowering bush. "I trust she will do the same."

A familiar figure appeared at the door of Château Auteuil. Ali, garbed in something plain yet expensive and well-tailored. Good. Mercedes was looking after her loan. Also visible, standing near an artificial pond at one edge of the large lawn surrounding the building, was Andréa. Outwardly he appeared unconcerned and blasé, but his face remained watchful, and his eye darted subtly toward them.

"Dangerous." Laffw barely mouthed the words. "Very dangerous."

On the other side of the lawns, perched on a beautiful little patio, Mercedes was working at something on a datapad. Laffw raised her arm and called out. Mercedes rose and gave a polite bow. Laffw advanced across the grass onto the patio and bowed gracefully, her lips splitting into a wide smile.

"Mercedes Solari, you are the picture of grace and hard work. Did we choose well?"

"Very well. I trust all went well with the research?"

"So, it is business before pleasure." Laffw rose and became deliberately stiff. "Yes, all went better than expected. I only had to call in two favors. I have the documents you wished. Shall we discuss them here?"

Mercedes gestured at the surrounding decorated posts. "I've got signal jammers in all of these. Gaspard installed them for me. If anyone wants to hear us, we'd have to be shouting, or they'd have to be within a few feet of us. Especially with this noise."

Mercedes gestured illustratively. The dome had its own semi-captive bird population, and they were in the midst of multiple crescendos. Laffw nodded and sat down, dismissing Bapti with a wave.

"Before we begin, how is Ali behaving for you?"

Mercedes considered. "Very well. She's an excellent servant. It helped me get used to having servants. I used to have no-one except a secretary when I was duchess."

"Ali was well trained in obedience before I found her. Soldiers make excellent serfs, and crippled soldiers are grateful for what they are given. And Gaspard? Where is he? I expected him to be near you."

"He's in Amasian City. He said he had some urgent business there that might prove useful."

"You give him a great deal of freedom."

Mercedes's eyes flashed as she responded. "You don't trust him?"

"He was your superior once. Now he is your inferior. In Kavki culture, it is considered foolish to take serfs whose role was so dramatically reversed."

"Guard he was and servant he may be, but I also owe him much, and he's been willing to suffer much for me. I trust him, and so I give him more leeway than I might another who was a stranger to me."

"Like Andréa?"

"Since you say it openly, yes. He's here so I can keep an eye on him."

Ali appeared with a tray of refreshments. She gave the briefest of bows and departed. Laffw eyed her retreating form, then accepted a proffered cup of some Kavki brew from Mercedes.

"Ali has changed. Are you giving her enough discipline?"

"I saved her life earlier."

"So did I, but I do not also let her become so casual in deference. Humans are so odd with how they treat their lesser citizens."

"I think it's your people who would appear odd to our eyes, Laffw."

"Compromise is the foundation of democracy, or so it is said."

Mercedes leaned forward. "I'm curious, Ambassador. Feles and human law punish serfdom very severely, while the Kavki appear able to hold as many as they like."

"That is a typical human misunderstanding. We do not have complete freedoms in that regard. Should a serf do something totally against their master or mistress's command, we cannot punish them out of hand. With overt disobedience, we are obligated to just cut them loose and let happen what will happen. They can find other employment outside our systems if they choose."

Mercedes grimaced. "I think we should change the subject. Time for business."

"As you wish."

Laffw drew the datapad from its pouch and slid it across to Mercedes. She watched keenly as Mercedes flicked through an opening table of names, noting the flashes of recognition. After a minute, Mercedes looked up.

"These are half of my former cabinet. I remember some of these were among those who led the insurrection and attempted to restore my power. And I take it these people have been disposed of?"

"Yes."

"You've yet to impress me. I did some of my own research on the journey here, and some of these people have been dead for years. Many died as part of the insurrection."

"Not all died. About half the names there survived. Some were imprisoned. Others had their reputations ruined to the point they could never enter politics again. Ancient Earth's legacy of dirtying all who disagree with the popular mood casts a long shadow."

"I take it all of these cases were handled by Prosecutor de Granger?"

"His manipulation of the law was poetic. With the complete, or at least unquestioning, support of Duke Vorn-Solari and his cabinet, his rulings went unopposed. The duke may have believed you dealt with for good, but Granger wanted to leave you with no edge should you escape from the d'If."

Mercedes shrugged. "Can't say I'm surprised. Granger always liked a belts and braces approach. Can the survivors be contacted?"

"I have already been making arrangements through appropriate channels, naming no names as yet."

"Which one can't be contacted?"

"An old friend of yours. Artorius Noirtier. Dead nearly eight years."

"I… see." Mercedes seemed to struggle with a strong emotion, but quickly rallied. "For any who are imprisoned, I take it there's a means of releasing them?"

"Always. Granger is a shrewd type, but he cannot hide or redirect everything. Especially from the likes of me. In the right hands, the right defense council can overturn every conviction. The most complete set-up is always the easiest to overturn."

Mercedes showed a bitter smile as she scanned through some of the case histories and reports. "That's the de Granger I remember. Sly and stupid, with some racism for good measure. My father told me about a few of these people, and I found out a little more. He could've found a dozen things to really finish them if he tried. And to think he is lauded as New Dubai's fount of wisdom in law. Duncan's proving to be more idiot than schemer. What about the Ekri land dispute?"

Laffw gestured at the datapad. "All there, though I do not see why you wanted me to research it. It matters little in relation to you."

Mercedes's smile returned, this time triumphantly smug. "Some things can't be found out officially. Where you have connections, Laffw, I have insider knowledge. Knowledge I kept within me for ten years in the d'If. Knowledge I learned from my father and from Noirtier."

"What knowledge?"

"Patience. You'll like it better as a surprise."

Laffw narrowed her eyes. "Do not brush me off too often, Mercedes Solari. I will let it pass this time since you seem so certain, and we are still quite early in this affair, but do not make a habit of it. You may regret it."

"Very well. But don't hold your breath for anything happening in the next few days. We have enough here for individual assaults on each, but my aim is to bring them all down in a short space of time. Maximum impact, minimum effort, leaving the least time for them to marshal their defenses. And in the spirit of being more open and honest about my actions, do you want to know my next moves?"

"If you please."

"Very well."

Mercedes shifted in her seat and whistled across the lawn at Andréa. It took a few minutes for the young human to reach them, walking at a leisurely pace. Laffw smiled still, but beneath her face she scowled. She knew a disreputable type was almost inevitable, but this one was worse than she had imagined. A sly, slinking thing without respect. Why Mercedes kept him on was a mystery to her. One more thing to ask her, and hopefully receive an answer.

Andréa stopped before the pair and nodded his head in a mock deference. "Hail to thee, my benefactors. I hope I haven't been called to break up any disputes. Negotiation is not one of my strong points."

Laffw might have responded harshly, but Mercedes got up and smiled. "Not at all. I called you here to let you know exactly what you're doing over the next few days. For the benefit of our mutual partner in this enterprise."

"Understandable."

"Here's the full details." Mercedes thrust the datapad she had been work-ing on into Andréa's hand. "Read the plan, then delete it. And don't deviate from it unless absolutely necessary."

Before Andréa could take the datapad, Laffw snatched it from Mer-cedes's hand. Her eyes scanned through the lines of text. Then she stared at Mercedes Solari.

"This is your plan?"

Mercedes nodded, and Laffw had to make an effort to control her voice. "Are you quite mad? This would never work."

Mercedes only smiled. A smile on loan from the deepest darkest oceans, assured of its hold on all things.

---

THE MOMENT THE datapad was snatched from her hand was the closest Mercedes had come to snapping in many years. Damn Laffw, why couldn't she just behave like she was supposed to? That's what she wanted to say, but she dared not. The rest of the meeting was a mixture of taut and polite, and her self-control had almost reached breaking point. Patient she might be, but there were limits. It took the last sliver of Mercedes's self-control to walk at an even pace away from her benefactor, clutching Laffw's precious datapad in her hand.

Once inside, she quickened her pace and took the small lift up to the second floor. Here was her office, a space more personal than anything else in her life. She had set this place up herself, and no-one was ever allowed inside. Shedding rough emotions like an itchy cloak, she stepped into her large, white-colored gaming space. Time to get lost in another world and let her subconscious rebuild her composure.

Locking the door and laying the datapad on a shelf, she picked up a pair of VG goggles and toggled through the selection of AR games she had pur-chased. She remembered her little collection of virtual escapes from reality, for the times when she didn't want to work and hated the official blathering of her father's cronies. In here, she was in control, following a set script she understood and could memorize. Several had gone off the market during her time in the d'If, but a few remained in updated formats.

"Yes, this one will do. *Dance-Dance AUGMENT.*"

The rhythm action separated her from reality, making her move her arms and legs in time to the smooth beats. The lead singer's vocals guided many of her movements, tapping or stepping on symbols surrounding her shaped like musical notes. It recalled a simpler time when she was a teen and Gretchen was barely out of childhood. They had played together in co-op on the easy setting, usually to the same pieces from a band with a particular slow and predictable pattern. They had still played when they were both adults, Mercedes on the brink of becoming the next duchess.

"Yes, you were there." She spoke in time to the music, the rhythm of her remembrance merging with the melody. "You'd just met Duncan at that function. You were love-struck, so bright and cheerful. Those innocent eyes, such a joy to see."

If only she had known what would come. It was that same song playing now, and as she moved, tears flowed from Mercedes's eyes. So many lost memories, so many reasons to stop. But she never stopped. If she did, she would be betraying herself and all she had done to survive in the d'If. As she concluded her final spin and arching reach to the side, she raised her head to the heavens and could not hold back the tears that threatened to overwhelm her reason.

"No one can understand me. No one, no one in the whole Cluster, in the whole Universe."

With a swift motion, she killed the song and pulled off the goggles. All but throwing the goggles back on the shelf and grabbing the datapad, Mercedes went to her small study-office, banging the door with enough force to rattle some of the fixings. Her eyes drifted from the datapad to a book she had left there from earlier. A copy of *The Count of Monte Cristo.* Picking it up, she looked at its archaic language and laughed.

It was a foolish book. There were parallels to her own little tale, but there was one thing wrong with Dumas's version. He wrote a happy ending for his protagonist and showed mercy where none was deserved. With a single flick of her finger on the screen, the book was deleted from her digital library. She wouldn't be swayed by such childish notions as mercy or forgiveness and redemption. Vorn, Granger, Laurent-Leblanc. Through ignorance or malice, they had taken everything from her except her life, and almost took that in turn. Now she'd come back to reclaim all she'd once had, and no motion of mercy would stop her. Ever. Spinning round and staring through the window at the garden below, her gaze became regal and hard. She would carry this through. Whatever it took.

Emerging, she found Ali waiting for her. "Ali, send a message to Gaspard. Tell him the plan's going forward. He knows what to do next."

---

GASPARD GLANCED UP from his datapad. It would be raining soon, the water pattering down on his head or drifting down in soft silvering curtains. The d'If hadn't had rain on its upper levels, and he'd never gone down into the mining complex where condensation from the venting tubes caused clouds to form and produce sheets of grimy drizzle. This rain was pure, untainted, and harsh on his fur. A sign of his liberation if there ever was one.

He rechecked his comm. This was the time and place, a smaller alley in the Upper Residential District near one of the cheaper apartment towers. The signal ID had stirred strange mixed feelings within him. A guard from the d'If, a remnant of his old life come back out of nowhere. It had come at the best moment when his mistress needed outside help. Perhaps they could arrange this together with Andréa, cut out the need to involve any other third party. They all shared a murky past, so all had a reason for keeping quiet. If they brought in anyone else, there might be only one way of keeping them quiet.

A shape appeared, a male Feles in a hooded top. This must be it, but…. No, it couldn't be. It shouldn't be. That build, gait, the color of the fur. It had to be some nightmarish coincidence. The Feles stopped a few paces away and lowered his hood. A sickeningly familiar smile crossed his lips.

"Hello, Gaspard. I see you've moved up in the world."

The bottom fell out of Gaspard's mind, clattering down into a bottomless abyss that immediately rushed up to flood his heart with twisted mixtures of feelings. What the hell was Echo doing here?! Gaspard put the thought into words with a few more curses. Echo shrugged and spoke as if he were describing a job change.

"Was with a work gang near the outside of the station, caught one of the guards and forced my way into one of the emergency shuttles. The blast from the d'If disabled us, and I repaired it. Didn't need the guard. I hopped over to Cape Life, then found out you'd been there."

"You didn't follow me? And how'd you get hold of that caller ID?"

"I took the ID from a passing corpse during the escape. And sorry to disappoint you, but finding out you were at Cape Life was sheer chance. No name given for you, but I'd know your face anywhere. You and Prisoner 74."

Gaspard bit his tongue, restraining the automatic correction on his lips. He mustn't know, not yet. Echo stepped forward, his smile broadening into that wide soft expression he'd used when they did... it.

"I didn't know you'd gotten yourself such a cushy job. Got yourself a place? Makes me feel quite lonely."

Echo's hand felt along Gaspard's chest. He wanted to pull away, but those eyes held him in place. The new scenery vanished, and they were back inside the d'If interrogation cell with the cameras off and Gaspard getting ready to pay for Echo's mercies. Then the rain started, the illusion broke, and with an effort he pulled away. Echo smiled, clearly letting him.

"So why were you looking around for possible helpers? 'A small job, good pay, discretion required.' Come on. Out with it."

No choice. He had to tell him now. Gaspard forced out as much as was needed, as little as he could afford, and more than he wanted to say. Echo listened with a half-cocked head, then laughed as the contracted tale concluded.

"Well really, that's a lark. I think I can find someone. Several someones in fact. And I'll help, too. Don't worry, Gaspard. Now that I'm here, you've got nothing to worry about."

Gaspard wanted to die. The rain was falling harder now, chaining him next to this thing he didn't want to touch, yet didn't want to leave. His heart screamed in agony.

---

FOR HERMA, TRAVELING back from her school in the early afternoon following some scheduling mix-up, trams could be the most infuriating transport imaginable. Slower than cars, they were often crammed with people, though today her tram was empty. But while her allowance could pay for taxi rides or other similar means, she preferred frugality and caution. More than her mother did with those fancy things she wore half the time.

"Excuse me."

Herma glanced up, shocked by the familiar voice, and saw the face of an eager-looking boy with a soft face and off-blonde hair starting to lose its darker streaks. Her stomach tensed. If there were any way out of being next to her betrothed, the Marquess Malcolm Vorn-Solari, she would have taken it. But he could report back easily enough, and then her parents would find out, and the whole weary round of recriminations would start up again.

She made her tone as completely neutral as possible. "Yes, Malcolm?"

"Can I sit here?"

"If you like."

Malcolm sat, and for some minutes they rode the tram in silence. No-one else got on as they paused at a stop. Might as well say something. Being silent was almost worse than moving away from him.

"How was school for you?"

Malcolm spoke with irritating casualness. "All right. I got some decent marks. Still don't have much of a handle on maths. Hope I'll be able to get some people to help when I'm Duke."

He had the same infuriating manner, the same casual expectation of assistance that among so many other things had infuriated her when they first met on his mother's estates on Argo.

Two years ago, at the tender age of ten, the idea that Herma was engaged to be married was almost like something from one of her treasured fairy tales, and her parents seemed so excited. But then she'd met the duke's eight-year-old son, and only her training in manners had prevented an immediate and rude response to his attempts at a greeting. With permission from their parents, Malcolm had taken her for a walk through the grounds of his grand mansion.

As they walked, he had grown worse. The boy had rambled on condescendingly about his toys, his parents, the new things in the shops that *his* family could afford but chose not to buy. After enduring this for half an hour, Herma had snapped. She looked the boy straight in his puckish face and unloaded her own doses of venom. His silly clothes, ostentatious mannerisms, utter deafness to anyone other than himself, and condescending insults that made light of those less than he was. Perhaps he considered himself above everyone else, like the tyrants of Ancient Earth? Perhaps he should find someone who would agree with his idiotic view of the world?

All that and more poured from her mouth, and she hadn't seen the innocence in his eyes, the truth of childhood's unthinking acceptance behind those rude remarks. Her sharp almost-parental tone had sent him rushing back to his parents in tears and led to her being grounded for a week until she formally apologized to his parents with the muffled insincerity of an angry child. It was a month before the next arranged meeting, and it was only with an effort that she remained civil.

Since those awkward early exchanges, they had met five times. She still didn't care for him that much, but she knew her earlier rebukes were made based on surface impressions. But the damage was seemingly done. Around her he became shy, jumpy, and outside his parent's company chose not to speak beyond frosty acknowledgments and forced courtesies. Her opinion had further soured, and she continued to see a spoiled brat without even the wherewithal to understand when he had been in the wrong.

"Never mind a husband. How can he lead a planet?" she had said to one of her friends.

It seemed like a complete impasse. He refused to be taught, and she refused to bow to one so unworthy of loyalty. The marriage was scheduled for when both came of age, and until then all she could do was wait. Those stupid books on her shelves had lied to her. There were no happily-ever-afters for people like her. She, as New Dubai's next generation of nobility, had to exist in a world without the comforts of normality.

But here on the tram, seated next to each other, Herma got a chance to look him over once more. Yes, he had changed a little since they had spoken two years before. She had expected to meet him at the ball, but he avoided her on purpose. Now he came up to her? Maybe he wanted her help with something.

Realizing she had been silent for some moments, Herma chose to reply to the young boy's remarks. "I'm quite good at maths. We are to be married, after all, so I could become your little helper." She quickly recalled herself, "Erm... I'm sorry, that sounded wrong."

"No, it didn't. I understand."

"You do?"

Yes, definitely something had changed. Malcolm looked at her with the fearful innocence of one afraid to put a foot wrong during an exercise. Biting his lip, he spoke with the fear leaking into his words.

"Could you help me with it now?"

"If you like."

Unbelievable. Unaccountable. Why was she doing this? Malcolm was getting out his schoolwork datapad, and she was checking over his sums and calculus, pointing out some wrong sums and a few digits carried over incorrectly. He spoke with deference, almost with modesty, as he accepted her criticism. She had to ask.

"Why the sudden change?"

Malcolm smiled, a sheepish expression. "My father. He told me to stop being silly and talk to you like a normal person. Don't know what he meant by that. I just never talk with many people like you."

"Like me?"

"Normal people. No, that's not…. How do I put this? People who don't suck up to me."

"I suppose not."

"And thanks for the help. Especially with that last one."

"Not a problem. I think that question's jinxed. It took me a week to solve that one. It may be the mathematical principle behind one of the basic White Engine functions, but I swear it was concocted by a sadist."

"Only until you think about it. Of course it follows that route. Simple when you think about it. So, what's your weak study spot?"

"Well…." Herma squirmed in her seat, feeling on edge once more. "I've been lagging rather with my history. I still haven't got the pre-human era that well."

"I didn't think they taught it."

"For New Dubai, my school's pretty cosmopolitan."

"Would you like some help with that? My father's been teaching me a few things my tutor doesn't seem to know."

"I suppose that's what parents are for. All right."

For the next ten minutes, the two children worked over Herma's homework. As they finished, the tram started to slow again, and a voice announced their stop at the Assembly Building. Malcolm was just getting up when he paused and looked at her.

"Erm…. Would you like to come with me? I'm meeting Pappy there."

Herma's stomach turned at the thought of meeting his parents, but it might be best to show any hatchets were in the process of being buried. "Yes, I think so. I was scheduled to visit you tomorrow, but since we're already together…."

She let the sentence hang as the pair got down off the tram. An unseasonable burst of rain was drenching Amasian City, and the news flash said the weather control towers had been scheduled undergoing maintenance, so no moderation was possible. Malcolm was just pulling up the hood of his jacket when Herma produced and unfurled her umbrella, secured in her schoolbag after seeing the weather forecast.

"Here, we can both get under this."

They did, but only just. Huddled together under the dark umbrella, Herma and Malcolm went the few dozen meters from the tram stop to the imposing yet modestly-decorated Assembly Building.

The pair ducked into the entrance, and Herma shook off her umbrella on the mat. A drone approached them, and Herma expected it to scan. All it did was glide past and round, almost bumping into one of the front hall's ornamental columns. Frowning at the drone's strange behavior, Herma barely noticed Malcolm walking up to the reception desk, then walking back.

"Must be out or something."

"Hmm? Out? No one's there?" Herma looked, and indeed there was no-one at the desk. "But that's silly. Someone must be there."

Walking up to the desk, she pressed the small buzzer she assumed would get someone's attention. First in a short series of presses, then a single prolonged buzz, then finally supplemented with a call out.

"Hello? Anyone? Is anyone there?"

Malcolm spoke from behind her. "It's all right. They're probably busy. We can use the waiting room over there. Pappy will be out soon."

Herma looked at her watch as Malcolm went into a nondescript door across from the desk. Yes, there wasn't long to go before the session finished and the duke would be available. But still….

There was something like a crawling feeling along the back of her neck. There was something wrong in this place. A wrong atmosphere. The air was heavy and wet with it. She again pressed the buzzer and shouted this time, finally getting up on one of the stools and banging the counter as loud as she could. Even with all this noise, no-one came. She supposed she'd best go wait with Malcolm.

Face crumpled, stomach dancing with unexplained butterflies, she walked toward the door. It loomed in front of her, her footsteps echoing as if in a cathedral. She stopped short of the door, her hand reaching out for it. Something in the pit of her stomach told her to run, run as far as she could as fast as she could.

Just as she withdrew her hand, the door opened and another hand, an adult human hand, reached through and grabbed her by the wrist. With the briefest of screams, she was yanked inside, then something was clamped over her mouth. There was a smell from her chemistry class, and a sickly-sweet taste on her lips. Then her eyes rolled back, and she was sinking into a sea of black unconsciousness.

Her last words trailed off in an incoherent mumble as she fell.

"Mal… colm…."

# FILE 9

## INGRATIATION

*I once asked a man about how best to infiltrate a social circle.
He said, "Can't be done." I knew he spoke truly. He had tried it
himself without success. I then asked a woman the same question,
and she smiled coyly. "It can be done," she said, "if you know how."
She did not enlighten me. But I take her meaning. She infiltrated
by not seeming to infiltrate. Everyone always suspects you're trying
to get one up on them, but if you set the right stage, you can fool anyone.*

—Excerpt from Fingal Dee's "Getting Ahead"

PERFECTLY TIMED. THAT'S what Mercedes thought of her arrival at the
Assembly Building with Ali in the driver's seat. There were Law Officers everywhere, and a couple of important-looking cars. Sliding out and blasting past the
cordon, she pushed into the front hall and saw a small crowd gathered around
one of the waiting room doors. It included a few familiar backs. A Law Officer
approached and spoke with the usual soft sternness of their position.

"Ma'am, you're not allowed in here at this time."

Mercedes turned, the picture of affronted indignation, and almost shouted. "I have a serious matter to report to the House."

"No-one's allowed under orders from Grand Prosecutor de Granger."

"Is the Grand Prosecutor here?"

"Yes, but—"

"That simplifies matters. Please tell him that the Baroness Clarisse wishes
to see him about a matter of life and death."

"Ma'am, I can't—"

"What's going on?" Granger broke away from the group by the door and approached Mercedes with a strained indulgence. "I'm sorry if I appear brusque, Baroness, but we have serious matters to attend—"

"So do I. My ward Andréa has been kidnapped."

The change in Granger's face was almost comical. His eyes widened and started, his jaw became slack, and his fists clenched. If Mercedes hadn't been focusing on her role, it might have made her laugh. The whole display lasted a mere second, then his self-control reasserted itself and he responded curtly.

"I think you'd best come with me."

Mercedes allowed herself to be led into the small group. She immediately recognized Duncan, but the other faces were strange to her, a paunchy human with a pained face, and a sleek female Feles who looked like a Synod Enforcer.

"Baroness, the duke you know. This man is Hans Berggarten, and this is Synod Enforcer Saqara Yarin who is visiting on a mission."

Yarin nodded. Before any more could be said, Berggarten all but exploded.

"What the *hell* is the point of introducing each other? We're losing—"

"Please, Berggarten, calm down." Granger's control was admirable. "Baroness, have you received any message concerning your ward in the past hour?"

"No. At least I don't think so. I'll check."

Mercedes produced the comm and scanned through recent messages. She found the message she expected, putting on a suitable frown for her audience. She drew in breath with a hiss, extending the comm with a shaking hand. Yes, they were buying it.

Her voice shook believably. "What does this mean?"

"It means that someone has been very foolish." It was the Synod Enforcer who spoke, much to Granger's obvious chagrin. "His Grace's son the Marquess Malcolm Vorn-Solari was kidnapped just over an hour ago from this very room. Also with him was his fiancée Hermathruda Berggarten. This message was left here."

Granger picked up a datapad and showed the baroness its message. It was identical to the message she had, an assurance of safety, then a demand for one million yuren in non-traceable currency. It sounded convincing enough. She had hummed and hawed over the wording for an hour the previous day. She looked from Berggarten to the duke to Granger.

"Is it true, then?"

"Yes." Duncan was struggling to control his emotions. "My boy. My little boy."

"And my daughter." Berggarten almost shouted. "That silly girl. Getting herself involved in this."

It was time to strike a less combative note. "No-one here is to blame except the bastards who took them. We should blame them above all. Not the children, and not ourselves."

Berggarten looked startled at the calm down, then nodded. "Yes. Forgive me, Baroness. It's just a lot to take in."

Granger took charge of the situation. Give him his due, he was competent at organizing things. Like searches, court cases, and coups.

"We must act at once, find them, and bring these villains to justice."

"How exactly did they pull this off in the first place?" Yarin spoke coolly. "I take it the whole building staff weren't in on it."

Granger struggled not to sound embarrassed. "Apparently, most of the staff were redirected by a false alarm to other parts of the building, the few that stayed were drugged, and the security footage and surveillance drones were sabotaged. We've had a report of an unscheduled delivery vehicle which left when the kidnapping must have happened. This was carefully planned. I've already got a trace on the vehicle, so soon—Yes, what is it?"

A Kavki officer entered with a message. She whispered into Granger's ear, then retreated Granger clenched his fists and kicked the nearest empty chair.

"Damn it all. It seems the vehicle was found, but the occupants weren't. And they infected the local camera network with a scrambler virus and completely wiped the vehicle's travel log."

"So, we can't follow them?" Berggarten once more despaired. "Then we'll have to play along for now. Get the money. One million each."

Duncan's face darkened, and he surprised Mercedes with his next words. "I know I can manage that. The Assembly will grant those funds willingly enough to keep Malcolm safe. But what about you? You can't afford that much all at once."

"I must." Berggarten sounded in torment. "It's my daughter."

Time for her cue once again, it seemed. The pair would end up wrangling for hours on the subject if she didn't step in. The message signal bleeped convincingly from her comm, and she checked it dutifully.

She gave the lightest of coughs. "Pardon me, but if you wish, I can help with this matter."

Duncan sounded less than thankful. "That's very generous of you, Baroness. But I can't ask you to pay our debts for us."

"This isn't debt. It's extortion." She was surprised at the emotion she could muster for her performance. "And I wasn't talking about paying a single yuren. That was a message from one of my agents."

"Agents?" Yarin's ears pricked.

"Yes. You see, I didn't come here just because of Andréa. There's something more here that I may have invited to your doorstep."

Granger's eyes snapped over to glare at her. "Explain yourself."

Like a fish to a lure, as predictable as ever. In her best impression of the agitated woman, she spun her tale of a small kidnapping gang from Cape Life who might have followed her to New Dubai after a failed attempt to capture her, possibly going after Andréa as a form of revenge. Malcolm and Herma were obvious targets when they arrived here, so they must have local contacts or similar. Methods included staking out a target's usual habits and finding points in their day when they were least protected. Common practice with more vulnerable victims was to take the money and leave a corpse behind. It was all very convincing and dramatic, just the sort of thing to appeal to Duncan, though Yarin's face seemed to think less of this tale.

Granger nodded, seemingly satisfied.

"In any case," Mercedes concluded, "we can't let it continue. Such a thing must not be allowed to stand on New Dubai, let alone any other of the Cluster's Capital Worlds."

Granger's expression fell. "Do you intend to hunt them down and save their victims? Such fantasies won't help us."

"No mere fantasy, Grand Prosecutor."

"I can't allow you to do that. It's completely against procedure."

"I have every respect for the law, Prosecutor. But there's little time to dally. My servant Ali can find them in half the time it might take official forces. We have experience with them, and you do not. Yarin's input could be useful."

Mercedes indicated the Synod Enforcer with a gesture. There was a moment's quiet, then the woman spoke with emphasis.

"Under normal circumstances, if there were not such a threat, it might be wiser to have the authorities handle this. While unorthodox, in this case it might be better for a private individual with suitable means to perform the initial investigation. These gangs have ways of keeping tabs on the authorities in these times that they didn't have a century ago. But this is risky. Are your servants able?"

"Perfectly."

"Then while they observe us, we observe you. When you find their hideout, let the authorities handle it. I'm sure they are competent on this world."

"Eminently." The smug tone of Granger's reply was nauseating.

"Then," the Synod Enforcer returned her gaze to Mercedes, "I think we need say no more. Unless there is anything further?"

There was nothing further. Mercedes left, the picture of the hesitant yet confident ally. It was almost touching how much Duncan cared. There was probably more to him than at first glance, maybe something of what Gretchen saw in him. Back in the privacy of her car, she tore away the itching mask and saw her grimacing reflection in the tinted window. What was she thinking, empathizing with that man? She'd been the one to arrange this affair in the first place. What next? Sparing him from his just retribution?

There was no time or need for any kind of mercy here. If Gaspard did his job, the trail would be laid and provide enough traces she could believably follow it. The greatest issue was Yarin. The Synod Enforcer was an undeniable wild card, harder to trick than two distraught fathers and a prosecutor keen for action. So long as everyone played their part, all would be well.

She glanced up at Ali's reflection in the rear view display. "Are you ready?" The reflected eyes dipped for a moment, a nod of ascent. "Good. Good."

Her mind drifted back to her meeting with Laffw earlier in the day, uncomfortable on so many fronts. She had considered complete honesty up to a point but decided against it long before reaching New Dubai. She would tell what she wanted only when needed. And as to the other matter, that was clearly off limits. But with that Synod Enforcer on planet and probably asking discreet questions, time was running short.

The Grand Assizes. That was the finish line, her planned denouement. Hopefully everyone else would play their parts accordingly.

———————————————

AFTER A QUICK glance to left and right to check for any unwanted eyes, Gaspard passed into the kidnappers' hiding place. It was an old apartment complex with adjoining storage area, abandoned following the folding of its owners and as yet unoccupied officially. The slow drip from a leaking water pipe was the only sound during his ascent, with everyone on the upper floors keeping as quiet as possible. As he reached the fourth floor and knocked, the door opened, and a gun barrel poked out.

"Password."

"Salazar."

The door opened enough for Gaspard to slip inside, then slammed shut as the guard pressed against it, weapon still at the ready. A quick glance showed Gaspard that everyone was present, even Andréa and Echo.

It had been a touchy operation, with Echo getting the building's tech shut down, then Andréa and Gaspard getting inside ahead of the children and hiding. The pair walking into the waiting room had been good luck, as had the complete lack of struggling from the staff as they were knocked out. The feeling was almost exhilarating, though soured by Echo's sickeningly familiar form on the journey there and back, and now waiting for him at an obscure and rubbish-filled end of the corridor.

Ignoring Echo's face with an effort, he reached the door of the cell where the two children were held. Andréa leaned next to the security panel, its tiny display showing the captives. The thumping of tiny fists sounded on the other side of the door. Switching on the security feed beside the door and turning up the sound, the scene unfolded.

The boy Malcolm was the one pounding and shouting. *"You can't keep us here. I'm the duke's son. I order you to let us out."*

The girl Herma was visible on one of the two basic beds, the only furniture in the room. She looked at Malcolm, then sighed and shook her head as he resorted to kicking the door.

*"Just stop, Malcolm. They won't listen. Haven't you figured it out? We're being ransomed. And I'll not make any bets about what they'll do to us if they don't get the money."*

*"Pappy will pay."* Malcolm was now storming up and down in front of Herma. *"He won't rest until I'm found, even if that means paying those people what they want. He'll come for me. I know he will."*

*"Both our parents will come, but you won't speed anything up by shouting."*

Malcolm glared at her for a moment, then his face fell, and he sat beside her, crossing his arms in a huff. Herma seemed to reluctantly put a comforting hand on the boy's shoulder. Their voices became low, indistinguishable.

An unexpected smile broke across Gaspard's face. There was an unquantifiable charm in the children's interactions, something he had never experienced before. His face softened, and he raised a hand to the screen. He wanted to comfort them, to tell them everything would be all right, that they wouldn't be there much longer. Then Andréa's hand reached up and tapped his fingers. His face showed no empathy for the children.

At once, Gaspard was himself again. "You ready?"

Andréa smiled unpleasantly. "Are you?"

Gaspard winced and averted his eyes, and Andréa's smile grew slightly wider. The human gestured at Gaspard's hand, then at his own chest and face. The meaning was clear. Two swift punches later, and Gaspard opened the door and threw Andréa into the cell and slammed the door. Gaspard looked at the display once more. The children saw another victim, winded and raw from an assault. Sympathy was clear in their faces, and Herma was the first to offer help. Gaspard switched off the surveillance monitor and went to the nearby window that looked out on the street below.

As expected, there she was. A regal-looking Kavki with her face concealed by a veil, standing and looking directly up at the building. Ali, here for the arranged signal. Glancing around to make sure no-one could see, Gaspard raised his hand to the glass. Ali nodded and within seconds was round the nearest corner and out of sight. Gaspard turned, and Echo's face almost pressed into his own. Echo pursed his lips, and Gaspard pulled back as if from a dangerous animal. The other seemed unruffled, merely cocking his head.

"Well, aren't you going to say a proper hello?" He glanced down at the street where Ali's form had been a second before. "We haven't talked properly yet."

Gaspard's mouth was as dry as sandpaper. He was frozen, unable to move away from Echo as he pressed close and laid a hand half-across his own on the sill. Confused and dreadful emotions rushed through his mind. He'd hoped and almost prayed that everyone from the d'If was either dead or far away from him. Then that signal, the meeting, the realization that Echo was still there in his life, still looming large with that unsettling smile. It had been the work of minutes to explain how Echo escaped and trailed Gaspard from Cape Life to New Dubai, and the work of seconds to get Gaspard to spill every detail of his current role. Now here they were, back as before.

Damn him. Damn them *all*. Why didn't he just chuck it and leave? Why? Because he hadn't the guts. He was unable to stand up to Witton, to Mercedes, to Echo. Anyone. That brief emotional storm flashed with a few strained words.

"This isn't the time for flirting."

"Was I flirting? I thought I was just starting off an interaction. You have my apologies. But you seem troubled. Something you want to say?"

Gaspard bit his lip so hard it started to bleed. He wanted to let Echo die here with the others when Ali was sent in, but the foul seed of whatever bound Echo to him blossomed into a treacherous flower. The words were forced from his mouth, a warning given without willingness of what was to come. Echo's eyes didn't change a fraction as he spoke. After several minutes of silence, Echo spoke with an irritating laconic drawl.

"Thanks for the warning. Didn't know you'd graduated to being complicit in multiple murder. Though I suppose the d'If prepared you for it."

"You always were full of it."

"Perhaps, and you always took it. I'm also aware that you warning me is probably in direct violation of your employer's wishes. And if that's the case, you've just opened yourself up to a whole world of hurt." He paused. "Hmm. 'World of hurt.' Such a quaint human expression. Kind of like our *'gaskeh-dyf'* in terms of meaning."

"You always liked using human terminology. For anything."

"You never objected. Said it helped make things more…. What was the word you used?"

"I could pretend it was a human pushing into me with my permission. Better than seeing what it really was and why."

"You're still clinging to that excuse? If you had any real reservations about our little trysts, you'd have run me in on the spot and be damned to the consequences." He leaned close to Gaspard's averted cheek. "But you didn't. You let me do what I wanted because you wanted it yourself. You had all that control, but you wanted someone controlling you in turn without orders or punishments. Don't try to deny it." He chuckled. "Oh, it's good to be free again. To say whatever I want without anyone listening. To freely confront someone too cowardly to face who and what they are."

"You're a sick little shit."

"I'm not the one who was kinky for human males and kept a little stash of relevant visual stimulation in his office for the long night shifts. Oh, yes, I found out about that. What did you say to that guard once? You're drawn to their inflexibility."

"Shut it."

"Personally, I like both Feles and Kavki. Kavki in particular, as so many of them modify their bodies. God, that one from the lower levels was a juicy piece of—"

"Shut up!"

Gaspard's yell shook the corridor. He hoped and prayed someone would come see what was happening, but no-one came. Echo looked at him, a satisfied smirk splitting and twisting his face.

"I like you when you're angry."

"Echo, just stop. If you want to go, go. Otherwise, you're dead. If you're lucky, I'll have another use for you."

"Is that a promise? Is this really the old Gaspard I'm talking to, or was that regret I heard just now? Hard to tell with you."

*"G'qy,* I deserved better than you."

"Pardon?"

Gaspard's mouth opened, then shut again, tongue sticking to the sides of his mouth. Echo's mouth was bent close, lips pouting very slightly, a sight sickly sweet. No, he wouldn't do it. *Couldn't.* But he wanted to. A storm of antithetical emotions focused on Echo. The urge came all at once to punch, kiss, strangle, embrace. Why couldn't he just leave this pervert in the past where he belonged? Of course, there was an answer, the answer in Echo's eyes. He was a coward, as incapable of pushing away Echo as he was of betraying Mercedes to her enemies. Yet hadn't he just done that by warning this worm of what was coming? For one wild second, he wanted to die where he stood, but even this he couldn't do. Finally, he forced out some words.

"Why did you find me? Answer that message?"

"Silly, you can guess the reason. You can't have so easily forgotten what we meant to each other for all those years."

"I remember what we were." Anger finally became dominant, and Gaspard almost spat the words. "A horny prisoner and his whore."

"And who caused that in the first place?"

It wasn't true. It couldn't be true. Gaspard couldn't be responsible for this horrible situation. He was suddenly back to his first year in the d'If when he attempted to change a couple of work schedules to ease up on a few of the prisoners. Echo had found out and promised discretion in return for a favor. The same kind of favor Gaspard had paid to keep Mercedes safe.

Closing off his heart had been the only way to survive after that. He ignored the cries and grime, cutting himself off from everyone and everything but the routine, losing his mind to fantasy while his body was used to pay for Echo's influence. Becoming like the drones which patrolled the hallways and assembly rooms. Now, just as his heart was waking up, Echo's presence recalled the old scarring. Gaspard spoke sharply.

"Blackmail, that's all it was. Bloody blackmail."

"Oh, really? I seem to remember you enjoyed our little trysts—"

Before Echo could say another word, Gaspard grabbed his throat and forced him against the wall, cutting off that smooth snide voice. Echo remained leaned against the wall, breathing with an effort, eyes boring into his own. Gaspard's claws extended slowly, pressing against the pulsing jugular.

"One more word, Echo. Just one… more… word."

Echo didn't oblige, and Gaspard pulled away, all but running away from him. He'd cast his die now, saving Echo when he could have abandoned him to death and freed himself. But could he have left Echo there? No. He knew it and hated it. Echo would always win with him, his little toy. Gaspard wanted to scream.

---

FORTY MINUTES. THAT was how long Ali had been waiting since Gaspard made the signal. Why was the human keeping her waiting so long? It did not make sense. The sooner she went in and fulfilled her orders, the better. She disliked these tasks on principle. She had seen too much death in the Human-Ekri Conflict to enjoy inflicting more on those unable to put up a fair fight. If there were any humans there, they could die, but as to the others?

Why did she need to kill everyone there? What was the point? It was all some idiotic half-baked power play that had nothing to do with her personally.

There he was. Gaspard, coming out in a hooded garment. And behind him was someone else, another Feles she did not recognize. They went in opposite directions, though the unknown Feles cast an unsettling look toward Gaspard. Now was the time to give the signal to Mercedes. Several minutes passed after she gave it, then the confirmatory return call came. No words. No verbal message. Only a single sound signal. Enough to be understood. It was time to begin.

Ali stepped round the corner into view of the building and immediately saw her entrance. No-one was in sight as she crossed the road at a quick walk, although the hum of shuttles and cargo vehicles overhead disturbed an otherwise tranquil scene. She reached the door into the main building and listened. No sound came from within. Stepping back, she raised her foot and slammed it against the primitive manual lock that held it fast. The lock broke under the impact, and the door swung open.

The Kavki on the other side of the door never knew what hit him. Before he could cry out, Ali shot forward and struck him hard on the neck. He crumpled to the floor, killed with a single blow. Ali pressed forward with barely a pause, listening for any sign of an ambush ahead. The noise she made would surely be heard, even if their only response was puzzlement at one of their compatriots slamming a door. She moved fast, but her mind lingered on the past.

It reminded her of her last mission, the storming of a sniper's nest on Axiom a month before the Siege of Cataaka was brought to an end. It appeared like an afterimage as she ran. Her squad scaled the building from outside and in, a building much like this. The hostages had died long ago, the first abandoned when food and water supplies were stopped by human blockades near the system. Squad mates had died, but the sniper had fallen. Then the gunfire from a concealed human foot soldier had torn into Ali's neck, shredding her vocal cords, nearly blowing away her spinal cord, and piercing her torso. That day had taken her voice, and now she replayed it without prompting. She felt no fear, only a dull humor at such sentimentality.

Ali found a stairwell and began her ascent at a run, her blade and parts of her clothing flashing with reflected light from the emergency lighting strips along the wall. Two more of the kidnappers—a Kavki and an Ekri—appeared as if from nowhere and saw her. They drew their guns and aimed, but that second's pause was enough for Ali to close the gap. Two quick strikes, and the guns fell from their stricken hands. The Ekri was swiftly dispatched with a thrust to the heart, but the wounded Kavki instead toppled over with a cry of surprise and pain, plummeting the two stories down and landing with a sickening *thud*.

A thud. Like the body of the foot soldier that had been picked up by a Feles on Ali's squad and hurled to his death. She lingered for a moment, relishing the sound. Humans had won the Human-Ekri Conflict, and their spell of forgetfulness had spread across the Cluster, blinding all to the plight of veterans. Only Laffw's employ had saved her from the empty life of an unwanted being, forgotten in a slum. A single thought pierced her mind as she cleared the last set of steps. All humans could die, and still, it would not be suitable recompence.

Ali burst through the door onto the third floor. The guard just inside immediately turned, reaching for the gun at his side. A single stab with her blade through the human's heart sent him crumpling to the ground. The few remaining emerged, hearing the commotion and realizing something was wrong. Ali darted to avoid one's sights and saw another heading in the direction of the hostages' quarters. There were four, three humans and a Feles. The Feles seemed the wisest and backed away at once.

Four targets, three within range, all easily dispatched with her hands. Just like the targeting system she had been tested on by Laffw and Bapti when brought over for evaluation. It was unusual for Ali, a free-born Kavki with military training, to be selling herself as a serf. But for one such as her, wounded and marked by association with the Human-Ekri Conflict, entering the serf market was the only sensible option. Being Laffw's political assassin did not align with her personal moral code, but she was the property of her mistress. It was the way of the Kavki.

Three lay dead, their necks broken. The fourth was punching a code into the hostages' room. Even as Ali ran, she considered the futility of this action. She was at too great a distance to close the gap before the desperate Feles could get inside and use one of the hostages as a real human shield. Mercedes's comedy was on the point of turning into sincere reality. The door opened, and the Feles dived inside at the same moment Ali snatched out, catching a fold of fabric in her fingers that snapped away, the friction causing a spike of pain across her palm. She skidded to a halt and turned, staring into the room.

The two children, Malcolm and Herma, were hiding behind Andréa, who stood in a protective stance like the noble figure he portrayed. The Feles was pointing a gun at the three, glancing between them and Ali. His voice came in stammering, high-pitched gasps.

"If you wanna see them live through this, you'll back away from that door."

Ali looked from hostages to kidnapper, then slowly backed away. This was not the time to launch foolish assaults. Better to sway this panic-stricken Feles into letting his guard down. Mercedes's orders had been clear. Kill all the kidnappers left in the building once Gaspard had departed. As Ali retreated, the Feles moved forward toward the door, struggling to keep his gun trained on two targets at once. Then Andréa burst forward and tackled the Feles.

Ali stared, momentarily dumbstruck. Andréa was wrestling with the Feles, hands clamped round the weapon and pulling it in all directions. No, not all directions randomly. He was steering it toward something, someone. Even as she started forward, her keen eyes picked out Andréa's finger sliding into the trigger guard, pressing the Feles's struggling finger down. On impulse, Ali threw one of her blades at the feet of the struggling pair, throwing off whatever aim there might have been. The gun barked, and there was the twang of a ricocheting bullet. One of the children let off a high-pitched scream. It was Herma. The bouncing bullet had struck the wall within an inch of the children's heads.

Ali dived in and grappled both human and Feles, separating them with a dexterous move. Just like her old instructor said, use the forces of the limbs to your advantage and defeat them with their own strength. She threw Andréa back against the wall, but the Feles aimed his gun and fired again, forcing Ali to dodge the bullet's searing arc. It struck the wall behind her, then there came another scream. She righted herself outside and saw the Feles kicking Malcolm away while locking Herma in a vice-like grip.

Malcolm yelled like the child he was. "Let her go."

Ali scanned the situation. This was the worst possible scenario. Andréa's foolish action had agitated the Feles past the point of reason. He might do anything at this point, even kill Herma. Ali briefly glanced at Andréa, who was righting himself. They made eye contact, and for the first time in many years Ali's heart was chilled. The look in that face, in those eyes, was nothing like the sly young man employed by Mercedes. There was something more there, a deep-set madness that overwhelmed all rationality while preserving a scheming intelligence. What was he up to?

There were sounds coming from the lower floors. Sirens, some kind of kerfuffle. The Feles looked even more alarmed. Ali readied herself, but Andréa acted first. With a heroic cry, Andréa charged out of the cell, flinging a pillow at the Feles's face. For a split second, Ali stopped breathing. She expected a gunshot, the human girl's brains splattering across the wall. There was a shot, but it was Andréa who let out a cry of pain and collapsed, hissing and cursing as he clutched his bleeding knee. Herma broke away from the Feles's slackened grip, and Ali made her move. The strike was swift and clean, directly across the windpipe. The Feles fell with a spasm, hands briefly scrabbling at the air before he slumped to the floor and went limp.

Stumbling from the cell, Malcolm rushed over to Herma and turned her face away from the bodies, then averted his own. For a moment, an adult visage came across the boy's cherubic face, a man taking responsibility for one precious to him. The child quickly reestablished itself and looked on the point of being sick. Ali still wore her wet weather cape, and she bore no stain or mark of violence. A single fluid motion drew the cape from her shoulders and draped it over the two children.

Herma looked up at her with tears in her eyes. "Th—thank you."

There are moments which last an eternity. *Thank you.* It was such a simple phrase, but she had only heard it once in these past thirty years. Laffw had never said it, nor had Bapti or Mercedes or even Gaspard. He was polite, but never to that extent. But this child, a complete stranger to her, had spoken with that simple honesty. It was warming, like stepping into a ray of sunshine after hours spent in a dark and dank cavern.

The moment was brutally shattered as Law Officers rushed in. They pushed past Ali, clearly aware of her identity. One of them covered up the body, another produced a flask of something for the children, while yet another attended to the wounded Andréa. It was a few minutes later when that sly human Prosecutor de Granger appeared, closely followed by the duke, another man Ali presumed to be the girl's father, and Mercedes. While Herma remained collected when her father came over, Malcolm rushed into the duke's arms. Mercedes went over and knelt by Andréa, who looked the picture of pain and pride.

Granger's voice cut in. "Lady Clarisse, is this one of your people?"

"Yes. This is my servant, Ali."

"Well, all I can say is that what she did was both brave and foolish, and if it hadn't been for that Synod Enforcer, I'd be advising you both be put under arrest for reckless endangerment of lives."

Mercedes glared at Granger. "Do you think we might attend to the wounded before arguing over protocol? I'd rather my ward's knee didn't get infected."

"He saved us." Malcolm's voice peeled out in the confined space. "Saved us from that Feles. He—he protected us."

"He *did* shelter us." Herma spoke in a more controlled tone.

Mercedes looked at Ali. "Is that true?"

Ali's gesture was answer enough. She knew Mercedes's little codes. Others would see a general gesture of acquiescence, but Mercedes saw more than the others. She saw the slight suggestion in Ali's hands, the flicker of her eye. The signs were plain. He *seemed* to defend them, but....

Mercedes spoke to the duke. "I hope my actions haven't caused more harm than good in this instance, Your Grace. If I've endangered your son and his betrothed through my actions, I humbly beg your forgiveness."

"Don't." The duke's smile was disarming. "I fear Granger was a little hasty in rebuking you. Your servant saved not only your ward and my son, but my son's fiancée. Yes, people were hurt, but it might've been much worse."

"I can't thank you enough for your understanding, Your Grace."

There was a time of silence as Ali followed Mercedes and the small group out of the building, while Medicos were summoned to attend to Andréa. Once outside and under umbrellas to fend off a fresh fall of rain, Ali took up her place behind Mercedes, and the duke spoke once more. In his face shone the sincere gratitude of a father who might have lost everything.

"If you please, Baroness Clarisse, I'd like to visit you and give you proper reward for your service."

"Just a visit from you would be more than reward enough. I think my ward will be confined to the city for some time, so I'll be staying in my apartment in the Upper Residential District. You may come whenever you wish."

"Expect me in one week. Now, perhaps you would like a lift somewhere?"

"Your Grace is too generous, but I parked my vehicle nearby, and my other servant Gaspard is waiting for us. I can only again express my happiness at restoring your child to you."

"Then until next week, Lady Clarisse."

"Until next week, Your Grace."

Mercedes nodded to Granger and Berggarten, then turned to leave. Ali followed her down the street. Mercedes glanced at her, the eyes flashing with an unsettling keenness.

"Did Andréa try to shoot one of the children?"

Ali nodded.

"Which one? The boy?"

Again, Ali nodded. Mercedes remained silent as the pair made their way back to her home.

# FILE 10

## ACQUAINTANCE

---

*The many and varied speeches from superior to inferior are a fascinating
study to any student of psyche. It shows how one views the other,
and if you can find examples of the reverse, provides interesting contrast
for long-term study. But for all your research, you can find little to no real
examples of the ideal relationship; a meeting of equals. Sadly such relationships
are not to be found publicized by the press in this universe.*

—Excerpt from Fingal Dee's essay "On Relationships"

AS YET ANOTHER guest was shown out in the long and boring parade of
official visits, Laffw continued to lounge in her chair, the end of her Smoker
playing against her lips. Finally, she took a long, deep inhale of the pale mist
within the Smoker's beaker, then exhaled the saccharine vapor with dreamy
relish. She must look the very image of frivolity and decadence. But when the
door closed and no-one was in view, her eyes lost their dreamy quality and
flashed with the razor-like intelligence her closest allies remarked upon.

As much as she enjoyed things like the Smoker, she retained her wits. The
Smoker was filled with nothing but the mildest pleasure, laced with artificial
scents to give the right impression. When on missions, nearly all of her decadence and frivolity was the clumsiest act. That so many still fell for it was
insulting. Perhaps they were dulled to the possibility of danger, or they did
not consider her a threat except when she might brandish a weapon at them.
After all, what was she? An upstart official with no real breeding, nothing in
the elitist world of the Synod's lower ranks, or the regressive society of New
Dubai. All chose to underestimate her, and all would be sorry.

Glancing out the window of the Kavki Embassy, positioned among the higher floors of the Diplomatic Center in the heart of Amasian City, she contemplated her incoming fortune. She, a Kavki "mudder" who had worked her way up through the Tri-Solar Hegemony with cunning and coyness, was now one of the most powerful diplomatic figures in the Cluster. A fashion icon, a political weapon, a force to be reckoned with by the wisest. And soon, crowning all other achievements, mistress of one of the richest Capital Worlds. It would be a coup to live in shadow history.

She smiled, turning over to take another draft from her Smoker, laughing out a cloud of vapor before twirling her finger through it to make stunning patterns before it thinned and faded. Her fingers continued to play in the air, creating hypnotic lines against the lighting strips set into the jasper-red roof. Her hand swept down onto a nearby alarm pad, which summoned Bapti from an adjoining room.

The Kavki serf gave a slight bow.

"You summoned me?"

"Bapti, have you received any updates from Ali recently?"

"None."

Laffw frowned, the Hooker's stem clenched in her teeth. "Half a week, and not a word. Nothing from Ali, or from Mercedes. Even after that mess with Andréa. Why she involved him like that…."

"I had wondered why you agreed to the plan."

"Because I know Mercedes. She prefers working alone, and overt intrusion would cause her to rebel violently and upset her plans. We both play for high stakes, mine higher than hers. Had I known Andréa would act in that foolish way, I would not have agreed."

"If you please, I was going to speak with you about Ali."

"You have an opinion on the lack of communication? Well, out with it."

"It is difficult for me to say. I hate thinking such a thing about a comrade. I fear we may be losing her to the human."

"Losing her? To *Mercedes?*" Laffw gave a short, sharp laugh. "I doubt that. Just because she saved Ali at Cape Life? Ali is not one to be swayed by such an action coming from a human."

"Why are you so certain of her loyalty on that account?"

"Are you so blind to who she is? She hates humans. Hates them with a bitterness greater than many an Ekri could ever do. You remember what she lived through during the Human-Ekri Conflict, do you not? What you both lived through?"

"I remember. The difference is I survived my ordeal and came out whole and able to live. She did not. It might be easy for one with Mercedes's skills to turn her away from us."

"Do not dismiss her because of her misfortune or her injuries. She is canny, knowing, and has more experience of the dark side of the world than both of us combined. Remember that when judging her loyalty. I bought her knowing what she suffered, and even without the nanomachines in her blood and the chip in her shoulder, I own her body and soul. As I own you."

"And we are both grateful for your generosity." Bapti bowed.

Laffw's face twisted into something between scorn and satisfaction. "You are kind to remember your place, Baptintilik Q'tosten Dakke. And I trust Ali-adriden Adakram P'fetrae also remembers. She would never forget her place for a human. Now, on another subject, you have studied this world. I would have your opinion. Mercedes's knowledge of it is deep, but I wonder if it is not tainted by her association with it."

Bapti considered. "I think it is lacking. There is something about such a freedom of social movement that gives me to contemplate dark futures. Not to mention the exclusion of other Cluster peoples from positions of influence. Also, the elitist social structure which supports the Dukedom is in need of ousting. Perhaps we should take steps to ensure these things change before the future duchess has a child."

Laffw let an ironic smirk cross her lips. "That would not be well done. You know as well as I do that tyrants are soon deposed. We must introduce some cultural reforms and persuade the people that they no longer need such a ruler. All they need is a regional government answering to the Tri-Solar Hegemony. We take a percentage of their trade profits, have a hand in the largest administrative issues…. We need not be a constant presence to make a profit. That is how the Synod works."

"I see. Your wisdom is, as always, faultless."

"Not quite. You have yet to ask me about the other matter."

"Other matter?"

"Yes."

"If you mean any potential gains on the stock market, I assumed that would go without saying, as humans put it."

"You are correct. When the time comes, we shall be ready to buy and sell just the right stocks. It could shift the economic balance of power for decades. And who knows, one step further up the ladder toward the Synod."

Bapti nodded, though she had disbelief in her eyes. For one such as Bapti, any but high-born Kavki reaching the Synod was laughable. There was something to be said for that attitude. It was the highest administrative authority in the Cluster, covering hundreds of solar systems, thousands of inhabited worlds and satellite bodies, perhaps millions of station colonies and other space-faring groups. But why then not reach for it? All the peoples had reached for the impossible before. They had reached for fire, hunting tools, farming, building, sea crossing, flying, and finally the transcendent step beyond the atmospheres of their worlds into the great unknown.

To Laffw, the Synod was a trace of that ambition given physical form. It was a means to grasp the impossible, to fly close to and beyond the sun and find a seat in the very heavens. She spoke of it to her serfs, but very few others. Her dreams and ambitions were private, and to the world she showed only her veneer of false vapidity and the changes to her body. On an impulse, Laffw glanced down at the additional fingers she had added to her hand. Kavki were naturally born with four digits per hand. Now she had five. A useful tool when shaking hands with local dignitaries was not to startle them with an unfamiliar grasp.

"Bapti, when is the appointment with my stylist?"

"This evening. One hour after dinner."

"Good. That gives me plenty of time to see our dear baroness. I want some straight answers from her about that stunt she pulled with Andréa and Ali."

———————————

IT WAS ONE week after their last meeting when Duke Vorn-Solari appeared in an armor-plated car with escort to visit the Baroness Clarisse. He had originally intended to visit in the afternoon, but an emergency meeting with the Synod forced him to reschedule and cancel a different appointment to make it. He could have just brushed her off until another day, but he wasn't that kind of man. He would fulfill his obligation to the woman who saved his son and go to Apartment 231 of the Yakam Apartment Building in the Upper Residential District.

As the duke entered, escorted in by the Kavki servant Ali, he glanced around him. He hadn't been here before, but there was a familiar kind of smell. It made his stomach knot slightly. As he waited, someone shuffled in a nearby room as if getting dressed or doing some other form of preparation, with a muffled yet ethereal singing. He smiled. It seemed the baroness had a fine voice. And in a strange way, it reminded him of a scene long ago, when he'd courted Gretchen, a lonely-looking heiress on a balcony of an Argo estate, singing to the distant birds.

The baroness emerged in a simple trouser suit, her mask in place as ever, her blonde hair allowed to droop casually across the mask. The Kavki Ali emerged behind her and went to a discreet corner.

The baroness bowed. "Your Grace, I'm deeply honored."

"I'm pleased you could see me earlier than planned. I had to schedule a meeting with the Synod for this afternoon. I can't stay very long."

"I understand, Your Grace. Would you like a drink?"

Duncan thought about the timing. "Just a small one, and mild. Have you got Q'ylian liqueur?"

"We have everything. Ali, a small Q'ylian liqueur for His Grace, and New Sol Tea for me."

Ali nodded and prepared the drinks. The baroness motioned toward the two most comfortable chairs, looking out over the Upper Residential District and by extension a large portion of Amasian City. Once they were settled and had their drinks, the baroness opened the next phase. Her tone was light but seemed clipped and calculated in a way that put Duncan automatically on edge.

"I trust your son is recovered?"

"Quite. He's a tough lad."

"And the young Berggarten?"

"She's quite all right, in no small part due to your ward's bravery. How is he now?"

"The reconstruction's going well. He should be out in a few days. I would ask, will my servant suffer any consequences?"

"I talked with Granger about it. There's evidence that all of those in the building either attacked first or were prepared to. She shouldn't have any fears."

"That is good. I was planning to hold a celebratory party at my country house, for my ward principally but also for the quick resolution to all this. I'm inviting several of the locals. I was wondering…. Would you and your family care to attend if you have the free time? Maybe the Berggartens can also come."

"I don't see why not. My attendant can provide some dates when I'll be free. It'll give me the chance to thank your ward in person. And I'd like to get to know you better. People with your resourcefulness are not to be overlooked in the current climate."

"What climate would that be?"

"Times are a changing, Lady Clarisse, if you'll pardon the expression. The White Oil boom won't last forever, and we've got to keep this place relevant. I won't deny my predecessors were formidable politicians, but they were running New Dubai into the ground with their pride."

"Why is that?"

"They didn't want to bring in outside help for the White Oil mining process. They wanted to finance the whole thing themselves, create their own equipment, drawing funds from all the other old families, bring in unofficial off-world help. It would've bankrupted the families, and probably the planet. White Oil mining's expensive for a reason."

"So, the Synod still has a monopoly on White Oil mining equipment. Sorry if I sound ignorant, but there's little mainstream news awareness in the Outer Worlds."

"They get a cut of the proceeds, but we're still making twenty times the amount of trading money we did before the White Oil deposits were found. We've become more powerful than the old duke could've dreamed. It's just the morale booster humanity needed after the Human-Ekri Conflict."

"Yes, it's understandable. By the way, is there anything new about this legal battle between Granger and those Ekri refugees?"

"Nothing. As far as anyone's concerned, they don't stand a chance against Granger. He's the best Grand Prosecutor this planet's ever seen. Laurent-Leblanc's lucky to be represented by him."

"I thought this was Granger's fight alone?"

"True, but Laurent-Leblanc's the one putting the claim in on the land."

"Are they still on the planet?"

"Yes."

"Tell me… I've always been curious. What are your thoughts on his companion, Hydee?"

His stomach knotted again, as it always did with uncomfortable subjects and unwanted memories. "Well, that's a difficult question. I don't have much opinion about it myself, but Granger doesn't like it one bit. He's a bit stiff about that kind of thing. I guess that's one of the few things I agreed about with my predecessor, the right for people to be with whom they liked."

"I have not seen many prominent figures outside humans on New Dubai."

"That's the old guard. It's difficult to go against them. I mean, they're the ones who got my predecessor out of power before she died. People like you, Lady Clarisse, make this world go round. You serve the people."

"Yes. The people." The baroness seemed to think for a moment, then her eyes flashed back to Duncan's face. "When I met Hydee at that event last week, she seemed less than energetic. Is she unwell?"

"She has delicate health. Something of a recluse because of it. She stays at Laurent-Leblanc's country estate most of the time."

"I see. One other question, if I may. What does her name mean? It doesn't sound like a traditional Ekri name."

"Well, it's an Ekri word according to Laurent-Leblanc. In the Ekri tongue, Hydee means 'devotion.'"

"I see. How interesting. Oh, but I must be delaying you. You surely have many other appointments."

"No. I'm free for the next"—he checked his watch—"half hour. Unless you've got another appointment."

"No, not at all. Not elsewhere. It's just I'm also expecting the Kavki Ambassador Laffw here, and I don't know whether you'd like her company."

Now was his chance, an opportunity delivered on a platter. "That's fine. I wouldn't mind talking with her about something."

Almost on cue, like a majestically dressed whirlwind, Laffw entered with a snide-faced Kavki serf hot on her heels. The serf took up a position next to Ali, while Laffw bowed with the grace of a deity, her new robes flowing like rippling smoke.

"Lady Clarisse, I apologize for coming early. And—My, my." She bowed again, even lower. "Your Grace, I am honored. Your presence overwhelms me. I had no idea I would be enjoying your company."

She giggled, and her eyelashes fluttered for a moment. The duke smiled, willing to indulge her performance. She sat and asked for an exotic drink from Ali, which was delivered within a few seconds. Laffw talked in a light and airy tone, as if her remarks meant little and her understanding was less. She spoke of fashion, of the charity ball, of other things equally vapid, and only a light flurry over the recent kidnapping affair which had filled the news. Somewhere he could slip in his question. As they were discussing gardens, Duncan decided to spring that question.

"Talking of gardens, I understand you stayed for a time at Cape Life, Ambassador. It has sumptuous gardens, but Cape Life must be quite crowded this time of year."

"Yes, it is," said Laffw, "and it was the cleaning season in the recycling plant, so there was a terrible smell through most of the place. The air purifiers in my mansion kept me from the worst of it."

"And I suppose you met the baroness there?"

"Yes. Oh, yes, it was wonderful. There was some strange affair about a few rogues going missing on one of the lower levels, but otherwise it was sheer bliss. I am quite sure my mansion was an influence on her. It quite reminds me of her new country estate."

"Where is that exactly?"

The baroness's eyes flashed again. "It is a beautiful place. And I bought it for a steal. I pity its former owners, abandoning such a place."

"What's it called?"

"Château Auteuil."

The name elicited unpleasant memories of a foolish happening from before he met Gretchen. The knot in his stomach twisted into something resembling a hangman's noose. He gripped the glass just a little tighter as he answered.

"I'd heard it was up for sale. The previous owner was unwell and had to move, or so they said. So, it's now the property of the baroness. Interesting."

———————

MERCEDES LAUGHED ONCE the duke was well out of earshot. It'd been amusing seeing him control himself after the mention of Château Auteuil. Then he had done his best to keep the subject glued onto Cape Life, without much success. Finally, after several more minutes of circular conversation, the duke had to excuse himself, begging other business. Laffw gave him a jocular farewell, waving her drink around her with a wild and skillful gesture. Mercedes simply sat with a slight smile on her face until she could laugh in safety. Inside, she was screaming. The lies he had told about what she'd been trying to do. That was the story they came up with? But at least he hadn't recognized her.

With a final bow of the head, the duke was gone. With Mercedes herself again, Laffw's manner changed at once. She put down the drink and looked hard at her hostess.

"Interesting man. I did not realize he could be so charming."

Mercedes pulled the mask away, still laughing. "He doesn't recognize me. I looked him straight in the face, wondering if he might. You'd think he'd remember someone like me, even in passing. He didn't even notice. A few years, a mask, a change in hair color, and I'm just a stranger to him."

"And your dear sister?"

"She hasn't met me yet. Any reason for your visit beyond casual chatter?"

"I am very cross with you, my dear." Her deliberately light tone belied the bite in her words and flash in her eye. "Andréa's behavior during Ali's little performance was reckless. You could endanger our entire scheme, especially if one of the kidnappers decides to spill the beans, to use a human saying."

"There weren't any survivors. You can relax. I admit it was a risk, but it paid off. Are you going to say now I didn't tell you enough at the outset of this stage? I think I was quite frank with you."

"Frank or not, it was foolish. And you of all people should have seen the potential for such actions in him. Why did you allow it?"

Mercedes smiled. "Shrewd as ever. It was on purpose, of course. I knew he might take such risks, perform such actions, but I didn't want you to interfere. I needed it to look entirely natural. You might've sent in Bapti or someone else to ensure things went as planned. I didn't want that. I need Andréa to feel he's a trusted member of our group. I also needed to ingratiate him in some suitable fashion. Now he's in a perfect position."

"Perfect position for what?"

"Well, Ali didn't tell you anything, did she?"

"She has not been communicating with me."

"Yes, on my orders."

"Why exactly?"

"Security, principally. Best the fewest knew until everything was finished. But… did you know Andréa tried to shoot the young Vorn-Solari? Not overtly, just in a way that'd have it pass as the kidnappers' work."

"Why would he do such a thing? And why keep him on afterwards?"

"Because…. Well, you'll see in due time. Make a nice surprise."

"Mercedes Solari, this is getting to be a bad habit. How am I supposed to help you if you keep me in the dark?"

"The less you know, the better." This was expected, having to reassure the business partner, show they were safe. "Plausible deniability is a useful tool when used appropriately."

Laffw's face was the picture of displeased resignation. "Have you a timeline in mind for your grand scheme, or are we improvising everything?"

"Rarely do I improvise, Laffw. I've got it all planned out. We need all the pieces in place before the Grand Assizes next month. At those Assizes, Grand Prosecutor Granger will be concluding his case against the Ekri refugees. That case will fail, and in addition multiple appeals will be put forward. The appeals will be for my former cabinet members."

Those few key allies. Her father had disliked them, especially Noirtier, so she had cultivated their friendship. And true friends they'd been, though they did little to prevent her fall.

Laffw continued speaking. "I am glad to have made my contacts in advance. It may take all the time between then and now to get the paperwork in order."

"It will be the grand culmination of my plan. From the heart of New Dubai's elite circle, I'll bring the whole lot crashing down. We'll both need the time and will be working against it."

"I understand." Laffw smiled. "It is cruel indeed. And you, the lost ruler of New Dubai, appear from nowhere, bringing justice to the planet so long under the yoke of the usurper."

"If all goes well, I won't be appearing from nowhere. When, or if, all goes as I've planned, I'll be off world before anyone can stop me. The baroness will vanish and be left as a figure of ignominy related to what shall appear, and from her long captivity the former duchess will be liberated to take control of a shaken world."

"By the way, I have one question."

"Ask, and ye shall receive. Perhaps."

"I find your new home at Château Auteuil quite delightful. But why did you settle there? Was it mere sentimentality? Or does it factor into this great scheme of yours?"

"You'll see. Oh, yes, you'll see. If you can make it, come to my party and you'll begin to see the scope of my plan. And you'll see all my victims together in one place. Won't that be something?"

"I apologize, but I am booked."

"Oh, dear. Well, I'll happily tell you all about it."

Laffw sipped her drink, looking sidelong at Mercedes. In her eyes was the glow of victory, a glow Mercedes knew was a warning sign, but also the light of suspicion. Mercedes must watch her this coming month. Watch her like a hawk.

---

"DUNCAN, THE SYNOD'S been calling all day." Gretchen was standing outside their home, a concerned expression on her face, as her husband returned. "I've done my best to explain that you were very busy, but—"

Duncan threw off the odd feelings in his heart. "It's fine, Gretchen. I'll see them. Then, if you like, we can go for a walk. I think Malcolm needs the exercise. He hasn't been out much since that horrible ordeal."

"Good idea. I'll get him down."

Duncan ran through to the private Comm room, tossing off his coat into the arms of a servant drone. He arrived in the black-paneled room, puffing a little. He scanned in and waited for the display to activate. He only just got himself looking respectable and calm as the Synod Representatives appeared before him. Among them was Minister H'dryn, but she was the only member present that Duncan recognized from the previous session.

*"The Ministers of the Synod acknowledge the transmission of Duke Duncan*

*Vorn-Solari, current ruler of the human territory of New Dubai. This emergency meeting of the Core Synod is now in session. Duke Vorn-Solari, have you any news on the matter we discussed when we last spoke?"*

"I've done my best with both Laffw and this baroness she befriended there. But I have had little time for thorough inquiries. My son was recently kidnapped. You understand."

Minister H'dryn nodded. *"We understand. We have similarly had such confirmation, but there has been some difficulty tracing any connection between the Dagger's death and Ambassador Laffw. There remains some ambiguity about the evidence we have. You have already met our chosen agent in this matter."*

Duncan nodded in turn. "Yes, I have, and I've got information. I'm now on speaking terms with the Baroness Clarisse, and she is close to the Ambassador. I have confirmed definitely that both were on Cape Life during that time, and I may be able to learn through her some further information at an event she is staging at her new country estate."

*"Do so, and report to us when you do. This must be settled swiftly. One other thing. We have received news of strange inquiries being made about the cabinet of your predecessor, Mercedes Solari."*

"What of it? Those people don't know when to quit."

*"It was very specific inquiries surrounding their conviction and Grand Prosecutor de Granger's role in gathering evidence against them. There were also investigations into other members of the former duchess's cabinet who were forced to retire from politics due to unfortunate circumstances."*

"Who initiated the inquiries?"

*"There were no names, but the contacts we traced lead back to Ambassador Laffw."* Minister H'dryn was frowning. *"We cannot help but consider the possibility that our investigation and these inquiries are related."*

"You want me to continue on my end?"

*"Of course. Report to us if anything comes up. But do not mention anything about the inquiries. They may be a separate matter and will be treated as such until concrete evidence is found."*

"I shall do so."

The display shut off, and the duke breathed a sigh of relief. He made his way slowly back into his study proper, slumping into a chair and falling into a fitful sleep. His dreams took on a fever-like quality. He saw his predecessor, his sister-in-law Mercedes, resting on a blood-drenched throne. He too was covered in blood, and bodies lay around him. The throne was in his place of nightmares, the place he had long thought forgotten. Château Auteuil. He stared down in front of him, seeing the writhing woman in the midst of painful labor. The child's bloodied head came out, and the face was the face of—

"Duncan?"

Duncan started awake. Gretchen was leaning close to him, her face worried. She crouched down next to him and placed a hand on his.

"Duncan, you need rest. You're looking half-dead."

"I'll be fine. I'll just get myself some coffee and—"

"No. No stimulants. They're bad for you when you're in this state. Come with me into the garden. It's lovely weather out there. You sit down, and I'll get you some Sy'jen Tea to help you relax."

Duncan allowed himself to be led into the garden and seated in one of the two wicker chairs. The sun was behind some clouds for the moment, but the day was warm, and his spirits instantly calmed as he leaned back and relaxed. Here, he once more seemed to be on another planet. The tea, when it arrived, instantly soothed him as if he were being given a drug. The sun came out, shining with its orange-yellow radiance, and the duke of New Dubai fell into a deep sleep.

The next thing he knew he was started awake by a tap on his arm. It was his son, Malcolm, grinning from ear to ear.

"Hi, Pappy. Sorry to wake you. I've got great news. Herma's agreed to come round this week."

"Hmm? Eh?" Duncan looked at his son, still in a dozy state. "What did you say?"

"Herma. She's coming to visit tomorrow."

"Sorry? What did you say? Well, I mean I heard you, but I thought you and Herma didn't get on."

"I—Well…." Malcolm's face grew crimson. "She's grown on me. And she's got some good qualities. I was thinking of asking her on the hot spring trip the week after next. I'd really like to show that little place in the garden where I've been arranging the rocks."

"Well, that's great. Because I was going to invite Herma's family, anyway. I'm glad you two are getting on better. By the way, you're okay?"

"Yeah. I'm fine. I've got to thank that man Andréa for helping us."

"Andréa? Oh yes, the baroness's ward. You like him?"

"Yes."

"Well, you'll get another chance to meet him soon."

Duncan told Malcolm about their invitation, and the boy was over the moon. "Can Herma come, too?"

"She's invited."

"Great."

Before Duncan could say any more, Malcolm was skipping back down the steps and running along the path toward one of the secluded groves. Duncan watched his son go with a smile on his face, assured he was recovering from his ordeal. Dropping back off to sleep, he was woken up by the peel of evening birds. The sun was approaching the edge of the estate wall, the temperature had dropped, and a quick look at his watch told him it was nearly dinnertime. He'd been asleep for over an hour. No dreams though.

Dinner that night was quiet, but there wasn't any strain. Conversation was relaxed, and the food was enjoyed to the full. With dinner finished, Malcolm went to his room to get some of his homework done, and his parents decided on an early night after so much excitement and pressure. As they settled, Gretchen made the comment that "even rulers desire rest." She'd used it on their wedding night.

As they lay together in the soft sheets, Duncan struggled to get to sleep. His mind drifted back to their first night together. Gretchen had slipped away from the stifling ducal abode with her sister's unexpected help, and in the flat Duncan had taken in Amasian City they had finally consummated their love. Not "right and proper," but hardly a sin as his prospective father-in-law would say. He grinned, remembering the motions that caused the unfastened bed to shift a little under them. Then that look Gretchen's sister had the following day—combined protectiveness, understanding, mischief, and warning.

But as he remembered Gretchen's sister, the indomitable and mysterious Mercedes, his mind lingered for some reason on the baroness. Three hours later, he woke with sweat on his brow. A vision had tormented him in another nightmare. He had imagined the baroness sitting on that throne in Château Auteuil, now with everything so drenched in blood that the whole room stank of it. She had reached up and pulled away the mask, revealing the youthful face of Mercedes Solari. Duncan had stood immobilized beneath her gaze, and as she reached out toward him, her face melted. All of this in that place. The place that now belonged to the baroness.

Gretchen had been roused by his wakefulness and placed a hand on his chest. "My love, what is it? You're shaking."

"I just had rather an unpleasant dream. Like... like someone walking over my grave."

"What you told us at dinner, about the baroness's invitation. I think you need that party more than Malcolm does. Is something wrong?"

"Well…. It's just funny. My dream had her in it. And Mercedes."

"Poor Mercedes. But I hope you're not being won over by a mysterious masked woman."

Gretchen was joking, but the tense seriousness of his face made this remark fall as flat as stale beer. The two settled back down to sleep, but for Duncan his sleep was fitful, and the morning came with dark shadows under his eyes. Looking at himself in the mirror of his private bathroom, he sighed and pushed his nightmares to the back of his mind.

"Mercedes is gone. Gone forever now. Best look to the future. And play the game with this Baroness Clarisse."

# FILE 11

## MASQUE OF AMBIVALENCE

*Oh to see the lights at night, that leap and play*
*all to stay the coming of eternal night. We must*
*and must and must begin to see the dawn's dwindling.*

—Excerpt from Fingal Dee's "Cold Worrier"

AT HIS COUNTRY estate a mile from the suburbs of New Dubai, Laurent-Leblanc sat at his desk making the final adjustments to his speech to the Representative House the following week. He had been sitting for the past hour, writing, typo-searching, and copy editing, then writing again. Then there were the reports on current military statistics and recruitment, the usual monthly summary of psychological and physical health reports. His backside felt like it needed both. It was a tiresome but necessary grind.

He ran through his speech once again, the speech he'd been mulling over for the past fortnight, a state address on the merchant navy, its precious collection of shuttles and fighters protecting their transport ships from pirate attacks and natural disaster. All to preserve their precious White Oil export. Hopefully this address would open the way for official sanction to expand the available resources and make sure the merchant navy kept up with demand. This he could only do with the full backing of both the duke, the New Dubai Representative House, and the Synod Representative. The duke was a given, always was. The representatives too were easily persuaded. But for the Synod....

Rising achingly from the desk, he headed out through the large patio door and walked toward the small luxurious-looking house built in an enclosed section of the grounds. This was Hydee's house, her private sanctum gifted by him to her when she had come of age. Whenever his mind was troubled, Hydee's talk eased it. It needed easing. This talk needed to convince the Synod to allow for more military force, something they had tightly controlled since the Human-Ekri Conflict. The duke had been coy during his address the previous week, but he would have no qualms about expanding the merchant navy were the Synod to agree. It was at least possible. New Dubai was giving the Cluster more White Oil than it knew what to do with, and the Synod could not afford to refuse their demands.

Thinking about the Human-Ekri Conflict, and now on the threshold of Hydee's house, Laurent-Leblanc hesitated. Would he be permitted to enter? Could he speak with her today? A quick glance at the small pad assured him she was open to visits. A light press, a slight pause, and he sighed with relief. She accepted the call. The door slid open, and he passed into the heated, gilded interior. It felt a little like walking into a temperature-controlled bird cage. At least that's what Granger insisted on calling it behind Hydee's back. But this wasn't a cage. She could leave it whenever she chose. She had the choice. Yet she didn't make it.

Hydee was sitting in the front room, slowly plucking at a native harp-like instrument she called a Sytri. She was playing a complicated tune that bounced between 2/4 and 4/4 time signatures, her long fingers plucking the strings with the expertise of lifelong dedication. Laurent-Leblanc stood and gazed for some moments, awed at the supple movements of Hydee's fingers over the instrument, creating a melody that soothed and haunted all at once. It was the song of that same bird he struggled not to acknowledge, a plaintive call to the wilds beyond the cage's velvet-covered bars. A motif of ignorance and pleading.

Many had called Laurent-Leblanc a hater of Ekri, but this was an Ekri he had nothing but loved since plucking her from the rubble of Cataaka thirty years ago. He had no measure of Ekri beauty, what an Ekri would consider good looking, whether it was her scale tone, the length of her limbs, the smooth flat surface of her chest, or the hints of a crest around the edges of her face. But to him, she was perfection, a subtle calling from lost yesterdays when the Ekri walked in glory. Hydee continued playing for another minute before pausing and looking at her guardian. Her glass-like shallow-set eyes met Laurent-Leblanc's, her soft voice rippling through the air.

"You received an invitation from the Baroness Clarisse. Will you go?"

After a moment's silent asking for her permission, Laurent-Leblanc settled on the couch next to her. He rested an arm about her shoulders. He had heard many whisper their ignorance of whether his feelings toward Hydee were familial, romantic, or carnal. A plague on them all and their rumor mongering. His reply was as soft as her question.

"We'll both go. I'm not ashamed of you. And you shouldn't be ashamed of who you are. You're royalty. Remember?"

"Royalty without throne or treasury is not royalty, Shazika."

Laurent-Leblanc couldn't help smiling at this. The Ekri word *"Shazika"* had no direct translation into human languages, but it had been interpreted many ways depending on both human and Ekri dialects. He chose to use its meaning of "guardian" or "protector." He always struggled not to wonder what she might mean by it. He leaned a little closer, wary of her pulling away from him. If she did, he would leave at once.

"Royalty is royalty. The baroness would want to meet you. You barely spoke at the charity function. Please, Hydee. You've not been out since then. I don't want you to become a shut-in. You need to mix with people in society."

"I appreciate the sentiment, Shazika. But I do not feel safe. With this dispute with my fellow Ekri approaching its end—"

"Bosh." Laurent-Leblanc laughed, resisting the urge to place a comforting hand on Hydee's own. "Don't worry yourself about it. I won't let them take you and make you into their—What is it?"

A drone hovered in without warning. Laurent-Leblanc's sharp response stopped the drone dead in its tracks. Its mechanical voice sounded with a maddening calm.

*"Prosecutor de Granger wishes to speak with Laurent-Leblanc over NetCall. It is a matter of great urgency."*

"Ah. Hydee, you don't mind?"

"Go."

The simple word was neutral in tone, and Laurent-Leblanc was already feeling guilty at abandoning his charge even for someone like Granger. But duty called, and as he left, the harp resumed, this time with a melody in 2/8 time.

In his study, the display call alert was screeching with unusual violence. Granger never did have any patience. Settling himself, Laurent-Leblanc opened the view, and Granger's head and plainly-clothed shoulders appeared in view. Despite this blue-tinted truncated view, Granger's face still held the proud natural opulence that held everyone's attentions at the quarterly Grand Assizes. The same quality that Laurent-Leblanc despised. His greeting was as cold as he could make it without being rude.

"Granger. It's nice to see you, but what's the matter?"

Granger's voice was as grave as ever. *"You've got that invitation from the baroness to her country home at Château Auteuil?"*

"Yes."

*"I'm not easy about this. You've accepted?"*

"I'm going to. Why shouldn't I?"

*"No reason. I'm just unsure. This woman comes out of nowhere with enough money to buy several White Oil freight ships, and a mysterious ward from a family I've never heard of becomes involved in the unexpected and blatant kidnapping of the duke's son and his intended bride. You don't think that's strange?"*

"Stranger things have happened. Remember ten years ago?"

*"Don't remind me."* Granger's face became pained. *"I lost someone very close to me that day. Those damn loyalists, wanting their precious duchess back without thinking what it would do to all our pockets in the long term. Bringing a planet to its knees—"*

Laurent-Leblanc cut off Granger's fuming reminiscences. "I'm just saying stranger things have happened. It doesn't have to be a conspiracy against the duke. She's a stranger here. And a complete dandy from what I've seen."

*"No dandy. She's coy, watches everything, and misses nothing. I can see why Ambassador Laffw befriended her. I'm going just to get a better look at her. Is your pet going?"*

Laurent-Leblanc's face puckered into a grotesque parody of itself. "Her *name* is Hydee."

*"She… it…. The Ekri is your war prize. Don't forget that and paint yourself as any nobler than I am. And don't forget what you did to her fami—"*

"Granger, we may be allies in government, but keep following this line of talk and you'll lose that ally."

*"You always did take the side against me. When I wanted Mercedes dealt with, you sided with our weak-willed leader to have her sent to the d'If instead. I've spent ten years wondering if she'd break out of there."*

"But you said she was dead. Killed when it exploded."

*"Yes, but that's not the point. You always follow your own way, even if it's to the detriment of the entire planet."*

"You're exaggerating rather much today. As I said, if you don't hold your tongue, you'll lose my allegiance. And maybe your case."

*"We're both involved there, and you can't afford to lose that."*

"Want to push me? Go ahead. I've faced worse."

There was an unassailable truth in those words. He had faced worse. He had led a fleet to blockade a planet for two months, then sent a barrage of missiles down at its capital to end the fight quickly. And amid the ruins of that place, he had found a tiny wailing bundle in a corpse's protective embrace and taken the child to raise. Granger smiled, an expression dredged up from a foul bog.

*"My apologies. But don't forget my warning. Or what you hide from her every day."*

Granger shut off the call without any ceremony, leaving Laurent-Leblanc alone for some moments to contemplate. Finally, he pressed a button.

"Schedule in message to the Baroness Charlotte Clarisse. Tell her I accept her invitation, and that Hydee and I would be glad to come."

Again, deciding for Hydee. But could she decide for herself? Walking from the study into the large lounge, his gaze rested on its one large feature, a human-sized mirror. He stepped up to it and pushed a small button hidden within a leaf pattern. The mirror shifted to become a window looking into a hidden vault. Laurent-Leblanc's eyes gleamed for a second as he beheld the Ekri treasures he had kept here for over thirty years. All priceless, all undamaged, and all rightfully belonging to Hydee.

The one thing he lingered on in spirit was also the one thing he knew couldn't be seen. An ancestral treasure, an object of birthright. Hidden behind all those treasures was a coiled horned serpent of black and white ivory, adorned with little details in gold and jade. He had picked that up not a dozen yards from where the baby Hydee had lain. Hydee, Hydee, Hydee. The word he had chosen for her when she had become nameless. Devotion. Devotion to him, to this life. This life she'd only known through him, a life she wouldn't have had otherwise.

He quickly shut off the window, turning it into a mirror once more. He sighed and shook his head. Later. That was what he always repeated to himself when debating about whether to tell Hydee about her lost wealth and the cultural heritage of her people he had plundered as the spoils of war. Later. Later. Later. Perhaps after a whole lifetime when old wounds were forgotten. When she had forgotten. When maybe he had forgotten....

---

IT WAS THE day of the party, and as blackout shutters across the dome turned day into night, the festivities began in earnest on the specially-constructed party platform covering the lawn. Mercedes risked a quick glance through the window as she put her mask in place. The sight prompted a smirk both appreciative and disdainful.

*Psychedelic* was a term little used in the Cluster. It was an obsolete human word drawn from the culture of their Twentieth Century on Ancient Earth. Tied to visual effects, to atmosphere, to stimulants both legal and illegal, it was an archaic term from a lost time. But as the guests mingled down below after their long walk from the landing area, she could think of no other word to describe it. It was a psychedelic freakout, designed to impress and overawe, distracting from the hostess as a person.

Which is what she wanted. She didn't want to be a person. She was an enigma, a force of nature. The band was performing well. She always liked Ekri performers, and it would be one in the eye for some of the elites down there. Now just a quick check in the mirror. Yes, anything less like the stoic Mercedes Solari could hardly be imagined.

She gave a theatrical twirl, raising her leg in emulation of Ancient Earth artistic poses. She was dressed in a sun-yellow trouser suit with flared cuffs and a high collar, her current mask a mix of blue and gold. It was gaudy and tasteless to her eye, but in fashion at the moment on New Dubai, especially among Amasian City's upper echelons. The long-lost Commedia dell'arte given a second life.

She arrived on the ground floor and saw the others waiting. Andréa wore an emerald and purple tuxedo, which squeezed in all the right places and glittered from reflective material sewn into the fabric. Gaspard and Ali were also there, dressed in gold-trimmed suits tailored to their respective species. Ali in particularly looked resplendent with the fins across her head and graceful sheen of her waxy skin. All flare and glitter, like rotting mackerel under moonlight.

"All ready?" The others nodded. "Well then, let's give them something to talk about."

The walk toward the platform could not have been more dramatic or well timed. As she stepped up onto it, all eyes turned toward the small group. Mercedes bowed to the party and spoke in tones which carried through a lull in the techno backdrop.

"Welcome, friends and guests, to Château Auteuil. You've done me the greatest honor in accepting my invitation. My house is yours, so please enjoy the evening. Eat, drink, dance, and be merry. And tomorrow…."

She trailed off with a mischievous smile. Scanning the faces turned toward her, she caught those of the duke and Gretchen, of Laurent-Leblanc with his Ekri ward, of Granger eyeing her from a corner. Each had clearly expected a low-key garden party, not this ostentatious show. Regardless the crowd had clearly been won over by her display and outfits, with some even clapping as if she were an actress completing her star turn on a stage.

Mercedes grinned, raised her hand, and snapped her fingers. Several lighting rigs suspended from the frame of the dome sprang into life and played artistically across the staging area. The music swelled into an infectious beat, and Mercedes prepared to mingle. The comments were complementary, to her relief and satisfaction. It might have been too much, but they'd loved it. The music was noticeable without being intrusive, and the food was the best for all the peoples present. Conversation took hold, Mercedes played the perfect hostess, Ali was the perfect servant, and Gaspard took up a viewing position.

What a view of humanity could be seen. Fingal Dee and her partner Chatterly were in one section with a small throng around them, a column writer detailing the event for a social site, and then her targets noticeably distant from each other. As if they were avoiding contact. Perhaps they didn't want to talk shop. She quickly passed by Fingal Dee, exchanging a friendly word or two. Dee seemed in top form, spouting about the outrageous rumors about her being "entirely true," and how boring Granger was to talk to. Well, she wouldn't have to run that risk for much longer.

As she continued the slow progress toward Duncan and Granger, she considered the scene, imagining what she must look like in it. To pretend decadence was one thing, but to be decadent by nature was another. She could never be decadent. She knew too well what it led to. She'd watched it in her father, to a point in her ailing mother, and in the sycophantic courtiers who swarmed around her during her few months in power. Decadence was a terrifying drug, and those around her had rebelled against her weening attempts.

Mercedes timed her entrance to break Duncan and Gretchen away from the discussion of some Kavki oligarch with a lip modified to look like Cthulian testicles—pure show without function. With the hostess quietly enforcing priority, the oligarch moved away. Mercedes put on her best smile.

"Your Graces, I'm pleased you could attend."

Duncan smiled in turn. "Lady Clarisse, I'm more than impressed by your arrangements here. It's a wonderful sight to behold. It must've taken you some time to arrange."

"You'll forgive me when I say it was more Gaspard and Ali's doing than mine. I'm hopeless at staging such large events." A lie of course, but best to distance herself from the ever-efficient Mercedes in their minds. "No head for it."

"No shame in admitting someone's help. I'd never have gotten this far without Granger and Laurent-Leblanc at my side." He glanced over to where Andréa was talking with some other guests including the oligarch. "Your ward seems to have healed up quite well."

"Yes. He does me proud."

"Those features. That posture. He reminds me of someone I knew a long time ago."

"Probably one of the nobles that visited before you became Duke. Perhaps you met a branch of the Manfredi family?"

Duncan hesitated before continuing, and Mercedes barely suppressed her triumphant smile. "Your home is quite something. This land used to belong to friends of my father. They didn't fare well during the troubles ten years ago."

"Yes, it is wonderful. And restoring that house was well worth the price. I almost built an entirely new one. You should have seen the state of the place when I first took charge. Shoddy materials most likely. A pity. It and this land have quite a history. I don't know if you've heard of it. Apparently…. No, I'm just gossiping."

Gretchen broke in. "Please tell me. I'm interested."

"If you insist. Well, apparently, some twenty odd years ago, a relative nobody from beyond Argo had an affair with one of the human servants in his house. The affair left the girl pregnant, but she refused to have an abortion. The man, fearing a scandal that might jeopardize his planned career and alliances, attempted to have her killed. It wasn't an act of thought, just of impulse born from pure terror. A friend gave shelter to the woman until she gave birth. She died due to complications, and the baby was given to a trading family to raise as their own. The pregnant servant was sheltered in the very house which once stood here."

The duke had turned slightly pale. "An interesting story. Is there any truth to it?"

"No more than many another tale, at a guess. It's a good story, with the running theme that people with true nobility are few and far between."

Mercedes's eye locked onto the duke's. Yes, he had that same self-control which allowed him to stand up to her father when courting Gretchen. How well he used it now to keep his memories secret, his manners casual.

"And I'd say you were one of those few, Lady Clarisse. Oh, but, where are my manners? Lady Clarisse, this my wife, the Duchess Gretchen Vorn-Solari."

Mercedes bowed. "Honored to meet you at last, Your Grace. I have seen you only from a distance until now. And I am pleased I could help your son."

"We're indebted to you." Gretchen spoke with the voice of a grateful mother. "We couldn't have stood to lose our son."

"Indeed. I hope my little party is satisfactory. And please, be honest. Politeness is all very well, but honesty is of far greater value."

Gretchen looked around. "A little loud for my taste, but enjoyable. The music's also enjoyable. Quite reminiscent of some tunes I listened to when I was a girl." Gretchen looked at Mercedes. "You know, I think I've seen your face somewhere before."

Mercedes's stomach twisted as disaster loomed, but outside she remained calm and merely shrugged. "Probably at the charity ball. I was there that night. You likely caught a glimpse of me. Where is your son?"

"At home. He still needs rest after his experience."

"I understand all too well. Andréa was in such a state of shock, I'd rather not detail it. But all's well that ends well. Ah, here's the crescendo." The music was reaching a climax. "I love this band, don't you?"

"It has points. Those pieces of music are quite nostalgic."

"Do you wish me to change them?"

"No, it's quite all right. Thank you all the same."

"As you wish. Your Graces, if you will excuse me, I must see another of my guests. Time waits for none, even eternity." Mercedes bowed.

Duncan inclined his head in return, but Gretchen seemed suddenly frozen. She stood, rooted and stiff as if struck by a bout of some plague. Duncan and Mercedes rushed for her at the same moment, catching her arms as she started to slump. It was Duncan who spoke first.

"Gretchen, what's the matter? You've gone white."

"I.... It's just.... A moment."

Gretchen pulled herself up with an effort. Mercedes immediately had Ali bring both a chair and a reviving drink to revive her, then excused herself. Unconsciously, she reached up and felt the edges of the mask. It was still in place. What had happened? What had she done? Had Gretchen recognized her? Glancing back expecting the current duchess to be staring after her, Mercedes's unease lessened as Gretchen merely seemed confused. All she could do was carry on with her program. On to Laurent-Leblanc.

Laurent-Leblanc was standing close to the serving area with Hydee near him, a small drink in her hand. She looked the picture of meek beauty. A sickening sight in one with her lineage. Mercedes opened with a courtly bow and greeting. Friendly exchanges out of the way, she looked directly at the Ekri.

"Hydee Satkireae, I've long wanted to meet you again."

Hydee bowed her head. "A pleasure. I admit we have not met in person for some little time, but *Shazika* has told me much about you."

"*Shazika?* Forgive me, but I'm not familiar with the term."

Hydee quickly clarified. "He is my guardian. As you are that young man's." She glanced toward Andréa. "I am surprised to see him unhurt by his ordeal."

"My ward recovers quickly from injuries, especially with the care lavished on him. Though I dare say he is giving a somewhat inflated account of his actions to poor Granger over there. I must rescue him soon."

Laurent-Leblanc raised an eyebrow. "Your ward exaggerates?"

Best take more care with her words here. "Doesn't everyone exaggerate to some degree? Take a soldier. Wouldn't it be more than usual for a soldier to turn a narrow-won victory into a glorious success, glossing over any unpleasant details surrounding death tolls and unpalatable casualties?"

The general's reply was stiff. "I dare say there have been such people. But I dare you to find one in the last few conflicts which the Cluster has endured."

Mercedes made all the signs of apology. "I meant no offense. It was a mere observation based solely on human history. I was particularly remembering the Spanish invasions of Ancient Earth. Whole cultures were ravaged for their wealth and punished for believing something different from a single deity. There are, of course, less savory reasons for extermination and enslavement, but the Spanish were the ones I was speaking of."

"I see. I accept your apology. And yes, such victories are a sad reality of human history. Hydee, I must speak with Granger for a moment. Do you mind?"

After a nod of agreement from Hydee, Laurent-Leblanc pulled away to intercept Granger, leaving the Ekri along with Mercedes. Strange that he should ask permission from Hydee, one who was almost property. But then Laurent-Leblanc was never entirely predictable, an advantage in both his military and political career. She had counted on that once, but he had sided with Granger and the duke.

It was a simple matter to make light conversation with Hydee and get her more relaxed, then slip in a small question. "How's your guardian's case against those Ekri refugees going?"

Hydee started, then relaxed. "He expects complete victory. With Prosecutor de Granger on his side, what other ending could there be?"

"But if their claim is genuine, then they'll win."

"It cannot be genuine."

"Forgive me, but how do you know this? Does your guardian have solid evidence to the contrary?"

Hydee shuffled uncomfortably from foot to foot. "I do not know about such things. It is not my place or in my interest."

"Not your place to know, or not your place to ask… Highness?"

The Ekri started and looked into Mercedes's eyes. Those eyes, previously glassy and subdued, now shone with a long-disguised fire. There was life there, however much her luxurious imprisonment with Laurent-Leblanc had attempted to stifle it. Hydee glanced over toward Laurent-Leblanc, then back to Mercedes.

"If you knew what he has done for me, you would not speak so. My status is nothing, though he alone upholds it with me. He could have done anything to me, but he gives me a home and security. How you knew—"

"That you are the last heir of the House of Pakaa, shaman rulers decimated during the Siege of Cataaka which ended the Human-Ekri Conflict? I know this, and so much more. I know the system of Cataaka had lands on New Dubai through ancient treaties with humanity following their induction into the Synod. I also know the Ekri refugees currently involved in a legal battle with your 'guardian' are the latest generation of its rightful owners by this same ancient accord, and that they owe suzerainty to the House of Pakaa. And, to crown it all, I know that your House of Pakaa was destroyed in an unprovoked military bombardment during the Siege of Cataaka by a fleet commanded by none other than Viscount-General Henri Laurent-Leblanc."

The Ekri was grinding her teeth. "A lie. You lie."

"I never lie about such things."

"He could never do that."

"No one in history can say they know anyone who couldn't do that. That capacity is in everyone. Denying that is just naive."

"What are you?"

"It's who. I'm someone with reason to hate Laurent-Leblanc, as you are. Why don't you smite him and have done with it?"

She lowered her eyes. "You do not understand. You can never understand. Hush. He comes again."

Laurent-Leblanc saw Hydee's shaken state and put an arm round her. "Hydee, you're pale. Are you all right?"

"I fear my conversation overstimulated her," said Mercedes with a smile. "But I find her truly enchanting. You are to be commended on having such a wonderful person as your companion."

Hydee took some little time to respond, but when she did her recovery and control were admirable. "I thank you for your compliments, Lady Clarisse. If at all possible, I would speak with you again at a later date. Your stories are most intriguing."

"She could come to our house if she wished."

Mercedes smiled. "Yes. I'd like that. Now, if you'll excuse me, I must have a word with Prosecutor de Granger before my ward catches him again."

The baroness moved away, leaving Laurent-Leblanc ignorant, and the Ekri secretly shuddering. She approached Granger with some speed. He was clearly dreading another assault from Andréa, so her arrival brought him visible relief.

"Hello, Granger. I hope my ward hasn't been too trying."

Granger was struggling to be polite. "Well… I—I suppose… I can't say he wasn't interesting to listen to."

"You must forgive him. He gets carried away with himself. By the way, how's things on the legal front?"

Granger's face became relaxed. "Everything in that regard is going most splendidly. I'm confident in saying I've never lost a case yet, and I never will."

"Yes, I'd heard a little of some of your earliest major victories. Such as Edward Dulac."

Mercedes kept her face completely relaxed, a smiling mask of innocence beneath the secondary mask of expensive fabric and dyed hair. It was delicious to see Granger's face pinch, remembrance clearly galloping through his brain.

"I'd hardly call that a victory. Dulac was never brought to account for his perversions."

"True, but your diligence brought the scandal to light. You did handle the prosecution of Penzance Payran."

"I did. You seem to know something about New Dubai's old government."

"Names, little else. Laffw delights in talking scandal when she thinks one isn't listening. There is one name I would speak of in more detail who had quite a fascinating history. He was a former Count from Argo. I forget his exact name. Norteer. Natrier."

"You mean Artorius Noirtier."

"Yes, that's the name." Memories bounced into her mind, a kindly yet canny man who had tutored her in political theory, one of her staunchest allies.

"Yes, I remember the case well. He'd been siphoning money away from public projects without the Duchy's knowledge. The Synod comes down hard on embezzlement on such a grand scale. He was given a stiff sentence."

Prison for that upstanding person, her close friend? "And where is he now?"

"Dead. Six months into his sentence, he killed himself in his cell."

Mercedes's facade momentarily slipped. "Dead? He—" With an effort, she regained her self-control. "That's terrible. Did he…? Did he leave any note to say why he…? I don't wish to pry, but—"

"I understand. And it's an old case, anyway. No need to keep secrets. He'd smuggled in a datapad and left his final message there. He said that if he couldn't serve New Dubai, then life wasn't worth living anymore."

It took an effort to keep her voice detached. "Well, if he was guilty, then he got what he deserved. Anyone who abuses their position like that isn't fit to live. Be they Count, Minister, or even Grand Prosecutor, they all deserve punishment if they've abused their power."

"Yes. I quite agree."

Getting a man to dig his own grave had never felt so satisfying. "Now, I'm sorry, Prosecutor de Granger, but I must attend to other matters. I won't be away for long."

"Of course, Lady Clarisse. A pleasure talking to you."

It was all Mercedes could do keep herself under control. A quick tap of the comm summoned Gaspard from his position. He walked beside her as they reentered the house. Safely out of view, Mercedes tore away her mask as if it were a spider clinging to her face. Baring her teeth, she swung out sideways, her fist slamming into and cracking a nearby mirror.

"Damn him. *Damn* him."

Gaspard's voice was firm. "Mistress, calm yourself. You'll have your chance. You've learned something?"

"I've learned that whatever mercy I might have given Granger is no longer tenable. I won't let him go unpunished for what he did. He stained so many names, destroyed so many lives without pity or even a second thought. He's worse than Duncan and Laurent-Leblanc. I'll see him go the same way as Noirtier. No, I'll see him get worse. Far worse. Pay like for like. Measure for measure, as they say."

"Your orders?"

"Make sure everything is ready before the Assizes. That's when we strike. No delays, no matter the cost. Tomorrow, you'll visit the Ekri refugees and get them as much on board as they need to be. Also, if it hasn't happened within a few days, bring Hydee Satkireae to me. If possible, ensure it's without Laurent-Leblanc's knowledge."

"And the duke?"

"He's my affair. But you must keep a close eye on Andréa. Suck up to him if you must, but don't let him go off on his own if you can help it. Take him with you tomorrow."

"You think he—"

"I think he has a want of patience in his nature. And that's the last thing we need when we're so close. When the time's right, he'll be of use. I've already planted the seed for the duke's ruin. Although…."

"Although?"

"I think my sister recognized me. If she visits, she's to be admitted at once. Make sure Ali knows. I'll be back outside in a moment once I've composed myself. And…." She saw the slight graze on the side of her hand from the mirror. "Could you help get this sorted? Must keep up appearances."

# FILE 12

## FACING FACTS

*To say you have everything is arrogant.*
*To say you have nothing is defeatist.*
*Say you have something, but say it with humility.*
*You get fewer envious looks when you do.*

—Extract from Fingal Dee's "Wisdom in Wit"

FROM THE SHUTTLE window, Gaspard looked down at the arid land-scape of Alasaya, enclosed in the rain shadow of a large mountain range. In the nearing distance was an old water extraction tower from the planet's early colony days. Round the base of it, just coming into view, were the huts and facilities of Qalaa's Prospect, built from bits of scrap and salvaged materials. As the shuttle drew closer, small details emerged for him to see. There was a makeshift cultivation tower, a crooked-looking water extraction and purifica-tion plant, and battered solar panels to power their tech.

Didn't they get any supplies at all? Disputed their claim may have been, but why this complete lack of help? It didn't make sense. Not to him anyway. Perhaps that's what New Dubai did to those it considered unwelcome guests.

Andréa was in the passenger seat, yawning at the three-hour journey from Amasian City. "Aren't we there yet?"

Gaspard threw a sidelong glare. "It seems patience isn't one of your vir-tues. We'll be there in a few minutes."

"Good. And as for my virtues, I believe virtues are for the virtuous."

"You could at least not quote Dee at me."

The shuttle landed. Gaspard glanced out the window, seeing the Ekri guard standing ready with an outdated gun clasped in lean and knotted hands. It was a pitiable sight, these Ekri abandoned by the Cluster's laws. He remembered the summation Mercedes had given him before setting off that morning.

"In the eyes of the law, and many of the outlying human population, they're squatters. They received no official aid, no supplies to supplement the meager crop from the tower, and no equipment to maintain their water purification plant. They have to grow, buy, make, or maintain everything themselves. Many are sick, and a few have died. Because of their neglect, none of the Ekri are eager to meet outsiders. Approach with caution."

The ramp slid down, and Gaspard clambered out. Andréa was staying in the shuttle, lazy bastard. Gaspard hoped he wouldn't have to stick around him for much longer. At least the shuttle controls were biometrically locked, so Gaspard was the only one who could fly it. As he approached, the Ekri guard snapped to attention and pointed her weapon. Her voice was a bark close to desperation.

"Halt. Come no further."

Gaspard stopped as instructed, calling across the two-meter divide. "I wish to speak with your leader."

The sentry's crinkled face became slightly more crinkled. "Why would our *Sayydi* wish to speak with city-dwellers?"

Gaspard smiled in spite of himself and the gun aimed at his chest. The word *Sayydi* dated far back into Ekri history when they were principally a nomadic tribal people. The word translated roughly as Elder or Shaman and could cover any gender. All the peoples had something like it, but none had remained as affixed to a society.

He looked at the sentry, who was fingering the gun's trigger. It was just as Mercedes had predicted. Hostile, suspicious, yet showing some sign of needing friendship from somewhere. It was best to use a direct approach.

"I have no interest in bickering with a sentry. We've come with information related to your case against Laurent-Leblanc."

The sentry clearly doubted his words, but Mercedes had said information against Laurent-Leblanc would overrule any mistrust if it came from a complete stranger. Finally, the sentry lowered her weapon.

"I will communicate your request. If refused, leave at once."

The Ekri left, her face still sullen. Gaspard relaxed. A step sounded behind him. He turned to find Andréa approaching, his face wrinkled in distaste.

"Such glorious squalor. I don't understand why they want more."

"Andréa, behave yourself."

"Why? I don't have any reason to be civil to these people."

"There's plenty of reason. Now be quiet. I've got enough worries here without needing to shepherd you around."

"Oh, shepherd, is it? In some circles, if I didn't detest you and your friends, that might be taken in a very different light."

"God, you're a walking political embarrassment. You don't want to stand out in the sun like this. You'll fry. Go back to the shuttle where it's cool."

Andréa smirked, then gave a curt bow and left again. It was like sparring with a petulant little child, but orders were orders, and he had to tolerate him for Mercedes. It was all for Mercedes. It was a few minutes more before the sentry returned. She looked almost more on edge than when Gaspard had arrived.

"Our *Sayydi* will see you."

Gaspard followed her to a large tent-like structure near one of the solar panels. A wind caught his fur, throwing stinging sand into his eyes. There were other Ekri appearing, curious about the intruder, and they seemed unconcerned. Truly the Ekri hadn't changed, still of the desert and willing to walk with all its dangers and hardships.

Inside the large tent, settled cross-legged on a sippa mat and flanked by four more sentries, was a female *Sayydi* of considerable age. Gaspard took in long limbs and a stocky body, a mangled face speaking more of hardship than age, and a single working eye that stared out unblinkingly. Her rasping voice could barely be classifiable as female.

"We received a message about your coming yesterday, despite our communications being unreliable of late. But I had not thought you would arrive so promptly. Or be so pointed in your desires. I expected one of your people to be more circumspect."

"I apologize for any inconvenience. If you hadn't wished to see me, I would have respected your wishes."

"That I find difficult to believe. So, tell me, why does one from the city come to us? You say your business concerns Laurent-Leblanc, yet you are not one of his lackeys, nor affiliated with the law. Neither employs Feles willingly on this world."

"You want to bring him down. I'm authorized to help you."

The Ekri gave a single short laugh akin to a croak. "We Ekri have been alone for thirty years. We do not take kindly to anyone forcing themselves into our lives. We win our own battles, as we have done and will do again."

"Self-sustenance is one thing. Obstinacy is another."

"You are bold in your words. I wonder if they are your own or not. If you knew the truth of our situation—"

"I know it in full."

"Then speak and have done."

"You rightfully claim this land as your own by ancient treaty. Through Prosecutor de Granger, Laurent-Leblanc claims the land for himself and declares you as squatters to be removed. You have tried to contest the issue, but circumstances make this difficult. My mistress wants to bring down Laurent-Leblanc and Granger, which will enable you to settle here as per your accord, in addition to receiving aid. You also have another interest in Laurent-Leblanc. He holds the last treasure of your line."

Every Ekri in the room started and tensed, and the *Sayydi's* good eye narrowed with the shrewdness of age appreciating youth's wisdom. "Our princess is his, body and soul. If we take her without her consent, we play into that man's hands and give him due reason to turn us out and away. In any case, she has no knowledge of his true self and what he did during the Siege of Cataaka."

"She knows her position. And soon she'll know the full truth."

"What of it? She is as spineless as the eels which swim in the seas of the Kavki homeworld. She is no ruler. She is a puppet we may use to reclaim our right to stand as equals in the eyes of the Synod and the Cluster."

"Worse reasons exist. And I'm here to give you your chance. My mistress vows to restore your princess and your rights to this land if you do as she instructs. When the case is brought before the Grand Assizes, this is what you must do."

Gaspard ran through what he had memorized from the datapad. It was a fantastic scheme, almost unbelievable, yet somehow logical.

"Breaking and entering Laurent-Leblanc's home to get the final piece of evidence will be the hardest part," he concluded, "but my mistress will have persuaded your princess by that point. If you want it, I have a copy of the evidence you can present on the day."

Gaspard took out the datapad from his jacket and handed it to one of the sentries. It was in turn handed to the *Sayydi,* who briefly scanned its contents. It seemed to satisfy her, for her eye flashed with something like glee when her gaze returned to him.

"Why do you help us like this?"

"My mistress's reasons are her own. You'll likely know in time, but for the moment know you'll have what you want, at no extra cost. Just don't let them pressure you into dropping the case before the Grand Assizes. It will be decided in you favor."

The *Sayydi* seemed on the point of refusing, but finally she motioned to the guards who had quietly blocked the exit. They stepped aside, sullen yet obedient. The sentry gave the datapad back to Gaspard, and the *Sayydi* spoke with a level satisfaction.

"We will be there. If you do not fulfill your bargain, we will ensure you do not live to regret your betrayal."

Gaspard bowed, then made a sign with his hand. *"Ataka qaphokh."*

The *Sayydi* started. The last thing she expected from a Feles was a greeting in their native language, let alone the secret language of their tribe. She let out another croak-like laugh.

"Your mistress does her research. Very well. Please leave now."

Gaspard left under escort, satisfied at the impression he had left. It was the work of under a minute to get back to the shuttle and begin take-off. Andréa was lying in the passenger seat as before, his eyes staring off into space. Gaspard heartily wished Andréa abandoned in the desert and out of his charge. In the few hours they'd been together, Andréa's manners and attitude had brought all of Gaspard's worst instincts to the surface. There was something about him that made Gaspard wish him in the depths of the old d'If.

"Andréa, I want you to be honest with me while we're nowhere near Mercedes or Laffw or anyone else. Why did you really join us? You don't seem the type to snuggle up with scheming nobility."

"That's a harsh description of Mercedes. But I wouldn't say I joined you. It's a means of employment and personal gain, nothing more. I didn't know anything until I arrived at Cape Life. Once I knew more, I admit I hoped you'd choose me. The guy I want is the duke."

"What about the duke?"

"I'll tell you afterwards." Andréa smirked and looked straight out the window as the shuttle lifted off, his voice light in manner but holding a dark undertone. "Sticking together is better than staying apart, especially for those at the bottom of the heap. Do you think our employer will honor her side of things when it comes to the crunch? Will she look after you? Or Ali? Certainly not me. I'm playing a part. When it's time for me to leave the stage, she'll drag me off with a cane." Andréa rose, stretching his arms and yawning. "I'll leave the return flight to you. I need my beauty sleep."

Gaspard didn't object, didn't even speak. Before half an hour had passed, Andréa was asleep, and Gaspard was effectively alone. His heart ached for the city, for direction from Mercedes. Even for Echo, though that aching melded with the deepest disgust and self-loathing. His eyes closed, tears pushing out and flowing across his face. A human quote, a surprisingly apposite quote, was forced from his lips.

"Stars, hide your fires. Let not light see my black and deep desires."

---

IF GRETCHEN SOLARI had heard the world was ruined and the sky red and the grass around her dying, she would not have reacted. She had been lost in her own thoughts all day. She ate breakfast mechanically, skipping her exercises, canceling all social engagements due to "ill health," and sitting in the garden staring into space as if trying to penetrate the fabric of the universe. Her son had told her enthusiastically about his schoolwork, and she had simply nodded. Her husband had kissed her, and she struggled to respond to his touch, and he had gone away looking perplexed and hurt.

Finally, near lunchtime, Duncan approached her again as she wandered through their garden, touching this plant and that. He gently took her hand, the same gentle touch which had helped woo her heart.

"Gretchen, please talk to me. You look unhappy. You've not been yourself."

"Haven't I?"

"You've been staring into space since that party. What's the matter?"

Gretchen tried to answer without success. It had been nearly two days since the party at Château Auteuil, and a single sight still obsessed her imagination. The Baroness Charlotte Clarisse. The vaguely remembered resemblance leapt into her mind, and in place of the decorated mask and blonde hair, Gretchen imagined a face bearing scratch-like keloid scars beneath locks of dark hair, marring a beautiful and once-carefree face as they had marred their mother's. That face and the possibility of what might lie beneath the mask made her feel like she was being swallowed by some ancient beast's maw.

"I don't know, Duncan. I don't...." She looked at her husband. "What you told me about Mercedes, it was true. Wasn't it?"

Duncan stiffened. "What's that to you? That's all finished ten years ago. You must really be on edge if you're remembering that."

"You were more than a little on edge yourself on the way home." Gretchen almost sounded accusative. "I tried talking to you. So did Malcolm. All we got was silence."

"I had something on my mind. And I was tired. Anyone would be after that party. Maybe you're just tired." He put an arm round his wife's shoulders. "Forget about Mercedes. I know it's sad, but that's all finished. She's been dead this past decade. If you're going to dwell on the past—"

"All right." Gretchen's reply was sharp. "All right. I—I think I'll go for a drive. If you don't mind."

Duncan did not object. He looked too stunned to say anything in response to her sudden vehemence. She got up sharply and went back into the house. Regardless of what might happen, she had to know. She had to see this strange person who by the hour had become the living image of her long-dead sister. If she didn't, it would never let her rest.

Changing from her faux-Tudor frock into a simple trouser suit, she ordered the car to take her to the Upper Residential District. She had to try and see her, if only in passing. She refused to think about the real reason for her going.

She would just go to throw off this idiotic idea. She'd gone to her funeral, and Duncan had assured her Mercedes was dead. Besides, she needed to thank the baroness for a pleasant evening. Maybe if she repeated that enough, she'd believe it.

As she was driven to the baroness's apartment, the half-truth rolled round her head like a cracked egg, becoming ever more fragile as she approached her destination. The car drew up after half an hour navigating heavy traffic beneath the Yakam Apartment Building. Its surface, all cleaned glass and polished metal, was more imposing than it had any right to be. A single press of the button on her bracelet made the car begin its drive to a nearby parking space reserved for exclusive vehicles. Entering the building, she breathed a sigh of relief that no-one was there to recognize her.

The small console by the door displayed the building's residents and who was available to receive visitors. She heaved an involuntary sigh of relief. The Baroness Charlotte Clarisse was in and accepting visitors. She pressed the small display and spoke into the tiny mike in front of her.

"I'd like to see the baroness please. It's Duchess Gretchen Vorn-Solari."

Her name and title were spoken in a light tone, almost a whisper. A green flash appeared, showing that Gretchen could come up. The lift sighed as it took her to the upper floors. The walk down the richly carpeted corridor somehow reminded her of old sensational stories of prison executions on Ancient Earth, the long walk to whatever method was chosen to appease its sadistic onlookers. She pressed the small touchpad, ringing the bell.

The Kavki servant was the one who opened the door, the one called… what was it? Ali? She'd heard the name at the party. No need to worry about it if she were wrong. Ali conducted her into the flat's large and sparsely furnished living room.

The flat's occupant, standing at the window like a shadow, was dressed in a jade faux-kimono flashing with onyx scales in a dragon design. She turned and stared at her visitor, her mask today a cream-colored affair with filigree patterning in the shape of a butterfly. The baroness motioned to Ali, who poured out drinks before leaving the room. Gretchen's eyes followed Ali through the door, which didn't quite close behind her. The baroness's voice recalled her attention.

"Good day, Your Grace. How may I be of service?"

Gretchen might have given any number of answers, even followed her original plan, but instead she threw caution to the winds. "I'd ask the same of you—Your Grace."

The baroness stiffened momentarily, then relaxed and smiled. "I'm not sure I get the joke, Your Grace. I'm a baroness, not a duchess."

"You're a baroness now. But you weren't ten years ago. When I thought you'd died."

"That's true for both of us. And I don't understand what you mean."

"Ten years ago, on Argo. When you died of an illness—or so Duncan said."

"Your Grace, are you feeling quite well?"

"Drop it." Gretchen's voice became hard. "I know who you are, Mercedes." An old pet name jumped to her lips, a childish remembrance of two girls playing in the woods of the family estate. "Roly-poly, please don't shut me out. Tell me I'm not going crazy. If I've made a mistake, please remove that mask so I can be sure. I don't care what's underneath so long as it isn't my sister."

There was a prolonged pause, then the baroness sighed. With a half-hearted chuckle, she pulled the mask from her face. As the "baroness" fell away like a discarded cloak, the face of her long-dead sister stared out with something resembling her old sibling affection. But even as she spoke, the hard lines time had carved into her creased her face.

"I never thought I'd hear you call me that, Twinkle. Remember how my nickname started? When I was a baby, always rolling across the floor rather than crawling or standing up like a proper lady. I wouldn't expect you to use it here."

"And my little name. You said my eyes shone like stars in the night sky, twinkling past the city lights. Mercedes. Oh Roly-poly."

Years fell away before her, and she rushed forward to embrace Mercedes as if she were a little girl again. There was no responding hug, and for a horrified second it felt like she were hugging a statue of her sister. Gretchen pulled away almost at once, a question in her eyes.

Mercedes in turn averted her gaze. "When did you know?"

"At the party. You said, 'Time waits for none, even eternity.' That was the motto you chose when you became duchess. That's the last thing you said to me before…." Her tone became hard again, "Before you went back on your word and attempted to usurp my husband. Did you mean to say that? Were you just tormenting us?"

"Goodness knows. I must've been mad. I began to feel like myself that night." A genuine smile flashed across her sister's face. "Won't you sit? Our current pose is a little melodramatic."

Gretchen sat stiffly, while Mercedes reclined in her seat, clearly with a forced nonchalance. She picked up her drink and sipped it, but Gretchen left her own untouched. Something, an indescribable feeling, made her wary. Mercedes spoke after several minutes of silence.

"So, what shall we talk about? It's been ten years, after all."

"Yes. It has. What happened to you? Duncan told me you'd died. I went to your funeral."

"A closed casket funeral, of course. Oh, yes, I died. I died and got sent into my own little hell. I was too inconvenient. I'd be a liability alive and at liberty, and dead by arrangement I'd become a martyr. As a tragic figure whose sister carried on the proud family line, alongside the man who saved New Dubai's established system, I was quite safe. But where to keep me? Where else but the d'If?"

Gretchen started. "The... d'If?"

"You've heard of it?"

"Mother told me about it long ago. I never imagined it was anything but a tale to scare me if I was being naughty."

Mercedes's eyes fixed on her sister. "For ten years, I was kept there. Ten years in a tiny cell, looked at by every other prisoner who wanted to make me their tool, keeping my pride in the face of its sickening warden's attentions. My only friend, a Feles who didn't know anything about me. And for those ten years, I waited and never forgot the men who sent me there. Duncan Vorn-Solari, Henri Laurent-Leblanc, and Georges de Granger. They grew rich and fat on my legacy."

Some old resentment long buried rose to the surface, a vengeful serpent disturbed from rest to strike at the intruder. Gretchen's face crumpled into a puckish scowl.

"Mercedes, that's bullshit. You know damn well why you were forced out. You wouldn't accept that New Dubai needed outside help to tap our White Oil deposits. Without it, we'd have bankrupted ourselves and turned this planet into a backwater. You didn't have the stomach to admit we needed help from the Synod, so Duncan had to do something. For New Dubai."

"For New Dubai." It was Mercedes's turn to scowl. "Oh, sure. For New Dubai's elite who would have given that money and come under my control, I was ousted from my throne and left in the cold. For New Dubai, humans maintain their elitist fantasy with the Synod's silent approval. For New Dubai, your esteemed husband left the running of his political, military, and legal life to a war criminal and a two-faced crook. For New Dubai, those two destroyed my old parliament, smeared their names, and killed Noirtier."

"*What?*"

Gretchen couldn't help starting forward. Noirtier. The name so long forgotten rushed back into her mind, that old gentle man who'd been coaching Mercedes, almost like a father to them both. Mercedes's smile was unpleasant.

"Oh, you didn't know? I shouldn't be surprised. Count Artorius Noirtier, our mentor and friend, the man who was more a father than our own ever was, jailed for embezzlement. And since that was the finish of him, he chose death over shame. He killed himself, but it was those bastards who drove him to his death."

Gretchen was shaken to the core, struggling to maintain her composure. "I... I didn't know. I didn't know what happened to Noirtier. I'd heard from Granger that he died in prison. I didn't know—Oh, God, why is this happening?" Giving way, she glared at her sister. "Why are you doing this? For Noirtier? Is that it? Or yourself? Are you here just for your own petty vendetta?"

"Petty? I suppose it would be to you. You never were cut out to rule."

"We're not talking about me, but about you."

"I'm here to regain what's rightfully mine. And ensure those who wronged me and those close to me pay in full for their crimes."

What was she hearing? Mercedes had never talked like this before. Was she still sane? Had the d'If broken her mind?

"Mercedes, listen to yourself. You must stop this. I don't know what you're planning, but it has to stop. Didn't you read any of Mother's books? Those who pursue vengeance never find happiness. I've spent ten years wishing you back. I found happiness with my husband, with my son. I've only wanted you to make my life complete. Please abandon your quest."

"And if I don't?"

"My duty is to my husband, and to New Dubai. If you seek to bring it down, you're an enemy of our planet, and I must denounce you."

"I'm the enemy of the old state, which killed Noirtier."

"Stop playing with semantics."

"You should stop being blinded by that unworthy poltroon."

"What will you do then, eh? Kill me? Remove me? I won't keep silent otherwise, Mercedes."

Gretchen was breathing hard, anger and shame boiling inside her. The woman before her was becoming less and less her beloved sister. In her mind's eye, she was seeing a perfect portrait being slowly distorted and ruined by the light of sun and playing of rain across its unprotected surface. The transformation completed as Mercedes replied.

"You know, I always considered both our parents' deaths to be quite unusual. Mother was ill for so long after having you, and I knew Father wanted to move on. Her death was so convenient. Did you see it, too, that night? When he went into her bedroom without reason the night she died? Heart failure. Anything could have brought that on, but...." Her eyes flashed again, fixing on Gretchen's face. "And our father's own growing indolence, his lack of energy, the slowing of his wits. I know I had nothing to do with it, but you always loved Mother, as did I. She cared for us more than our father ever could. But hate him as I did, I'd never have killed him. Not then. But in some ways, you had more stomach than I. Children can do terrible things sometimes."

Gretchen's stomach clenched. A new image flew before her mind. The numerous afternoon teas she served her father, the tiny drops of stuff she put into it. Little drops taken from one of Argo's local plants, a poisonous plant kept purely for ornament. Slow, cold revenge for Mother, for all the years of putting state over family. Gretchen would never put the state over her own children, would never be like her father. Why else had she left every decision to her husband and focused on raising their son with love and kindness?

Mercedes's eyes narrowed. "Do as you will, and I shall do so, too. If truth is to come out, all truth shall. I'm sure your dear Duncan would agree."

"You think you can blackmail me? You're planning to ruin us anyway, aren't you?" Gretchen tried one more time to reach out. "Mercedes, do you really hate Duncan for what he did to you, or that he took me as his wife?"

There was no answer. How could there be? Gretchen knew of her sister's near-possessive love of her. A love which had driven away other suitors as being 'not good enough,' until Duncan so completely won Gretchen's heart that Mercedes was forced to concede. The marriage had happened, their father had died, and Mercedes began walking down this path.

Gretchen's voice abruptly broke. "Oh, God, Mercedes. What happened to you?"

An unsettling smile warped her sister's mouth. "I was met and fooled by three little piggies. The just soldier and political wizard. The faithful and honest watchdog of the law. The man who wooed my sister. What are they really? A mad dog, a serpent, and a fool who listens to them. They've written their ends and shall suffer as I did when they turned on me. The terrible knowledge of betrayal by those who are valued and trusted."

"Can't you just abandon it? This place... what you're seeking will destroy you. It destroyed Father, Mother.... It might've done me if Duncan hadn't been there."

Mercedes's face softened suddenly, and for a moment the supportive elder sister poked through the veil of bitter years. "You always were so monochrome in your views of the world. As for me, I've gone too far to turn back. I swore in that cell that nothing would stop me reclaiming my throne. If you wish to avoid the fallout in person, I suggest you go to Argo for a time. We've still got lands there, haven't we?"

"Yes."

Her sister's face hardened once more. "It's my duty, Gretchen. My burden. My curse if you like. If it's any comfort for you, Duncan's fate won't be too harsh. I'd not give you excessive grief. I will say you were too trusting, as is your nature. I still love you, Twinkle. Remember that. Now, I beg that you leave me alone. And if you don't want me telling your side of this sordid drama, I'd keep silent until the final curtain."

Gretchen rose, leaving Mercedes seated. She took a last lingering look at the sister five years her senior, the treasure of her life. A treasure soured by the passage of time. Struggling to keep nascent tears at bay, the duchess of New Dubai parted with her predecessor and began the long walk back to her car.

# FILE 13

## COMPLICATIONS

*Comments on "the best-laid plans" go back as far as Burns's original remark on the subject, and I do agree with the poet on this point. But that remark never took into account the mellifluous scheming minds raised in a culture where complex plans are a means of survival.*

—Excerpt from Fingal Dee's "On the Tragedy of New Dubai"

AMBASSADOR LAFFW'S PARTY was modest by her standards. There were only forty guests with almost as many companions, a small five-piece orchestra providing subdued background music, and the press presence outside was barely noticeable. The refreshments were also comparatively slight. She reflected with a nostalgic indulgence on one particular event where she had arranged a buffet containing seventy different drink types and ninety dishes from across the Cluster. Since it was in the heart of the city, no fireworks could be displayed, which for some must be a slight blot on their evening.

Laffw had dressed to dazzle, her gown putting most of the other frocks and coats on show to shame. She glided from group to group, making small talk with ease and exuding her usual impression of vapid affability. Once or twice, she glanced over to check on Bapti, who stood in a corner watching all, as was her duty. Dear, devoted Bapti. Everyone had a past, and hers was not one to emulate. Mother suffering psychotic fits, father killed during one of them, causing mother to be permanently sectioned. Bapti was left an orphan at the mercy of the system. Then along Laffw had come and granted her a life of luxury. She had taken to it as if made for the serf life.

She also noted Mercedes in her role as the baroness, working the pump handle of a gossiping couple with expert skill. She was impeccably attired in the Throwback Evening style, a suit with straight lines giving her figure even more sleekness. The other guests were the usual sort, weak and feeble in spirit and body, clinging to a facade of privilege provided by the unique social eco-system of New Dubai.

But while her face continued to smile, an unease grew in her gut. She glanced more than she might have done at Mercedes, that sleek and confident figure without a ruffle in her hair or her dress that was not intended. She was too calm, too collected, too sure of herself. That confident poise had first drawn Laffw to her, but now she began to worry about it. Even fear it? No, that was a ridiculous idea. She feared nothing a human could offer, no threat any person could possibly pose.

Ali was not there, and neither was the Feles. She would have to ask about Ali again. Bapti would be pleased at that. While working for the same person, the two had only ever maintained a stiff cordiality, masking cold resentment. Ali at being the "pitiable newcomer," and Bapti at being sidelined by Ali's "brisk and silent efficiency." Laffw scoffed at such trifles. She favored or ig-nored each equally and in turn, as was their due.

Her train of thought was broken as another guest entered, a female Feles. This guest seemed like all the others to the lay observer, but to Laffw she stuck out like a sore thumb. There was a cool intelligence and poise lacking in almost everyone else in the room. She was a complete stranger in an unusual out-of-season gown, a disguised Comm on her wrist, and eyes that darted from face to face like a watchful fugitive. Or a predator hunting their prey. She continued the line of small talk with an effervescent human merchant even as the Feles moved round the edges of the room.

"But it was too much. Just too, too much. I never would have believed it were it not for my being there. Just laser, darling."

*"Laser"* was the vogue word among the trading classes. To anyone of high-er intelligence, Laffw would have adjusted her talk accordingly, but there was no need for a merchant invited to fill out the numbers. Even as she spoke, her finger pressed the disguised comm at her waist, cuing Bapti. The serf raised her hand as signaled, and Laffw excused herself. Passing rapidly through the crowd, she bent close to Bapti's ear.

"Did you see that woman who entered just now?"

"The one with the hunter's look?"

"Hunter…. You may be right. I recognize her. She is no average Law Officer. She is a Junior Synod Enforcer."

"What business would a Synod Enforcer have here?"

"If you cannot guess, you are no true serf of mine. Bring the baroness here at once. We must protect our assets."

Bapti bowed and obeyed. Laffw immediately went into her private room, giving light dismissive waves to a few guests who tried to get her attention. Once in her office, she shed her party persona, becoming the cold and calculating politician. Less than thirty seconds later, Bapti led Mercedes in. Laffw turned.

"You saw the Synod En—"

Her words stopped dead at the expression on Mercedes's face. The human looked on the brink of panic. Now away from the chattering crowd, she started pacing up and down, fingers clenching and unclenching, face contorted with emotion. Never had Laffw seen Mercedes in such a state before. It unnerved her. If this strange new arrival upset this composed, almost stone-cold woman, it must be a sign of great trouble ahead.

"Yes." Mercedes answered Laffw's unfinished query. "I saw her all right, well before you deigned to summon me. She's got the smell of the Synod all over her. I don't understand."

"Why is she here?"

"I don't know. It might be something to do with the Grand Assizes or…."

"You think it is to do with Cape Life?"

"Maybe."

"But there is nothing else for a Synod Enforcer to be concerned about on New Dubai, is there?" There was a long pause, and Mercedes's agitation increased. "Is there?"

"I don't know. I guess not."

"Well, I shall speak with her. She cannot refuse an interview with the Kavki ambassador, and my curiosity would be quite natural. Bapti, get her in here, then leave us. Mercedes, you should stay unless the Synod Enforcer requests privacy, in which case wait outside. You can admire the flowers on the stand outside with Bapti. And try to act natural."

Mercedes took a few deep breaths and recomposed herself. It was so satisfying to be the more composed of the two, just like previous deals where she had been complete master of the situation from start to finish. As Laffw settled herself down, Bapti showed the Synod Enforcer in, then left with a curt bow. The Synod Enforcer, Saqara Yarin by name, made formal self-introductions, then looked at Mercedes.

"Baroness, it's been some little time."

Laffw's eyes darted to Mercedes. "You two know each other?"

"We met briefly over the kidnapping affair." Mercedes's smile was only slightly forced. "I'm delighted to meet you again."

Yarin nodded, then requested privacy. Mercedes nodded and excused herself, leaving with an almost impolite haste. Yes, she really was unnerved for whatever reason. Laffw laid a hand across the table, activating the small pad for the mic in the stand of flowers just outside the door. Bapti normally listened in, and now Mercedes would, too.

"Please, take a seat Synod Enforcer Yarin. To what do I owe the pleasure of your visit? I do not remember issuing an invite."

"I wasn't invited, Ambassador. I apologize for using my authority to gate-crash, but I have urgent business here."

"I am always willing to assist an agent of the Synod in anything. What brings you to New Dubai?"

"A mission. The Synod sent me here to investigate an incident on Cape Life. Since you were there at the time, we wanted to ask you a few questions. I've been sent to gather intelligence regarding your stay. Just routine, you understand."

"Of course. It must be hard work for one like yourself to cover such a large portion of the Cluster. If you can, could you tell me any details about this incident?"

"I have no reason not to do so. Nearly two months ago, a group of undesirables were summoned to Cape Life by an anonymous message. One month ago, the remains of one of those summoned was found in the lower levels of Cape Life. They've been identified as a noted Ekri assassin. This wouldn't concern us ordinarily, but this Ekri was a war hero to her people, and with the situation as it stands, we can't afford to offend the Ekri people by refusing to investigate the murder of one of their national icons."

"I do not see what this has to do with me."

"You were at Cape Life around the time the Ekri was summoned with the others. You or your staff may have heard something."

"Could the others who were summoned not tell you anything?"

"Some were tracked down and interrogated, but they claim complete ignorance. There's evidence of chemically induced amnesia. The remains of the Ekri were found near an access hatch for Cape Life's energy conduits. If the body were thrown in there, it would've been disintegrated, though why that wasn't done is difficult to imagine."

"How was this Ekri killed?"

"Shot with a handgun, a rare type. Not one issued except to high-level security staff. Since your network on Cape Life is so extensive, we wondered if you could give us any information. We would also like to question your servants, Ali and Bapti."

Laffw made her voice a shade more airy. "Oh, I hear things. But I was not there for business, just pleasure. Look, I do not remember much about back then. Tell you what, I can get my diary for that time, then you can come by my apartments this evening and we shall talk it over."

"That's acceptable. You can reach me at this address when you have time to talk. And now I'll be going. I've got other leads to follow up."

The two exchanged cordial farewells, and Laffw watched as Yarin left the room. Less than a second later, Mercedes and Bapti both came in, and as the door closed, Mercedes clutched her forehead and seemed on the point of staggering. For the first time in decades, Laffw's stomach twitched, the sign of a dire threat impeaching on her life. Finally, Mercedes slumped against Laffw's desk and spoke in a voice shaking with anguished despair.

"Gods preserve us, now what do we do? First Gretchen recognizing me, and now this—"

"You were *recognized?* Why did you not tell me?"

"It doesn't matter. It's dealt with. But what do we do now?"

"I do not know." Laffw's tone was icy. "It seems I was wrong to place trust in your precious Gaspard. But I am pleased you grasp this situation."

"I grasp it, all right. I can't let them find out about me. Not now."

"It is more than that." Bapti sounded almost as icy as Laffw. "If my mistress is even remotely connected with this death, her ambassadorship is forfeit. The Synod will cut her loose to save itself. And you will be left without any protection from your enemies. You are dead for sure." She turned to her mistress. "Please, may I kill that idiotic Feles?"

Mercedes's voice snapped like a whip. "We can't afford to enact recriminations now, even if Gaspard did bungle it. We've got to act fast. Couldn't this be something like... I don't know, false identification?"

Laffw shook her head. "Impossible, I assure you. Clothing or ID would not suffice. They would run DNA tests. And if they say that Ekri was a war hero, she was a war hero. And since she was not disposed of, we are all in danger."

Mercedes seemed about to speak, then stopped and slowly calmed down. "Only if this investigation gets any further in the near future. I think we can ensure it won't."

Laffw's eyebrow climbed up her forehead. "Are you proposing the murder of a member of the Synod Enforcers? Have you quite lost your wits along with your calm? You do not kill off agents of the Synod."

"Please, I can handle this."

"How?"

"It's better you don't know."

"I will know." Laffw shot up and bellowed the words. "I have just about had enough of your idiotic secrecy. Look where it has brought us. Your wish for secrecy has now dragged us to the brink of ruin."

Mercedes's voice was shaking slightly. "I understand your concern.... Look, if I tell you what I'm planning for my enemies, what will happen at the Grand Assizes, will you let me go ahead with my plan?"

Laffw frowned. If there were anything less at stake, she would cut her losses and run, throwing her partner to her pursuers as a suitable scapegoat. But the rich, the wondrous, the all-consuming wealth and status Mercedes had offered dangled before her once more.

"Tell me."

Words tumbled from Mercedes's mouth, words forming into an intertwining web of schemes and revelations. Laffw listened, first in growing disbelief, then with the kind of gleeful enjoyment that comes from watching others suffer. The scheme was beautiful, savage in its cruelty, mind-bending in complexity, and lethal in its efficiency. Even Andréa's place in things was explained, and his part in the final drama was so unexpected that Laffw gave a slight gasp, and even Bapti's jaw dropped.

Finally, breathless, Mercedes looked pleadingly at Laffw. "Now, will you let me deal with this? And with Gaspard?"

There was a prolonged silence. The party noises drifted in from outside, a reminder of her solid and secure life. But the future, that wonderful future of power and position, dragged her eyes and ears to fix upon the human who almost crouched before her. Finally, Laffw smiled and laughed.

"My dear, you were wise in a sense to keep that a secret. Had you told me at any other time, I would have dismissed it as the ravings of a sad, mad woman. But if that is how you treat your direst enemies, I would rather not know how you proposed to deal with the Synod Enforcer. Now, I think we had best return to the party. If you wish to begin at once, do so."

---

THE DAY AFTER Mercedes and Gretchen's encounter, Ali was ordering supplies for both her mistress's apartments and Château Auteuil. An unseasonable bout of rain forced anyone without an umbrella or personal transport to use weatherproof coats and hats. As she walked through the store fronts and sometimes inside to the many automated consoles for ordering goods, she listened to what was said around her.

Everywhere, people were talking about the same thing. Duchess Vorn-Solari canceled all engagements and left for Argo due to ill health. How detrimental it was to the duke's good image not to have his wife around. Grand Assizes came up with the Ekri case. How sensational. Another charitable donation was made by the Baroness Clarisse. Was she not the most generous of people? The final and most obscure was Ambassador Laffw holding a modest embassy function to which multiple diplomatic figures were invited, including a visiting Synod Representative.

Many chose to ignore these common lines of higher-tier gossip as they passed by on their business, but Ali remained alert. She listened attentively as one young couple talked with such vigor that their search for fresh party clothing was forgotten.

"Why is this newbie here? A Synod Junior Minister accompanied by an Enforcer?"

"You got it wrong, dear. The Enforcer arrived over a week ago."

"And the Ambassador doesn't know either one's here? That's what my father told me."

"Your father's privileged to know this how?"

"He's been assigned as one of the Law Officers at Ambassador Laffw's party. One of the other guests is Baroness Clarisse."

"Oh, wow. Now there's a dreamy woman."

"When did you see her?"

"That party she hosted at her home. Remember, I told you about it. Château Auteuil."

"Oh, yeah, I remember now."

"But what about this Synod Junior Minister? Why is the Synod sending anyone here at all? It's been quiet for the past decade."

The talk fell into meaningless channels, human channels, the channels that made Ali want to throw something at the pair and be done with it. This world was beginning to make her sick. So many humans completely absorbed in what they were doing, what they wanted, what they were aiming for. What about the Ekri in the desert? What about other peoples beyond their small world made rich by giving others the power to travel between the stars? Did they not think of them?

But the day was not entirely without a subtle charm. She was being followed, had been followed since leaving Mercedes's flat. It was the Feles Gaspard told her about, the one called Echo. She had never spoken to him. She only ever saw him at a distance. Why he would be following her was something of a mystery. Considering their twisted relationship, she expected him to be following Gaspard. Poor, lonely, clinging Gaspard. Why follow her today? It was only a second's thought to realize why. Gaspard usually did the shopping, but he was on another errand for Mercedes, so Ali had gone instead. Gaspard's recent delays in some of his errands started making a little more sense.

How long had this creature clung to him? However she felt about the situation as a whole, she felt a curious pity for Gaspard, strung to this strange Feles like a weight hung about his neck, dragging him down into an unknown abyss. She refused to quicken her pace, instead moving toward the less frequented end of the Commercial District. There was a media store, and she passed inside, moving at a sedate pace to the self-contained age-controlled adult content isle at the back.

She lingered just long enough for Echo to enter and see her pass inside. It was like the other parts of the shop, with two walls and a central chest-high stall filled with products for all tastes, though here as everywhere else it geared toward human needs and fetishes. Slipping to the other side, she crouched down as if to examine the available stock on the lower shelves. There was the slight hiss of the door opening, and Echo's shadow passed along the other side. Time to teach him a lesson.

In a single fluid motion, she leapt over the aisle, but then a Feles foot kicked up and struck her in the chest, throwing her back the way she had come. She righted herself instantly, and he ran for the exit. He almost reached the door back into the main shop when she grasped his ankle and dragged him off balance, then spun him round and kicked him along the floor. He slid to a stop beside a small stand of something that looked like a bondage series and did not try to run again as she approached.

Echo looked directly into her eyes. "Well? You gonna play out something from these vids, or take me to your leader?"

Ali's mouth creased into a grimace, then her hand shot down and plucked a small datapad from Echo's belt. It was a model with no net connectivity. Ideal for covert stalking, but also vulnerable if the stalker were caught. She stepped back, snapped the datapad in two, then left the way she had come. Echo was picking up the pieces, cursing. The datapad had clearly contained all his surveillance for the day. Video? A text log? She did not know, nor did she greatly care.

Alone again, Ali took a taxi to Mercedes's residence. Once inside the empty apartment, she went straight to her sparsely furnished room where a small terminal and Comm stood waiting. The next five minutes were dedicated to typing out a report, bare facts without any kind of embroidering. Once finished, her finger hovered over the send command. Then she placed it into draft along with the thirty other reports she should have sent to Laffw. Two months ago, she would never have done such a thing.

Emerging into the apartment proper, she gazed out the window, reaching up to feel along the lines of her scarring. Every time she saw a human, a ghost of that horrible day flashed into her mind with all its associated memories. But this city, so choked with the species she hated more than anything else, also woke something in her, a yearning for freewheeling travel, for the satisfaction of some kind of agency in what she did every day.

No. She slammed her fist into the glass. What was she thinking? She owed the Ambassador more than she could ever begin to repay. Without her, she did not wish to imagine where she might be right now, what she might be forced to do in order to live. Perhaps she could ask for an immediate relief of her duty and get Bapti to take her place. Bapti was completely loyal, raised from childhood by Laffw. That was it, not being around her mistress, around her thoughts and feelings. Around her world….

Her world? She gazed out again at Amasian City, taking in every squalid, decadent detail of the surrounding neighborhood. This was not her world, had never been her world. She had never set foot on anything that might have been her world. Her mistress Laffw, who had given her a new life, only went to places like this. Decadent, filled with sectarianism, the kind of dross the Synod had been extolled by others of the Kavki to curb. Did her mistress truly wish to sustain this wretched system for her own gain? She had done many questionable things, but always in the service of advancement. Had she not?

Her gaze flashed down to the road below, and she raised an eyebrow. Echo was there on a corner, and so was Gaspard. They stood close, and Echo appeared to be running his fingers along Gaspard's chin. The spasms of emotion were visible even from this high up, though it was difficult to tell elation from disgust. Gaspard rapidly broke away and crossed the street, almost running into a stream of traffic.

What power tied Gaspard to that Feles? Now he was here, free of the d'If, he could do whatever he chose. He was bound by no nanomachine leach, no boundaries. If Gaspard killed that parasite, Mercedes would not even bat an eye. Why did he hold his hand and endure such humiliation?

Her musings were interrupted as the door opened. Gaspard appeared again, back from his errand. He peeled off his coat and grabbed a towel hung by the door to dry his rain-spotted mane.

"Eugh. I hate rain. Always hated it when the vent systems dumped on us in the d'If. Why Mercedes wants some abandoned storage building for, I can't imagine." He looked up at Ali. "Anything interesting out there?"

Ali threw a look that told more than words could. Gaspard gulped, shuffled, glanced left and right, then snapped like an overturned spring. His voice quivered on the blade's edge between rage and despair.

"Why the hell'd it have to be you? I don't want anything to do with him, but what the hell can I do? Kill him? Expose him? Kiss him? It's not like I want him shadowing me all the time. Gksuk. But why am I talking to you? God, I wish you could do something other than stare at me like that. Why don't you?"

Ali opened her mouth. All the noise that could come from her ravaged voice box was a barely sentient rasping croak. Gaspard looked stricken, turning away from her. Her unused throat muscles ached from the effort, and she placed a comforting hand across where the scarring remained. Gaspard might have spoken again, but the apartment doorbell buzzed. Ali immediately went and looked at the viewscreen. Echo stood there. Gaspard pushed her aside and looked, then bared his teeth.

"Of all the nerve. Ali, leave us alone please. Don't come back in unless he tries something."

Ali did not know what else to do. She wanted to knock some sense into Gaspard, but it was not the place or time. She retreated into the bathroom and pulled the door closed. She stood like a statue as the front door opened and shut, then the padding of feet sounded on the carpet, and finally voices were raised in hissing conversation.

"That precious Kavki around?"

"No."

"Good. I don't like the way she kicks."

There was a short pause, then Gaspard's tired voice. "Echo, I've no time for your games."

"Then why let me in?"

"Why'd you come here at all?"

"You didn't give me much time to do anything out there. Besides, you can't do much in the rain. In here, however—"

"Don't you dare." It was impossible not to imagine Gaspard's twisted expression quickly brought back under control. "Why are you following us around? Me was bad enough, but Ali? I thought we'd cleared any debt between us when I saved you from being arrested for that kidnapping. Aren't you satisfied with that?"

"I'm not easily satisfied. You should know that. Gaspard, why're you still tagging along with her? The Baroness Clarisse indeed. We both know she's little more than an upstart escapee. The one you wanted kept safe at all costs.

I fulfilled my end of things, and what did you do? Run off with her and leave me and everyone else on the d'If to die."

"You know nothing about her." Gaspard almost bellowed. "You could never understand. You're just a bastard out for himself like everyone else."

"Everyone else? Do you include yourself in that regard?"

"I… I serve a higher purpose. I was nothing in the d'If, but I'm something here. I'm helping someone right a wrong done them which can't be forgiven."

"Salve for your conscience?"

There was a sudden, sharp silence. Ali risked a glance into the room. Gaspard held Echo by the neck. She expected him to throttle the Feles then and there, but instead Gaspard bent close and pressed Echo's forehead against his own. Ali could smell the mingled odor of sweat, souring rain, and sexual tension on both of them. It made her sick. Echo spoke again, his voice unchanged.

"Well? Why don't you do it? It would save you a lot of trouble. I'm not letting you get away so easily. I'll always be there, watching you."

Gaspard's teeth bared "I want to. Believe me, I want to so very much."

"Then why don't you?"

Gaspard seemed about to speak, but instead loosed his grip and turned away. He looked defeated, depressed by the weight of some strange knowledge.

"Just go, Echo. Please."

Echo gave a theatrical bow. "Since you ask nicely, of course. And if you need my help again, please call any time."

Echo left without another word. The moment the door closed, Gaspard slumped to his knees and cried, tears rushing down his cheeks. A terrible kind of pity stirred within Ali, and without hesitation she emerged from hiding and placed a comforting arm around the Feles's heaving shoulders. He turned to look up at her, and she asked the question with her eyes.

"Why do I put up with him? It's… it's because…." He was struggling to find any words, as if pushing against a long-sealed doorway. "Because he forced himself on me, and now I can't do anything else. My body's his, and it longs for him." Again, he saw the question in her face. "Why don't I kill him? I want to, but I can't. I just can't. It'd be like killing a piece of me. I don't know what it's like to feel anything else. I never got the chance to feel anything else, to feel any kind of… Gksuk! Not even killing him will grant freedom. He'll always be there, even if he's dead."

Ali swiftly crouched down in front of Gaspard, cupping his face between her hands. After a moment, she leaned in and pressed their foreheads together. Literature in Feles culture made this the classier version of a human kiss or the Kavki joining of forms. It was a sign not of love, but of a bond of emotion. Gaspard relaxed, shuddering with new emotion. And deep inside her, something woke and blossomed that had long been locked in the frosted confines of her heart, hardened by war and bitterness. A feeling of comradeship, the altruistic wish to aid another being.

The moment was brief, and the comm call shattered it. Ali answered as Gaspard quickly straightened up and took a few deep breaths. The call was from Mercedes, and it was the signal they had been instructed to respond to, the reason Gaspard went looking for that abandoned building.

*"I have a job, and it's urgent. Gaspard, come at once, and bring the Cape Life package you took from the Ekri. Ali, you will wait for further instructions."*

---

"IS SHE COMING round?"

Mercedes smiled at Gaspard's nod. The Feles finished setting up the lamp, all ready to produce the desired dramatic effect. It had been child's play, following Yarin from the party, catching up with her and asking for a quiet word, then quickly using a small gassing device to knock her out. Gaspard had arrived promptly, summoned by her even as she pursued the Synod Enforcer, and now they were setting up the perfect stage.

Mercedes placed the voice modulating mask over her mouth. *"Wake her up."*

Ali obeyed, jabbing her with an injector and pulling back behind Mercedes as Gaspard switched on the lamp, which shone directly down on Yarin. The two pulled back into the distant shadows, and Mercedes watched with satisfaction as Yarin lurched, slowly raised her head, and squinted into the gloom. Then she started twisting her wrists, pushing against the bonds. Now was the time to begin.

*"It's useless to struggle."* The voice modulator made Mercedes sound distorted, her tones robbed of gender. *"You won't be able to escape. My associate is very skilled with restraints."*

"Who are you?" Saqara barked angrily into the shadows. "I warn you, if you injure me or do anything to me, the Synod will be down upon this planet like—"

*"I have no intention of doing anything permanent to you. In fact, I wish to help you, but you must fulfill certain conditions."*

"What're you talking about?"

*"You're investigating the death of an Ekri at Cape Life. Ambassador Laffw is deeply involved in this, as is her servant Bapti, and a pair of recent friends. The Baroness Charlotte Clarisse, and her so-called ward Andréa."*

"The baroness…. *She* did this?"

*"Yes. She's as ruthless as her friend Laffw, and a social climber of the worst sort. Her ward is no ward, but a dangerous killer. And Laffw's in it as deeply as they are. You want to bring them all down?"*

"If you're speaking the truth…. Yeah. For the sake of the Synod."

*"Good. So do I. What would you say if I told you that it was Laffw who killed the Ekri and summoned those others to Cape Life for her own purposes?"*

"I'd say show me proof."

*"I've abundant proof, physical and otherwise."*

Mercedes took the box from beside her feet and held it just inside the light. It contained the pistol she had used to kill the Ekri on Cape Life, shining and still gloriously covered in evidence and ID signatures. Yarin looked at it, but even as she leaned forward, Mercedes drew back into the shadows and continued.

*"I've also got proof that she's conspiring to bring the trading wealth of New Dubai under her people's direct control through a secret deal with the current duke."*

"That I find difficult to believe."

*"You clearly don't know your prey. Laffw is unscrupulous and callous, entirely without morality, only interested in her own gain. I can give you all the evidence you need to bring her down. The Ekri won't stand for anyone, even an ambassador for the Synod, being complicit in the murder of a national hero of the Human-Ekri Conflict."*

"What's your interest in all this?"

*"Purely selfish. Our goals align, so I'm willing to help. But I've four conditions. No information must leak before the Grand Assizes, your sources for these documents must remain anonymous, certain documents I shall highlight as an attachment to the evidence you need must be shown to have been legally obtained*

*as part of an unrelated covert investigation, and Laffw must think you've been killed until the time is right."*

"Those are your conditions?"

*"Yes. And I won't waver."*

"I'm hardly in a position to argue."

*"Hardly. If you refuse, I'll kill you, then ensure the trail leads to Laffw, and that my evidence is released at an opportune time to destroy her."*

"You're that desperate to bring her down? Why?"

*"As I said, my reasons and interest are purely selfish. But I'm sure a Synod Enforcer isn't above making use of someone's grudge to fulfill the Synod's mission."*

There was a long pause. Yarin was clearly considering her options, and Mercedes could visualize them with ease. Refusal meant death, but acceptance still placed her life at risk from Laffw. But if she were to bring down Laffw, it would be the coup of a lifetime. What did she have to lose? The expected answer came.

"All right. You've got a deal. I'll disappear until everything's so cluttered with the Grand Assizes that they won't notice me leaving. There's a place I can go to stay hidden until then. But if you're fooling me—"

*"You have my word. We're going to knock you out again now. When you revive, you'll be free of your bonds, and the evidence shall be left for you under this chair. Guard it with all due care. You must vanish, completely and utterly, until the time's right. Sweet dreams."*

Another burst of the gas, and Yarin's head dropped like a stone. Mercedes nodded, and Gaspard opened the single door leading from the half-decrepit building in the Lower Residential District into the deserted street. Mercedes watched smilingly as Gaspard undid the restraints. Then she placed the boxed gun and a datapad containing all the extra evidence and leads required to destroy Laffw when the time came.

Outside in the soft rain, another thought struck her. Things were in motion now, and there was only one piece of solid evidence connecting Laffw and her true identity. Who could retrieve it? Gaspard she could trust, but it seemed impossible that he could get there. And Ali? How strong was her loyalty to her mistress? She would have to wait and see. Maybe chance, or cleverness, would provide the right scenario to test Ali's character.

# FILE 14

## HOT SPRING HORROR

---

*Families are always wonderful subjects for observation and deconstruction. They are prone to the most spectacular outbursts, and resolve conflicts in ways ranging from sycophantic to combative. They can destroy each other, or reunite around a common dislike. Such variety makes family conflict, and the ways it is either resolved or allowed to implode, a key tenant of fiction old and new.*

—Excerpt from Fingal Dee's essay "On Relationships"

THE CLOCK SCREAMED its alarm at Mercedes with the insistence such devices had held since their invention. She swiped at it with her usual morning gruffness. Had it been a physical object it would have hit the opposite wall. She slowly pushed herself out of bed and slid across the floor to where her dressing gown draped over the nearby chair. She pulled it on, and Ali entered with the day's first refreshment.

After the first gulp of strong tea brought feeling back to her, she shuffled into the living room, following the smell of breakfast. Seated in her usual position beside the window, she munched her breakfast. The sound blended with the humming and crunching of traffic on the road below, the rustling of trees, and the second pattering of rain in as many days. A quick gesture across the datapad next to the seasoning switched on the morning news bulletin, the announcer sounding as chirpy as ever.

*"Good morning and welcome to 24/7 Cluster. I'm Margaret Maye with the latest headlines. In the news today, tensions mount on both sides as the land dispute between New Dubai's government and the Alasaya refugees is prepared for the Grand Assizes, and we speak to Prosecutor de Granger's representatives about*

*the forthcoming trial. In other news, New Dubai's Duke Vorn-Solari announces unprecedented economic growth during this quarter, with White Oil exports fig- uring largely in the increase. The Cluster stock market closes with a profit despite a general fall in trading and a selling spree on farming exports from the cultivation plants on Hyden. And at the latest Synod summits—"*

Another gesture shut off the noise and brought up the morning's corre- spondence. It was a quick matter to skip through the advertisements, a few unwanted invitations to small parties, and an official invitation.

A smile slid across her face. "Invitation for myself and Andréa, for… Pa- paya Springs? Goodness, that takes me back."

The memories of her last time at Papaya Springs prompted a smile to cross her face. Hot springs fed by ancient volcanic seams a hundred miles north of Amasian City, they were both tourist attraction and ducal getaway. A famous love scene had been filmed there for an award-winning movie, and before that several less reputable movies used the hot spring's secluded corners as sets for their rapturous actors. To her, it represented her last year of innocence, before Duncan Vorn-Solari removed her from power and set her on this path. Gretchen had loved it, and they had shared an obscure pool together.

Gretchen…. Nothing had come out, and no-one had appeared to her and spoken to her using her own name. Duncan and his cronies would've moved at once had he known. She couldn't in all conscience blame Gretchen for her actions against their father. It was little worse than what she was doing now. Three lives, three careers, would be ruined by her. One at least would be destroyed utterly.

She pressed her Comm, and Gaspard appeared with a bow. "Mistress?"

"Andréa and I are invited to the Papaya Springs this afternoon. I've decid- ed to go, and I'll be taking Ali. You can have the day off."

There was a slight reluctance in Gaspard's reply. "You're most generous."

"Since you're here, I assume you know where Andréa is?"

"I placed a tracker on his collar this morning. He's in the Aslaan Casino."

"Of course. Today's when he gets his allowance, isn't it? I'll get him out of there and make sure he hasn't bet more than he can afford. Once I have Andréa, I'll be returning here for my luggage and going on to his apartment."

"I understand. I wish you a pleasant stay. And the best of luck."

"Thank you."

Gaspard left, still unsmiling. He had his own issues, but Mercedes cared little. She had her own mission, her own plans. It was the work of a minute or two to be dressed, then to summon a taxi and drive to the Aslaan Casino in the Commercial District. She remembered a time when physical casinos were illegal, another symptom of Vorn-Solari's indolence. Dropped off outside, she passed inside and forged into the casino's main gaming room.

It took little time to find Andréa, but she didn't hurry her approach. It appeared he was playing an Ancient Earth game. Baccarat chemin de fer. A quick glance revealed Andréa's modest winnings from across the table, although a few still had larger win tallies displayed beside their places. Keeping out of Andréa's line of sight, she watched as the current Banco slid a third card across to Andréa.

Mercedes knew enough about baccarat to know why this was. Andréa lacked the numbers to definitively win the round, so he had taken a chance and asked for a card. The Banco likewise withdrew a card, and everyone craned their heads. The latest bet was clearly high, and it was between these two alone. As the scene played out, each of the two original cards were flipped. The Banco totaled six, while Andréa had eight. Andréa's total money count shot up as his opponent's plummeted, and several eyes flashed at the winner. Mercedes came up behind Andréa and gave a light cough.

"Pardon me, but we need to talk."

Andréa turned nonchalantly, only fidgeting slightly as he addressed his patron. "I see you've come to enjoy the show. Sorry you've missed so much. And my final opponent's down." He turned to the table. "Thank you, everyone, for the game. I'll be going now."

After pressing a few buttons to transfer his winnings to the collection point at the main desk, he followed Mercedes from the room, the baccarat players watching him leave with a mixture of relief and disdain on their faces.

Once outside, Andréa smiled at Mercedes. "Your timing's terrible. I wanted to fleece that whole pathetic mob."

"You cheated, of course."

"I can't in this place. Just pure skill."

"That's as may be, but we have more pressing business. An invitation from Duke Vorn-Solari. You wouldn't want to disappoint the duke, would you?"

"Certainly not. I'd love to return to the duke's society. I'm pleased to have been so serendipitously interrupted."

Andréa's smile seemed innocuous enough, but nothing could dislodge Ali's report from Mercedes's mind. This young upstart had tried to kill Duncan's son, and what Ali had seen in his eyes… Mercedes could judge character quite well, and just as she knew Laffw was greedy and Andréa was sly, she knew Ali to be brave. To be frightened by a look alone was the sign of true darkness, and Andréa held that darkness within him. As she did, he wore a mask covering reality, but his was a mask of flesh and blood.

A quick check of the watch showed it was two hours before their flight to Papaya Springs. It was simple to lead Andréa to a small exclusive coffee house on the outskirts of the Commercial District. Once there, they sat at a corner table, well-lit yet inconspicuous. They drank some fine coffee sourced from fields from the south and ate wafers that—at least to Mercedes's palate—would have benefited from a dip in some bitter syrup to improve their taste.

"How much do you normally win there?" asked Mercedes over their second cup.

"Not much." Andréa shrugged. "Maybe 23,000. I try not to win too high or too often. They'd get suspicious otherwise. I'm protected by your luster, but little more. Give them half a chance, and they'd run me off this world without a second thought."

"Agreed. By the way, have you any plans once our business is finished?"

Andréa frowned. "You know, I hadn't really thought about it. Maybe go on a tour of the Cluster, or at least the Capital Worlds. I haven't been around them much. Mostly stuck to Outer World systems."

"Surely you had jobs in the Capital Worlds."

"That's different. You—Well, you do the job and get out of there. You don't have time for sightseeing. But with the payday from this, who knows? I might be able to buy myself respectability. My father was apparently respectable. Didn't stop him having an affair and dumping my mother."

"Is that what she told you?"

"It's what I know." Andréa became forceful. "I didn't know my mother. But I heard the story enough from my foster father. Some bastard nobleman had his fling, then refused to do right by her. In the Outer Worlds, it wouldn't be frowned upon. Here, her reputation would've been ruined. And people say we've progressed since the bad old days of Ancient Earth."

Why tell her this now? What was he doing? Was he justifying himself, preparing the way for some planned action? She had assumed in a way he knew nothing of his background, but if he did know.... Some subtle warning sounded in her mind, pushing against bringing him anywhere near the company of the duke and his followers. What then? Dump him? He knew too much. Kill him? Safer, but there would go her plan. Unless....

Yes, it was risky. Almost too risky, but she had Ali there to back her up if anything went very wrong. But what reward could she offer Ali? Her thoughts flew back to that first read of the old news in a bath aboard the *Hated Brilliance*. Then, she had wished nothing but ruin on her usurper, ruin at any cost. She couldn't back down now, but she could moderate the damage to one person's life.

Mercedes spoke as she thought and planned. "The more we progress, the more we remain static. If we had any concept of doing the decent thing, wars wouldn't happen. Nor would affairs, or vendettas, or anything like that. But then, oh, how sterile our poor dear humanity would become without those injections of abnormal normality."

"So, you despise our faults while admitting their necessity."

"That's me. A lady of contradictions."

---

ANDRÉA HAD TO run after Mercedes and Ali as they bolted up from their seats and made for the door to Shuttle Pad 12, where the announcement had just called them. Ali had appeared like magic carrying a small amount of luggage, and ever since their departure from the coffee house Mercedes had been taciturn. It felt like he was in detention. They quickly crossed the landing area to where a sleek private jet stood ready, the doorway flanked by an equally sleek serving drone.

The duke waited just inside as the trio entered, a winning smile on his face. "Baroness Clarisse, I'm so pleased you could accept my invitation. And I'm glad to meet you once more, Andréa. I'm looking forward to some time together at Papaya Springs. They say their medical benefits are beyond compare."

Mercedes smiled in turn. "I've heard something of them. I'm honored to have been invited, Your Grace."

"We'd best be seated. Well then, all set, and off we go."

The jet took off within ten minutes, settling smoothly into upper atmospheric flight. Andréa took in each passenger. Ali sat in the opposite corner to him, while Mercedes sat in one of three seats positioned round a table. The other two seats were the duke and his son Malcolm, looking excited and eager. Mercedes was talking. Andréa kept his ears pricked.

"Has your wife gone ahead of us, Your Grace?"

"Gretchen's not been feeling well. City living isn't entirely to her taste." A likely story, considering his employer's occasional reminiscences. "She's gone for a rest on her family estates on Argo."

"I'm sorry to hear that. I didn't expect there to be so few on board."

"There will be a few others there as well. Laurent-Leblanc and Granger. They've been working themselves silly for the Grand Assizes. I decided to enforce some time off before they keel over."

"A wise move. I'd hoped to give such a rest to both my servants, but Ali insisted on coming. I'm sure Gaspard will be having a relaxing time while I'm away. Tell me, what are these Papaya Springs like?"

Small talk about the springs followed, with Mercedes explaining that she might go into one of the steam rooms, but the natural spring baths were not for her. The duke nodded in understanding, and Malcolm jumped excitedly in his seat saying he'd be down there for a while. Andréa pretended to read a book on his datapad, listening intently and glancing up once or twice to check on them. The small talk segued into Mercedes speaking to Malcolm, her voice sounding genuine in its soft affection.

"I'm pleased to meet you under better circumstances. Tell me, how is your betrothed?"

"We've barely been apart."

"You know." The duke smiled as he spoke. "That kidnapping a few weeks back has really changed things for them. They used to barely speak. And now they chatter like they're already married. I'm looking forward to seeing her father walk her down the aisle."

"Down the aisle? I thought Ancient Earth churches didn't exist here."

"We're planning a wedding on the Moon of Astur. They've got loads of Ancient Earth facsimiles there. I don't want my boy getting anything but the best."

"Then I, in turn, wish him only the best. He deserves such a bride. Don't you agree, Andréa?"

Andréa nodded but said nothing. The small talk resumed, continuing for the next half hour until they reached Papaya Springs. Andréa's eyes never strayed for long from Malcolm. Malcolm Vorn-Solari, that spoiled little darling of the duke. The duke, that man, curse his existence and all that sprang from his feted loins. How long had he dreamed of killing him or doing something to him that would hurt him the way Andréa had been hurt?

Take something away. Take away what was most preciously, what was dearest to his heart. Yes, that was it. Here, now, during the flight or as they descended the steps from the jet, he could easily kill the duke. Too easy, too quick for what he wished that man to suffer. But Malcolm was different, a target that would wound the duke more than a hundred bullets. The half-formed thought wasn't new. It had appeared during the kidnapping farce when he tried to aim that gun, when Ali had interfered. Yes, that was it, at long last his chance to inflict what he himself had suffered for so many years. Just retribution, just as Mercedes had been planning.

In the large lounge area waited Laurent-Leblanc, Granger, the girl Herma, her parents, and a few others he didn't bother to recognize. Malcolm was all he needed to watch now, trusting to opportunity. Mercedes would protect him, would approve of these actions. After all, she wanted the duke to suffer, so his actions would be facilitating her wishes. There was a quarter hour of mingling, then they went to their changing rooms. Given suitable clothing for the hot springs baths, Andréa changed, hearing the duke laughing as he helped his son. Such happy sounds, sounds he had been denied.

Damn him. Damn them all. This would be the day. He'd show the duke what it was like to lose what mattered most.

The water was heavenly, almost distracting him from his plan. The duke and Malcolm were in an adjoining pool. The intoxicating steam caressed his torso, and his body slumped as if enraptured by the promise of divine pleasure. In truth, he dared not relax. His goal was too close. The duke's voice echoed in his ear.

"Ever been to a hot spring before?"

Andréa started and straightened up. "Not really. I'm sure my pores will be purged of anything even remotely harmful."

The duke grinned. "If you think this is good, try the spring water. I came here on my honeymoon, and I'm sure that helped both Gretchen and I conceive my wonderful boy. He's taken to this place so much that I'm convinced of it. He's a child of Papaya Springs."

"I see. Yes, places can leave impressions on the young, even when still in the womb. Buildings, even when long gone, leave strong memories. As if someone had stamped the mark of that place into the very soul of whoever was born there. It ties them to it, and those who lived within it, more than the strongest cord or chain ever could."

"Yes. Yes, indeed."

The duke seemed unnerved by Andréa's statement. Good. He deserved to be. A quick glance showed Mercedes in an observation room, talking with Hydee and Laurent-Leblanc. No sign of Ali's watchful face, so she must be in another part of the springs. Herma appeared and slid gingerly into a shallow pool. Malcolm joined her, and the duke shifted so he was within easy reach if either child got into trouble. The pair were so idyllically, so childishly happy that it made Andréa nauseated. Another reason to shatter it with his own hands, to turn the memory of this place into a cancerous pariah.

The opportunity was provided by the boy himself asking a question. "Pappy, could you show me Love Corner?"

The duke looked embarrassed. "Well… maybe later. I don't want you going there on your own."

Andréa raised his hand with a smile. "I'll take him, if you're willing. I saw it on one of the local maps. Unless you'd rather one of your people went."

The duke looked at Andréa, then pressed a nearby button. A drone appeared, obviously their companion. Or the boy's guardian, more accurately.

"This can go with the two of you. Malcolm, be careful and don't be too long. Some of the pools round there are way too deep for you."

"Oh, Pappy."

"Don't try to kid me. I know you haven't been keeping up swimming practice. Now, off you go."

A quick adjustment to make sure he was decent, and Andréa led Malcolm along a short path into an enclosed area that looked like the old carved cocoon of a geyser. Malcolm whistled as they approached an extra-large pool with gently steaming water. Just his luck, no-one in sight.

"Wow, this is incredible."

"Yeah, isn't it?"

Malcolm turned a concerned face to his escort. "Are you healed, Andréa?"

"Completely." Andréa smiled. "Thanks for asking. And you? Are you and your betrothed well?"

"We're both fine. But Pappy's become quite protective ever since those idiots tried to kidnap me. You know, I think your guardian'll get some honor in the next year for her actions. And maybe you will, too."

"That would be nice. If unlooked for. You know, I'm surprised there aren't more people around here."

"Usually are, according to Pappy. We've got the place to ourselves today."

"I see. Oh."

"What is it?"

"Look in that pool there. I'd swear I saw a fish."

"Fish? What'd fish be doing in here?"

"I don't know. Could you look? Your eyes might be better than mine."

Malcolm did bend over. The drone crept forward, ready to shoot in and rescue the boy if anything went wrong. In that moment, Andréa saw only his goal. All thought of safety, prudence, and waiting for a better time vanished from his mind. This was it, his opportunity.

With a swift action, Andréa reached down and twisted the lens of its eye, causing it to whirl away and flail. Malcolm was just turning round to see what had happened, but before he could otherwise move or speak, Andréa's hands grasped him round the neck and forced the boy's head and torso underwater. Malcolm's legs flailed wildly, kicking out, but Andréa held firm, his grip tightening. The boy's strength began to flag as water and hands constricted his breathing.

"Now he will know what it feels like. To lose what is dearest to you." A slight unhinged snicker broke from between Andréa's bared teeth. "He will know the pain before he dies himself."

And then, out of nowhere, a smashing pain exploded across the side of his face, and he was thrown bodily against the wall.

---

KEEP AN EYE on Andréa, for he will try to harm the boy. That is what Mercedes had told her when they were alone in the female changing room. It had been hard slipping into the male area where the duke and his son were, but Ali had succeeded and kept her eye on Andréa from a steam-wreathed corner. She had watched as Andréa went with the drone and the boy to an enclosed area of the hot spring with that deep pool and seen the man's action of disabling the drone's sight and attacking the boy.

Between that and her flat hand striking Andréa's face had been five seconds, but they were the longest five seconds of her life. As Andréa went flying, Ali pulled the boy from the water and carried him to the other side. He was already coughing and spluttering, and as she gently tapped his back, he began breathing normally. The frightened boy of two weeks past was there before her again, waking the strange feeling in her heart that had first stirred upon seeing him and the girl Herma, that had blossomed when comforting the distraught Gaspard.

A twisted voice broke in on them. "You!"

Ali twisted round, standing half-crouched and ready. Andréa had risen, recovered from her blow, and now looked like a fairy tale monster. He bared his teeth, his fist clenched into weapons with lethal intent. His breathing became hard and harsh like a growling beast. Ali gestured to Malcolm, who immediately ran back the way he had come. There was no way out. Andréa had burned his boats and would face the consequences.

"What do I care?" He was dribbling with rage. "You've messed it all up, you interfering, fish-faced bitch! I can't have the boy now? Fine, I'll have you, instead!"

He rushed forward, strategy clearly thrown aside in his rage. But though consumed by bloodlust, his blows were no less skilled. Her old training asserted its hold, her eyes narrowing into slits, her hands splayed and ready to deflect any blow. One blow was sidestepped, another deflected, and yet another crashed into a nearby rock formation and skinned one of the human's knuckles.

"Stay still, you shitty little fish with legs!"

The old slur awoke a stinging memory. Ali was held in a prison cell by some human captives, her mouth gagged, unable to retort as they called her all the usual names. "Walking slug," "fish out of water," "stinky on stilts," or "fish with legs." The distraction was momentary, but enough that he got in a hit. Ali stumbled back, her ribs screaming from the impact. Hot air came from a steam vent under her hand, a vent with a valve that controlled its flow into the environment. As Andréa rushed at her, she stepped aside and twisted the valve. A jet of steam struck the human, and he balked, covering his face and screaming.

He stumbled backward into the water, giving Ali a chance to shut off the valve and retreat into the sudden cloud. She was sodden, her robe drenched and skin dripping with condensing moisture, but she continued to stare at Andréa as he rose like a sea-washed specter from the pond and charged, his face and chest red and blistering. Without a second thought, she reached in and grasped Andrea's face, feeling blisters pop under her hand. Even as he gave a shrill gasp of pain, she twisted round and slammed his head into the ground.

His whole body relaxed, and Ali drew her hand away. Not dead, but stunned by the pain and the impact with the stone. Footsteps approached, so she drew back and leaned against the wall, cradling her screaming ribs.

The next half hour passed in a blur, with medical staff and Law Officers descending on the place. She rested in relative quiet in one of the cool rooms, her bruises treated and her cracked ribs diagnosed. Little to be done there but take some supplements to help accelerate healing and dull the pain. It did not surprise her when Mercedes appeared, looking haggard and strained but still defiant and controlled. Human and Kavki eyed each other, then Mercedes spoke.

"Thank you. You saved that boy and exposed Andréa for what he is. It serves both of us, does it not? You care for those children."

Ali nodded slowly. Mercedes bent down, then reached into a pocket and brought out what looked like another pill. She held it out.

"You can refuse this if you choose, but I don't think you want to go back to being Laffw's servant, do you? Not after all this."

Another slow nod. Mercedes nodded in turn.

"I thought so. I did some research, and Gaspard managed to get me this. These will destroy the nanomachine trackers in your system. As to the physical tracker, you can deal with that better than I. What's happening next will be difficult, so if you want to leave now, I will understand. Equally, if you feel unable to live beyond Laffw's circle, I'll dispose of this, and we'll pretend this conversation never took place."

Ali looked from the pill to Mercedes's face. A month ago, she would never have considered this offer. Here, now, in a world beyond Laffw, with those children and Gaspard in the forefront of her mind, she did consider. Mercedes was giving her the one thing she had either rejected or been denied. Her own choice. She reached tentatively for the pill, then the human's hand closed and withdrew.

"There is one thing. This pill doesn't come for free."

Of course, always something with humans like her.

"It's something to face in a world after Laffw, the concept of give and take. In exchange for me giving you this pill, you must take something from Laffw. A non-networked datapad kept either on or near her. Bring it to me, and the pill's yours. Are you still interested?"

# FILE 15

## PREPARATORY ACTIONS

*Deception is merely another word for progress. Or so people wish to believe.*
*We deceive without thinking and must think to redress or resist temptation.*
*It is our basic instinct to compete with others. The pride competes for the male.*
*The insects compete for the flower or the corpse. The tree resists the wind.*
*We all combat. It is meaningless to deny it. The distinctions come from individuals.*

—Extract from Fingal Dee's "Views on Devolved Morality"

THE FOLLOWING DAY, all of Amasian City was alive with gossip about the events at the Papaya Springs. Hints turned into words, words turned into sentences, and sentences into elaborate tales of the event which had nearly claimed the life of the Ducal heir. It became a modern myth, a tale of high society hiding a snake in its bosom, or—depending on who told it—a lowlife who sneaked in using a gullible member of their group that none would ever trust again. The trial was scheduled for the third day of the Grand Assizes, with Granger acting in his appointed role as chief prosecutor for the Dukedom.

Duncan presided over the meeting at his house, together with Laurent-Leblanc and Granger. It was too important to be a remote call. Face to face was essential. Duncan had delayed the meeting until he was quite sure he could leave his son alone. He didn't want to leave him, especially since Gretchen still wasn't there. Why the hell did she have to stay away now? He'd messaged her as soon as the confusion died down, and she had just looked blank. She said she couldn't be there and shut off before he could protest.

He barely listened as Laurent-Leblanc discussed what would happen at the Grand Assizes, which now included the case against Andréa for assault and attempted murder. Granger was assured of success in the case. Of course he thought that. He always did. His pride wouldn't ever admit the possibility of defeat. They were talking about seating, and Duncan's tongue finally loosened itself.

"I'd rather have the fewest possible for the Manfredi trial. Don't you think my son's suffered enough without people gawking?"

Laurent-Leblanc was curt in his reply. "If you wanted a low profile, you would not be the duke. Just have courage. There's no chance of an acquittal in this case."

"I hope so. I…."

Granger cocked his head. "What is it, Duncan? You haven't been yourself since yesterday. And it's not just your son."

"It's about the baroness." Duncan struggled a little before continuing, the feeling within sounding absurd on his lips. "When Andréa was taken into custody, I looked at her face. I couldn't see much from where I stood because of that mask, but what I did see was…."

Both men asked at once. "What?"

Was that a note of fear he could hear in his own voice? "Pleasure. Or satisfaction, maybe? In her face, and in her eyes, as if she'd just seen a terrific coup come off. I've only ever seen that expression once before. On a face I hoped I wouldn't see again."

Laurent-Leblanc cut Duncan off. "Stop overthinking it. You're stressed, and yesterday was a shock. You'd probably have been seeing staring eyes in the hot spring pools. All we have here is a gullible wannabe aristocrat and a clever man who took advantage of her. The whole thing will blow over in a few months, then we can all get back to normal. Speaking of which, isn't Her Grace coming home yet?"

"No. She still isn't feeling well. I can't understand it. I'll try contacting her again, but I don't think she'll come.

Granger spoke with an irritating calm. "Perhaps it's best she not come. Save her the stress. We don't need her here anyway. I suggest you get some rest while Laurent-Leblanc and I get back to our tasks. We've all got preparations to make. Then tomorrow we make history, and everything will be all right again. Eh?"

He glanced at Laurent-Leblanc, who nodded. Duncan nodded, too, albeit absently. He couldn't get that image out of his head, the baroness with a cool smirk on her face, the expression of a satisfied game master. Why was he seeing that face again? Why?

---

MERCEDES SIPPED HER morning tea with the usual calm. To her, staring out across the city from her usual spot, the gossip surrounding Andréa was of no interest. All she had to worry about was the next week or so, when her multilayered, intertwining plans would reach their end goal. During that time, it was all or nothing.

Gaspard entered at her signal. "Yes, Your Grace?"

Mercedes turned, her face unmasked and smiling. "Things are moving forward. I'll be moving to temporary accommodation later today. The sale of this place and of Château Auteuil have come through. Today is the last day I shall need your active help in this matter."

"Really?"

"Unless you wish otherwise. You must make sure Yarin gets off planet safely. Ali can't be with you at present. In four days' time, when the trial is adjourned and Andréa released on bail, I want you to deal with him before he can make any more trouble for us. And this time, make sure the body isn't found. I know it's hard on you, but I trust you to manage this situation."

"Yes, Your Grace."

"After the final verdict of Laurent-Leblanc's land dispute, developments will be swift. I can deal with any visitors, and once all is settled with Granger, I'll be traveling to Argo to deal with the final issue. After that, I'll head for my final destination and await developments."

"Yes, Your Grace."

"Before I forget, do you wish me to remove that sign from your hand? Do you have any plans going forward? Or would you rather remain here in my service?"

There was a long pause, and Gaspard seemed to be thinking. Finally, he approached and held out the hand. Mercedes produced the little laser, grasping the fingers and playing it across the Feles's palm. After a moment, she let the hand fall and fixed her gaze upon Gaspard.

"How long you have been at my side. How long, and through such terrible times. But all things must come to their end."

"Yes." Gaspard's smile looked almost heartfelt. "Any final orders of business?"

"Any engagements today?"

"None. There were three, but all were canceled by this morning's messages."

"Understandable." A thought struck her. "How's my stock with the local shops?"

"We're getting demands for payment. Our credit appears in question."

"Make sure all debts are paid before the Grand Assizes. Back to the subject of visitors, is Hydee still coming?"

"She sent nothing to say she wasn't. And I've made sure she's coming alone."

"How?"

Gaspard shrugged. "Ways and means."

"I see. Nothing too unpleasant, I hope. If you could, please stay and watch her. After that, you may carry out my wishes."

"Yes, as you wish. Oh yes, something else. Ambassador Laffw is coming. She will arrive within the next few minutes."

A sigh and a laugh. "Of course she'd come. Part of her role, I suppose. The counterculture ambassadorial icon, visiting the noble and disgraced alike. She's getting quite a kick out of all this now she knows what the ending's going to be. Speak of the devil, I think that's her. She's a little early."

Gaspard let Laffw in along with Bapti. The Kavki was dressed in a, for her, restrained and somber outfit. She bowed theatrically and spoke with a laughing tone.

"Hail the fallen dame. And may I congratulate you on your latest coup. Took me quite by surprise, yet it fits in so perfectly. I was right to trust the Synod Enforcer to you. And as to what will happen tomorrow at the Grand Assizes…. Did you hear the defendants of the Laurent-Leblanc case will be arriving today by a special flight? Oh, it is too exciting. I will not know what to wear."

"I'm sure you'll find something."

"True. Meanwhile, since your part is about to exit the stage, may I have my property back? Maybe I can get some answers about that lack of reports. And for all her faults, she is a most valuable serf."

Mercedes's shrug was perfection. "She should return to you within the day. Didn't want to be involved anymore, so I let her leave. I expected her to be back with you by now."

Laffw laughed again. "Oh, well, we can track her down if she is away for too long. She would never abandon me completely, after all I have done for her. By the way, when we last met you spoke of someone recognizing you."

Mercedes nodded, briefly explaining. The days since Gretchen left her apartment had been filled with nightmarish tension carefully hidden, except when she channeled it into her performance after the Synod Enforcer confronted them. She had heard nothing, and now Gretchen was off world. No-one had come calling, and nothing had been directed at her.

"I think," she concluded, "we can say there is no threat from that quarter. A good thing, too, at this late stage."

"As you say."

"Now Ambassador, as lovely as it is to see you again, I must ask that you leave within the next ten minutes. I have an important guest related to Laurent-Leblanc arriving very soon, and she may be more willing to talk if there were fewer intimidating figures in the same room as her."

"I see." Laffw eyed Mercedes. "Nobility meets nobility. I shall let you have your private meeting. All this in your plan, and even luck seems to favor you." She turned to her serf. "Come, Bapti. We have some errant property to locate."

Laffw left with a sweeping gate, with Bapti close behind. When they were definitely gone, Mercedes snorted.

"I'll be well rid of them and the end of all this." Her eyes turned to look down into the street. "There they go. And here comes my visitor. It's the day for being early, it seems."

A few minutes later, the hesitant-looking Ekri stepped inside. She wore a hood, which she pulled down to reveal features pinched and frightened. It was clear she had been contemplating turning back all the way up to this point, and now she was here it was like standing on the scaffold with the executioner. Mercedes gestured to a chair, and Hydee sat down sharply, almost painfully. Gaspard was in a discreet corner, and Mercedes settled herself down to the task.

"You came. That means you're at least willing to hear me out about what you should be doing tomorrow."

"Yes, I came." The Ekri's eyes narrowed. "But that does not mean I either believe you, or that I should follow any requests you have for me."

"I'm interested to know why or how I would be lying."

Hydee seemed to collect her thoughts. "When I was the tiniest child, my governess saved me from the bombardment that killed my entire family. I might have been left for dead there or raised and sold to Kavki aristocracy in the black market of Taltis. They would likely want me for my 'fine looks' and 'aristocratic roots.' But out of that rubble, as a helpless baby, I was plucked by a man who I might have been taught to hate had I reached an age of reasoned thought before the Conflict's end. He took me from that ruined place and brought me to his ship. We set off back to New Dubai, and he raised me, gave me everything I could ever need. He told me I was his ward, that I would be his heir. That he had never found anyone he could love as a partner, but in me he saw someone he loved like a daughter. He has always treated me as such."

"I see. Well, we all need balms for our consciences."

"You have no right to say such things."

Mercedes gave a sharp laugh and tore away her mask. "I have every right. I trust you can recognize a face."

The Ekri stared at Mercedes, then balked in her chair. "No. Impossible. He said you were dead."

"Yes. And I dare say he also said he couldn't stop the bombardment of Cataaka, or that your people fired first. Likely the latter as that is the official story. Perhaps he also mentioned the treasures lost in the bombardment which destroyed your home, treasures going back millennia. If so, you should read this."

Mercedes pulled a datapad from inside her clothing and handed it to Hydee. She took it and opened it cautiously. She read slowly through its contents, and her eyes grew wide and tearful. Mercedes restrained a smile, satisfied with the impact. She didn't hold back as her words cut into the Ekri's weakened position.

"That is a copy of an order from ex-Fleet Admiral Henri Laurent-Leblanc authorizing his private fleet to bombard the major cities of Cataaka and break its blockade of local flightpath from inside. It also details the entire plan, designated targets, and a special little addendum. 'Orders to be carried out with extreme prejudice.' And we both know what 'extreme prejudice' means in military documents. If you look at the bottom, you'll also see a little list of objects taken following the bombardment during rescue efforts. A suitable tally for his accountants, no doubt."

"How did you get this?"

"Research and a little influence in high places. He hid it well. It wouldn't do in the current climate to have to own up to cultural and humanitarian crimes against our current allies."

"But, I can't bel—"

"You can't believe your beloved Henri is capable of slaughtering everyone you hold dear, then stealing your heritage while he played the role of savior to a squalling babe? And now he seeks to deny the rightful claims of a people to whom you are the nearest thing to a queen. Truly a fitting end for the last of a noble Ekri dynasty."

The emotions crisscrossing the Ekri's face were a picture. Mercedes wondered if she would burst into tears or rip at the furniture. Instead, Hydee glared at Mercedes, then tossed the datapad away and straightened up.

"What do you want?"

"I want to see Henri Laurent-Leblanc ruined. Prosecutor de Granger and the duke are also on my list, but you have the option of dealing with Henri personally. After the Grand Assizes begin."

"Why at that time?"

"Because, on the first day of the Assizes, evidence will be shown that entirely disproves his claim upon your people's land and exposes Laurent-Leblanc and Granger for the snakes they are. Any attempt to nullify it will be countered by other factors."

"You really intend to bring them down?"

"Yes. What will you do now?"

"I... I must...."

"Do what you must as your people's leader?"

"Yes. It is my duty. As a ruler and an Ekri."

"I shall look forward to seeing his reactions, for I, too, shall be there. As will the duke and several members of the Synod's lower ranks. I can guarantee, Hydee Alasha Pakaa, it will be like no Grand Assizes before it."

Hydee took her leave after this final exchange. Mercedes nodded slowly. It was really beginning at last.

---

GASPARD HAD A difficult day ahead. Once he finished dispatching the mysterious parcel Mercedes wanted on its way, he set about his next task. It was easy enough to go to Saqara's apartment block at that time of day. Dressed in nondescript casual clothes, it was easier still to keep an eye on the front doors until a familiar figure stepped out, carrying a small suitcase. There she was, the Synod Enforcer. And before he could start, he felt an unpleasantly familiar hand slap his rump. Echo whispered in his ear.

"Like some help here?"

Gaspard's face crumpled. "Why're *you* here?"

"Ask a silly question. I take it we're following to keep her out of trouble?"

"Yes."

"Good. This should be fun and easy. Keeping tabs is my middle name."

That old, rusted joke again. Gaspard had long grown tired of this winking repetition that Feles didn't have middle names, even if they adopted names for the Cluster's common parlance. Settling with an exasperated sigh, Gaspard tried to ignore Echo as they followed Yarin. She took no taxi, but walked the five miles to Amasian City, where many private shuttles were parked away from the bustle of the city center.

It was a prolonged shadowing, right up to and inside the shuttle port. All the time, Echo walked at a short distance. Gaspard's mind drifted back to the kidnappers' hideout, back to the d'If, back to his life before the d'If. Stricken of any feeling, his mind dwelt in places beyond comfort, where Echo's face had loomed large, and he had felt the pain that was pleasure driving into his loins. What he confessed to Ali came back to him. What had he ever known beyond that brutal reality? Nothing, absolutely nothing except him. Him and his grinning face, that sickening look in his eyes.

Yarin passed through the shuttle port and went through the process of claiming her ship. With his keen hearing, he noted the wise precaution of registering the shuttle under another name. They hadn't been followed by anyone he recognized, and now she'd passed out of sight. His mission was done, he was free. At least....

Echo continued to shadow him, and for Gaspard it grew progressively harder to keep his cool. Finally, as they walked down a quiet street near the

Commercial District, Gaspard turned down a small alley. Echo followed deliberately, but after a few paces, Gaspard turned to face him.

"Stop it."

Echo's eyebrow twitched. "Excuse me?"

"I said stop it. Just leave me alone."

Echo's response was to push forward and force his tongue against his lips. Gaspard pushed him away, wiping his lips as if to remove some swatted insect.

"Eugh…. You always tasted foul, whichever end you use."

"My, you're in an independent mood today. What's brought this on?"

"I don't have any obligation to you. Never again. Just get out or my life. Leave me alone."

Echo's face broke into a sadistic grin. "Don't fool yourself, Gaspard Atarex. You say you want me out of your life forever, yet the first chance you get you call me back."

"You're the one who keeps coming back for more. What's the matter? Can't get enough of me?" The words tumbled out, buoyed along by a kind of insane courage. "Or are you so insecure in anything other than lust based on fear that you can't let go? Oh yes, that'd be funny. Bloody hilarious. You say I need you, but it's really you who needs me. No matter what you say, I don't need you, so I can just wipe you off my foot like the piece of shit you are."

For the first time in a long time, Echo's face twitched, the smile fading away to be replaced by a scowling look. Then Echo rushed forward before Gaspard could react, pinning him to the wall. Echo's hand reached down, clenching hard enough to cause pain, but the wellspring of courage continued to flow. Echo thrust his head forward, trying to press their foreheads together. The sign of domination or supplication, forced upon him again. Gaspard acted at once, headbutting Echo with all his strength.

The pain was sharp, and Gaspard stumbled in a momentary daze. He threw a punch at the vague shape that might still be Echo. The fist made contact with flesh. There was a grunting gasp, then a crashing noise. When his vision clarified, Echo was sprawled on top of a small heap of trash. The expression on his face was unlike anything Gaspard had seen before, almost exhilarating to see. The victim had rebelled against the tormentor, and now Echo was afraid.

"I don't have time for your sick little games." Gaspard's voice was alien to his own ears, cold and cruel. "I've got a few things to do for Mercedes, but once that's done, I'm leaving this planet. But there's one job I think is better suited to you than me. Believe it or not, Mercedes paid me while I worked for her. Andréa needs dealing with when all this is over. I'll pay you to do it, then we never see each other again. Got it?"

Echo stared balefully up at Gaspard, bared his teeth like a scolded wildcat, then slowly rose and brushed himself down. The two Feles stared at each other, a stare like felines of Ancient Earth sizing each other up anew after a scrap.

Then Echo laughed. "You win. And you don't have to pay. Think of it as repaying debts."

"No, I'm paying you. I won't play your games again. Just get out of my sight."

It was hardly believable to see Echo slinking away down the alley like the beaten animal he was. It wasn't a tactical retreat, not a false concession. He was truly walking away, defeated by his victim. It was almost unbelievable, but it was happening. He'd done it. He'd fended Echo off, engaged with his tormentor and won.

Gaspard walked in the opposite direction, across and through streets into a park near the Upper Residential District. In that park, alone with a new fall of rain, he stopped and turned his face to the sky. The water fell across his face and mingled with his tears. Not tears of pain or misery or exhaustion. These were the pure tears of victory. He raised his arms toward the sky and bellowed the single triumphant word untroubled by circumstance or any uncertain future.

"Free!"

---

IT WAS THREATENING rain as Ali passed into Laffw's embassy residence. Her window of opportunity was short. Laffw and Bapti would be with Mercedes for a brief period, then likely return here to attend to other matters now things were coming to a head. A vague sensation of regret and horror at her planned actions almost made her turn around and walk away. Why should she listen to Mercedes? How could she abandon everything, even consider such an action? What life had she outside what Laffw had given her?

Her answer came in the form of a vision, the memory of the two children she had protected, the Feles who had unburdened his heart to her and received unconditional support. Whatever kindnesses Laffw gave her, they could not coexist with her new purpose, making a life of her own, helping those who could not be help themselves. It was somewhat selfish, but when in her life had she been given the luxury of selfishness?

The two datapads pressed against her chest, weighing on her as she met one of the embassy staff in the front hall. "Aliadriden Adakram P'fetrae? What are you doing here?"

Ali produced one of the datapads, handing it to the staff member. There was a moment's pause as the staff member opened it and glanced at the heading.

"A report for Ambassador Laffw?" Ali nodded. "Would you like to deliver it in person?"

Again, Ali nodded and was shown into Laffw's quarters. Left alone, Ali went straight to Laffw's desk. Mercedes was a fool if she thought Laffw kept important documents on her person. One stray bullet, one targeted EMP attack, and the data would be lost. In her private residence, surrounded by the security of a nation, sealed away from prying eyes and hands, that was where it would rest. Placing the false report on Laffw's desk, she then opened one of the drawers and reached inside. Somewhere was an old-fashioned mechanical spring, unhackable and invisible to random intruders.

It was relatively safe. There were no cameras in this place by her order, and she trusted her serfs absolutely. And now, through this action, Ali was shattering that trust. Giving in to selfishness, she was abusing the bond of service and loyalty all Kavki serfs owed to their keepers. A sacred trust, almost a familial bond. But there were some things that trumped family, including one's own desires.

Her fingers found the switch, then she faltered. Conflict blossomed behind her eyes, and her throat gave a rasping croak of protest. What was she doing, betraying her mistress for a human's promise? Laffw had given her a home, food, clothes, unconditional support, and a reason for living after the horror of the Human-Ekri Conflict. But that had been among her people, within their social norms. Here, in the rest of the Cluster, the precepts of the Kavki counted for little, just as the Feles tribal loyalties, human blood relations, and the Ekri's Law of Vendetta were rendered next to useless beyond the strict bounds of their own worlds.

With a soft click, the panel popped open, a flip top disguised as part of the table's varnished decoration. There it was, the non-networked data-pad holding the contract binding Mercedes and Laffw's fates. A swift motion switched the two round, and the guilty datapad was secreted into the depths of Ali's clothes. She had barely closed the panel and the drawer when the door opened, and Laffw burst in with Bapti hard on her heels.

"Ali! Wonderful, I had hoped to meet you today. What is that there, a report? Your report? I am delighted to hear it." Laffw picked up the datapad and glanced through it. "Yes, this seems satisfactory. Ali, I wish you to return to Mercedes if possible, and if not, then shadow her. I wish to keep an eye on her during the next few days." She smiled unexpectedly. "For all your tardiness in some respects, you have been admirable in the performance of your duties. I commend you."

Ali nodded acknowledgement. Laffw turned and settled back at her desk. The interview was over, and Ali was dismissed. Ali walked from the room at a slowed pace, listening to Laffw's comments to Bapti.

"This meeting with the Synod Examination Committee is such a bore. 'Explanation of Kavki social conduct' indeed. Humans just will not understand that serfdom for us is not the same as their slavery. Do we beat our serfs? Treat them as lesser beings? Bind them forever? Leave them without legal rights? No! Just because humans have advanced a little, they think they can forget their pasts and take a puerile high ground—"

The closing door cut off the rest of Laffw's tirade. Outside the embassy, the rain was beginning to fall. Ali did not bother to protect herself but let the rain flow across her waxy skin and soak into her clothing. Before her, once Mercedes had held up her end of the bargain, there was a new life of free choice. Behind her, forever burned into her mind, were the tattered remnants of Laffw's trust in her.

---

AMASIAN CITY DETENTION Facility was the least comfortable interim prison Andréa had ever stayed in during his long career as part of the criminal classes. Its cells, isolated from contact with the outside world aside from a single terminal strictly controlled by its officers, were based on the Ancient Earth Supermax style popularized in the classical wasteland once hailed as the United States. In that cell were a bed, a toilet, a shower cubicle, a comm terminal with limited access, and nothing else. The forcefield separating the cell from the rest of the facility was transparent, allowing anyone to check on him when needed.

Outwardly, Andréa portrayed the picture of nonchalance. Inside, he wanted to tear the walls of his prison to shreds, to disembowel the guards and use their intestines to shin down the wall and then use as a garrote to kill every single one of his enemies. The duke, Mercedes, Malcolm, Granger, Laffw, Ali. Yes, Ali, curse that throatless Kavki. If not for Ali, the duke's precious son would be dead. Fitting retribution for…. He chuckled. Yes, fitting retribution, fitting for the duke to lose one son and—

"Hoy." A warden stood outside, "There's a private call coming through. It's your guardian, the baroness."

Andréa's eyebrows raised, then he went over to the terminal and accepted the call. The cell door suddenly became opaque, and he heard the hum of surveillance in the room shutting off. A private call indeed. How much of her mysterious fortune had this taken?

Mercedes's face was like a stone through the terminal's video link. *"Our time is brief, so listen. In two days' time, you will be indited for the attempted murder of the Marquess Malcolm Vorn-Solari. When the time comes for you to speak, you will tell them everything about your connection with the current duke. Your attorney will be able to produce all necessary to prove your claim. Both our wishes shall be fulfilled."*

"And what is that connection?"

*"Don't play games. You've known from the start. Why else accept my offer, play along this long, and try to kill Malcolm?"*

Andréa bit his lip, then smirked in his usual manner. "How long have you known?"

*"Since I saw your DNA profile while searching for someone to play your role. I've got a very good memory for official DNA documentation. I shall be in the Gallery during the Grand Assizes on the day of your indictment. After this happens, bail will be posted, and you'll be free to go where you wish, certainly to leave New Dubai. You have been most helpful with my plans. I will ensure you are suitably rewarded. So will Laffw. I hope you put on a good show."*

The video link shut off, leaving Andréa alone with his thoughts. He turned away from the screen, then raised his head and cackled. Oh yes, she'd played him very well, just as he thought he'd played her. Mercedes, Duchess of New Dubai, hadn't been the revenge-blinded fool he thought her. She, Laffw, and everyone else had used him.

"Duped."

His word addressed the space, coming out in a gasp. He'd been duped. It was all a set up from the very beginning. He had been tricked. Used. Manip-ulated. He paced up and down, his teeth bared like an animal in the throes of deepest passion. He would play her game, fulfill his role, but when the time came for his exit, he would have his own script to play. And if they dared remove him from the stage before he had his scene....

# FILE 16

## THE GRAND ASSIZES

---

*Remember the time we walked, ah me,*
*The time we danced neath falling leaves,*
*The time we laughed at the tripping child,*
*The time we never knew failure.*
*The time before I fell and died,*
*And you spent the money for the rent.*

—Verses from Fingal Dee's "Song for Idiots"

THE DAY OF the Grand Assizes dawned bright, although yet more rain was forecast for the afternoon. Thanking privilege for allowing swift passage past the congested roads to the Grand Court, and Granger's shrewd route choice to avoid the gauntlet of journalists at the front of the building, Henri Laurent-Leblanc emerged onto the floor of Courtroom A. Glancing up at the galleries, he saw very few people there. One of them was Laffw and her servant, the former wearing a rather gaudy gown. The second was the Baroness Charlotte Clarisse, her face an impassive stony mask.

Oh, well, might as well have them there instead of complete strangers. It was early yet, and few had arrived aside from essential court staff. He was glad of the lack of spectators, of too many people from the case. It gave him time to think, to reflect, to steel himself for what was to come. Granger had been confident from the first, for whatever reason, they would win hands down. Then he could tell Hydee something of the truth, give her a chance to be who she might be, free of those poisonous settlers at Qalaa's Prospect.

But where was Hydee? She should've been somewhere, if only in the gallery. She had slipped away from him, saying she needed to powder her nose, but hadn't returned. She must be all right. If anything had happened, there would've been a report by now. If those bastards from Qalaa's Prospect had done anything to her, it would be all the more reason to throw them off world where they belonged. Finally, the courtroom began filling up, and Laurent-Leblanc took his seat.

There were quite a few faces appearing in the gallery, and eventually it reached capacity, but still no sign of Hydee. Couldn't she bear to see this go through? She had been a little distracted and worried for the past several days, but she hadn't said anything to worry him. He had given her space, and she seemed thankful for it. The defendants walked in, including the *Sayydi* of Qalaa's Prospect, that old crone with her scathing eye.

Almost triumphantly, Granger entered along with his opposite number, the so-called "Feles Angelus" Grand Attorney Glas. The two exchanged a courteous nod, though their mutual dislike was clear to see and left undisguised. The scene was slightly marred as a force field was erected between the gallery and the courtroom, but safety must come before all. Good. Better to keep any potential agents from Qalaa's Prospect from doing anything to disrupt proceedings. He wouldn't put anything past them.

Yes, everyone had assembled now except the judge. Granger appeared confident. Glas was the portrait of non-committal assiduity, and Laurent-Leblanc struggled not to appear nervous. Be confident, charismatic, as he had before his men in the Human-Ekri Conflict even in the direst of times. Finally came the appointed judge, a Kavki known by the name Goddard brought from off world to oversee the case. Everyone rose as Goddard entered, then sat as she settled into her seat. Laurent-Leblanc took the chance to shuffle a little and get comfortable, then the Court Counsel gave a resume of the case, including the various evidence given on both sides, and both the testimony and opinions of key figures in the case.

It was Granger's turn first, and his voice echoed through the chamber with the magnitude and charisma of a stage actor. Goodness, he was so persuasive. The Ekri forfeited their claim to New Dubaian soil following the Human-Ekri Conflict peace settlements, and Qalaa's Prospect had continued to refuse aid and lived willingly in conditions one of his agents called appalling. Granger produced evidence of threatening and abusive messages sent to

Laurent-Leblanc by them, apparently showing their "clear prejudice and lack of legal standing beyond the use of scare tactics." Everything they'd arranged beforehand. His closing speech was triumphant.

"I feel," he concluded, "with all the evidence present, this court should deliver the just and right verdict in favor of my client, and put an end to this sordid dispute which has marred our judicial system for too long due to its plain clarity being muddied by the machinations of a group of bitter Ekri who refused to leave the past behind. I hope, too, that my client Laurent-Leblanc, a patriot of the highest order and unimpeachable member of our society, will no longer be troubled by a group who has allowed petty revenge to muddy this remarkably straightforward case."

Attempts at applause were silenced by the usher's stentorian voice as Granger seated himself. Goddard looked at Grand Attorney Glas with her narrow eyes.

"Have you anything to say on this matter?"

"I do, Your Honor." Glas continued to keep his face magnificently straight. "I submit that I, on my client's behalf, can provide evidence not only of their rights to the land, but of Laurent-Leblanc's complicity in a smear campaign of the most prejudicial kind."

Granger bolted up from his chair. "Your Honor, I must protest."

The courtroom was humming with murmurs, with many looking shocked at the Attorney's accusation. Laurent-Leblanc looked at Granger, and his stomach dropped. The Grand Prosecutor, his ally on so many political battles, looked unnerved by this statement. Goddard looked hard at the Feles.

"I hope this evidence is compelling, Sir Glas. You make a serious accusation."

"The evidence is compelling and reliable, Your Honor. If I may continue?"

"You may."

"But Your Honor—"

The Kavki's voice cut Granger off. "The Grand Prosecutor will kindly not speak out of turn. If he must speak, he will raise an official objection while his noble colleague finishes presenting his evidence."

"Yes, Your Honor. I beg your pardon."

Granger sat down looking like a scolded schoolboy, and Glas asked for the large display to be activated. This done, he connected a datapad and brought up documents to correspond with his statements. Laurent-Leblanc watched

Glas and saw the unmistakable. There in the Feles's movements and attitude was the unflappable knowledge of certain victory, the same confident body language Granger had held until barely a minute ago. As Glas spoke, the court became deathly quiet.

"I would draw attention first to the ancient agreement which ceded the disputed land to the Ekri House of Pakaa, who previously held suzerainty over a large portion of Ekri territories prior to their destruction during the Siege of Cataaka. It gives them stewardship over the Alasaya region of New Dubai, which is too harsh for others of the Cluster to inhabit comfortably, as part of the settlement of Humans three centuries ago."

Goddard's tone was icy. "You have already stipulated this, Attorney Glas. Is there something you wish to add?"

"Yes, Your Honor. I wish now to draw attention to the terms of the Treaty of Cataaka by which the Human-Ekri Conflict ended. And to a specific clause by which treaties pre-dating the duration of the Conflict— which ceded land or influence to the Ekri—would not be infringed upon by anyone. I would remind the court that the Treaty of Cataaka was ratified and enshrined by the Synod itself, and still holds true. This means, contrary to what my colleague has argued, my clients have every right to settle the Alasaya region."

Goddard's face shifted but remained composed. "We have heard nothing of this before."

"That is true, Your Honor. My offices have tried to gain access to Synod legal records for this case but were denied access. It is only two days ago that I received special permission from the Synod to examine the Treaty closely, which overrode the previous block placed upon it. I discovered access through New Dubai's terminal system was blocked by an executive order."

"From whom?"

"Viscount-General Henri Laurent-Leblanc. His digital signature was used to block all access to the Treaty of Cataaka and associated documents."

There was a flurry of chatter through the entire chamber, and the usher once more had to raise her voice to obtain silence. The memory of an obscure document appeared before Henri's eyes, a document thrust forward by Granger as a precautionary measure, something to use in case things got ugly he had said. Was this what he meant, hamstringing them? What the hell was going on? Even if he hadn't known about it, why had it come out now, today of all days? The judge looked at Prosecutor de Granger.

"I trust you knew nothing of this highly irregular incident, Prosecutor?"

"I knew nothing of this, Your Honor."

Granger's face didn't move as he lied to Goddard. Laurent-Leblanc's hands clenched slightly, and he looked into Goddard's eyes.

There was no emotion in the Kavki's face as she replied. "I hope that is true. Have you anything further to add, Attorney Glas?"

"I have, Your Honor. I would next like to address the claim made by Prosecutor de Granger of my clients refusing outside aid and sending threatening messages to his client. As to the former, my offices have only been able to secretly visit the area due to undisclosed sanctions put on travel through that region by Viscount-General Laurent-Leblanc. Again, his signature has been identified beyond any possible doubt. The sanctions stipulate any attempted legal or voluntary aid for Qalaa's Prospect is to be halted, and covert patrols are to be kept to prevent unofficial aid reaching them. Furthermore, messages supposedly sent from Qalaa's Prospect have been analyzed by data cryptographers from the Synod and—"

Granger rose sharply. "Objection. When did the Synod become involved in a domestic dispute?"

Glas spoke with force, and for the first time sounded emotive. "With all due respect, Your Honor, this no longer falls into the category of a local dispute, and due to the circumstances surrounding the information block on the Treaty of Cataaka, the Synod has become an interested party, so their contributions to this case are valid."

"Objection overruled, Prosecutor de Granger. Continue, Attorney Glas."

"Thank you, Your Honor. When the Synod's data cryptography department looked at the threatening messages and denials of aid provided by Laurent-Leblanc as part of his defense, it was discovered that the signals were faked. They were sent by those same covert units preventing aid from reaching Qalaa's Prospect and disguised themselves using Ekri coding to make it appear as if the settlers were refusing aid and threatening Prosecutor de Granger's client."

Goddard looked at Prosecutor de Granger. "Does your client have anything to say about these very serious accusations?"

Laurent-Leblanc tried to speak, but Granger spoke before him. "My client, the Viscount-General, denies all of these charges and makes no comment on how his signature was used. I would ask whether someone in his household didn't steal it for their own use."

"What is your response to that, Attorney Glas?"

"I'm bound to disagree with this supposition, Your Honor. To input his digital signature requires two things. His personal datakey, which is kept on his person at all times, and his sub-dermal ID chip, which interacts with a nearby terminal to authorize use of the datakey and the signature. The lack of either part of this makes use of the signature invalid and nullifies any document or other use it is put to."

"Is there any way either the datakey or the ID chip could have been copied?"

"It is a matter of public record that each datakey design is unique and each template is destroyed afterwards to prevent forgery. As to ID chips, they're designed to work only as part of a living person's body, and on an individual level with the assigned DNA. Replicating the ID chip would be a long and laborious process and far too conspicuous for secret work, while the datakey can only be replicated by stealing and dismantling the original. The loss of a datakey is reported immediately and its authorization revoked, making such a tactic impracticable."

The judge was clearly moved by Glas's arguments. "I must admit the evidence is quite strong. But have you any evidence as to why Laurent-Leblanc would go so far to discredit the settlers of Qalaa's Prospect?"

"Yes, Your Honor. I have a witness who can testify as to Laurent-Leblanc's motives for his actions. She is waiting to be summoned."

"Then do so."

There was renewed murmuring as the Court Council pressed the button which would summon scheduled persons to the enclosed witness box. It was a special compartment to the left of the judge's bench, designed so its surface could shift from transparent to frosted as the need required. As it changed, Laurent-Leblanc almost leapt from his seat. Hydee was standing there looking regal and wondrous. Several spectators whispered until the usher called for silence. Goddard's voice took charge.

"The witness will state her name."

Hydee kept her eyes on the judge, away from Henri. "My first name is

Hydee. To those on New Dubai, I am known under the surname Satkireae. My true name and title is Hydee Alasha Pakaa, last surviving heir to the House of Pakaa, of the Ekri's home planet Cataaka."

"Can you prove this?"

"Yes. Attorney Glas can provide records of my birth, registration, and heritage prior to the Siege of Cataaka, in addition to DNA verification. I was born one year before the Siege."

There was a pause as Goddard squinted at the datapad. "This is satisfactory. Now, Hydee Alasha Pakaa, what is your relation to Laurent-Leblanc?"

"I was rescued by him from the ruins of my palace following the bombardment of Cataaka's capital, an event which ended the Siege."

"Objection, Your Honor." Granger was not to be restrained. "The fact that Laurent-Leblanc was forced to bombard the city is a matter of public record. What bearing does this have on my client's supposed motives?"

Laurent-Leblanc looked toward Hydee. She still wouldn't look at him.

"I would ask that the court remembers the circumstances at the time of the Siege of Cataaka. Neither side held a definitive advantage, and both military commands were hesitant of using brute force for fear of reprisals. Laurent-Leblanc holds that he was fired upon before giving the order to use orbital bombardment. I must reveal now this is not what occurred that day. My people never fired until after the bombardment began."

"Objection." Granger bounced up from his seat once more. "I must protest against this. This person has no evidence to support her claim."

Now it was Glas's turn to cut in. "Your Honor, we can provide evidence gathered by the Synod on this matter from surviving data records from Cataaka."

"Objection overruled. Prosecutor de Granger, Attorney Glas, you will please allow the witness to proceed without further interruptions. Hydee Alasha Pakaa, continue with your statement."

"Before I continue, I feel I must clarify that while I was too young to remember what happened, I have recently discovered information on this topic. Laurent-Leblanc ordered his fleet to open fire on Cataaka, with main targets being both military bases and civilian centers. The capital city, where the Pakaa house resided, was the worst casualty. My entire family was killed, and it was only through the sacrifice of my nursemaid that I survived the bombardment."

Glas nodded before asking his next question. "What is your relation to the people of Qalaa's Prospect?"

"They are from a clan which has ancient ties with my own. In a sense, I am their monarch. But such titles have been denied to me."

"Why is this?"

"I am known as Laurent-Leblanc's ward and have received care from him since I was a child. But until recently, I knew nothing of the full circumstances of how he found me. I was found by Laurent-Leblanc in the rubble of my former palace when he led a team down to ransack and remove its treasures."

Granger, who had turned brick red over the past few seconds, bounced up and almost exploded at the judge. "Objection. Your Honor, the witness can't possibly provide proof of this."

"Prosecutor de Granger, you have been warned once." Laurent-Leblanc had to admire the judge's withering gaze forcing Granger back into his seat. "While an unwarranted interruption, it was a sensible concern. Can you provide evidence for your claims?"

"I can if Attorney Glas is willing to bring in an object. His clients may be able to identify it."

Goddard nodded her consent, Glas gave a signal, and a side door opened to admit two human porters carrying a shrouded object. The tension in the gallery was palpable. Laurent-Leblanc's stomach twisted and plummeted into the abyss. A great gasp broke from the gallery as the object was placed on Glas's desk and revealed. It was a serpentine statuette of black and white ivory embellished with gold and jade. Glas asked that the *Sayydi* be called to try and identify the object.

The judge looked at Hydee. "How did you get this?"

"I gained access to my guardian's private documents. Acting on information given to me about his actions, I found his secret storeroom and discovered my people's treasure. Treasure which rightfully belongs to the Ekri. The item before you, I believe, is a sacred totem forged by the Pakaa clan some seven hundred years past."

"Can the *Sayydi* identify this object with all certainty?" asked Glas.

The *Sayydi*, who had been seated in silence up to this point, looked long and hard at the object before nodding. "It matches descriptions in our records, and the symbols on it are our ancient tribal sigils. We had presumed it lost during the bombardment."

Glas spoke once more. "Records presented to us will show this object was looted from the destroyed palace home of the Pakaa family by a platoon led by Laurent-Leblanc, who went down onto the planet without authorization from Space Command."

Goddard turned an impassive face to the prosecutor's desk. "Does Laurent-Leblanc have anything to say on this matter?"

"My client does not wish to—"

"Quiet, Granger. You've done enough damage." Laurent-Leblanc spoke sharply, rising and turning toward Hydee.

There was an audible gasp from around Courtroom A. Laurent-Leblanc looked from the *Sayydi,* to Glas, to Goddard, and finally to Hydee. Words formed and poured out limply with no force behind them.

*"Why,* Hydee? Why now? What have I ever done to you? I've tried to save you from these parasites. I raised you to be my daughter. I would have told you everything."

Hydee's answer held no warmth. "When?"

There was a sudden flurry of chatter from the galleries, and under its cover Henri let out the softest of sobs. No tears came, nothing else to show the deep despair filling him. The usher called for order and silence, and Goddard's voice took charge once more.

"If there is any further disturbance, I shall clear the court. Also, Laurent-Leblanc will kindly sit. This is a most serious case. I must retire to consult with my Court Councils for the case on this matter. Let us please remember that we are concerned with the rights of the residents of Qalaa's Prospect to settle the Alasaya region of New Dubai, not any other incidents that may have come up in regard to this charge. We shall weigh the facts on both sides before giving a final verdict."

Goddard rose, and everyone else followed suit. With the judge departed, everyone relaxed and sat once more. Hydee had vanished from the box, gone who knew where. Henri felt Granger's occasional angered glances, Glas eyeing them, even the people in the gallery staring down at him. What could he do? Some had risen and left to stretch their legs, but most seemed too excited to move. Lashing out wouldn't do anything, and what could he do? He was a public figure, respected and awed and feared all at once, and if he knew anything about people, they loved to see the mighty fall. Hadn't that been what Granger and he counted on to bring Mercedes Solari to her knees ten years ago?

After nearly an hour, everyone was summoned back to their places and rose. Henri hadn't moved, still in a slight daze and seeing a ghost of Hydee on the witness stand. The Council and Goddard reappeared last and sat, prompting proceedings to resume. After arranging her papers, the judge spoke.

"The plaintiff and defendant will please rise." They responded to this, and after further shuffling of papers, Goddard delivered her verdict. "Due to overwhelming legal evidence in favor of their claim, and fresh evidence brought of the defendant's complicity in attempts to sway the case in his direction, we have decided to dismiss this case with prejudice. No further attempt shall be made to contest the claims of Qalaa's Prospect to settlement rights in the Alasaya region. Furthermore, this court shall begin consultation for possible prosecution of Viscount-General Henri Laurent-Leblanc for harassment, abuse of authority for personal gain, attempts to pervert the course of justice, and potential connection to cultural and war crimes against the Ekri during the Human-Ekri Conflict. This case is dismissed."

"All rise." The usher's voice was like the bell tolling at the end of all things.

For the next few minutes, Laurent-Leblanc only knew buffeting, calling, shouting, questions that went unanswered, and answers to unasked questions. The general exit from the Grand Courts was the most chaotic seen in years. Reporters rushed out ahead of everyone else, preparing to send off reports of the whole trial. The spectators were almost all chattering to each other as they tumbled down from the gallery.

On the steps, half-hidden behind one of the ornamental pillars, Henri saw Ambassador Laffw among the crowd, then a small crowd of Duncan's representatives sweeping down and brushing aside the few remaining journalists trying to wheedle comments from witnesses. Granger ducked over to him.

"Let's get you out of here. We can salvage this. Don't worry. When the appeals court—"

"I won't appeal."

"What? You won't appeal? Why?"

Granger looked startled, but Henri simply met his gaze. "It's true, isn't it?

I've never denied truth. I didn't deny it when we deposed Mercedes Solari. I don't want Hydee to be dragged into a courtroom again."

"If you hadn't gone soft over a whining lizard—"

Henri's fist struck Granger before he could think, feel, or do anything else. Granger crouched, winded by the blow, as Laurent-Leblanc charged down to where his car was waiting. Anyone who might have stopped him pulled away as if he were a predator passing through a heard of prey.

In his car on the way to his country estate, the next hour was like a nightmare. As he looked through the window, every face seemed to glare at him accusingly, and every light was like a camera flash. As he passed the large news screens in the city center, reports on the trial lit up the screens outlining the accusations set to be brought against him. Regardless of their truth, he began to fume. What right had these people to judge him? He'd saved them from the tyranny of Duncan's sister-in-law. She who would bankrupt the planet rather than seek outside aid. He had risen up from nothing, an infantryman, to help lead a planet.

But even as the bitter memory almost reached his lips, he recalled a tiny Ekri baby, wailing and clawing the air amid rubble, cradled in the dead arms of another female Ekri killed by the last blast from his flagship's cannon. He could have left the baby there and gone with his soldiers to plunder the ruined palace. He could have fired one shot and put the creature out of its misery. Instead, he picked it up, ordered forty percent of spoils be given to him, and decided to raise that child as his own.

A vague impression pushed aside memories and recriminations aside, linking Hydee's mental state to a party. No, before that. The Big Splash Ball when they had first met the Baroness Clarisse. The baroness, with that strange mask across her face. Was she involved in this? He had to be sure. Laurent-Leblanc redirected his car's course to the Yakam Apartment Building. The baroness wasn't at home, but he still rushed up to her door and banged on it, bursting in despite the building manager's protests. It was quite bare.

"Where is she?"

"She went to her country estate." The building manager was almost hysterical with terror at this emotional onslaught. "But she left a message should anyone call. Here."

A datapad with volumetric playback function changed hands, and back in his car Laurent-Leblanc saw a sigil printed on an adhesive strip across the underside. His sigil, his mark that was crest of office and reminder of his military victories. Activating the recording, he watched as a bust of the baroness appeared, flickering slightly as its AI-driven simulation synced with the pre-recorded messages.

*"Good day to you, Henri Laurent-Leblanc. If you're seeing this, I'm no longer at home. This platform can answer any question you desire. I spent some time perfecting it so it would explain everything to you.*

Laurent-Leblanc's first question was a bellow of rage. "Lady Clarisse, what is the meaning of this?!"

The head did a mechanical jerk sideways. *"This platform has a limited number of responses. Kindly rephrase."*

It took some minutes for Laurent-Leblanc to calm down. "Fine. I'll play along. I would like an explanation of your conduct, Lady Clarisse. For reasons I can't fathom, you've engineered my ruin through a string of lies and trickery."

*"Neither lies nor trickery have brought you down, Laurent-Leblanc. Only your actions have brought this upon you."*

"You dare speak to me like that?"

*"This platform has a limited number of responses. Kindly rephrase."*

"Do you know who I am?"

The baroness's voice was level and cold. *"I know you are a Viscount-General whose military and political influence have helped Duncan Vorn-Solari succeed as duke of New Dubai. I know before that you were a Fleet Admiral in Space Command during the Human-Ekri Conflict thirty years ago. That is official. What will become known is you launched an assault on Cataaka without authorization, causing terrible loss of life and looting the Pakaa family of its wealth. Wealth which could have been used to restore Cataaka to glory. You also raised the last member of the Pakaa line as your own while keeping her in the dark about your past and plundered wealth. And, whatever your reasoning, you decided to deny the Ekri settlers of Qalaa's Prospect their rights and slur them using underhanded tricks. Have I suitably summarized your life?"*

"I should charge you for defamation of character."

*"It wouldn't do you any good, Henri."*

Laurent-Leblanc became more incensed. "You dare use my first name? We barely know each other, and you—"

The bust suddenly cut him off, her face twisting into a satisfied sneer. *"Oh, we* do *know each other. So very, very well. Think back, Laurent-Leblanc. Back ten years, to a woman you threw from her rightful throne for the sake of your own greed. A woman from whom you took a planet, giving it into the hands of a man too weak to change the status quo. Think back to a little gathering of men, a trio of stooges in conspiracy. Duncan Vorn-Solari, Georges de Granger, and you. Together you hoodwinked the entire Cluster and secured positions of power for yourselves, all while preserving the old order whom my father couldn't corral for all his bluster. All while sending a woman guilty only of wishing to give her world its chance to a decade of purgatory in the d'If. Granger engineered it, you supported it, and Duncan approved it. Look, Laurent-Leblanc, on the face of the past."*

The recording flickered once more, and Laurent-Leblanc watched as a hand—the hand of the baroness—reached up and removed the velvet mask covering the right half of her face. Laurent-Leblanc let out a strangled cry, his eyes twitching in their sockets. Mercedes Solari, a decade older and still implacable, stared at him from the display.

"No." His hands shook, almost losing their grip on the device. "No, no, no, no. This is a trick. It has to be a trick."

*"No trick, Henri."* Mercedes's facsimile smiled. *"My due retribution. Revenge is a sweet dish when served as cold as this. Your reputation, your wealth, your cult of personality all are destroyed. Or will be in the next few days. You've lost everything, just as I did when you betrayed me. The others will join you soon. What fate awaits you now I care not. You can't touch me, and you can't denounce me now. Who would believe you? Officially, I'm still dead."* The display glitched again. *"This is all the recording holds. Ending."*

The display shut off, and the datapad closed down. Slumped in that seat, all he could do was laugh. Even Granger couldn't browbeat an image, and what good would it do to argue with the inevitable? He knew Mercedes. He remembered her careful and cunning nature. If she was still alive, he'd be as good as dead within the day. It might be better to rob her of the pleasure, a last act of revenge. Dimly, as if in a dream, he heard Mercedes's echoing laugh of triumph, the triumph she had imagined over New Dubai's elite, unheeding of the social collapse she might herald.

"She deserved what she got." His voice sounded uncertain. "Trying to bring down the elite and set herself up as the world's absolute power. In the end, I guess I did, too. Our sins aren't so distinct."

It was another half hour before he reached his home, getting out of his car and walking toward his house in a kind of trance. Then he stopped, turned, and saw Hydee's little home, the home he built just for her. The door was open wide, almost as if inviting him in. The black hole where his heart and mind had gone pulled him toward that door, tugging him along the corridor to Hydee's old chambers.

He didn't expect to see Hydee but didn't expect what was there. An Ekri was standing in front of the empty sofa. Laurent-Leblanc stopped, let his head fall sideways, and spoke with numbing lips.

"Yes?"

"I have been expecting you, Henri Laurent-Leblanc."

"Why… you… here?"

"I am here on behalf of the House of Pakaa to deliver retribution. I have been asked by our monarch to make it as swift as possible."

"By… Hydee?"

"Yes. She made this request on behalf of her house. The Right of Vendetta must be fulfilled, to purge the blight from our tribe and our princess. At her personal stipulation, I am to make it as quick as possible. Are you prepared?"

Prepared? Was anyone ever prepared for death? He could fight, fly, do what he could to reclaim his position. But what was the point? If he knew Mercedes, she'd have planned everything out carefully, and Granger and Duncan were doomed by this point. Just like him. So, what now? What to do? How long had he tried to save Hydee from being the slave of the *Sayydi*, those sly and skulking priestesses who were like so many versions of Mercedes, guiding their planet by and for their will alone?

"Can you give her one last message?"

"If you wish."

"This is my message. I'm sorry. I failed. Now… live."

Laurent-Leblanc had made his last words. The Ekri drew a needle-like blade from the sheath at his belt and held it up.

"This will prick your heart. It is laced with poison. You will be dead in but a second."

Unbuttoning his jacket and shirt, Henri pulled aside the fabric to reveal the bare skin above his heart. The needle glinted as it was thrown through the air, and as it sank through the flesh, he felt no pain. At least it was better than a public trial. And in a way, he was dying on his own terms. A last wish flashed into his failing mind. Even if Duncan couldn't escape pain, he heartily wished Granger the worst death any man could die.

# FILE 17

## TO FIND DISORDERED MINDS

---

*Oh bitter was the wind that winter's night,*
*When Death's hand came knocking in time to the clock's toll.*
*I stir, I watch, I wait as the door swings in like arm outstretched.*
*I want to run, or hide, or fight. But all of these are meaningless.*
*What can you do with It? It has been with us from the first.*
*To escape It is to escape life. I watched as It approached,*
*its hand held out like a friend. "Time's a come," It said. "Will ye come?"*

—Extract from Fingal Dee's "Death's Progress"


GRETCHEN'S FACE FLICKERED in the display on Duncan's desk. *"I'm sorry, but I can't."*

"Why won't you come back? I need you here. It's all gone mad today. I need you. *Malcolm* needs you."

*"I need you, too. You could come here. Can you manage that?"*

"I've got far too much work to do."

*"Please, you really should come. If only for a day or two."*

"It'll take half a day to reach Argo from here."

*"I know, but...."*

Gretchen's voice could be so pleading and persuasive. Almost like her sister, though turned to familial bonds over courtly scheming. Duncan sighed and smiled.

"All right. I've got one other thing to deal with today. Something big that came up. Once that's dealt with, I'll be sure to come."

*"Thank you."*

Gretchen's hand appeared in the display for a moment as if to reach out and touch her husband, then the vision shut off. Duncan settled into his seat and pondered the day ahead. It would be a hard one. He was exhausted, drained of all energy, and not looking forward to the press coverage later that morning. If his servants hadn't been all drones, they might have resigned from the onslaught of snappish remarks he couldn't control.

After all, what was he supposed to have done yesterday? Granger had been the one who'd made a fool of himself. The Qalaa's Prospect trial had been an abject humiliation, with everything after that coming in a surreal and dead-ly flow. The verdict, the scrum of reporters, Laurent-Leblanc's extraordinary outburst, which he could still feel as a bruise across his stomach, and the news of his death by Right of Vendetta mere hours before the *Sayydi* had left with Hydee for Qalaa's Prospect.

The evening had been full of news, gleeful news of defeat and death, news that shook the planet and prompted outpourings of both grief and scorn in equal measure. It seemed many enemies were emboldened by his death to speak against him, bringing further upon further accusations to tarnish his name. Maybe Duncan should've known, but he didn't want to know. Laurent-Leblanc and Granger had gotten him into this planet's cursed social system and kept him there, allowing him to woo the woman he loved. He hadn't been as idiotic as his sister-in-law, trying to bankrupt and disempower them and putting them all against her. Granger had met with him late in the evening and brushed off any impact on him with aplomb.

"It doesn't matter in the long run." Granger had spoken as if addressing a courtroom. "The Cluster existed on their White Oil exports, so they turned a blind eye to it. New Dubai's society was none of their business as long as strong exports continued, and the interstellar cruisers carried freight and peo-ple from system to system without fuel crises every few years. And since I'm the best bloody prosecuting lawyer on the planet, one failure won't bother many of them too much."

Malcolm's smiling appearance and the chance to settle down with him for an evening as father and son had been a blessed breath of sanity. Sometimes he wondered why he'd bothered with all this ducal business, but Granger and Laurent-Leblanc had insisted he step up after Mercedes had proposed what she did. Gretchen didn't want anything to do with the post, and many more would've rebelled against the replacement of the Solari line, so Duncan had taken Mercedes's place.

Guess he wouldn't be allowed to forget about that. First the d'If exploding like that, then these bloody messages.

He looked at the small stack of datapads he had found waiting in his private office, delivered by a drone well before he'd woken up from a night of troubled dreams. He hadn't expected any messages following the previous day's debacle. It was a little-acknowledged truth that reputation was everything on New Dubai. If reputation—good or bad—vanished, a person had nothing to recommend them. But these were different, a selection of appeal alerts related to the former duchess's household and power base. Granger had said once that any such appeals would be copied and forwarded to him. Amazing that Granger kept such a trivial promise.

He'd picked up the first without thinking and seen the name and original charge. Dulac, possession of human child pornography. Payran, bribery and solicitation with intent to threaten. Crespi, mishandling of trust funds. Lacar, blackmail and solicitation to falsify poll results. Then one name stood out above the others, bringing with it the memory of a stern old face framed by locks of white hair. Noirtier. Artorius Noirtier, imprisoned for embezzlement and committed suicide six months into sentence.

Rereading it twice more did nothing to change what was written. He vaguely remembered Granger saying that Noirtier was dead but.... Noirtier, that strange, harmless-looking man who was as shrewd as anything. That's what had made it so shocking. Not the embezzlement, but that he'd been willing to do it at all. But the evidence had been there.

But there had been one on the bottom. *Sender withheld.* Only a few people or groups in the entire Cluster could withhold message ID in messages to him.

After he read what was typed there, he looked through the attached proofs and documents. That last had been the worst, the *coup de grace* to his mood for the day. Within the half hour, he'd ordered Granger's mail stopped by executive order, then insisted that he come at once. The next hour had been a torment, his call to Gretchen his only relief. Now he was resolved. He'd finish his meeting with Granger, then he and Malcolm would travel to Argo.

No, damn it. He had to attend Andréa's trial. He'd send Malcolm off first, then follow once the trial was done. He'd have to find someone to replace Granger for that, someone reliable and unaffiliated.

It was half an hour after the summons when Granger appeared, looking controlled but still slightly flustered. His voice was cold, official.

"You wanted to see me."

Duncan winced at Granger's statement. "Sit down. I'd rather we didn't linger on this."

Granger sat down, and Duncan paused for a moment. His voice had become suddenly sharp and harsh, almost like hers. The two men seated on opposite sides of the desk, the morning light shining in upon them, the air of coldness.... Yes, it was a mirror of that scene when he had come with Laurent-Leblanc and Granger to see Mercedes, putting the case to her and forcing her to step down from her office. Not that she'd kept to her word, but the atmosphere was the same, a kind of doomed finality to a relationship. Nevertheless, he would be polite to this man who within a few hours had become a stranger to him.

"I've summoned you here for a number of reasons. First, Laurent-Leblanc."

"Ah, yes." Granger's face puckered and sneered all at once. "He was quite unbalanced at the end. Probably explains why he let that Ekri kill him. We can salvage this."

*Always* that same bloody saying, even in the face of complete ruination. "You know what the Synod are like for interfering in other cultural practices."

"Oh, we needn't interfere. It's just some additional smearing that's needed. Maybe bring an action for murder. After all, Ekri don't have any real rights on this planet. We can keep on pressuring them, and—"

"There will be no charges filed, nor any investigation, nor any action taken on your part. I order it."

Granger bolted up from his chair. "What?"

"Sit down, Granger."

For a moment, it seemed Granger wouldn't do anything. But instead, stiffly, he returned to his seat.

"I guessed you were doing something underhanded, but I didn't like to interfere. Then. Things are different now. I've received some interesting alerts today regarding a series of appeals."

"Yes. All defeatable, I assure you."

"I don't think we want to contest them, do we?"

"I really don't understand you, Duncan—"

*"Your Grace,* if you please."

Again, his voice sounded alien, cold, taut as a bowstring about to fire an arrow. Granger shuffled a little and cleared his throat. "Your Grace. Those were valid convictions...."

"I thought so at the time. I didn't like my sister-in-law that much, so I was willing to... well, let some things slide. But to start off," he picked up the datapad in question, "you convicted Dulac *in absentia,* and since then he's been unable to return due to that conviction."

"Yes. So?"

"Very convenient."

Granger appeared flustered. "What are you trying to say?"

"The evidence, those filthy website addresses and datapads full of smut that were found in Dulac's apartment.... Where did you get them from?"

The flash of anger across Granger's face was clear but momentary, and he rapidly recovered composure. "I don't find such jokes amusing, Your Grace. Especially when it accuses me of falsifying information."

Duncan sighed, shaking his head. It felt like addressing a toddler that had taken a sweet and denied it a few hours later. "When I first ascended as the duke, I trusted both you and Laurent-Leblanc. But you were both rotten. Laurent-Leblanc a war criminal, and you a keeper of justice more crooked than I'd ever imagined. My rule for the past decade's been built on lies. I've read the information sent to me about you."

"What information?"

Duncan pressed on without answering. "I couldn't believe it at first. But everything about it was true. Dulac, Payran.... Even that old man Noirtier. All innocent."

Granger licked his lips, the subtlest of actions but telling enough. He'd been put on the defensive and was feeling under threat.

"You seemed satisfied at the time. With their imprisonment, I mean. On legal and accurate grounds. I can present my evidence against if that will—"

Duncan raised his hand in a hushing gesture. "Please, spare me the legal gibberish, Granger. I'm going to take steps. I'm going to hold an emergency meeting with the Synod, and I'm sure they'll want to appoint their own people to investigate such a grievous number of offenses. Until this matter is looked into, you're suspended from your duties indefinitely."

"What the hell? You seem to be under a misapprehension, Your Grace. Someone is trying to frame me. A cunning frame using this recent crisis and your undoubted sorrow at Laurent-Leblanc's death. Show me the sender of these ridiculous accusations. I'll tear them apart before your eyes. I'll make sure whoever sent them is never believed again. I'll—"

Once more, Duncan heard his voice from another place, tired and harsh. "For your own sake, just stop. It's gone on long enough. I'm going to order those appeals fast-tracked and all the evidence re-examined by a new Prosecutor and the Synod's data analysts. I've also asked that a new Prosecutor handle the case against my son's assailant. I'm sorry. You've left me no choice."

Granger looked like someone had punched him in the gut, stripping him of all his wind. It was a half-beaten man who rose with a pathetic shell of aloofness.

"I… see. Well, if it's not too much of an inconvenience, I will take a walk in one of the local parks. If that's all right, Your Grace."

The acid resentment was palpable. Duncan nodded, and Granger left, his back erect and his face turned impassive as stone. Alone again, Duncan's head sank between his hands. God, it would be good when all was over. He almost wished Granger would just vanish from sight, disappear in the woodwork of the world so he could get on with being the duke, with being a husband, with being a father. His eyes raised to the ceiling.

"If there is anything divine in this universe, please hear me. Can't this all be over for at least one day?"

---

MERCEDES SMILED TO herself as Granger appeared on the path ahead of her. Bapti's warning into her near-invisible earpiece had been well timed. Seated on that bench, letting the sunlight stream across her blue-and-red robes, she cultivated the impression of being a sprite. As Granger approached, his eyes focused on her. His face changed in recognition, then his pace quickened toward her.

"Yes." Her words were barely a whisper, spoken through stiff lips. "Yes, that's it. Come into my parlor, little spider."

Granger stopped abruptly next to the bench. He appeared to be seething with strong emotion, and Mercedes gave a bland smile.

"Good day, Prosecutor de Granger. Won't you sit down?"

"I prefer to stand."

"As you like. Is something the matter?"

The question was calculated to goad, and it did. His face became a twisted caricature, and he spoke with such force that speckles of his spit pattered across the arm she rested along the back of the bench.

"*You. You* are at the bottom of all this. You're the bane of my existence ever since you came to this world. Who are you? What did I ever do to you?"

Mercedes looked around. There wasn't another soul to see, no drones to catch them on camera. All as Laffw and Bapti had arranged. Actions spoke louder than any words, and her action had more than its intended effect. As she pulled away the mask, Granger stumbled back, shocked momentarily into inarticulate silence.

Mercedes grinned. "Not who you expected? You know, I'm really shocked that a mask, some new clothes, and a bottle of dye was able to fool so many of you, especially you. Always so astute, so knowledgeable of the grudges people can hold."

Granger's voice was slowly returning. "Mercedes… Mercedes… Solari."

"Yes, Georges." A malicious tone crept into her voice. "Mercedes Solari, back from long and painful exile in the depths of the d'If at the fringes of the Outer Worlds' territories. A pleasure to meet you again. How long has it been since we last had tea together?"

"I…. You were *dead*. You died when the d'If was destroyed. I told the duke you'd died."

"You told poor Duncan what he wanted to believe, like always. Did you tell Laurent-Leblanc about the d'If's destruction? It would've made that message I sent him much more impactful. Before the Ekri had their just revenge."

"You… you killed him."

"I never touched him. I merely facilitated his exposure as a coward and cheat. As a murderer. Just as I've exposed you as a liar and a hypocrite. And likewise as a murderer."

Granger's eyes flashed from left to right. "How did you know I'd be here?"

"I've had my allies watching you all day. Laffw has really been enjoying the spectacle."

"Ambassador Laffw? So she's in on this?"

"Yes. She got me out and allowed me to find the bits of my wealth you didn't manage to get away from me. Then it was a simple matter of insinuating myself into this cancerous thing you call high society and sowing the seeds for your demise. This world's really gone downhill since I was last here."

"You've been behind this all along. The attack on the Marquess, Laurent-Leblanc's fall, and these horrible accusations against me."

"Accusations imply that it's as yet unproven. My claims are fully proven. And are ratified by the Synod."

"By your tame Ambassador."

"Not only her. By the Synod. Diplomatic channels are very useful. So long as nothing was known, I imagine the Synod were willing to turn a blind eye to one planet's domestic troubles, but you didn't use your legal powers against your own people. You used them against the Ekri who had a right to that land. One has to ask, where would it end?" Her smile became a grin as the emotion rushed across Granger's face. "Yes, that's it. That's the look I wanted to see. The feeling I had that day. My father and I gave you the most precious of all gifts, our trust. And what did you do?"

"We stopped you from turning it into your personal playground. No power should be absolute, but you wouldn't accept that. You would've destroyed those who made this planet work to sate your pride, for the White Oil to be all ours. By asking for help and funding from the Synod, we maintained our prosperity."

"You let the old order root itself even deeper, a cancer on this world. Where's the other peoples of the Cluster enjoying this prosperity? The old order, your order, keeps them out. The White Oil remains ours, and we're the ones who keep it flowing. The other peoples must watch from the borders while we revel in our wealth."

Granger laughed, a hollow pitying sound. "You must be mad. What sane person would destroy the elite of a planet and take complete control of its funds and government? You would've bankrupted the planet and sent it into a spiral of decay. You're no better than the tyrants of Ancient Earth who held complete command over the lives and deaths of their people."

"Spare me the hypocrisy. You've done worse than anything I'd planned. When I tried to drag this planet into the modern day, you threw it back in my face and locked me away with the Cluster's stinking remnants. Then gave my world's new riches to moribund families without the guts to accept the inevitable truth. Well, now I've found something to throw back at you. That same truth."

"And what truth is that?"

"Humanity's isolation is over, and this world's the last major holdout. In years to come, we'll mingle with the Cluster and become a united whole, free from the sectarian thinking you've helped preserve here. And if I've got to become a tyrant to ensure that happens sooner rather than later, so be it."

Granger straightened, his composure visibly recovering. "I'll have you both for this. For Laurent-Leblanc. You'll spend the rest of your days in the deepest, darkest prison imaginable. You're so sure of your success that you've blurted everything out." He pulled at his lapel, revealing the tiny recording device set into the back of its pin. "And with this, you've signed your own death warrant."

Mercedes's eyes flicked from the lapel pin to his face. "So, you still have that old thing. I'd have expected you to get something better."

"You're finished, Mercedes. You've fallen for the oldest villain's downfall in the book, the need to talk."

She laughed, a high mocking laugh that sounded off to her own ears. "And you've fallen for something, too. Do you think I'd have told you anything or met you at all if there'd been the slightest chance of you revealing me? That thing hasn't been recording or broadcasting since you came within three yards of me. And I doubt anyone would take your word alone. No, don't move." Granger had started, and Mercedes raised a warning hand. "You're being covered. Bapti is an excellent shot. Not the way I hope you'll go, but she will shoot if she has to."

Granger was sweating, visibly struggling to stay calm. "You're still going to pay for this. If you insist on toppling me, I'm dragging you down, too. As I said, you've signed your death warrant."

"You did that yourself at the event you attended. Remember? I asked you about Noirtier. You answered without so much as a twitch. You must've really hated him to do that. You knew the kind of man he was."

"He was like you, a reactionary who'd have ruined the planet. But I—"

"Salvaged it? Always that tired old phrase. The refuge of a bigot who'd let this planet fester if it served his interests. You know, if you'd been even half-way decent about anything you've done, I wouldn't have needed to do this."

"You're going to kill me?"

"No. Death's too simple. Too merciful. The three of you, under your guidance I've no doubt, condemned me to a very slow and horrible death in the depths of the d'If. I thought it only right that I do the same. Laurent-Leblanc may have been the one to mobilize the elite against me, but you pulled the strings. You're the puppet master who makes this world dance to any tune you desire. Any who displease you are removed, and any who threaten the system are made its public enemies, as you did with all my old government."

"You speak of your government as if they were some group of chess pieces you can move around a board."

"That coming from you? Talk about hypocrisy." The grin grew broader still. "You see, Georges, I left Laurent-Leblanc's fate to chance. But not you. You I had to be sure of. But none of you deserve just to die. You must suffer as I suffered, be humiliated and vilified by the people who once fawned over you as if you were Ancient Earth's Second Coming. Then, perhaps, you can feel death's release."

"I won't let you—"

"Now."

There was a distant *"phut,"* and Granger gave a hiss and clutched at his neck. The tiny soluble dart had struck home, just as Bapti assured her it would. Mercedes rose from the bench and faced Granger, cocking her head slightly, adopting the tone of a headmistress addressing the less well-endowed members of a class.

"Have you ever heard of Compumentia? It's the human name for an enzyme unique to Kavki physiology. It's a key part of their regenerative capabilities and allows them to adapt their bodies the way they do with minimal impact. Ekri can handle it without too much difficulty, and it's been used to treat war wounds or similar injuries. But it's also got some peculiar side effects on Feles and humans. To Feles, it's a deadly poison which causes organ failure. To humans, it triggers what can best be described as a toxic psychosis. It's almost entirely untraceable after a day or so, and there's no antidote."

Granger's eyes widened. "You… you wouldn't dare—"

"It'll already be taking effect now. Laffw said it'd take effect in five to ten minutes for an average-sized human."

"You… bitch. This is murder."

"No, not exactly. I'm not actually killing you. You'll probably have a long and comfortable life ahead of you in an asylum. Maybe nursed and cared for when you don't have the brains to feed yourself or change your clothes. Grand Prosecutor Georges de Granger, I bid you farewell. We shall not meet again."

Mercedes took the path at a brisk walk, leaving Granger standing by the bench. There were two other people just coming into view up ahead, maybe five minutes' walk away. No one she knew, but even so, best to replace her mask. She reached a bush and ducked behind it, watching through a gap in the foliage as the human couple approached Granger, who was leaning against the bench. They approached, seemed to recognize the figure, and appeared to ask whether he was okay.

His reply was a yell that carried clearly to her ears. "Silence, or I'll have you removed and executed for contempt of court."

Goodness, it had worked faster than expected. She watched, grinning like a demented clown, as Granger turned away from the stunned couple and wandered down the path, occasionally staggering as if his sense of balance had gone. As he passed by the bush, she heard him repeating something, a phrase from an obscure Ancient Earth poem.

"Had not the duchess some share in the business? Had not the duchess some share in the business? Had not the duchess some share in the business?"

The local Law Officers would find him soon enough, take him into medical custody, and then would begin the long process. He would be taken in by the authorities and given some final abode where he couldn't harm himself. To live the rest of his life in quiet ignorance, away from her.

For a brief moment, she was sick and disgusted by the whole affair, but only the briefest moment. She would never falter, never waver. The burning desire to reclaim her throne renewed. Laurent-Leblanc had been left to his own devices and accepted death. Duncan would come next. Gretchen she would treat with what kindness she could. Faces and deeds drifted through her mind. Noirtier and her other allies, her own suffering, the Ekri of Qalaa's

Prospect, and others unknown who had likely suffered at his hands. This act she would never regret.

Bapti appeared at her shoulder. "Was that well done?"

"*Brilliantly* done."

"Before we part, my mistress wishes to know…. Did you have any hand in Ali's desertion?"

Mercedes's eyes locked with those of the Kavki, implacable and unyielding. "Would it matter if I did? We can talk about it later. I think I'll return to my new rooms. You go back to Laffw. All that's left now is watching Andréa's little show, then the journey to Argo, and on to the arranged destination." Her next words were little more than a whisper, spoke to a nearby bunch of flowers as Bapti retreated from sight. "Two down. One to go."

# FILE 18

## THE ONE WHO LIVED

*When we came to cliff's great height,*
*We looked upon the sea below.*
*And I, in seeing such a great cascade,*
*knew our love was short and slight.*
*I longed for days of first romance,*
*When all the world was sleek and bright.*
*I longed for days now gone for good,*
*and heard you quietly slip away.*

—Stanza from Fingal Dee's "Love's Sickness"

NEW DUBAI WAS in shock on this final day of the Grand Assizes, the day when Andréa Manfredi would be tried for the attempted murder of Marquess Malcolm Vorn-Solari. All were distracted from this otherwise sensational trial by a double tragedy that Herma only just understood. The disgrace and death by vendetta of Viscount-General Henri Laurent-Leblanc, and the sudden mental breakdown of Grand Prosecutor de Granger had hit like dual thunderbolts. She'd been brought by her parents, but now found a place to sit near Malcolm, who'd been brought with his father the duke.

"Hello."

Malcolm smiled. "Hi. Nice to see you. I'm glad you're here. I couldn't face this alone."

Herma hadn't smiled so broadly for some time. "My parents have been insufferable recently. Ever since the news broke yesterday about Laurent-Leblanc."

Malcolm revealed his ignorance, so Herma told him about the tragic events. He was shocked but took the news well.

"And now this news about Prosecutor de Granger's illness," continued Herma. "It's making my parents say terrible things. They're saying the duke's not the best leader if his associates meet such terrible fates, and…."

Malcolm frowned. "They're thinking of canceling the engagement?"

"I don't know. I've tried asking Mother, but she doesn't answer. I daren't ask Father. I don't want you getting hurt by all this."

"I'll try asking Pappy and Mammy. We're going there later today."

"Where is your mother now?"

"On Argo."

Herma looked at Malcolm's puckering face. She laid a hand gently on his shoulder. "Something bothering you?"

"Herma… why did you change your mind about me? I feel like you've been kinder to me lately."

"You've matured. We all do at some point. Well, *most* do. You aren't so wrapped up in your position. And when we were held hostage all those weeks ago, you didn't think about yourself. You looked after me."

"Of course. That's what anyone would do."

Herma shook her head regretfully. "Not anyone."

"You mean like your parents?"

"They know being poor. And I'm afraid they'd do anything not to return to that state again, even at the expense of…. I don't know what's going to happen in the future. But—I never thought I'd be saying this to you—I hope it involves the two of us."

Malcolm placed a hand on hers. For a moment, he seemed almost like an adult taking the hand of his beloved. But no, they were both still children, open to the whims of their parents and the rules of society. She was eventually summoned back by her parents. It was a struggle getting through the gallery, which was packed almost to capacity. Finally, the court ceremony began.

She settled near the front so she could see and watched Grand Attorney Glas and an up-and-coming Prosecutor called Syruis Akwar appear, along with twelve jurors balanced by gender and people from across New Dubai. Then the guards escorted the prisoner in. Andréa looked defiant even in plain clothes. The gallery broke into whispers, quickly checked by the usher's voice.

Finally, the judge Goddard appeared, and the ceremonial cycle of the court was completed.

Andréa stood in the dock with a strange expression on his face. There was calm acceptance, but also a smug confidence that made Herma both anxious and angry. How dare he sit there smiling like that? Yes, it was a smile, not very well disguised. Goddard's voice took charge, a clear contralto bell in the stuffy clamber of metal, wood, and glass.

"Andréa Manfredi, you are charged with assault and attempted murder against Marquess Malcolm Vorn-Solari. How do you plead?"

Andréa raised his head and looked directly at the judge. "If you please, Your Honor, there is a slight error in your indictment. Andréa Manfredi is not my real name, and I do not feel able to be charged under it."

There was a murmur within the court, as if someone had spoken a forbidden word. The usher banged her staff to restore silence. Goddard responded, her voice unchanged.

"Then please state your true name."

"Before I say anything further, I would ask that you clarify a point. Have you monitors in this courtroom that measure my physiology and would detect any attempt to lie?"

"Of course."

"Then I'm content, Your Honor, to answer any questions."

Herma's stomach twitched. Why was he doing this, making sure of something that must be obvious to anyone? Courtrooms always had that kind of thing installed. It had become a fictional trope to subvert their use. Her eyes remained fixed on Andréa, though Goddard's voice remained the backing soundtrack to her thoughts.

"Now that clarification has been made, you will please state your name. Or if you cannot, state the names of your parents."

"Your Honor, I wasn't named at birth, though my foster parents gave me the name of 'Boy' or 'Runt' more often than not. The name I most commonly took for my business was Bernedetti, which many in this court may recognize." There was a visible and audible discomfort among some of those present. "I don't know my mother's name, as I was taken from her within minutes of my birth, but I did discover the identity of my father and the events surrounding my conception."

"If you know your father's name, say it."

"Duncan Vorn."

There was a sudden rush of speech through the court. Herma darted a glance at her prospective father-in-law. His face looked like a mask, stiff and unnatural, while he reached out to grip his son's hand as if for support. Andréa *must* be lying. He couldn't be. The usher's staff did little to quell the gallery's sibilant murmurs, and it took Goddard's stentorian yell to quiet the court.

"Silence in court. Prisoner, remember that you are under oath. We will not tolerate such jests in this place."

"It was no jest, Your Honor. It's the absolute truth. My father is the man once known as Duncan Vorn. Now Duncan Vorn-Solari, Duke of New Dubai. If you want to quibble, you could say that I believe I'm speaking the truth."

The prosecutor spoke. "Your Honor, this is madness. He must be deranged."

Andréa's reply was irritating, delivered in such an annoyingly assured way. "If you doubt me, have my DNA examined. Your current duke's DNA should be on public record."

Goddard's words didn't match her even tone. "This is highly irregular. You may be removed for contempt of court. But since this will little delay proceedings, I think we can accede to your request."

No one was asking the duke anything. He wasn't even speaking. Herma looked again, still saw only the mask. Malcolm was next to him, looking confused and terrified. The whole process was carried out in a matter of seconds. A sample of Andréa's blood was taken and compared to that of the duke. The results were positive, a filial match between Andréa and Duncan.

The judge's calm had been broken, and she snapped at the prisoner. "Explain this at once."

Andréa nodded, so sickeningly smug. "I must start with events prior to my birth, but be assured they are the truth, supported by documents I've given to Attorney Glas. Duncan Vorn was having a secret affair with a servant on the estate of a friend on this planet. This friend was the former owner of Château Auteuil. He was young then, a carefree man expected to do such things. But I needn't elaborate on why such a fling under the nose of a leading member of New Dubai's elite would cause a scandal, especially since one of those men was a close friend. I was born just over twenty years ago at Château Auteuil. My mother died giving birth to me, and I was sent away to a foster family on Vorn's order. Once I was old enough, I ran away from their cruelties and made my living any way I could. Which eventually brought me here, before this court and into my father's sight."

Herma all the time wanted there to be a sign, an alarm, a tell that this was some cruel practical joke. But nothing happened. No sound came. Truth, like a terrible stinking specter, was smothering Courtroom A. The cry from the duke made her and half a dozen others jump in their seats. She saw him rush toward to the gallery's balcony rail and stare down at the prisoner, his face white and frenzied. Andréa turned and stared up at the duke.

The duke seemed to croak rather than speak. "That night. That night at Château Auteuil. I knew I'd seen your face. I thought I'd seen it in some report, but… it's her face. Christine. My Christine. I—I never meant to…. Forgive me."

Everyone was stunned at the duke's apparent admittance of his indiscretion. The judge was struck dumb, the Councils were dithering, the jury looked at each other, the galleries were echoing with chatter, and even the stern usher seemed petrified. But two figures weren't caught up in the chaos. One was the baroness, the other the Kavki Laffw. The flesh squirmed across the back of Herma's neck. They were enjoying it.

Andréa's face had twisted into an expression of demonic fury, an insane rage breaking free of control. His voice rose in a shrieking challenge to the duke's words.

"Forgive? You dare ask *forgiveness* of me? You abandoned my mother and me, hid us away like shameful baggage, and left me to the delicate mercies of those monsters the law called parents. I scraped and lied and killed to live, while you married an heiress and sired a 'legitimate' child. That child had all the love that should've been mine. I hate you. I hate you *all*. All your gilded clothing and stuck-up morals, but you're no better than us. Hell, you're worse. You never suffered anything for your sins. Your wealth and charitable *mea culpas* cleansed you in the eyes of your adoring, sycophantic public. Now you've seen what your beloved leader's really like. A bastard's father, the sire of a criminal. What does that say about your precious nobility?"

Herma covered her ears just in time, as Andréa let out a hissing stream of invective that caused even greater chaos. The prisoner was rapidly restrained and removed, the court adjourned, and everyone left in a disordered scramble.

———————————

ON THE EVENING of the trial, Andréa sat in his cell with a strange smile on his face. It was as if his dreams were coming true. He had seen his father's face, and seen that father humiliated and broken. He may have been intended as a tool of Mercedes, but it was worth it. It had been nearly twelve hours since he was dragged from the court. After that first outburst, he didn't resist. What would be the point? He would be free very soon. The bail would be posted. After all, his actions still rested only on one person's word. And that person had been conspicuous by her absence.

"Tables turning." His words were mouthed behind his hand, a whisper to his secret self. "The pawn becomes a knight to fell the queen and her array of pawns. Not long now."

The minutes ticked by, and eventually the moment came. The guard on duty came up to the door and opened the cell.

"Get up. Someone's posted bail for you. You'll be getting a tracker bracelet, and if you fail to appear for your next trial…."

The words droned on, passing Andréa's ear. As Mercedes had said, bail was posted. An exorbitant amount no doubt given the severity of his crime but posted nonetheless. A bracelet was attached round his wrist, a tracker to stop him going away a certain distance or entering certain areas. He was led out into a day overcast and shaded by heavy rain.

The final words from the Law Officer stuck in his ear. "A car's waiting for you near the corner of the next street, down that alley. It's your ride. If you take off that bracelet, we'll know."

Andréa knew there was no car. Or at least, the car was not for him. He was a danger, and whether Mercedes knew it or not, he'd be removed. A tragic incident staged to look something like a suicide or an accident.

He walked briskly, the weight of the tracker bracelet chaffing his wrist. He turned down the alley pointed out by the guard, and saw the figure in the distance, wearing a waterproof top with a hood pulled over his face. The outline was unmistakably that of a Feles. So, Mercedes had sent her pet to take care of things.

Andréa approached with a smile.

"Glad to see you again. I didn't expect to be released so promptly. I suppose my testimony had a greater effect than anticipated. I hope you've got a means of taking off this bracelet. I could do it myself, of course, but…."

The Feles did not respond. Andréa approached slowly, maintaining his friendly expression even as he noted his enemy's hand staying in the pocket of his coat. The Feles took a step forward, a microsecond of hovering imbalance as one foot transferred to the other. Andréa lunged forward and struck with his hand, throwing the Feles off balance. Andréa's free hand grasped the Feles's coat and tore out the contents of the pocket. It was a short razor-sharp knife, the kind used by assassins.

"Hmm. Very nice. Time for a little payback."

Andréa shot forward, his instincts taking over. His opponent was too slow, and soon pinned against the wall. There was something wrong about the way he moved, something unlike Gaspard's usual movements. But that didn't matter. Mercedes must have sent him, so he must be Gaspard or someone close to him. Either way, this would be a message.

Andréa plunged the knife into the Feles's back up to the hilt. The Feles let out a hoarse cry of pain, soon overtaken by gasping gurgles as the blade was driven home again, and again, and again. The ground beneath them became stained with a crimson scum, while the Feles's contortions grew weaker. Finally, he slumped completely, and Andréa pulled away. The knife was put to a final use as Andréa inserted its tip into the bracelet's pinhole lock. As the bracelet clattered to the floor, Andréa let his mouth curl around in a rictus expression. The rain was already washing the blood from his hands.

"Now it's time to leave. Time to pay a visit to my dear father's family on Argo and make sure that bitch gets everything she deserves."

---

GASPARD PACED UP and down. Echo should've been back by now with Andréa's blood on his hands. If this was an example of service when he wasn't being paid in rape, he was glad they wouldn't be meeting again after this. They'd arranged everything remotely, not coming into contact except to confirm the kill. Mercedes had to know for sure, as did Gaspard. Andréa was a danger to them all.

"Come on, come on. God, if you're doing this to spite me, I swear I'll—"

He turned sharply, then stopped, eyes widening. A familiar outline emerged from the thickening rain, Ali in wet weather gear. She approached at speed and stopped just in front of him, a strange expression on her face.

"Ali? What are you doing here?"

A look, a shrug, and an unexpected smile was enough. She was here of her own will and keeping an eye on things.

"Has something gone wrong?"

Ali's reply was to gesture down the street toward the alleyway where Echo was supposed to meet Andréa. Gaspard's heart lurched and he let himself be pulled along by the Kavki, barely noticing the rain soaking into his leggings and through the gaps in his coat. They turned into the lane's shadows, and it was less than a second before the crumpled figure came into focus. Gaspard walked forward slowly, seeing the ragged breathing of his old tormentor. He stopped a few paces short, struggling to control himself.

"Echo...."

Echo's eyes opened painfully. He looked into Gaspard's eyes, a weak but still ironic smile crossing his face.

"So, you *did* come looking for me. I thought you'd given up on me for good. I... I wanted to see you one last time."

"Don't think this changes anything. Where's Andréa?"

"Gone... after... your boss. And her... family."

Gaspard looked at Ali, his eyes asking a question. She shook her head. There was no point helping him even if they'd wanted to. Turning back to Echo, Gaspard felt the storm of emotions rise anew. Lust, disgust, guilty affection, revulsion, all mingled into a single indescribable whole that couldn't be named or admitted. Echo coughed, sending a spurt of blood across his chin, then stared up at him with fading eyes.

"Even if you wanted to, I don't want to be saved. I... I want to die with my illusions intact. Andréa would've killed us both. He mistook me for you, and... if you really want...." His face twisted with dying pains. "Vistaz. That's my... real name."

A lump like a rotten fruit bulged in Gaspard's throat. "Name. My true name's... Qaloch."

"And?"

"And I hate you. Vistaz, I hate you. You're a sick piece of shit."

Echo's mouth split into a grin showing bloodstained teeth. "That's… the… sp—"

The last word vanished in a final gurgle. Echo's eyes rolled up, his body relaxed, and he slumped down onto the ground. Gaspard walked carefully over to him, checked his pulse, then closed the lolling eyes. He turned to Ali.

"You saw it happen, didn't you?"

She nodded.

"And you did nothing?"

Her expression spoke volumes. Hadn't he wanted this resolution? Alive, Echo could've pursued him for who knew how long. Gaspard hadn't the stomach to kill anyone, nor could he have betrayed Echo to the authorities. This was the best way, for all its gruesome qualities. He rose and approached Ali, his voice sounding unpleasantly calm.

"I assume you know exactly where Mercedes would go?" Ali nodded, and he continued to speak in the same level tone. "And you want to help that boy, don't you? And the girl?" She again nodded. "Then we haven't got time to waste. We must go to Argo."

# FILE 19

## DUCAL PRIDE AND POWER

*That year was seen as a terrible time. So much loss of life
that some thought the world itself might crumble into space.
This was of course an exaggeration, but something close to the truth.
I felt it myself as I looked upon the scene presented, and pondered
my own view. I had seen some, if not all, of the players. And I
knew not what drove such a terrible episode of bloodshed.*

—Excerpt from Fingal Dee's "On The Tragedy of New Dubai"

HERMA WANTED TO scream. Shut in her room like an animal, her life was once more subject to another's whim. It had happened immediately after coming back from the trial. Her father had taken her into their living room and told her in the tenderest way possible that her "heart's wish" would be granted.

"Had I known what that scoundrel was like, I would never have allowed you to become tied to his son. I know you have never liked the match, so—"

"Father I—"

"Please, my girl, don't interrupt. This is for your own good."

After many long-winded words, the plain facts emerged. The engagement between Malcolm Vorn-Solari and Hermathruda Berggarten would be officially dissolved by the end of the day. She would be free to find the attentions of young men who were better suited and she would like more. All through her father's hollow platitudes, Herma wanted to hit him. When she was finally shown up to her room, her father locked her in. Her family refused to trust her. They knew she had overcome her revulsion at the match and refused to let her to jeopardize their future.

"A curse on them. On them both."

Herma finally screamed, lashing out at her desk and knocking several objects to the floor. She rubbed her hand where it had struck the wood, then looked out the window. She saw her future through that window, a future she now detested more than she had her arranged marriage with Malcolm. Malcolm, pompous and brattish, yet mellowing with age and acquaintance. Now, when he most needed her support, she was being pulled away from him by hands she had grown to detest.

It took no time to think. Pulling a small box from the compartment in her bed, she drew out her little bank card and checked its balance. There was just enough for a one-way shuttle ticket to Argo. She changed from the stifling gown her parents had chosen into a plain trouser suit and boots. Stuffing her card and a few other bits in her pocket, she set her media player to her favorite setting, chose a lengthy playlist, then went to the window.

If anyone had told Herma a year before that she would be sneaking out of her house to reach Malcolm, she would have called them idiotic or insane. The large sill supported her weight as she shuffled out and closed the window. The Berggarten house was built on three levels with a flat terraced roof housing a garden. An emergency ladder stretched down the corner of the house just out of view of the gate. Her room was on the top floor, and by standing tall and reaching up, Herma grabbed onto the edge of the garden wall and hauled herself up. After checking the garden was deserted, she clambered over the wall and tumbled into its border.

Quickly moving to the ladder, she began her climb down. She tried not to look down as she descended rung by rung, her stomach doing somersaults as freak winds buffeted her. There was a break in the rain that had persisted over the past few days, but the ladder was still damp to the touch, and her hand slipped more than once. When she reached the ground, she breathed a deep sigh of relief. Next was getting out of the small residential area where her house was placed. It was an enclosed piece of suburbia with a local shuttle port within two miles' walk. All she needed to do was get there without being spotted by her parents.

It was easier than she had imagined, quite simple to clamber up onto the boundary wall and through the one-way forcefields which kept unwanted people out. Then she ran round the back of the house and emerged into the main street out of sight of her house. From there it was a simple walk to the shuttle port, where she purchased a ticket for Argo. It involved a change at Amasian City Shuttle Port, then several miles' walk from Argo Shuttle Port to the duke's estates. It would be late evening on Argo before she arrived.

Boarding the shuttle was the most nerve-wracking part of the adventure. Someone might stop her, ask her where her parents were. But even on New Dubai, people could recognize an independent young girl when they saw one. She put on an air of confidence as she mounted the stair behind an adult couple and presented her ticket. No-one questioned her. All she had to do was keep up that facade.

At least, she assumed so. But as she was settling down for the prolonged flight and felt the gravity field fluctuate with warp activation, her eyes caught a pair of familiar figures on the seats across from her own. A Feles and a Kavki, figures she remembered seeing alternately with the Baroness Clarisse. What were their names again? She remembered the Kavki was called Ali. And the Feles was…. Some instinct told her the baroness was involved in some way, and her servants might get her there with less fuss.

"Excuse me."

The Feles, the one nearest to her, turned and gave an engaging smile. "Yes?"

"Is the baroness on board?"

"Baroness? I don't understand."

Herma glanced at the Kavki. "Your companion's the servant of the Baroness Clarisse, isn't she? And I think you're one, too.

The Kavki looked at the girl, and the Feles seemed uneasy. "I don't know where you could've got that idea."

"Show me another Kavki on New Dubai that's got those scars. I know who she is, and I guess you're that other servant. What'd you want in Argo?"

Herma's face was serious, and the Feles clearly understood something, even if it wasn't the full truth. He spoke with a solemn gravity.

"Herma Berggarten, our former mistress is en route to Argo, and we want to make sure nothing happens to Malcolm Solari. If you wish, you can come with us. It will be risky."

Herma considered it for some little time. Could she trust them? She had little choice at this point, and they seemed sincere. The Kavki even looked concerned, almost… caring? Without them, she didn't have the money to get to Malcolm's home except by walking, which might take hours. She didn't know exactly how far away their estate was from Argo's main shuttle port, didn't know how to find a taxi, and didn't know how to do anything else beyond her scatterbrained plan.

"Very well. But you'll help us in return. Help Malcolm and me get away from this place."

Both the Feles and the Kavki nodded, and Herma sighed with relief. There was still the chance she had to run for the hills if this were a trap or double-cross, but that didn't matter anymore. She'd forgotten her age, very young by human days even today. On Ancient Earth, she would have been considered unreliable, unable to move about without adult supervision. But within her had grown a resolve that now wouldn't be quelled. A resolve to see this ordeal through to the end, to allow herself and Malcolm to forge their own future.

———————

ON THE PLANET Argo, the northern hemisphere was well into autumn, the leaves turning shades of brown and gold dropping from the trees. Sitting at his study window, Duncan contemplated the mass of Ancient Earth plants that had been cultivated, salvaged, and grown into a vast forest on this verdant world, one of humanity's later acquisitions within the Cluster. The wind blew, bringing with it a fall of leaves across his view. The fall of his reputation seemed to mirror those twirling, nutrient-starved leaves.

He'd always liked it here on the ducal estates. It was a relatively modest house far removed from New Dubai's culture, held a nostalgic quality due to its chosen trees and bushes, and was surrounded by stands of wilderness allowed to go fallow once universal welfare and cheap cultivation towers had alleviated general hunger. There were no living servants, only drones floating or rolling around the building. They were comforting somehow, without judgment or opinions or anything beyond their programmed duty. It had come with Gretchen upon their marriage. Mercedes had been almost thankful to give it to them, her old family home far removed from New Dubai.

Thought she'd get them out of the way so she could carry on with her plans. Duncan almost laughed. He remembered the day Granger and Laurent-Leblanc strode across the lawn toward them and told them about what they'd planned. It had really been over ten years. Nearly eleven now.

He rose and looked into an ornamental mirror positioned between two pieces of artwork. His face was drawn, sullen, with a set look in his eyes he couldn't place for a moment. Then it hit right between the eyes. It was the kind of expression prisoners were said to have had on Ancient Earth when under sentence of death. He barely noticed his hands twisting in and out of each other, his legs shuffling as if in an agitated dance. Finally, he swore and turned away from the mirror.

Damn them all. Their whispers, their lies, their scheming. He wished he had never agreed to any of this. He'd spent ten years in hell.

Everyone had turned on him, but it wasn't for him to blame them. His poor Christine might've laughed at them, but he could never laugh. He'd brought this on himself with foolish love, by listening to those who shouldn't have been given the chance of grasping power. New Dubai was humming with rumor and gossip, and closing his mail had been a necessity to save himself and his family from the flow of abuse and hollow consolations. He refused the people's pity and their bile. The last one he had seen before shutting it down was from Fingal Dee. It was just one paragraph amid a sea of white space.

> So, the mighty fall. Condolences are hollow, and glee is wicked. So let me just say this. To paraphrase a poet of Ancient Earth, let the good you do live after you and the evil be interred with your bones. But as I once said, no good deed is remembered when the evil is so much more exciting.

God, Fingal Dee had such a vicious tongue when she chose. Why Mercedes liked her at all was quite impossible to know. But it was still the kindest thing anyone had said since Andréa's trial.

Where was Andréa now? He'd been released on bail somehow, then vanished. A dead body had been found, a Feles with a false ID and no accessible DNA record. There was a security ring round the estate, but for whatever reason he didn't think they'd stop Andréa. That young man, the son he should've acknowledged from the first, was out there somewhere and ready to take revenge against him.

*Revenge.* Why was that familiar? Why did it strike a chord in the depths of his disorderly mind? Laurent-Leblanc, Granger, himself, all brought low. Almost as if…. But that was impossible. The d'If had been destroyed, and she hadn't been reported as surviving. If she had, Granger would've thrown a fit. There's no way she would've waited any more than she did before attempting her reforms that would've bankrupted New Dubai's ruling families to fuel their White Oil industry, in addition to making her the planet's supreme leader. Maybe if she hadn't tried to do both at once, maybe she'd have mellowed by now if she had survived. Maybe if she saw Malcolm, things might begin to mend in some way.

As if on cue, the door opened, and the boy's face peered inside. Duncan looked up, becoming the smiling father with an effort.

"Come in, Malcolm."

The young man entered gingerly and stood some little distance from his father. His eyes were turned down, as if avoiding his gaze or afraid to look at his father's face.

"Pappy, I want to ask you something. It's… personal."

"Go ahead. I'll always tell you anything. Within reason, of course."

Duncan's laugh was light, but Malcolm's face remained serious. "I… I want to know…. That horrible man, Andréa. Is he *really* your son?"

It took some moments for Duncan to answer. His head fell, and he twisted and fiddled with his hands until the fingers grew sore.

"Yes. It's true. It was a fling. Nothing serious."

"But it *was* serious." Malcolm spoke with the innocent indignation of childhood. "You said when you married Mammy, you'd never loved anyone else. That you were free of anything else. But you had a son. Wasn't that something else?"

"Malcolm, I can't expect you to understand. Sometimes, when you're an adult, you have to keep secrets from others. Especially if you're a ruler."

"That doesn't make sense. You told me to be honest, a leader who wouldn't lie to his people. How can I not lie when my father lied?"

"I told you that so you wouldn't make the same mistakes as me. Parents make mistakes, and in an ideal world they make sure children don't make the same ones. Just as I told your mother nothing because I didn't want to hurt her."

"That doesn't make sense."

That repetition struck like a bullet. Father and son stared at each other, Duncan struggling to find any words to answer the boy's impassioned statement. Then the front door alarm sounded, and Duncan broke away.

"Stay here, son. Don't come until I call."

Malcolm nodded, still frowning in anger. Duncan reached the study door and opened it carefully. Squinting through the crack, he watched as Gretchen led someone quickly down the hall and pushed them into the living room. The silhouette was hideously familiar. What the hell was the baroness doing here now?

Like the activation of a falling block store shining on a display, the final section of the puzzle fell into place, and he saw what a blind fool he'd been. Stupid, slow, complacent, mindless. Malcolm had come up behind him.

"Is something wrong?"

"I mean it, Malcolm. Stay here."

Leaving his son in his study, Duncan walked stealthily to the living room door. Pressing an ear to it, he heard the two voices, his wife and....

"Why the hell did you come here?"

"Simple. Two of my three enemies are dealt with. I can't allow your husband to escape the consequences of his actions."

"After everything you've done, you want to punish him more?"

"I owe it to you as much as to myself. You want to live the rest of your life knowing what that man did? What he tried to do? He may have been led astray by Granger and Laurent-Leblanc, though I doubt anyone could be as entirely ignorant as that, but he's still culpable for Andréa. And letting those others have their way with my world."

"Andréa. Yes, a man you dragged here to show him up."

"That's neither here nor there."

"You've been planning a long time."

"Longer than you want to know. And now everything's coming together. Just two small matters, and I'll be ready to make my return."

"What matters?"

"The first is your husband."

Duncan threw open the doors and spoke in his darkest tone. "Yes, the first matter is me... sister-in-law."

Gretchen looked as white as snow, and as the other turned she removed the mask that had been part of her disguise. God, he should've seen it from the start, from the first time he'd seen her up close. The hair was a different shade, the clothes different, that mask hid the scars, but that poise and arrogant tone was still there. He should've seen it ten times over, but he didn't want to see it. Now he had to see, to admit to himself what a blind fool he'd been.

Mercedes's mouth curled into an unpleasant expression. "How right you are, brother-in-law. May I say I'm almost shocked I got to this point. Good plans aside, I should've been rumbled ten times over."

"I've been abominably slow, I'll admit."

"Poor qualifications for a duke—even for such a backward planet as New Dubai."

"If you've got anything to say, just say it. We're past the point of posturing or justifying our actions as anything but a family squabble."

"As you wish. You never did stand on ceremony. Put simply, you're finished, and there's little you can do to stop my triumphant return to power. Your two stalwart supporters are ruined, you are disgraced, and soon the full truth shall be known about your duplicitous actions. I offer you and Gretchen the same offer you gave me. But this time, I shall leave no avenues open for a return."

"Yeah, and that stopped you?"

"You are better than I am at keeping a promise. It's one of your better qualities, I have to admit."

The two glared at each other, then Duncan felt his own mouth curling up. "If I had a glove, I'd throw it at you. That's the traditional human way of demanding a duel, isn't it?"

Mercedes's laugh could be darker than an eclipse. "Yes. Very suitable for a planet stuck in our kind's past. We needn't be that theatrical, though it *would* be in character with the society you helped preserve on New Dubai. One question. Which should be considered the offended party? By your lights, we both may qualify."

"Either suits me."

"In that case, I'll leave the choice of weapon to you."

"Rapiers. In the Shadow Glade. Ten minutes."

Mercedes adjusted her cream-colored gloves. "I accept."

"Mercedes, Duncan, *please.*" Gretchen stepped between them, grasping her sister's shoulders. "Surely this can be resolved some other way."

Duncan's voice sounded alien to his ears. "No, Gretchen. There's no other way now. Your sister has guaranteed that. I take it you still know your way, Mercedes?"

"Of course. I'll be waiting."

Mercedes pulled herself free of Gretchen's grasp and stalked from the room. Gretchen trailed after Duncan as he went to the cabinet in his study, which held dueling blades, lengths of metal with edges made from heated plasma conduits. In shape, they looked like an Ancient Earth relic, but on their highest setting they could cut through steel. As he pulled open the cabinet and took the blades down, Gretchen grabbed his arm.

"Please, Duncan, take her offer. We can leave this behind."

Duncan looked into his wife's pleading face. "And let her win outright? No, Gretchen. This is our only chance to take a stand."

"But she could kill you."

"I know. But I must. It's my duty to you and myself. Do you really think she'd let us be free after everything she's been willing to do? Whatever happens, keep Malcolm safe."

Deaf to any further pleas, Duncan strode out of the house and into the woods surrounding their home. Ten minutes later, he passed into the small clearing where Mercedes waited. She had tossed off her skirt and small cape, showing the practical leggings and boots beneath. He in turn removed his coat and tossed it over a tree branch. She didn't look round as he approached with their weapons, only turning when he coughed and held out the blade.

"They're both the same, I assure you."

Mercedes took the blade and activated it. "I believe you. You know, you're the only person who ever fought me to a draw."

"I was going easy on you. Didn't want Gretchen to think less of you."

"How civil. Well, let's get this over with."

"Yeah, let's. *En garde,* Mercedes Solari."

"*Touché,* Duncan Vorn."

The two backed away a few steps, activated their blades, and made the sign. It felt like a strange pantomime scene, or a sequence from some Ancient Earth fable, but it was real. This was a real fight, a final confrontation for their futures and honor. And deep in his heart was the crawling fear, the unspoken knowledge that he might not win. The thought faded into nothingness as the sizzling clash of metal rang in his ears.

———————————

GRETCHEN'S STOMACH TWISTED and twitched, pushing at her conscience. The knowledge of any possible future following this idiotic duel clawed at her mind. What could she do? How could she stop it? She couldn't ever persuade Mercedes of anything, and Duncan was a stubborn man for all his kindness. She wanted to run out and stop them, to throw herself between them. But how the hell was she to do that?"

"Mammy, what's Pappy doing?"

Gretchen's heart felt like it was about to burst. "He's— it's a private talk."

"Who was that woman?"

"She's—she's my... sister."

"Sister? I don't remember you having a sister."

"Well, it's been a long time. And... and...."

She couldn't do it. How could she tell him about their past? She hadn't known the full extent of Duncan's transgressions until Mercedes and the media revealed them over the span of a fortnight. But what about her part? A second child who saw her father kill her mother, who took her own kind of petty revenge on his health and well-being, the quicker to allow her sister to take his place. Her sweet, protective, strong-willed sister. Strong-willed, or was it stubbornness? Sweet and protective, or possessive?

"Mammy?"

"Stay here, Malcolm."

"No, I don't want to."

The memory of that raging man in Courtroom A came back. "Fine, come on. But don't interfere."

She grabbed her son's hand and set off at a run for the Shadow Glade, with its ring of copper beeches cloaking the ground in darkness each autumn. It was a little over five minutes run to get there, but it felt like five hours stumbling round roots and bushes, following the old winding path now half-covered by fallen leaves. It was starting to rain, a soft autumnal shower that peppered her hair and weighed on her clothes. In the distance, a hissing, spitting sound reached her ears, and the sparking clash of plasma flashed through the trees. Then came scuffles, grunts, breaths, and exclamations.

Finally, at the edge of the clearing, the dramatic scene unfolded. Duncan had always been a fine duelist, but Mercedes was perhaps the best. Yet something hindered her movements, either age or lack of practice, for Duncan was holding his own, even pushing back against her onslaughts. Their blades glowed only faintly, but the slightest contact would still burn and scar. Malcolm pulled at her clothing, but she thrust him back with material authority.

"Stay here."

Gretchen advanced slowly, staying close to the edge of the trees. The conflict before her was something from a nightmare. The rain had strengthened, undoing the careful styling of her sister's curling locks. She looked old, worn, bitter, but still defiant. She didn't want either to win but couldn't bear that either should lose. The hand of familial and the hand of married love had taken either arm and were tearing her in two.

Duncan had the advantage. Mercedes's ankle snarled on a rootlet, and she tripped, tumbling a little and rising with a wince. Her ankle must have twisted, and Duncan saw it. He stepped forward slowly, holding her at sword point, the glowing tip of its plasma resting so close she must feel its heat. His voice had become cold.

"Do you concede?"

Mercedes's own voice was also cold, bitter, and angry. "Do you really think you'll be safe if I do? Will your wife be safe? Or your son? No, that should be *sons.*"

"Going back on your words. Why did I expect that?"

"Words given without sincerity hold no meaning. Don't you know that?"

Duncan shook his head. "No. I guess not. We neither of us thought this duel would end in an honorable fashion."

"No. Well? What're you waiting for?"

Torn apart. Being torn apart. All her life, she'd been torn apart by her different loves. She couldn't lose either, couldn't let either carry on with this farce. Whatever madness was in her, it couldn't be ignored.

Gretchen ran forward. "No! *Stop!*"

Duncan turned, and Mercedes shuffled away from him. Duncan looked at the pair, his face a mask of disbelief and disappointment.

His voice cut like the blade he wielded. "Leave, Gretchen. This isn't your concern."

"It's not my concern that you're about to kill my own sister? My only family outside you and Malcolm?"

Mercedes laughed. "You mustn't get sentimental, sister."

Duncan cut across Mercedes's jibe. "Gretchen, don't get in the way. She's a danger to us and this world. Look what she's done to Laurent-Leblanc and Granger. Whatever their crimes, they didn't deserve what she gave them."

Mercedes smiled in an unpleasant way. "You think this world has any kind of justice or need for fair and altruistic dealing? No. There is no higher justice in the universe, let alone the Cluster. You're still too naive to see things for what they really are. I more than accept it. I've embraced it. Whatever comes, I won't grieve for my victims. I've pursued my goals and will accept my fate."

Duncan raised his blade. "Then your fate is to die with your goal thwarted."

"Duncan, no!"

Before Duncan could strike, Gretchen reached out and pulled his arm to one side. Mercedes lunged forward, and Gretchen was thrown back on the floor. Duncan was back on the defensive, and the rain mingled with Gretchen's tears.

"No. Please, stop. Both of you, stop."

They were deaf to her, their faces and bodies consumed. The madness broke across her mind like waves across the rocks. Her father, her mother, her friends. She'd lost them all. She couldn't lose her sister, her husband, her son. No, she couldn't lose them again.

*"Stop!"*

She barreled forward, hearing a distant boy's cry, the singing of two plasma blades aimed with a mutual fatal aim. She dived forward, and her world became a fog of pain.

---

MERCEDES BARELY UNDERSTOOD what had happened. She and Duncan had been charging at each other, their momentum carrying them forward. Then Gretchen's form appeared between them, and their dual weight pushed the heated blades into her flesh. Both combatants threw themselves back, then Duncan caught hold of Gretchen as she tumbled backward. The wound had only partly cauterized, so blood began seeping across her clothing.

"Gretchen." Duncan's voice was painful to hear. *"Gretchen...."*

Light was fading fast from Gretchen's eyes. The blades had gone through her chest and must have pierced her lungs and heart. A hollow rattle sounded inside her, the remnants of her heart crying out for the last of her family's death. Her sister's eyes opened, then her arm rose weakly, reaching toward her.

"R... oly-pol... y...."

Mercedes's mouth formed words without sound. "Twinkle."

Gretchen's mouth twisted into a pained smile. Then her eyes glazed, her breath ceased, and her hand dropped to the ground. A child's sharp cry split the air, the boy Malcolm from the edges of the clearing. He was just standing there, frozen in horror. Duncan picked up Gretchen's body and carried it to the edge of the clearing, then returned and picked up his sword. Mercedes could've stopped him, but her pounding heart rooted her feet. Fury, a rage like that of Typhon roaring at Olympus, filled her heart. Duncan met his son's eyes, made a sign with his hand, and the boy turned his face away.

Duncan turned to Mercedes, flicking his blade's heat to a white-hot glow. "Maybe you didn't plan this, but you've really had your revenge now. Your own sister, the woman I loved, killed by us in front of my son. Your own nephew."

"So?"

The response was flat, hollow, almost mocking. Foreign to her ears. Duncan bared his teeth, his voice a growl of rage.

"So to hell with everything else. It's you or me now."

Mercedes finally smiled, the rage bursting to the surface as she pushed her sword's heat up to match her opponent. "Yes, nothing else matters in this moment. Fate has delivered a sweeter revenge than I ever could. But she was still my sister. So then, *en garde.*"

"*Touché,* you bitch."

The rain hissed against their blades, creating streams of steam through the air. The rage married with a cold calculation, blocking the pain from her ankle and the sorrow in her heart, focusing on a single goal. Duncan Vorn would die today by her hand. Her revenge, complete and absolute, would be fulfilled.

Finally, the moment came. Mercedes had successfully blocked Duncan's attacks, ducking as he took a desperate swing, which cut halfway through one of the surrounding trees. Mercedes was hampered by the pain in her ankle, and as she stumbled out of the way of another swing, she pretended to let down her guard. The rage-blinded Duncan seized his chance and lunged. She hopped to one side, and he stumbled past her, exposing his back. She swung her blade down and cut into the back of his neck. The plasma sank with ease into his spine, cutting through the vital nerves. Duncan slumped to the ground. Death was immediate.

Mercedes stumbled back, briefly overwhelmed by pain and emotion. Another scream sounded, and she was dimly aware of Malcolm rushing forward and tumbling down next to his father. Duncan's head lay at an unnatural angle, the wound an ugly line of singed darkness. The boy's voice broke through the patter of rain and the raging of her mind.

"Pappy. Pappy. Get up. Pappy!" Malcolm turned and glared at Mercedes. "What've you done?"

Mercedes looked down at the boy. He looked so pathetic, so unready to face this cruel world. The world she'd stepped into the moment she was born, the world her father had left for her when he died. One crude mistake had cost her everything. Now she had gotten everything back. But what about this pathetic little child, the remnant of her brother's ill-gotten gains. The boy was looking up at her with a terrified expression.

"You. Why? You *monster!*"

Mercedes thought the words, speaking in a flat tone almost unlike her own. "I've completed my quarrel. The three I wished to topple have been toppled and will trouble me no more. All that remains is you."

Mercedes raised her sword as if about to strike the boy, then stopped. She had willingly left Laurent-Leblanc to his fate, gladly facilitated Granger's madness, joyfully struck down her brother-in-law, schemed, lied, and cheated to take back what was hers. It would be the matter of a second to strike this boy down, to rid herself of the last remnant of her past. Sever the past. Kill it with a single stroke.

Her hand hovered, questioning, the blade hissing in the drizzle, ready to slice the boy's head in two. She knew the risks if this child lived. He had seen his whole world destroyed, his life ruined, and seen the woman who had done it. He would do as she did, wait years and then return. It's how humans worked, an eye for an eye until the floor was red and white with gouged eyeballs squashed under the stumbling tread of the half-blinded. Better to kill him now, to end his misery and the danger to herself.

But no. She wouldn't—*couldn't*—let this final remnant of her sister die. Looking into Malcolm's face, nearly a dozen others stared back from his eyes. Gretchen, Duncan, Laurent-Leblanc, Granger, Gaspard, Ali, Andréa, the old warden Witton, the Ekri at Cape Life. Those dead because of her, those dead by her hand, those dead or ruined through her catalysis. They all stared up from the eyes of this young boy, the child of his sister's innocent love. Guilt fell upon her like the headman's axe.

Suddenly, unhinged to her own ears, she laughed. Who'd have thought it? After everything she'd done, she couldn't kill a child. She had caused death and madness, ruination and scandal, all in the name of her goals, and at the last she couldn't kill a little brat who would surely come for her again. Deactivating the rapier and tossing it to the ground, she looked down at Malcolm, her voice an impish blend of impassivity and emotional torment.

"Do as you will in the years to come. If I were you, I'd leave this place. It poisons the soul. It poisoned me, my parents, your parents, their friends, the sycophantic nobility of New Dubai. But maybe, just maybe, you've got a chance. To end this farcical cycle."

"Don't tell me what to do!"

"As you wish. Just remember."

Malcolm seemed about to speak but lowered his head. Nothing more was here now, nothing but useless memories. Her throat rattled, a half-hearted laugh drowning and restraining bitter sobs. Then, slowly, she turned and limped away from the clearing.

# FILE 20

## CRUEL RESOLUTIONS

*The consummate ruler keeps many strings ready to their bow.*
*This may seem a cliched analogy, but it remains true to this day.*
*They remain aware of any threat, ready for any attempt to seize power.*
*And they react with the swiftness of Ancient Earth's Venus Fly Trap.*
*That is how they endure. And how they prosper. And of those who survive,*
*they either flee or wither beneath their gaze. So history tells us.*

—Excerpt from Fingal Dee's "Politiká"

RAIN PATTERED DOWN as Herma passed through the estate's gate and down the long pathway through the surrounding woods. She ran ahead of Gaspard and Ali, who seemed to be taking a measured pace. It had been a hard journey from the shuttle port, with Gaspard needing to hijack a vehicle and take a circuitous route round surrounding patrols. They had no wet weather gear, and all three were soon drenched. Pausing at a branch in the path, Herma flicked locks of dripping hair from her eyes.

"That must be the way to the house." She pointed down the well-used path. "Eugh, this rain. I'll be glad to get inside somewhere. I hope the duke understands."

Neither of her companions responded. They seemed preoccupied with their own thoughts and troubles. Finally, they reached the house, Herma clutching her side where a stitch had formed. She looked at the house, then froze.

"Something's wrong. Why are those windows open on a day like this?"

Gaspard had come up next to her and was looking about them. Suddenly he gave a hiss, like a stifled gasp. Herma turned and saw a figure limping parallel to them, heading toward the path, a woman in sodden clothes sprinkled with half-washed blood, her hands shaking, hair hanging over a scarred absent face. Was that the baroness? But she looked so different, almost alien.

The woman stopped, turned to look at them, then spoke in a flat voice. "You want the duke's family? Follow the small trail over there to a clearing surrounded by copper beeches." She pointed to illustrate. "You'll find them there." Her eyes flashed toward Gaspard and Ali. "It seems you've made your choices. Don't get caught."

A fear gripped at Herma's heart and thoughts. The woman looked half-mad, twisted and tortured by some strong emotion. Her voice was so mechanical, her eyes flat and dead as if she couldn't see anything. Finally, she turned and limped away from them.

Before she was out of sight, the three ran along the indicated route, and with each step and stumble fear gnawed at Herma's heart. They eventually reached the small clearing and beheld the dreadful scene. Herma felt sick but couldn't turn her face away. The duke's body lay in the middle of the clearing, the duchess rested on a kind of repose on its edge, and Malcolm was kneeling next to the duke with a blank expression.

Herma managed to stumble forward and kneel next to Malcolm. She gripped his hand. It felt like a block of ice and barely returned her grip. He continued to stare vacantly as she took his shoulders and shook him gently.

"Malcolm. Come on, we need to leave here. Malcolm. Malcolm, please say something. *Malcolm.*" She looked toward where Ali was checking Gretchen's body. "Is she…?"

Ali turned and shook her head. Gaspard appeared from her peripheral and gently picked up Malcolm, carrying him like the soaked and exhausted child he was. There wasn't any need for instructions, no need for words. The three made their way back to the house and passed in through the open patio doors. Away from the rain in the heated house, her senses gradually returned. Gaspard had placed Malcolm in a chair drawn near to the fire, and Ali had vanished somewhere. Gaspard did his best to dry off the boy, then Herma, then himself with some pieces of cloth taken from the furniture.

A few minutes later, Ali returned with a tray bearing three cups. She handed them round to Gaspard, to Malcolm, then Herma. Herma didn't know where the drink had come from, or even clearly what it was, but it warmed her. Malcolm seemed to have recovered enough to take notice of his surroundings. He saw Herma, then looked round at Gaspard and Ali, then he balked, and his arms started flailing.

"No! No! Not you. Get away! Get away!"

Herma rushed up and gently caught the boy's hands. For a second, he fought her grip, then relaxed and slumped back into the chair. With an effort, Herma kept her calm and raised Malcolm's drink to his lips. He took some, then turned away, his eyes growing abruptly steely and blank. The same expression she'd seen on that woman's face.

"She killed them." Even his voice had become mechanical, flat, like hers. "My aunt killed them."

"Your *aunt?*"

"That woman. She was my aunt."

The illumination was swift and violent for Herma, who clutched the chair arm so as not to lose her balance. "I… this… you…"

Malcolm continued in the same mechanical tone. "I'll kill her. She killed them, so why shouldn't I kill her?"

Herma looked at his face. The laughing boy who had enjoyed being with her, who had been so arrogant and then so apologetic and gallant, was rapidly dying like a plant withered by flame. Now that face was cold. The face of an avenger. The face of that woman.

"No." Herma grabbed his arm and shook him violently. "No. I won't allow it. I won't let you ruin your life the way your aunt's ruined her own and so many other people's."

"Has she?"

"Yes, she has. She killed your parents, Malcolm. Your *parents*. Who knows what she does to anyone who crosses her. I saw her, and she didn't even look human. She looked like an animal stripped of its sanity. I don't want you…. You can't become like her. You *can't*. I won't let you."

"Herma, I'm the Marquess Malcolm Vorn-Solari. I'm the next duke of New Dubai."

"You're Malcolm, my friend. My betrothed. My love. Yes, *love,* and I mean it. My parents wanted to drop the whole thing, to dissolve the engagement to save themselves. I don't want that. I want to be with you. Not as a figurehead or an object or a convenience. But as Herma."

Malcolm looked at Herma, looked at her with a face still flat and dead. Then life blossomed, and he dived forward into her shoulder and sobbed. She cradled him as he acted his age, crying and sobbing openly without any gender or social stigma to tie him down. Maybe she would get the chance to cry like that one day, when they were far away from here. When she could just be Herma, and he could just be Malcolm. Maybe it wouldn't work, but she could at least try.

Gaspard spoke now, his rough deep voice a contrast to Malcolm's shrill sobs. "If you wish, I'd like to help you. Ali and I, we both wish to help you. This isn't an obligation for us. It's our choice. You see, when we were traveling here, Ali did some research. There's this planet she knows, Ceres Novus, an agrarian planet far removed from the center of the Cluster. It's not like New Dubai or Argo. Humans, Feles, Ekri, and Kavki coexist there. You can even have mixed families. If you're willing to have us as your guardians, we can make our home there on one of their free land areas and live a self-sufficient life. It wouldn't be easy, but it's better than this place. You don't have to. It's your choice."

Herma didn't need to choose. Just the thought of what Gaspard described was like heaven. She would've gone there that second had the shuttle been waiting. She turned to Malcolm, who was wiping his tears away. His voice was still uncertain, doubtful.

"Yes… I think that sounds nice." He looked out the patio doors. "Who's that out there?"

Gaspard turned and squinted through the rain. Herma too squinted, and all three recognized him at the same moment. Malcolm gave a near-shriek, Herma's blood ran cold, and Gaspard's voiced gave a single, vile retort. The Feles rose slowly.

"You two, stay inside and take cover. Ali, you'd best come with me. We've got a mad dog to put down."

---

THE MOMENT GASPARD saw Andréa on the lawn, standing like the crazed specter of some ancient warrior clan, he felt an impassioned rage in his soul. Not for Echo or any others who might have fallen to him, but for the children. They wouldn't be harmed by him ever again. He walked to the patio doors, opened them just enough to slip out, then walked forward toward the human. Ali slipped out behind him and slammed the door.

Andréa called across the lawn, his voice a ragged shadow of its former self. "I thought I'd killed you. Guess you didn't have the stomach to finish me off and got someone else to do your dirty work. Well, now their blood's on your hands. And here we are. I've finally got another shot at that little brat. I'd hoped to find my father and mother-in-law here. Maybe even her. Then I'd have them all. I'd wipe that whole abhorrent line from the face of the Cluster. But it seems my former employer has already done her work. I saw her from where I was hiding, leaving with such a look on her face. A pity. But at least I've still got the boy to toy with before I leave for my next job."

"You're sick."

"That's none of your business. Step aside, Gaspard. This doesn't concern you anymore."

"That's where you're wrong. There's no escape for you, Andréa. This is the end for you."

Andréa's mouth broke and stretched into a rictus grin. "So be it. I guess I can handle a broken weed like you."

Andréa had been standing with hands in pockets, and now there was a flash from one of them as the concealed gun was fired. Gaspard and Ali both threw themselves to one side, but the bolt caught Ali in the shoulder. She tumbled and fell, head fins drooping from the sudden pain, clutching the wound as purple blood oozed across her fingers. Gaspard ran for cover as Andréa fired another shot, scorching the ground near his foot. Another shot, another dodge, and this time Gaspard smelt the singeing of fur as the bolt just missed his head.

There was an ornament in the ground near Ali, something carved of stone about the size of a datapad cell. Gaspard's eye caught hers as she snatched it up and hurled it. The object struck Andréa's gun on its power cell. There was a crackling, and Andréa dropped the weapon with a sharp cry of pain. Then Ali frowned, seeming to remember something. She glanced at Gaspard, an expression worthy of a whole sentence, and made for the woods at a run. Why was she leaving? She must have her reasons, but…. Andréa watched Ali's apparent flight and laughed.

"Typical Kavki. Cowards in the face of a real fight. Well then, it's left up to the true warrior races of the Cluster."

Gaspard nodded, baring his teeth. "Yeah, and no cheating with guns."

The two crouched like wrestlers, and Andréa drew his other hand from its pocket. In it was clutched a blood-crusted knife, likely the same knife Echo had taken to kill Andréa, that had been used to kill Echo. Gaspard gritted his teeth. Andréa had an advantage, but he hadn't spent most of his life in the d'If without learning to deflect and confiscate a prisoner's homemade shiv.

They circled for a time, then Andréa dove in for a low blow. Gaspard side-stepped, grabbed the knife hand, and twisted. If he had to break the human's wrist, so be it. Then Andréa's foot struck his knee, throwing him off balance. Within a second, Gaspard was pinned to the ground with Andréa on top of him. In a moment of tunnel vision, Gaspard saw his hands wrapped around Andréa's wrists, the knife held back inches above his throat, and Andréa's grinning face hovering behind the hilt.

"You'd better hope there's a life after death. I'm gonna make sure you'll be begging for it by the time I'm finished."

Gaspard glared up. He could hear small footsteps running across the lawn, and for a moment his strength slipped, and he felt the tip of the knife scraping against his throat. Then there was a childish yell, and a small flying form tackled Andréa. Free from the human's grasp, Gaspard quickly rose. Malcolm. He grabbed the boy and pulled him away.

"Get back inside, now."

The pull had been a second too late. Andréa slashed, and Malcolm screamed as the blade sliced into his arm, a trail of blood sprinkling the grass. Gaspard all but threw Malcolm behind him as Andréa rose, ready for another assault. The human ran at them, but Gaspard tackled low and grabbed his legs, flinging him down. Before Andréa could recover, Gaspard was on top and twisting the knife from his hand. The sound of snapping muscle and crunching bones under his fingers was followed by Andréa's pained screams. The knife dropped from the human's pain-shocked fingers.

Gaspard reached for the blade, but something stopped him. A strange impulse, an echo of a young and innocent Feles guard coming to the d'If, overjoyed at having employment, imagining prisoners reforming under his gentle guiding hand. He'd made a vow that day never to kill in anger or in a rage, only in the performance of his duty. Even then, when he'd been forced to shoot a prisoner who had taken a hostage, he'd done so reluctantly, feeling the pain of the shot as if he'd been that prisoner.

The moment's distraction was almost fatal. Andréa punched up with his good hand and threw Gaspard back and off, then a sharp pain wracked his thigh. Through the red fog, he saw the knife stuck into his calf. Andréa started toward Malcolm again, but Gaspard lurched over and again grabbed Andréa's legs, holding him back. The human turned, his face a mask of insane rage.

"I've had enough of you."

Andréa's hands fastened like vices around Gaspard's throat. Malcolm ran forward again, but Andréa kicked out viciously, and the boy fell to the ground. Gaspard struggled and clawed against the human's insane strength, his vision slowly blurring and reddening at the edges, his ears singing as the life was choked from him. Then he heard the sound of familiar feet leaping across the grass, a hiss in the rain-soaked air, and the sound of hot metal slicing through flesh. Andréa's face at the center of the red haze contorted with sudden pain. Then his grip relaxed, and he tumbled sideways.

Rising and coughing, Gaspard looked at his opponent. Andréa lay, eyes and mouth open in pain and shock, a still-glowing rapier stuck through his heart. Ali crouched down and tended to Gaspard's wound. A bunch of what looked like medicinal moss was stuffed into the wound on her shoulder, and she worked with her usual speed and precision. Malcolm was rising, groaning, and holding his stomach as the cut on his arm continued to bleed. Another figure approached, the girl Herma looking drawn and frightened. Her voice cut through the patter of rain.

"Is it over?"

Gaspard's voice was a hoarse groan. "Yes. It's over."

He looked at Ali's face, that impassive expression above the scarred neck and well-toned body. On that face, that pallid visage, with its scarred throat and deadened eyes, was a warm smile of relief.

---

A DAY LATER, before anyone knew about the duke's death, a small party boarded a shuttle to Ceres Novus from Argo Shuttle Terminal 2. They were two human children, a female Kavki, and a male Feles. They were inconspicuously dressed, and while the boy looked depressed, the girl was composed, and the other two were quite ordinary, if a little battered. Their ID cards showed them to be a small family, Kavki and Feles partners with adopted human children.

Gaspard expected them to be stopped. By the airport authorities, by Law Officers, by the household of the duke, even for whatever reason by Mercedes. But they weren't stopped. Ali's skills at creating their ID's had gotten through everything, and soon they were on their way off Argo and away from the horrors they had been living through for the past... month? Yes, it was around a month they'd lived through, though it felt like an entire year of his life had gone by.

Aboard the shuttle, Ali directed them to a compartment with a table and four adjustable seats so they could be together or separate and all be in private. They settled themselves along with the other passengers, the announcements were made, an in-flight menu was delivered for after they began the week-long warp journey to Ceres Novus, and they were familiarized with the bed functions of each seat.

As they climbed out of Argo's atmosphere, Malcolm Vorn-Solari twisted in his seat and looked down at the planet's receding outline. Despite the deep sadness he must be feeling, he still had that lively, innocent look. Herma seemed content, keeping half an eye on Malcolm at all times. The future for him was still uncertain, full of awkward questions. Ali watched them all, but also seemed more relaxed. Almost happy.

And what about him? What was the future before him now? A Feles without a clan, a lowly prison guard used and abused by those around him, saved by the most unlikely of figures. Whatever happened now, he would always remember that. Mercedes had helped him, saved him, given him this window into a world beyond the d'If, a world that woke his spirit and let him walk tall and free. Now he had a family to look after, a future to plan out.

It would be hard. It would be difficult. There may be times when each of them might wish to be somewhere else. Sooner or later, they might break apart and go their separate ways again. But for the moment, for this one glorious moment, he belonged. And that belonging he would treasure for the rest of his days.

LATE SUMMER CAST its wonderful light across Amasian City, a beautiful sight to see in her own identity. Mercedes Solari, herself whole and entire for the first time in years, stretched her arms and laughed. This was it, the final curtain. She hadn't felt this kind of anticipation in years. Everything had been building up to this point, every move and countermove in her elaborate plan culminating to this moment.

It hadn't been too long delayed, but her inner wish for immediate expiation had needed to be restrained. After the final scene at Duncan's home, Laffw and Bapti had whisked her away from the scene as quietly as they had brought her there.

A few weeks later, news outlets revealed the former Duchess Mercedes Solari was still alive and in hiding, having escaped a decade-long imprisonment. She had worked from the shadows, far away from the grisly scenes, to secure the evidence required for a peaceful return to power. The fallout had unfolded as predicted on Argo and New Dubai, and voices rose from unspecified quarters for the return of the old order. No-one mentioned the baroness. Why should they? She wasn't anything to do with Mercedes Solari.

"And here I am." She spun a little on the spot, a spontaneous pirouette of pleasure. "Here I am for everyone to see and adore once more."

Ever since then, the great and the good had been trooping in and out of her new offices for some little time. Even the slight and sullied came there from time to time, begging favors and forgiveness. The judiciary were also coming at a nigh-endless rate regarding a recent spate of pardons that needed approval based on new evidence related to each plaintiff's case. She'd approved nearly all of them, with a few exceptions. The nobility had come, of course, and this time she'd been more careful with them.

A light flashed from her comm. Laffw had arrived at last. She unlocked the doors and waited. Ambassador Laffw burst in wearing one of her most resplendent outfits. Mercedes, more modestly dressed in her traditional Neo-Tudor style and her graying hair cropped short and cleaned of its dye, smiled for her visitor.

"Ambassador Laffw, I'm pleased you could make this appointment."

"As am I." A pause for emphasis. "Duchess Mercedes Angael Quistor Solari."

Mercedes wagged a finger. "Let's be accurate about this. I'm not the duchess *yet*. There are formalities to go through, court cases to be resolved, secrets to be revealed."

"Oh, yes. I remember. Still, such matters are mere formalities. In private, I think we can call you by your true title."

"Yes. Care for a drink?"

"Most certainly."

Quiet, friendly talk.

Quiet, friendly banter as if nothing were going to happen.

Laffw spoke casually. "Very fortunate, Andréa being found dead."

"Very. They're pinning the duke's murder on him. They haven't found Malcolm, so they're assuming he's dead, too. Truly the people have mourned."

"People?"

"Oh, sorry. The *elite* have mourned. The people seem to have been mostly ignorant of what happened until the mainstream news was allowed to cover it. And in addition, before the duke's body was discovered, the mysterious Baroness Charlotte Clarisse vanished. Investigations into her background revealed that her supposed fortunes were all but non-existent. It was a truly terrible thing. The state reimbursed all concerned, of course."

"All for the best, I'd say."

"It's all been very distressing. So many people consoling me, condoling with me on the misfortunes New Dubai has suffered in my absence. So much business to attend to."

"Yes." Laffw swirled her drink. "Speaking of business, I think it's time we begin concluding our own. I must congratulate you on your plan. It worked magnificently. Especially the few adlibs you needed to include. Now all that remains is our little agreement."

"Agreement?"

"There is no need to be coy, my dear. I believe you can still remember the terms of our agreement. For my aid in getting you back here to reclaim your status and enact your vengeance, the Kavki were to have"—Laffw's fingers moved like a conductor as she recited the terms—"suzerainty over New Dubai for the lifetime of the Duchess Mercedes, thirty percent cut of all mining and trade proceeds, support in political, financial, or military matters related to the Synod or internal disputes, fifty percent White Oil access from the new mines for their duration. Yes, that was it. A fairly modest price if I do say so myself."

"Yes. Quite modest. Considering what we both did to get it."

"We each performed our part."

"Yes." She couldn't help letting a smile cross her lips. "Laffw, do you remember an analogy you made when we first met? To chess. It was about removing the most mobile pieces and making pawns change sides."

"Yes, though you made the most of the analogy. What of it?"

"There was one part of the chess analogy you overlooked. In order to further the game, pieces must be sacrificed."

"Yes, I had forgotten that. What of it?"

"I sacrificed Andréa, Ali, Gaspard…. And now *you.*"

Laffw's eyes narrowed. "I hope you did not mean that seriously. You would not want to see me displeased."

"Do you remember the day we first found Andréa? The Ekri assassin debacle was terribly convenient. Wasn't it?"

"Convenient? Explain yourself."

"Finding Andréa was the purest fluke, but after that, getting in at least one assassin who wouldn't fall for the drugged drink stunt was a natural part of the plan. As was killing her with one of your weapons. I think you should look at this. It's a copy of a memo I received from the Synod this morning."

Laffw snatched the datapad Mercedes took from inside her jacket. Mercedes had read it with such satisfaction when it arrived that morning, a message from the Synod to keep Ambassador Laffw and her serf Bapti under observation, and if necessary, under restraint until assigned Synod Enforcers came to assist them in a murder inquiry. Laffw threw the datapad to the ground, her face contorted with barely-controlled emotion.

"How…. You… you set this up. You arranged it."

"Right from the start. It was simple to get Gaspard to plant the body and the weapon where they would be found. A national hero to the Ekri people found dead at the hands of a Kavki. What would the Synod think about that? A little investigation would reveal the salient facts. You, consorting with wanted murderers, conniving with a massive deception that led to the death of New Dubai's ruling nobility, and killing a hero of the Human-Ekri Conflict. The crowning proof, the weapon that killed the Ekri being reliably identified as being a specific type assigned to diplomats and their staff. And there was only *one* diplomat aboard Cape Life at that time. Wasn't there."

It was a statement of fact, not a question. Laffw, for the moment, seemed unconcerned. She yawned, then smiled, asserting dominance.

"You forget. I have proof of our agreement. If I must be felled, assuming I am, you shall be dragged down with me."

"You mean this?" With a swift action, Mercedes drew the stolen datapad from within the desk, holding it by one corner. "Ali got it for me in exchange for her freedom from you. You haven't heard anything from Ali, have you? I daresay you won't ever again. I wiped this the day I got it, then overwrote and reformatted it a dozen times. The original data's irrecoverable. And don't bother bluffing, you'd never make a copy of something this dangerous. Not when you were so sure."

Holding it like a stinking thing, she went over to the office's rubbish chute, opened its door, and dropped the useless datapad down. Turning round, Mercedes watched the delicious effect. Laffw clenched her glass until it cracked, the shards dropping onto the carpet. She gripped the arms of her chair, staring with growing rage at Mercedes. Mercedes continued talking in a level, matter-of-fact tone, reveling in the victory over her former benefactor.

"It's funny. You knew I was a scheming, manipulative bitch capable of destroying so many lives, working out a plan lasting months. But whether through ignorance or greed, you didn't consider the possibility I'd betray you. That I'd entrap you without destroying myself. On the whole, I think you were the most naive of my pawns. You imagined yourself a player, but you're just a piece on the board. A pawn. No, that's not quite right. You were a queen. You moved the furthest and the widest. You allowed me to turn the pawns against my opponents, taking the pieces one by one until all that remained was the king. And without the other pieces, the king is at a huge disadvantage. Caught without protection, it was a simple case of checkmate. A pawn victory, in this case, necessitated the sacrifice of many other pieces including the queen. But unlike a game of chess, these pieces have wills of their own, so they need a little preparation."

Laffw's face looked twisted, pallid from shock. "You are a scheming monster. You fell your enemies, and with the same cool calm you betray your allies."

"Betrayal indicates some kind of trust. Yet neither of us trusted the other. You're the foolish one, believing I'd sell my planet's sovereignty. You left yourself open to this. You've only yourself to blame that I succeeded."

Laffw finally started up from her seat, towering over her former ally. Mercedes wasn't a woman to be bowed, and she stood her ground. The two stared at each other for some moments before Laffw spoke with a bitter, venomous tone. "I can still bring you down, Mercedes Solari. I can destroy you just as you destroyed me."

"Really? Without that datapad, who'd believe you? You'd say anything to save yourself. And besides...." She chuckled at the thought. "A woman coming back after ten years in exile, concocting such an elaborate and complicated scheme of revenge, so reliant on luck and the ignorance of a planet's nobility. Who'd believe that was anything but a trashy plot by some writer of sensational fiction? Or the tale of a politician desperate to save their own skin?" A thought struck her. "If it's any consolation, you probably won't be imprisoned or anything like that. Your career's finished, but you'll still be alive. It's more than I was in your position."

"How can you possibly be like this? How can the craven woman I rescued from the d'If be you?"

Mercedes's reply was sharper than she ever thought she could be. "You saw what you wanted to see. I trust the Synod will make swift work of you. Your people won't have one iota of my world. The Solari family have and always will control these lands. Any who attempt to take it will feel our wrath. As you now know."

There was an aching silence. Laffw seemed suddenly to have aged and shrunk, and as Mercedes moved to the window and looked down at the Synod Enforcer vehicle drawing up, Laffw let out a half-stifled sob. Turning back, Laffw straightened up and turned cold eyes upon her.

"Goodbye, Your Grace. I fervently hope we shall not meet again."

"The feeling's mutual. Goodbye, Ambassador."

Laffw turned and all but dashed from the room. For a while, there was silence. Then Mercedes heard a scuffle outside. Turning back to the window, she saw the Synod Enforcer vehicle, with Bapti being roughly pushed into the back of the vehicle. A few minutes later, clearly summoned by those who waited, Laffw walked down the path to the pavement with a stiff grace, going over to where her car waited. A Synod Enforcer waited there, and she spoke briefly to them before getting inside. For a moment, there was stillness, then the Ambassador's car and the Synod Enforcer vehicle moved down the road and out of sight.

Left alone, her drink forgotten on the small table, Mercedes looked back on her accomplishments. A slow but sure victory out of impossible odds. Chance, luck, and skill had all played into her hand. Now she was victorious.

Witton Mondego, Gaspard Atarex, Ali, Bapti, F'thodish Azd Laffw, Andréa, Henri Laurent-Leblanc, Georges de Granger, Duncan Vorn-Solari. And… Gretchen. All had fallen. The way was clear forever more. And if Malcolm came back one day, what did that matter? If he did kill her or depose her, he'd inherit a shell of a world, an echo of his father's glory. No matter how long it may last, she had achieved her ambition. Roly-poly, Prisoner 74, the baroness were all dead and gone. She was once more who she always was, who she was born to be. Mercedes Solari, Duchess of New Dubai.

Milton Keynes UK
Ingram Content Group UK Ltd.
UKHW011827061123
432058UK00013B/242/J